The Best AMERICAN SHORT STORIES, 1982

Selected from
U.S. and Canadian Magazines
by John Gardner
with Shannon Ravenel

With an Introduction by John Gardner

1982

Houghton Mifflin Company Boston

Library of Congress Cataloging in Publication Data
Main entry under title:

The Best American short stories, 1982.

1. Short stories, American. 2. Short stories,
Canadian. I. Gardner, John, date. II. Ravenel,
Shannon.
PS648.S5B4   1982   813'.01'08   82-11972
ISBN 0-395-32207-3

Printed in the United States of America

V 10 9 8 7 6 5 4 3 2 1

"K. 590" by Nicholson Baker. First published in *The Little Magazine*. Copyright ©
1982 by Nicholson Baker. Reprinted by permission of the author.

"Harmony of the World" by Charles Baxter. First published in *Michigan Quarterly
Review*. Copyright © 1981 by Charles Baxter. Reprinted by permission of the
author.

"Cathedral" by Raymond Carver. First published in *The Atlantic Monthly*. Copyright
© 1981 by Raymond Carver. Reprinted by permission of the author.

"Lamb Says" by Rosanne Coggeshall. First published in *South Carolina Review*. Copyright © 1981 by Rosanne Coggeshall. Reprinted by permission of the author.

"Dancing Ducks and Talking Anus" by James Ferry. First published in *The Literary
Review*, Vol. 25, No. 1, published by Fairleigh Dickinson University. Copyright ©
1981 by James Ferry. Reprinted by permission of the author.

"The Girl Who Was No Kin to the Marshalls" by Anne Hobson Freeman. First
published in *The Virginia Quarterly Review*. Copyright © 1981 by Anne Hobson
Freeman. Reprinted by permission of the author.

"The Power of Language Is Such That Even a Single Word Taken Truly to Heart
Can Change Everything" by Alvin Greenberg. First published in *StoryQuarterly*.
Copyright © 1981 by *StoryQuarterly*. Reprinted by permission of the editors.

"The Café de Paris" by Roberta Gupta. First published in *MSS*. Copyright © 1981
by Roberta Gupta. Reprinted by permission of the author.

"Good Rockin' Tonight" by William Hauptman. First published in *Playboy*. Copyright © 1982 by William Hauptman. Reprinted by permission of the author.

much like most of last year's. But if I were to point to a faintly discernible trend I would say this: A new seriousness seems to have settled over North American short fiction. I don't know for sure what the reasons are. I suspect our culture, or at least a segment of it, may finally be tiring of the self-consciously trivial artistic practice Americans favored in the age when we wanted to seem as wearily elegant and intelligent as post–World War I Europeans — the age that produced, in its belated flowering, Fitzgerald and his progeny: writers like O'Hara, Updike, and Cheever — not great-hearted writers, generally, not writers racked by philosophical anguish (put off, in fact, by any too direct philosophical earnestness), but shrewd and precise, if faintly pessimistic, chroniclers of manners in our time. Recent fiction from South America (Márquez, et cetera), with its urgent concerns and unabashed earnestness, has perhaps made our prevailing fashion seem anorexic, an effect intensified, I suspect, by the usual thinness of "experimental" or "meta" fiction of the sort much touted, of late, in universities. (This is not to deny that unconventional fiction may be powerful. Consider "The Continental Heart.") And I suspect the visible decline in the quality of American life may also have had some effect. Staggering unemployment figures, the crack-up of the liberal dream, the startling rise of simplistic religiosity and of philistine fascism (represented by book burnings and school board censorship of American classics old and new), the apparent failure of the civil rights dream of the fifties and sixties and of the universal human rights dream of the seventies, our apparent blind rush toward nuclear gunboat diplomacy — indeed, what seems to some the brutish stupidity of many of our national policies — these woes and others have, ironically, proved kind to fiction. It's hard to write thin slice-of-suburban-life fiction when all the supports of our weary, self-regarding ennui are collapsing and the only noise besides the writer's increasingly earnest voice is the strident tinkle, up and down the street, of TV.

The new seriousness does not often express itself in directly political fiction. Sometimes political evils of a previous time — mainly World War II — are held up in implicit comparison to the way things are now ("Shelter the Pilgrim," "Proud Monster"); and sometimes political evils play a background part (as in Joyce Renwick's old-fashioned, realistic story of commissars and nature, "The Dolphin Story"). But on the whole, fiction in 1981 expressed not a political but a personal seriousness of concern. The father-daughter story, represented here at its noblest in "Prize Tomatoes" (also a story about aging), is one obvious expression of this seriousness. Nostalgia stories often have a similar impulse. "Good Rockin' Tonight," like another Elvis story I liked, Lynda Sexson's "The Apocalypse of Mary," does not simply go back to the good old days of Elvis; it contrasts our more innocent experience — part foolishness, part holy idealism — with our present anger, sense of futility, and determination to escape this evil adulthood imposed by dutifully greedy businessmen and politicians, fake religionists, and above all those fake sophisticates who say, "We can no longer be like that, we must not naively imitate ourselves," or — as Nick told Jay Gatsby, to Gatsby's wonderful indignation — "We cannot relive the past." Elsewhere, as in Joanna Higgins's gentle and beautiful "The Courtship of Widow Sobcek," the new seriousness reveals itself in an unapologetic acceptance of religion as one of life's meaningful, ordinary values. If simplistic religiosity took a good deal of drubbing from serious writers in 1981, a number of serious younger writers show a comfortable acceptance of "real" religion — Christianity not only in Oates and Updike, where we've learned to expect it (disguised or no), but in many other writers; Native American religion in stories like James Ferry's "Dancing Ducks and Talking Anus"; slightly nervous but unapologetic Jewish religious feeling in Fred Licht's "Shelter the Pilgrim" and in many other stories presented or mentioned in this anthology.

The seriousness I speak of shows, I think, in the apparent preference, among many younger writers, for stories with real characters in them, stories in which something actually happens, stories in which the author shows frank concern, not self-protective, "sensible" detachment. Except in MacMillan's "Proud Monster" — a set of sketches — every story in this collection is suspenseful, a quality fairly common in the short stories published in 1981. Except in a very few magazines, like the *Mississippi Review*, which specialize in novelty, we seem to be well out of the experimental seventies, though it can hardly be said that fiction has gone back to where it was before the wave of experiment began. Some stories in this collection (Renwick's, Higgins's, Rosner's, Hauptman's, to name a few) show no particular influence of the experimenters; more commonly the new fiction (at its best) has domesticated the previous decade's innovations. Alvin Greenberg's "The Power of Language . . ." has a more or less conventional beginning, middle, and end but takes place on an island floating out into the Atlantic, carrying with it a herd of wild pigs that are beginning to behave in, to say the least, odd ways. "Lamb Says" is a love story rich in realistic detail, utterly lifelike except for one trifle, the persuasive but impossible central character. Raymond Carver's splendid story "Cathedral" develops Carver's own earlier experiments to create a much more conventional and at the same time much wilder kind of fiction. The experimenters' ways of enriching texture and avoiding the "exhaustion" of a literature that had too long played the same old notes have become, in the hands of the new generation, devices for enlivening the oldest game in the world, the telling of stories.

Not that the new seriousness is universal. When Faulkner wrote fiction in the present tense it was as startling as when the French took up *vers libre*. But present-tense narration has now reached plague level. The trouble with this technique as it is generally now used is that instead of giving the immediacy or eternal *Now* sought by Faulkner (in *Light in August,* for example), it has a *New Yorker*ish way of putting events on ice, presenting people and the things they do — however dull, however outrageous — with a sophisticated, ironic, timorous objectivity that often seems calculated to remind us that writing and reading stories may not be, for well-dressed, well-educated grownups, defensible activities. More often than not, these stories turn out to be not stories at all, not even interesting anecdotes one might tell at a party. "Edith is slicing ham, paper thin. It pleases her that she can slice it thinner than the machine can do at Safeway." The present tense turns out to be, itself, the message: One may with great sensitivity watch things happen — how the family behaves when the middle-aged father dies, how a young woman comes to feel at home in her new apartment in the Village — but one is silly to *expect* anything. Life, if one wishes to call it that, goes on; consciousness is all. If, a third of the way through such a story, we flip to the end, we find that (a) whatever story there may have been has been taken back: the central character realizes that nothing has really happened or ever will; or (b) the central character is hurtling toward the ground, having fallen out of a helicopter, and the experience isn't as exciting as he'd rather hoped it might be. No one denies that a passionate writer can use the present tense to set the page on fire, but most writers who adopt this style do not make burning pages their primary goal. In most of this fiction, in other words, detail and fine writing take the place of events, and the emotion seems dated, the weak suspiration of the vaguely dissatisfied seventies.

Another throwback to less urgent times is what I would call "case history" fiction, stories that present, with care and precision but no thematic or dramatic purpose — no concern about character growth or increasing understanding — exactly what it is like (for instance) to fall in love with a thirty-year-old man when you're a girl of fifteen. Mary Robison's story "Coach" at first glance seems such a story. It has the usual precision and flatness of tone, the usual deadly accuracy of observation, the predictably vivid characterization. But Robison's story comes in the end to real wins and losses — not life plodding on in its usual narrow-shouldered, deferential way, but serious changes in the wind, whispered forebodings. In comparison, the true case history pales.

What chiefly reveals the new seriousness is the energy of these stories — the energy that comes of passionate imagination, careful and considered style, firm authorial commitment. All of the stories in this collection, like a great many other stories published the same year, have *drive*. Very often the drive comes from the central character's entrapment and fierce struggle to escape, as in "Prize Tomatoes" — the story of an old man imprisoned by a daughter's concern — or "Good Rockin' Tonight," or "Exchange Value," an eerie story of two young blacks' obsessive self-entrapment. (In all but the last of these the struggle is successful, and even in "Exchange Value" there is still hope. Occasionally, as in R. E. Smith's "The Gift Horse's Mouth," the victory is a flat-out triumph.) Sometimes the story's drive comes from the writer's bold seizure and deft manipulation of materials theoretically too hot to handle, as in "Shelter the Pilgrim," Licht's moving story of a young Jewish idiot-savant whose friends are forced to abandon him to the Nazis, or Milton's "Coming Over," or Ferry's "Dancing Ducks and Talking Anus." Sometimes the drive comes from brilliant execution of what can only be described as a bravely lunatic idea, like that in "Lamb Says."

•

I've said enough now, I hope, to give notice of my biases and principles of selection. I might mention that I've tried to avoid selecting parts of novels and have avoided translations. I tried hard to find a really good piece of science fiction, but the sci-fi short stories I was able to get my hands on, both in "literary" magazines and in "popular" magazines, all turned out, ironically, to be mundane. Here and there one finds a story that's fascinating, even thrilling, but somehow nothing ever comes of it. (This has not always been true and surely will not always henceforth be true, but it was true, I think, in 1981.) I tried to choose stories in various styles representing various bases of life experience (Canadian stories, stories from the U.S., stories of various regions — North, South, East, West — stories about blacks, whites, Indians, males, females), but in the end nothing that got into this collection got in for any such reason. These are, simply — to the best of my knowledge — the best North American stories, or definitely among the best, of 1981.

JOHN GARDNER

The Best
AMERICAN
SHORT
STORIES
1982

RAYMOND CARVER

Cathedral

(FROM THE ATLANTIC MONTHLY)

THIS BLIND MAN, an old friend of my wife's, he was on his way to
spend the night. His wife had died. So he was visiting the dead
wife's relatives in Connecticut. He called my wife from his in-laws'.
Arrangements were made. He would come by train, a five-hour
trip, and my wife would meet him at the station. She hadn't seen
him since she worked for him one summer in Seattle ten years ago.
But she and the blind man had kept in touch. They made tapes
and mailed them back and forth. I wasn't enthusiastic about his
visit. He was no one I knew. And his being blind bothered me. My
idea of blindness came from the movies. In movies, the blind
moved slowly and never laughed. Sometimes they were led by
seeing-eye dogs. A blind man in my house was not something I
looked forward to.

That summer in Seattle she had needed a job. She didn't have
any money. The man she was going to marry at the end of the
summer was in officer's training school. He didn't have any money,
either. But she was in love with the guy, and he was in love with
her, etc. She'd seen something in the paper: Help Wanted —
Reading for Blind Man, and a telephone number. She phoned and
went over, was hired on the spot. She'd worked with this blind
man all summer. She read stuff to him, case studies, reports, that
sort of thing. She helped him organize his little office in the county
social service department. They'd become good friends, my wife
and the blind man. How do I know these things? She told me. And
she told me something else. On her last day in the office, the blind
man asked if he could touch her face. She agreed to this. She told
me he ran his fingers over every part of her face, her nose — even

her neck! She never forgot it. She even tried to write a poem about it. She was always writing a poem. She wrote a poem or two every year, usually after something really important had happened to her.

When we first started going out together, she showed me the poem. In the poem she recalled his fingers and the way they had moved around over her face. In the poem she talked about what she had felt at the time, about what went through her mind as he touched her nose and lips. I can recall I didn't think much of the poem. Of course I didn't tell her that. Maybe I just don't understand poetry. I admit it's not the first thing I reach for when I pick up something to read.

Anyway, this man who'd first enjoyed her favors, the officer-to-be, he'd been her childhood sweetheart. So okay. I'm saying that at the end of the summer she let the blind man run his hands over her face, said good-bye to him, married her childhood etc., who was now a commissioned officer, and she moved away from Seattle. But they'd kept in touch, she and the blind man. She made the first contact after a year or so. She called him up one night from an Air Force base in Alabama. She wanted to talk. They talked. He asked her to send him a tape and tell him about her life. She did this. She sent the tape. On the tape she told the blind man about her husband and about their life together in the military. She told the blind man she loved her husband but she didn't like it where they lived and she didn't like it that he was a part of the military-industrial complex. She told the blind man she'd written a poem and he was in it. She told him that she was writing a poem about what it was like to be an Air Force officer's wife in the Deep South. The poem wasn't finished yet. She was still writing it. The blind man made a tape. He sent her the tape. She made a tape. This went on for years. My wife's officer was posted to one base and then another. She sent tapes from Moody AFB, McGuire, McConnell, and finally Travis, near Sacramento, where one night she got to feeling lonely and cut off from people she kept losing in that moving-around life. She balked, couldn't go it another step. She went in and swallowed all the pills and capsules in the medicine cabinet and washed them down with a bottle of gin. Then she got into a hot bath and passed out.

But instead of dying she got sick. She threw up. Her officer — Why should he have a name? He was the childhood sweetheart, and what more does he want? — came home from a training mission, found her, and called the ambulance. In time, she put it on the tape and sent the tape to the blind man. Over the years she put all kinds of stuff on tapes and sent the tapes off lickety-split. Next to writing a poem every year, I think it was her chief means of recreation. On one tape she told the blind man she'd decided to live away from her officer for a time. On another tape she told him about her divorce. She and I began going out, and of course she told her blind man about this. She told him everything, so it seemed to me. Once she asked me if I'd like to hear the latest tape from the blind man. This was a year ago. I was on the tape, she said. So I said okay, I'd listen to it. I got us drinks and we settled down in the living room. We made ready to listen. First she inserted the tape into the player and adjusted a couple of dials. Then she pushed a lever. The tape squeaked and someone began to talk in this loud voice. She lowered the volume. After a few minutes of harmless chitchat, I heard my own name rasped out by this stranger, this man I didn't even know! And then this: "From all you've said about him, I can only conclude —" But we were interrupted, a knock at the door, something, and we didn't get back to the tape. Maybe it was just as well. I'd heard enough, anyway.

Now this same blind stranger was coming to sleep in my house.

"Maybe I could take him bowling," I said to my wife. She was at the draining board doing scalloped potatoes. She put down the knife she was using on the onion and turned around.

"If you love me," she said, "you can do this for me. If you don't love me, okay. But if you had a friend, any friend, and the friend came to visit, I'd make him feel comfortable." She wiped her hands with the dish towel.

"I don't have any blind friends," I said.

"You don't have *any* friends," she said. "Period. Besides," she said, "goddamnit, his wife's just died! Don't you understand that? The man's lost his wife!"

I didn't answer. She'd told me a little about the blind man's wife. The wife's name was Beulah. Beulah! That's a name for a colored woman.

"Was his wife a Negro?" I asked.

"Are you crazy?" my wife said. "Have you just flipped or something?" She picked up the onion. I saw it hit the floor, then roll under the stove. "What's wrong with you?" she said. "Are you drunk?"

"I'm just asking," I said.

Right then my wife filled me in with more detail than I cared to know. I made a drink and sat at the kitchen table to listen. Pieces of the story began to fall into place.

Beulah had gone to work for the blind man the summer after my wife had stopped working for him. Pretty soon Beulah and the blind man had themselves a church wedding. It was a little wedding — who'd be anxious to attend such a wedding in the first place? — just the two of them, and the minister and the minister's wife. But it was a church wedding just the same. What Beulah had wanted, he'd said. But even then Beulah must have been carrying cancer in her lymph glands. After they had been inseparable for eight years — my wife's word, *inseparable* — Beulah's health went into a rapid decline. She died in a Seattle hospital room, the blind man sitting beside the bed and holding on to her hand. They'd married, lived and worked together, slept together — had sex, sure — and then the blind man buried her. All this without his having ever seen what the goddamned woman looked like. It was beyond my understanding. Hearing this, I felt sorry for the blind man for a minute. And then I found myself thinking what a pitiful life this woman must have led. Imagine a woman who could never see herself reflected in the eyes of her loved one. A woman who could go on day after day and never receive the smallest compliment from her beloved. A woman whose husband would never read the expression on her face, be it misery or something better. Someone who could wear make-up or not — what difference to him? She could, if she wanted, wear green eye shadow around one eye, a straight pin in her nostril, yellow slacks and burgundy pumps, no matter. And then to slip off into death, the blind man's hand on her hand, his blind eyes streaming tears — I'm imagining now — her last thought maybe this: that her beloved never knew what she looked like, and she on an express to the grave. Robert was left with a small insurance policy and half of a twenty-peso Mexican coin. The other half of the coin went into the box with her. Pathetic.

•

So when the time rolled around, my wife went to the rail station. With nothing to do but wait — and sure, I blamed him for that — I was having a drink and watching TV when I heard the car pull into the drive. I got up from the sofa with my drink and went to the window to have a look.

I saw my wife laughing as she parked the car. I saw her get out of the car and shut the door. She was still wearing a smile. Just amazing. She went around to the other side of the car to where the blind man was already starting to get out. This blind man, feature this, he was wearing a full beard! A beard on a blind man! Too much, I say. The blind man reached into the back seat and dragged out a suitcase. My wife took his arm, shut the car door, and, talking all the way, moved him down the drive and then up the steps to the front porch. I turned off the TV. I finished my drink, rinsed the glass, dried my hands. Then I went to the door.

My wife said, "I want you to meet Robert. Robert, this is my husband. I've told you all about him." She closed the porch screen. She was beaming. She had this blind man by his coat sleeve.

The blind man let go of his suitcase and up came his hand.

I took it. He squeezed hard, held my hand, and then he let it go.

"I feel like we've already met," he boomed.

"Likewise," I said. I didn't know what else to say. Then I said, "Welcome. I've heard a lot about you." We began to move then, a little group, from the porch into the living room, my wife guiding him by the arm. He carried his suitcase in his other hand. My wife said things like, "To your left here, Robert. That's right. Now watch it, there's a chair. That's it. Sit down right here. This is the sofa. We just bought this sofa two weeks ago."

I started to say something about the old sofa. I'd liked that old sofa. But I didn't say anything. Then I wanted to say something else, small talk, about the scenic Hudson River. How going *to* New York, sit on the right-hand side of the train, and coming *from* New York, the left-hand side.

"Did you have a good train ride?" I said. "Which side of the train did you sit on, by the way?"

"What a question, which side!" my wife said. "What's it matter which side?" she said.

"I just asked," I said.

"Right side," the blind man said. "For the sun. Until this morning," the blind man said, "I hadn't been on a train in nearly forty years. Not since I was a kid. With my folks. That's been a long time. I'd nearly forgotten that sensation. I have winter in my beard now," he said. "So I've been told, anyway. Do I look distinguished, my dear?" he said to my wife.

"You look distinguished, Robert," she said. "Robert," she said.

"Robert, it's just so good to see you." My wife finally took her eyes off the blind man and looked at me.

I had the distinct feeling she didn't like what she saw. I shrugged.

I've never met or personally known anyone who was blind. This blind man was late forties, a heavyset, balding man with stooped shoulders, as if he carried a great weight there. He wore brown slacks, brown cordovan shoes, a light brown shirt, a tie, a sports coat. Spiffy. He also had this full beard. But he didn't carry a cane and he didn't wear dark glasses. I'd always thought dark glasses were a must for the blind. Fact was, I wished he had a pair. At first glance, his eyes looked like anyone else's eyes. But if you looked close there was something different about them. Too much white in the iris, for one thing, and the pupils seemed to move around in the sockets without his knowing it or being able to control it. Creepy. As I stared at his face, I saw the left pupil turn in toward his nose, while the other made a futile effort to keep in one place. But it was only an effort, for that eye was on the roam without his knowing it or wanting it to be.

I said, "Let me get you a drink. What's your pleasure? We have a little of everything. It's one of our pastimes."

"Bub, I'm a Scotch man myself," he said fast enough, in this big voice.

"Right," I said. Bub! "Sure you are. I knew it."

He let his fingers touch his suitcase, which was sitting alongside the sofa. He was taking his bearings. I didn't blame him for that.

"I'll move that up to your room," my wife said.

"No, that's fine," he said loudly. "It can go up when I go up."

"A little water with the Scotch?" I said.

"Very little," he said.

"I knew it," I said.

He said, "Just a tad. The Irish actor, Barry Fitzgerald? I'm like that fellow. When I drink water, Fitzgerald said, I drink water. When I drink whiskey, I drink whiskey." My wife laughed. The blind man brought his hand up under his beard. He lifted his beard slowly and let it drop.

•

I did the drinks, three big glasses of Scotch with a splash of water in each. Then we made ourselves comfortable and talked about Robert's travels. First the long flight from the West Coast to Connecticut, we covered that. Then from Connecticut up here by train. We had another drink concerning that leg of the trip.

I remembered having read somewhere that the blind didn't smoke because, speculation had it, they couldn't see the smoke they exhaled. I thought I knew that much and that much only about blind people. But this blind man smoked his cigarette down to the nubbin and then lit another one. This blind man filled his ashtray and my wife emptied it.

When we sat down to the table for dinner we had another drink. My wife heaped Robert's plate with cube steak, scalloped potatoes, green beans. I buttered him up two slices of bread. I said, "Here's bread and butter for you." I swallowed some of my drink. "Now let us pray," I said, and the blind man lowered his head. My wife looked at me, her mouth agape. "Pray the phone won't ring and the food doesn't get cold," I said.

We dug in. We ate everything there was to eat on the table. We ate like there was no tomorrow. We didn't talk. We ate. We scarfed. We grazed that table. We were into serious eating. The blind man had right away located his foods, he knew just where everything was on his plate. I watched with admiration as he used his knife and fork on the meat. He'd cut two pieces of meat, fork the meat into his mouth, and then go all out for the scalloped potatoes, the beans next, and then he'd tear off a hunk of buttered bread and eat that. He'd follow this up with a big drink of milk. It didn't seem to bother him to use his fingers once in a while, either. He used his bread to scoop beans.

We finished everything, including half of a strawberry pie. For a few moments we sat as if stunned. Sweat beaded on our faces. Finally, we got up from the table and left the dirty plates. We didn't look back. We took ourselves into the living room and sank into our places again. Robert and my wife sat on the sofa. I took the big chair. We had us two or three more drinks while they talked about the major things that had transpired for them in the past ten years. For the most part, I just listened. Now and then I joined in. I didn't want him to think I'd left the room, and I didn't want her to think I was feeling left out. They talked of things that had happened to them — to them! — these past ten years. I waited in vain to hear my name on my wife's sweet lips: "And then my dear husband came into my life" — something like that. But I heard nothing of the sort. More talk of Robert. Robert had done a little of everything, it seemed, a regular blind jack-of-all-trades. But most recently he and his wife had had an Amway distributorship, from which, I gathered, they'd earned their living, such as it was. The blind man was also a ham radio operator. He talked in his loud voice about conversations he'd had with fellow operators in Guam, the Philippines, Alaska, even Tahiti. He said he'd have a lot of friends there if he ever wanted to go visit those places. From time to time he'd turn his blind face toward me, put his hand under his beard, ask me something. How long had I been at my present position? (Three years.) Did I like my work? (I didn't.) Was I going to stay with it? (What were the options?)

Finally, when I thought he was beginning to run down, I got up and turned on the TV.

My wife looked at me with irritation. She was heading toward a boil. Then she looked at the blind man and said, "Robert, do you have a TV?"

The blind man said, "My dear, I have two TVs. I have a color set and a black-and-white thing, an old relic. It's funny, but if I turn the TV on, and I'm always turning it on, I turn the color set on. Always. It's funny."

I didn't know what to say to that. I had absolutely nothing to say about that. No opinion. So I watched the news program and tried to listen to what the announcer was saying.

"This is a color TV," the blind man said. "Don't ask me how, but I can tell."

"We traded up a while ago," I said.

The blind man had another taste of his drink. He lifted his beard, sniffed it, and let it fall. He leaned forward on the sofa. He positioned his ashtray on the coffee table, then put the lighter to his cigarette. He leaned back on the sofa and crossed his legs at the ankles.

My wife covered her mouth, and then she yawned. She stretched. She said, "I think I'll go upstairs and put on my robe. I think I'll change into something else. Robert, you make yourself comfortable," she said.

"I'm comfortable," the blind man said.

"I want you to feel comfortable in this house," she said.

"I am comfortable," the blind man said.

After she'd left the room, he and I listened to the weather report and then to the sports roundup. My wife had been gone so long I didn't know if she was going to come back. I thought she might have gone to bed. I wished she'd come back downstairs. I didn't want to be left alone with a blind man. I asked him if he wanted another drink, and he said sure. Then I asked if he wanted to smoke dope with me. I said I'd just rolled a number. I hadn't, but I planned to do so in about two shakes.

"I'll try some with you," he said.

"Damn right," I said. "That's the stuff."

I got our drinks and sat down on the sofa with him. Then I rolled us two fat numbers. I lit one and passed it. I brought it to his fingers. He took it and inhaled.

"Hold it as long as you can," I said. I could tell he didn't know the first thing.

My wife came back downstairs wearing her robe and pink slippers. "What do I smell?" she said.

"We thought we'd have us some cannabis," I said.

My wife gave me a purely savage look. Then she looked at him and said, "Robert, I didn't know you smoked."

He said, "I do now, my dear. First time for everything," he said. "But I don't feel anything yet."

"This stuff is pretty mellow," I said. "This stuff is mild. It's dope you can reason with. It doesn't mess you up."

"Not much it doesn't, bub," he said, and laughed.

My wife sat on the sofa between the blind man and me. I passed her the number. She took it and inhaled and then passed it back to me. "Which way is this going?" she said. Then she said, "I shouldn't be smoking this. I can hardly keep my eyes open as it is. That dinner did me in. I shouldn't have eaten so much."

"It was the strawberry pie," the blind man said. "That's what did it," he said, and he laughed his big laugh. Then he shook his head.

"There's more strawberry pie," I said.

"Do you want some more, Robert?" my wife asked.

"Maybe in a little while," he said.

We gave our attention to the TV. My wife yawned again. She said, "Your bed is made up when you feel like going to bed, Robert. I know you must have had a long day. When you're ready to go to bed, say so." She pulled his arm. "Robert?"

He came to and said, "I've had a real nice time. This beats tapes, doesn't it?"

I said, "Coming at you," and I put the number between his

fingers. He inhaled, held the smoke, and then let it go. It was like he'd been doing it since he was nine years old.

"Thanks, bub," he said. "But I think this is all for me. I think I'm beginning to feel it," he said. He held the burning roach out for my wife.

"Same here," she said. "Ditto. Me too." She took the roach and passed it to me. "I may just sit here for a while between you two guys with my eyes closed. But don't let me bother you, okay? Either one of you. If it bothers you, say so. Otherwise, I may just sit here with my eyes closed until you're ready to go to bed," she said. "Your bed's made up, Robert, when you're ready. It's right next to our room at the top of the stairs. We'll show you up when you're ready. You wake me up now, you guys, if I fall asleep." She said that and then she closed her eyes and went to sleep.

The news program ended. I got up and turned the channel. I sat back down on the sofa. I wished my wife hadn't pooped out. Her head lay across the back of the sofa, her mouth open. She'd turned so that her robe had slipped away from her legs, exposing a juicy thigh. I reached to draw her robe over the thigh, and it was then I glanced at the blind man. What the hell! I flipped the robe open again.

"You say when you want some strawberry pie," I said.

"I will," he said.

I said, "Are you tired? Do you want me to take you up to your bed? Are you ready to hit the hay?"

"Not yet," he said. "No, I'll stay up with you, bub. If that's all right. I'll stay up until you're ready to turn in. We haven't had a chance to talk. Know what I mean? I feel like me and her monopolized the evening." He lifted his beard and he let it fall. He picked up his cigarettes and his lighter.

"That's all right," I said. Then I said, "I'm glad for the company." And I guess I was. Every night I smoked dope and stayed up as long as I could before I fell asleep. My wife and I hardly ever went to bed at the same time. When I did go to sleep, I had these dreams. Sometimes I'd wake up from one of them, the heart going crazy.

•

Something about the Church and the Middle Ages, narrated by an Englishman, was on the TV. Not your run-of-the-mill TV fare. I wanted to watch something else. I turned to the other channels.

But there was nothing on them, either. So I turned back to the first channel and apologized.

"Bub, it's all right," he said. "It's fine with me. Whatever you want to watch is okay. I'm always learning something. Learning never ends. It won't hurt me to learn something tonight. I got ears," he said.

We didn't say anything for a time. He was leaning forward with his head turned at me, while his right ear was aimed in the direction of the set. Very disconcerting. Now and then his eyelids drooped and then they snapped open again. Now and then he put his fingers into his beard and tugged, as if thinking about something he was hearing on the television.

On the screen a group of men wearing cowls was being set upon and tormented by men dressed in skeleton costumes and men dressed as devils. The men dressed as devils wore devil masks, horns, and long tails. This pageant was part of a procession. The Englishman said it all took place in Málaga, Spain, once a year. I tried to explain to the blind man what was happening.

"Skeletons," he said. "I know about skeletons," he said, and he nodded.

The TV showed Chartres Cathedral. Then there was a long slow look at Sainte-Chapelle. Finally the picture switched to Notre-Dame, with its flying buttresses, its spires reaching toward clouds. The camera pulled away to show the whole of the cathedral rising above the skyline.

There were times when the Englishman who was telling the thing would shut up, would simply let the camera move around over the cathedrals. Or else the camera would tour the countryside, men in fields walking behind oxen. I waited as long as I could. Then I felt I had to say something. I said, "They're showing the outside of this cathedral now. Gargoyles. Little statues carved to look like monsters. Now I guess they're in Italy. Yeah, they're in Italy. There's fresco paintings on the walls of this one church."

"What's fresco painting, bub?" he asked, and he sipped from his drink.

I reached for my glass. But it was empty. I tried to remember what I could remember about frescoes. "You're asking me what are frescoes?" I said. "That's a good question. I don't know."

The camera moved to a cathedral outside Lisbon, Portugal. The differences in the Portuguese cathedral compared with the French and Italian were not that great. But they were there. Mostly the interior stuff. Then something occurred to me and I said, "Something has occurred to me. Do you have an idea what a cathedral is? What they look like, that is? Do you follow me? If somebody says *cathedral* to you, do you have any notion what they're talking about? Do you know the difference between that and a Baptist church, say? Or that and a mosque, or synagogue?"

He let the smoke issue from his mouth. "I know they took hundreds of workers fifty or a hundred years to build," he said. "I just heard the man say that, of course. I know generations of the same families worked on a cathedral. I heard him say that, too. The men who began their life's work on them, they never lived to see the completion of their work. In that wise, bub, they're no different from the rest of us, right?" He laughed. Then his eyelids drooped again. His head nodded. He seemed to be snoozing. Maybe he was imagining himself in Portugal. The TV was showing another cathedral now. This one was in Germany. The Englishman's voice droned on. "Cathedrals," the blind man said. He sat up and rolled his head back and forth. "If you want the truth, bub, that's about all I know. What I just said. What I heard him say. But maybe you could describe one to me? I wish you'd do it. I'd like that. If you want to know, I really don't have a good idea."

I stared hard at the shot of the cathedral on the TV. It held a minute. Then it was gone, and the view was of the inside with rows of benches and high windows. How could I even begin to describe it? But say my life depended on it. Say my life was being threatened by an insane Turkish bey.

They took the camera outside again. I stared some more at the cathedral before the picture flipped off into the countryside. There was no use. I turned to the blind man and said, "To begin with, they're very tall. Very, very tall." I was looking around the room for clues. I tried again. "They reach way up. Up and up. Toward the sky. They soar. They're like poetry, that's what they're like. They're so big, some of them, they have to have these supports. To help hold them up, so to speak. These supports are called buttresses. They remind me of viaducts for some reason. But maybe you don't know viaducts, either? Sometimes the cathedrals have devils and such carved into the front. Sometimes great lords and ladies. Don't ask me why this is," I said. He was nodding. The whole upper part of his body seemed to be moving back and forth. "I'm not doing so good, am I?" I said.

He stopped nodding and leaned forward on the edge of the sofa. As he listened to me, he was running his fingers through his beard. I wasn't getting through to him though, I could see that. But he waited for me to go on just the same. He nodded, as if trying to encourage me. I tried to think what else I could say. "They're really big. They're massive. They're built of stone. Marble, too, sometimes. In those old days, when they built cathedrals, men aspired to be close to God. In those days God was an important part of everyone's life. This was reflected in their cathedral-building. I'm sorry," I said, "but it looks like that's the best I can do for you. I'm just no good at it."

"That's all right, bub," he said. "Hey, listen. I hope you don't mind my asking you. Can I ask you something? Let me ask you a simple question, yes or no. I'm just curious and there's no offense. You're my host. But let me ask if you are in any way religious? You don't mind my asking?"

I shook my head. He couldn't see that, though. A wink is the same as a nod to a blind man. "I guess I'm agnostic or something. No, the fact is, I don't believe in it. Anything. Sometimes it's hard. You know what I'm saying?"

"Sure, I do," he said.

"Right," I said.

The Englishman was still holding forth. My wife sighed in her sleep. She drew a long breath and continued with her sleep.

"You'll have to forgive me," I said. "But I can't tell you what a cathedral looks like. It just isn't in me to do it. I can't do any more than I've done." The blind man sat very still, his head down, as he listened to me. "The truth is, cathedrals don't mean anything special to me. Nothing. Cathedrals. They're something to look at on late-night TV. That's all they are."

It was then he cleared his throat. He brought something up. He took a handkerchief from his back pocket. In a minute he said, "I get it, bub. It's okay. It happens. Don't worry about it," he said. "Hey, listen to me. Will you do me a favor? I got an idea. Why don't you find us some heavy paper? And a pen. We'll do something. An experiment. Sure, you can do it. You can. We'll draw one together. Get us a pen and some heavy paper. Go on, bub, get the stuff," he said.

•

So I went upstairs. My legs felt like they didn't have any strength in them. They felt like they did sometimes after I'd run a couple miles. In my wife's room I looked around. I found some ballpoints in a little basket on her table. And then I tried to think where to look for the kind of paper he was talking about.

Downstairs, in the kitchen, I found a shopping bag with onion skins in the bottom of the bag. I emptied the bag and shook it. I brought it into the living room and sat down with it near his legs. I moved some things, smoothed the wrinkles from the bag, spread it out on the coffee table. The blind man got down from the sofa and sat next to me on the carpet.

He ran his fingers over the paper. He went up and down the sides of the paper and the edges, top and bottom. He fingered the corners. "All right," he said. "All right. Let's do her."

He found my hand, the hand with the pen. He closed his hand over my hand. "Go ahead, bub, draw," he said. "Draw. You'll see. I'll follow along with you. It'll be all right. Just begin now, like I'm telling you. You'll see. Draw," he said.

So I began. First I drew a box that resembled a house. It could have been the house I lived in. Then I put a roof on the house. At either end of the roof I drew spires. Crazy.

"Swell," he said. "Terrific. You're doing fine," he said. "Never thought anything like this could happen in your lifetime, did you? Well, it's a strange life, bub, we all know that. Go on now. Keep it up."

I put in windows with arches. I drew flying buttresses. I hung great doors. I couldn't stop. The TV station went off the air. I put down the pen and closed and opened my fingers. The blind man felt around over the paper. He moved the tips of his fingers slowly over the paper, over what I'd drawn, and he nodded. "Doing fine," he said.

I took up the pen, and he found my hand once more. I kept at it. I'm no artist. But I kept drawing just the same.

My wife opened her eyes and gazed at us. She sat up on the sofa, her robe hanging open. She said, "What are you doing? What in the world are you doing?"

I didn't answer her. The blind man said, "We're drawing a cathedral, dear. Me and him are working on something important. Press hard now," he said to me. "That's right. That's good," he said. "Sure. You got it, bub. I can tell. You didn't think you could. But you can, can't you? You're cooking with Crisco now. You'll see. Know what I'm saying? We're going to have us something here in a minute. How's the old arm?" he said. "Put some people in there now. What's a church without people, bub?"

"What's going on?" my wife said. "Robert, what are you doing? What's going on?"

"It's all right," he said to her. "Close your eyes now, bub," he said.

I did that. I closed them just like he said.

"Are they closed?" he said. "Don't fudge."

"They're closed," I said.

"Keep them that way," he said. He said, "Don't stop now." So we kept on with it. His fingers rode my fingers as my hand went over the rough paper. It was like nothing else in my life up to now.

In a minute he said, "I think that's enough. I think you got the idea," he said. "Take a look. What do you think?"

But I had my eyes closed. I thought I'd keep them closed a little longer. I thought it was something I ought not to forget.

"Well?" he said. "Are you looking?"

My eyes were still closed. I was in my house and I knew that. But I didn't feel inside anything.

"It's really something," I said.

JAMES FERRY

Dancing Ducks and Talking Anus

(FROM THE LITERARY REVIEW)

I SUPPOSE YOU'VE HEARD that Renée douched herself with sulfuric acid. You may think this the beginning of a dirty joke, like the ones tree men like to tell on their breaks. But I don't think you could laugh once the story is told, laugh, perhaps, like my grandfather could laugh with his whole heart at the Trickster's most terrible pranks. I have not reached that point. We laugh, surely, that we may not go mad, laugh even at the most horrible things. God help me that I cannot. I still scream silently inside, scream as Renée must have when the acid began to ravage her flesh. The ambulance attendants saw the rough trench of teeth marks across her knuckles, as if she had jammed a fist in her mouth, the blood welling up from the exposed bone, smeared like some hideous clown make-up over the tight lips. She had not screamed aloud, that is certain. The only sounds she had made, so say her neighbors, were the sounds of love: the gasps, the moaning, the small, shrill cries. They had gotten used to hearing her and Larry together. They thought nothing of it. I was the one who found her. Not Larry. Over the phone her strangled voice, which at first I did not recognize, cried, "Ned! God! Oh, God!"

Larry, sixty feet above me, is singing to the tree.

> *Ladies love outlaws*
> *Like babies love stray dogs.*
> *Ladies touch babies*
> *Like bankers touch gold.*
> *Outlaws touch ladies*
> *Deep in their souls.*

I yell at him to quit serenading and cut the limb. He grumbles
something, scrambled by the wind, fiddling with his tie-off rope.
He's slow today, distracted, fussing too much over an easy take-
down. I remind him to back-cut the limb. He snarls, "I know, I
know!" jerking the saw into an angry sputter and dropping the
limb with an indifferent warning bark: "Headache!" He doesn't
have his mind on his work entirely, which is dangerous. Accidents
happen that way. People get hurt. When I told him, "Renée's
spread-eagled in the burn unit with her insides gutted," he just
said, "Renée who!" I don't know why I didn't smash him then. I
suppose I was still afraid of him. Renée is not on his mind now.
Perhaps he's thinking of me, here on the ground, waiting, watching . . .

For days Renée lay like a fallen tree in that hospital bed. And
for days all I could do was sit quietly and watch her face; while
awake, a face of stone, with eyes that seemed not even to stare, as
if she had gone blind also; but when asleep, forced into unconsciousness by the doctor's drugs, a face lit from somewhere
beneath by a procession of flickering grimaces, deep frowns, a lip-
biting look of almost unbearable apprehension, and once, an open-
mouth gape of such extraordinary awe that it caught my breath. I
tried to imagine what she was dreaming, but I couldn't. Sometimes, when the silence became too heavy, I would tell her an
Indian tale, as I used to, one of Wakdjunkaga's more amusing
escapades. She had always liked these Trickster tales, but I could
not tell whether she was listening now. I would even take the
chance and reminisce about happier times . . . fishing trips in the
mountains with Larry and me . . . rainy football games, huddled
under tarps and baseball caps, sipping Southern Comfort . . . riding horses hard across high, stony pastures, leaping the rock walls,
racing toward the forest fired with autumn . . . playing gin rummy
in the back of a truck going to pick apples . . . drinking and singing
songs and playing mumblypeg on the wooden bar tables, where
she would always lose, I would always win, and Larry would be too
drunk to care . . . None of these memories had any effect on her.
And I, who now spent every hour not working or sleeping at the
hospital, was not only becoming a stranger to these memories but
to the continuing life from which they had been borne.

My grandfather once told me that there was a certain pain that
purified. Because of the pain, some Indian ceremonies may seem

like mere torture to outsiders. But beyond the pain there is something else, if only one can get beyond the pain. The inside is reduced to ash, as the sun has touched you, sanctified you. And then you are filled with the holy vision. As it was with my grandfather once, though all such ceremonies were banned by the government. Through secret rites, the vision was obtained: *As an eagle, he followed the shadow of his prey into a dark cave to the center of a great mountain; there, Grandmother Spider lay on her web waiting. He was arrogant, like all birds of prey, and told Grandmother that he had no enemies and feared no one. Grandmother smiled her beautiful and terrible smile and told him that his fight was beautiful but that his boasting was wasted on her. He would be her prey soon enough, returning, as all must, to her dark womb.* When I first heard this as a boy, I was afraid of Grandmother Spider, but my grandfather said that sometimes fear is the mother of love, and that I should learn to love Grandmother as one both feared and loved the Great Spirit. He never explained his vision, if any explanation could be given. He had done too much just to reveal something ordinarily so personal. He knew the old ways were dying, and I think he was afraid I would not have a vision of my own to help lead me through life. I wish now I could tell him that I have had my vision, though in no way that he nor I could have ever foretold.

My father did not believe in visions, nor did he care for the stories my grandfather told. They were just myths and superstitions to him. He left the reservation before he was sixteen and worked building roads. Now he rides a huge earth-moving machine, tires as tall as a house, the wide steel blade carving up the land as easily as one hoes weeds. I grew up learning that money may buy you a house in the suburbs but does not promise you a place in the community. When the neighborhood kids played cowboys and Indians, I was never a cowboy. I disobeyed my father and went to visit my grandfather many times before he died (it was an old man's death, alone, in the night; I cried because I had not been there). He told me it was bad to disobey my father, probably thinking of how his son had disobeyed him once, but even worse to disobey one's heart. I too would leave home, but after my grandfather returned to Grandmother Spider, I no longer returned to the reservation.

•

Larry and I argue over how to drop a limb. He just wants to let it run, falling freely without any check on the rope. He thinks it will

miss that expensive hedge. Maybe he doesn't care. I know a risk
like that is bad business. This tree is taking too long and I have to
keep prodding him. He's usually a maniac in a tree. He neither
knows nor cares much about them, but once one needs to come
down he'll have it in pieces on the ground so fast as to seem to
leave a vacuum in the air. He swings carelessly from limb to limb,
ripping away with chainsaw snarl amidst clouds of sawdust and
blue oil smoke, dropping limbs with fly-casting precision. This
slow, methodical chewing away at the tree is not his style, not what
made him the best climber I had ever seen. Any other day we'd be
sitting on the stump already, taking a coffee break, recalling great
drunks, big trees, fish that fought till our hands were numb, girls
we never had but wished we did. Something about sitting on a
stump, especially a fresh one, with a friend, laughing at the past,
good times or bad, or what times we would have once the work
was finished. It's true stumps hold great power. Some trees refuse
to die. Slender shoots will rise from the blunt stump, slim fingers
fragile in appearance yet charged with the enormous energy of a
hundred miles of roots locked into the force of the earth. Grandfather told me how he would wait patiently for hours when he
found such a stump, wait, cradling his rifle, trying to make himself
part of the forest, wait until a rabbit appeared, wait still until the
animal had eaten the tender green tips of the budding stump, wait,
in no hurry, raising his rifle carefully, aiming, breath held, then
. . . CRACK — sending the hot shell to explode the rabbit's head,
knife ready to lay the animal open on the stump, devouring
quickly the heart while it was still raw, hot, and trembling. Thus,
so he used to tell me, he gained some of the great power of the
tree through his brother the rabbit. Larry and I, however, will not
sit on the stump of this tree. I will quickly cut it flush with the
ground and load it with the rest of the downed trunk, raking the
sawdust and shoveling it into plastic garbage bags.

   Larry used to be foreman of our crew when I first started. He
was just out of the service, a Vietnam combat vet, and he was such
a terror in a tree that I felt the same way I felt when I saw a twister
chew a wide path through an apple orchard, tossing and grinding
up trees as if they were going through one of our mechanical
chippers. Larry taught me everything I know about tree work, but
I was never too successful in teaching him about the trees themselves. And then there came the day when he was no longer head
of the crew, when he forgot to respect the power of a tree, even in

its death. It was about a year ago around this time, when we were taking down a big elm like this one close into the front of a house. Larry was in prime form, busily dropping the crown of the tree at our feet. He had such a momentum going that we had a hard time keeping up with him, the next limb crashing to the ground before the previous three or four were sawed and loaded. He swooped down on his rope and was ready to take off one of the huge leaders, a primary limb of the tree that branched out from the main trunk. It was at least twenty-five feet long and as big around as a truck tire. I told him it was too close to the house to be taken off in one piece. He shrugged. No sweat, he said, tie it off with the one-inch bull rope. I've seen tractor pulls with one-inch hemp where it would go most of the day without as much as a fray, but when that section cracked off and began to gain momentum in the air, I think everyone knew in an instant that we were dealing with something more than we could handle. The limb snapped that bull rope as if it had been packaging twine, whipping the exploded end in a great arc ten feet over Larry's head where he stood high in the tree. He didn't even react to get out of the way, but like the rest of us watched in awe as that piece of tree, tied only in the middle now, moved as I knew it had to, swinging ponderously like a huge battering ram straight into a solid brick wall, smashing through it in an explosion of broken brick and dust, driving with terrifying, unmerciful force right into the heart of the house. Even Larry looked a little stunned, though he tried to laugh it off, saying that there must have been a weak section in the rope. He tried to blame me, since I usually made it a habit to check all the ropes in the truck. I shook my head. The tree's revenge, I said, knowing that the rope was as sound as it could be. Needless to say, they wanted to fire him, but then I was Larry's friend and defended what I thought was just his recklessness, reminding them they'd be losing to some other company the best climber in the area. Economics won out, as it usually does, but now I run the crew, despite the color of my skin. I know trees, I give them results, the work gets done, quickly, neatly, no customer complaints, and I've never had an accident on a job yet. Larry still does the take-downs while I work the ropes from the ground, checking his carelessness, chanting to myself a death song for the tree: "Everything passes away, but the earth endures . . ."

I ease the limb down Larry has just cut, swinging it out away from the hedge where it falls harmlessly to the ground. I untie the rope and haul it back up to where Larry will tie the next limb off. I wish we were on a trimming job, where I could be up there myself. I take off my glove and flex my scarred hand around the rope. It is still stiff but growing stronger. I could climb now. My grandfather, as was the custom, had scars on his arms from cuts by his own hand, signs of grief at the deaths of his mother and father, swept away in an epidemic of smallpox. I, in turn, have a scar on my shoulder nearest my heart for my grandfather's death. And now, a fresh one across my knuckles for Renée. She still lives, but at the time, just after she was admitted to the hospital, I felt something in her had surely died, been burned away, leaving the eyes like cold cinders, reflections of the ash within.

At those times I remembered her as I once knew her, bouncing toward me, on the edge of sprinting, her black hair shining in the sun and lifting up from the sides of her face like the wings of a bird. My heart rose with it, jammed into my throat so that I gasped with a choking pain I'd never felt before. I called her Raven, breathless as she was from running. She laughed and teasingly called me a superstitious savage. She liked to listen to the stories my grandfather taught me, sitting with her legs tucked up and her head tilted on a hand, that raven hair swept behind a small, china-white ear. I knew she did not believe those tales, but it was enough just to have her listen. To her they were like the fairy tales she had heard when she was young: Snow White, Cinderella, Rumpelstilt-skin. Larry's war stories, however, she believed without hesitation, because, as they say, he had the scars to prove it. They seemed no less fantastic than my ancient warrior tales. Larry made the stories both funny and terrifying at the same time, funny, I was soon to realize, at the time they happened and not merely in the retelling, and certainly no less terrifying now than then. He would tell of the elaborate games and practical jokes they played to relieve the boredom or ease the tension of the long stretches between the savage firefights, the ambushes that left the survivors picking up the pieces of their buddies and dumping them in plastic bags. Larry had the scars from one such skirmish that earned him a Purple Heart and the Bronze Star. I asked him once about some longer scars on his arms, since they looked so like the scar on my shoulder. He said he got those in Saigon in a knife fight with a French pimp. I didn't know at the time whether to believe him.

My grandfather would have appreciated Larry's war record; he was a warrior, I can imagine him saying, he fought bravely. Was there any difference in cutting off the ears of the enemy dead, as some had done in Vietnam, and the taking of scalps? My grandfather would understand the brutality of the kill. I could only wonder at my own revulsion at what seemed cruel and savage acts. Perhaps I was only trying to seem more civilized to Renée, who eventually refused to listen to Larry's stories anymore. "Ned," she would say, "tell me about the Deer Woman of the Ponca." I did not want to speak of the Deer Woman, who was a destroyer, seducing and mutilating young braves, and who I had feared more as a child than Grandmother Spider. To Renée, I suppose, anything must have seemed better than the horror of Larry's memories.

My grandfather said once that death had two faces: one, sad and beautiful; the other, grinning and terrible. There was the time, when he was still young, a lightning fire made a wide scar on the timbered slope of a high ridge. When the medicine men of the tribe went up in solemn procession to say healing words over the earth's wound, my grandfather trailed along secretly, not allowed at such ceremonies yet nevertheless curious like any young boy. His rifle went with him, as it always did when he went into the woods. High on the ridge, with smoke still hanging heavily among the unburnt trees, he met a huge, terrible spirit, a dark, gigantic figure suddenly appearing out of the choking haze, trailing smoke as if forged out of the remnants of the fire. Wailing horribly, it crashed blindly through the forest toward my grandfather, slashing in crazed fury at anything in its path. The greatest fear my grandfather could remember had rooted him to the spot like the trees around. He tried to remember a warrior song to bring him courage in the face of almost certain death, but this awful spirit swooping down upon him swept away all thought and left only the fear and a crushing shame at his foolish disobedience. When almost upon him, the creature reared up with a ground-shaking roar, and the lone thought came to my grandfather that this thing surely must be death itself. He wondered why he should be so afraid of death. He felt his arms lift his rifle high over his head in silent recognition of his fate. It was then, when he had given himself up to this dark force, that the smell of singed fur and flesh swept over him, and he recognized the creature for what it truly was — a great black bear caught in the fire and mutilated almost beyond recognition. My grandfather does not remember firing, but he killed the bear with a shot and skinned it on the spot, crying tears mixed with relief, sadness, and anger. He saved the skin but buried the rest, knowing the meat was too full of fear to eat. He made a robe from the scarred hide, wearing it proudly on solemn occasions, where he was no longer a child, and everyone in the tribe from then on called him Burning Bear. He always considered this his true initiation into manhood, though four years would pass before he would go through the tribe's formal rites and achieve his vision. He would never fear anything ever again, living or spirit, not Grandmother Spider, not even the Great Spirit itself. He remembered sadly, but with no small pride, when he had looked terrible death in the face and lived.

In the dusk of a ripening fall day, watching from the high hospital window the failing light, the shadows gathering like flocks of black geese in the tree-choked streets, lights blinking and slowly coming awake, I told Renée of my grandfather's meeting with the burned bear. The telling of the old Indian tales had been like talking to myself; there was no sign of her listening as she used to. But I hadn't told her this story before — it was part of a separate, personal heritage that I kept to myself — and this time, even in the dimness of the room, I sensed a change; and as my eyes became accustomed to the gloom, I saw that her eyes had softened and, now as I watched, were slowly filling with tears, like water filling a muddy footprint, tears that streaked heedlessly down her face and hid in the darkness of her hair. I felt my heart grow weak, and I took my bandaged hand and squeezed until my eyes began to water from the pain. Blinking back the shimmering blur of water, I saw Renée's hands, bandaged also, rise trembling from her sides as if they were not a part of her, the two white-bandaged hands rising in the dimness like the alien spirits my grandfather said he saw leaving the bodies of people recovering from an illness, the white hands rising and falling in one unbroken arc until they slowly covered her face. She sobbed silently. I waited for the longest time until she had quieted, and then left to change my bloodied bandage.

Being in a tree is like being in the hand of God. I know that. I did not have to learn that from anyone. You must learn to trust the limb you're tied to; it is flexible but strong; it yields to your weight, acknowledges your presence, yet will not break, will support you even though you might be its destroyer. Once a Mohawk I know, who works the high steel, took me up to walk the windy beams forty stories above the city. He was part of a riveting gang, a bucker-up, wrestling steel all day on the building's skeleton, striding those narrow beams as if they were picket fences. I sensed the great power the Mohawk talked about in these steel and concrete mountains. "We put them together to last," he boasted, as we stood amidst the heaving cranes, the winches straining at their loads, the riveters machine-gunning the red-hot rivets into place. I certainly have no fear of heights, clambering about as I do on the swaying tops of hundred-foot beeches, but I was glad when I was back down on the ground. Being up there reminded me too much of the time as a boy when my father let me ride the huge earth-moving monster for the first time. Great excitement turned to a nightmarish fear, as if I were trapped on that machine, never able to get off, riding it forever. I cried, but for some reason my father would not stop, which only made my fear worse. The machine went on until I wet my pants and my father was forced to stop.

•

This elm we work on is diseased and must be taken out, burned, destroying the contagious fungus, but I do not like to see its dismembered limbs scattered about my feet. I yell for Tom to hurry and load these branches. "Do you want to be here all night too?" He's grumbling nowadays too, having to do more work since Danny was laid up in the hospital. He wasn't hurt on the job. He got in Larry's way, and it might as well have been like getting pole-axed by a falling limb. Tom gives me a dark look, tugging fitfully at the branches. I know I can't hold the crew together now. Nothing is the same. We do our job.

It is not only for business reasons that I want to get this job done as soon as possible. Renée is leaving the hospital today after so many weeks, and I need to be there, to take her home to my place. I keep prodding Larry, always careful, though, that he doesn't do anything crazy. I once saw him drop a limb on a power line because it was in his way and he didn't want to spend the time lowering the other limbs around it. The line ripped away from the house and lay on the damp lawn, its exposed end smoking. Larry just stared at it while I cussed him out. Suddenly he threw his handsaw down — at first, I thought, aimed at me, but landing right on top of the power line. It spit vicious blue-white sparks that hissed and crackled in the grass. Larry told a young neighborhood boy hanging about to go fetch his saw, but I took a pruning pole instead to pluck it away from the naked line and hand it back to him. He would not take it at first, staring at the blade shot with the sinuous streaks of the power's passage, staring with what seemed the first hint of fear I had ever seen on his face. Finally he laughed, swung down and grabbed the saw, slashing the air as he carried it up into the tree again.

"I loved him." Renée had spoken all of a sudden out of the dark, lying in the hospital bed. This was the first thing she had said since being admitted the week before. I was sitting silently in the dark, out of Indian tales and fond memories, and not knowing what else to say, when she said simply, "I loved him." I knew she had. It wasn't that. I think there was something else we dared not speak of, that perhaps could never be spoken of, at least directly, like one cannot look directly at the sun without risking blindness. Everyone, the police, the doctors, her own family, had wondered what had driven her to this mad act. Once it was known she wasn't pregnant, the sheer self-destructiveness of her actions became all too apparent. Yet there was always the nagging question that no one could reason away: If she had, in fact, wanted to kill herself, she not only had done an awful job of it, worse by far than those who gulp pills or slash veins yet eventually call someone, but she had subjected herself to what one doctor estimated as "an intensity of pain only experienced voluntarily by madmen and martyrs." The doctor shook his head. "You can't believe how much damage there was." She would probably regain only minimal feeling around her vagina, even with the extensive reconstruction they could do. As for children . . . "Absolutely out of the question," the doctor said. "She's very lucky to be alive." I waited, but she said nothing more. I patiently waited, making in the back of my throat the whispered roar of wind in the tops of trees.

I remembered spending most of a day cabling a lightning-split tree, covering its wound with the thick, gray asphalt dressing, tracing with my fingertips the jagged, splintered etch of the bolt's passage. Something incredible was written there, I felt, the creator's signature just as much as the spiral fall of a maple's winged seed, but something that was not yet for me to know, if I was to know at all. Renée and I huddled under a tree once during a thunderstorm. We had been walking in the park waiting for Larry. She was troubled. She said her skin felt prickly. I said it was the electricity in the air. She said Larry was drinking too much. He broke things. I asked her if he had ever hit her. A sudden flash of lightning startled the dark look on her face. Her wet hair hung limply down the sides of her fragile skull. She gripped my arm as the thunder boomed about us. She was afraid of the thunder. She wanted to move because she was afraid that lightning would strike the tree. I told her it wouldn't dare spoil our fun. She huddled against me, nervously fingering a button on my shirt, twisting it until the thread broke. We seemed shy and innocent like children. I held her as I would hold a trembling bird that had fallen from a great height. Her heart raced, her breasts straining against my chest. The storm beat around us, drenching us in warm, almost soothing rain. When Larry came in his car, tires hissing like coiled black snakes on the shiny asphalt, I would not go with them. Renée ran splashing, awkward, hair heavy with rain. Nearly slipping, she caught herself, pausing an instant to look back. It wasn't the look I expected. Driving at night, I had seen many a rabbit dart out right in front of my wheels, frozen a moment in the glare of the headlights, too close, you always think, to escape from being mangled, but never would you find a trace of blood or fur on the car the next morning. I had seen so many rabbits do that, I began to think it was a game with them, some sort of test of courage. In that brief exposure there was never the surprise or terror one might expect, but a richer fear born of known risk, charged with an excitement that burned red in those wild eyes. It was that look that I saw in Renée just before she disappeared into the car, whose rain-streaked windows I could not see into. I stood sodden in the downpour, wanting the lightning to tear through me, to burn out the excitement and fear I now felt. I knew she wanted him, desperately, shamelessly, almost fatally. I was afraid for her.

"Don't let him see me," she spoke again, startling me out of my thought, and then nothing, silence, except for the wind in my throat, though I waited until the nurses had to kick me out; nothing until the next day, her gaze not yet shifted from the ceiling. She ran a small, delicate tongue over her thin, cracked lips and in a voice that seemed to find the very strength to speak almost too much for it, said, "Once we went driving in the rain. Not going anywhere, just driving. Driving and singing along with the radio.

'Help me, Rhonda, help, help me, Rhonda . . .' " She gulped, gnawed her lip, blinking, her eyes beacons in the dark. Without thinking, I made a move toward her to calm her into silence again. Though I had waited and prayed for so long to hear her voice again, suddenly I was afraid of what she might say. I caught myself, standing just inside the glow of the bed lamp, and let her words run over me. "He just went faster and faster and I became afraid and told him to slow down but he wouldn't and just kept going faster and faster and I put my hand on his hand on the wheel and he clamped my hand to the wheel, he held it hard against the wheel until I cried out in pain and then he took his hands away and put his foot further down on the gas pedal, he was laughing while I tried to steer. He rolled down the window to let the rain blow in, and he just laughed, the rain hissing, the radio crackling with static, as we went faster and faster, and I was crying, and he still laughed . . ."

Later on that night, after leaving the hospital, I stopped in at what used to be our favorite bar. I knew I needed a drink, several, in fact, but I think also I was hoping to find Larry there. What I would have done if he had been I can't say exactly, but I'm glad now I didn't get a chance to find out. The headless concrete deer was still there by the door. Larry and I had stolen it off the lawn of a rich old lady we did a trimming job for, and donated it to the bar in a sort of compensation for all the mock fights we had staged over Renée to liven up a dead evening. The customers used to hang their hats and coats on the antlers until one day Larry came in and blasted the head off with that sawed-off .12-gauge he had brought back from the war. I happened to be there, and I could see he was speeding a little, but when he swung down on the rest of us in the place, pumping in another shell, I knew that most of that look came from someplace else, someplace I couldn't even begin to imagine, some crazed, dark, furious, knife-edge place that so terrified me that I found myself looking for a way to escape. Yet while smoke and dust still hung in the air, Renée came rushing in, breathing hard. Larry swung at her with the shotgun, but she stepped back out of the way. They stood staring at each other while I searched the bar for a weapon. But before I could act, Larry just tossed the gun at Renée and stomped out. I learned later they had argued over some simple, silly domestic thing, not putting the milk away or leaving his boots lying about, and he had suddenly flown into a rage. As I watched, Renée slowly pumped the remaining shells out of the gun and gave it to me. Her hand was shaking. She said, "I don't want to ever see it again." It's no good for hunting, so I broke it down and buried the pieces in separate locations miles apart.

"He had scars on the back of his legs," Renée said. I had come to the hospital after supper still nursing a hangover from the night before. I had almost not come. But when I realized the reason for this was not so much my physical condition as a distinct fear of hearing what else Renée had to tell, I knew I could not abandon the vigil, avoid what had been started the night before with her first words. I sat up now, resisting the pain in my head, and looked at her. She had one bandaged hand thrown across her eyes, and unlike the headlong rush of her words yesterday, she spoke very slowly and deliberately, with long pauses between sentences. "From shrapnel, was all he would say. I touched them. But I don't think he had much feeling there. He would never tell me how he got them. I was afraid to know. I had heard too many of his war stories. We were lying in bed once in the dark. He was smoking. I couldn't see him. I smelled the smoke. We had just made love. Now he was off someplace. I could never tell where. I was tracing the lines of his scars, not thinking, just touching. Then suddenly I was asking him what had happened then. He didn't say a thing, just touched the glowing end of his cigarette to my thigh and went on smoking in the dark. I cried and tried to rub the pain away." She was quiet then, and I thought it had passed. Then she was speaking again: "Then in the dark I couldn't smell the smoke. And then I felt his hand on my leg. I jerked away when he touched the burn. He held my leg. Then he kissed the pain. He sucked the burn." A longer pause then. I wanted her to be done, but somehow I knew she wasn't. "We made love again," she said finally, "and I couldn't feel the burn anymore."

I stood close to her then and took the bandaged hand that lay by her side. She fingered my bandage with her bare fingertips. Her other hand lifted away from her eyes, and for the first time they looked at something besides the gloom gathering at the ceiling. She looked at me. Her eyes were wet like stones in the rain. I ripped my bandage away and she took my hand in both of hers, tracing the stitched scar. The skin of my hand burned and burned. The sheets whispered of a shudder through her body. I stood and

waited in the dark, staring at her, watching a sheen of blue electricity on her hair so black around her pale face.

"I had a nightmare the other night." Her voice was keen and
true like the blade of an axe, and twice as hard. "I was lying in a
field in the sun. I was lying naked in the sun. And a strange shadow
came over me." She passed a gauze-covered hand in front of her
face. "And I felt cold. Then I saw a huge, black bird come down
out of the sun. And it started eating . . ." Her voice broke then.
Her grip tightened on my hand. "I couldn't move," she said, her
voice recovering its edge. "It pinned me to the ground, its claws
digging into me, and it pecked at me. It began to peck at me. It
kept pecking at me. I couldn't yell. I couldn't move. A big, black
wing covered my face. I couldn't see, but I felt it slowly, steadily
eating away at the middle of me." She then took my hand and
guided it under the sheet to the mound between her legs. My hand
found neither hair nor skin but only rough gauze and a rubber
catheter. I had felt her voice bite into me, her words chopping
down into me, slashing deeper with each hot stroke, but when she
pressed my hand upon her ravaged middle, I felt a pain like a hot
wind blow through me as if I were no more than a cloud, and
everything was driven out except the dark vision of the bird
swooping down, hearing the thunderous beating of wings and feeling the burning rush of wind and seeing the bird, big and black
and looking like no one or nothing I had ever seen, daylight or
dark, waking or dreaming, huge and awful, beating down on me
until I was smothered with darkness, and I heard Renée scream,
screaming not here or now lying in this hospital bed silent again,
but sprawled on the cold tile floor of her apartment's bathroom,
one hand still methodically squeezing the empty syringe as it begins to crumble and melt from the acid that it held for a moment,
the other hand stuffed in her mouth, the jaws tightening, hot
nausea rising and searing her throat, her head rolling back and
forth on the cold tile, her breath coming in short, spasmodic gasps,
her legs writhing uncontrollably, methodically pushing, pushing
out, heels trying futilely to dig into the hard, slick tile, as if she
were trying to climb backward out of a deep pit, a liquid fire
burning through her until there was nothing left but the pain, the
scream high and long, like the sound an animal makes when it
bites off the leg caught in the jaws of the trap, hearing now the
scream she never uttered as I stood beside her and the darkness

of the bird passed through me and I was beyond it bathed in light, and I felt Renée holding my scarred hand to herself, feeling the quiet rise and fall of her body with each breath. I took my hand back and held it against my chest, feeling my own shortness of breath. The wound tingled, but there was no more pain. She frowned at me in concern and was about to say something. I shook my head. "Sleep," I said. "I am here to protect you from the nightmares." I took my hand and stroked the electricity from her hair, my hand alive with the energy, stroked her head until she slept.

•

A couple of days ago the weather was bad and we couldn't work. The crew spent the day drinking in a small bar at a country crossroads. I sat sipping beer by a window, watching through the streaked glass the hollows of the earth fill up with a cold mist. The trees, half-bare now, were quiet, dreamy in the cold autumn rain. I saw in my mind an image of Renée holding a bright orange mum cupped in her hands like a little fire, her face warming to the flower's glow. I kept this image in my head like Renée had held the flower. I heard Tom and Danny playing pool, the click of the balls like the rattle of bones. Roy Acuff was singing about the Wabash Cannonball on the jukebox. The trees seemed to float in the mist, their bright colors muted in the gray light, smudged by the steady drizzle, until they seemed more like spirits.that had gathered here to pay their respects to me, the earth's new child. I felt humbled, yet strong and infinitely worthy. I heard Larry at the bar drinking and singing lewd songs. He started to dance with the barmaid, holding her close and whispering in her ear. She leaned into him, giggling, tossing her hair. Then I saw the bartender come around the bar at them with a paring knife he'd been cutting lemons with. I was smelling the lemons and watching some of them roll off the bar onto the floor as the man came at Larry. The girl turned out to be his wife, but he couldn't have known he was coming at a man who had survived a dozen VC ambushes. Grabbing a cue stick from Danny, Larry smashed the bartender in the face. The guy staggered back into a table, where he sat a moment on the edge, his face blossoming with blood, before sliding off onto the floor. His wife started screaming. Larry swung the stick around and cracked her in the middle. She went down in a heap, gasping for air. Wielding the stick, he then started to smash practically everything in the place: lights, bottles, glasses, windows.

Danny tried to stop him but got the stick broken over his head.
Larry turned on Tom then, who, glancing at me, said, "This isn't
my fight." He fled out into the rain. Larry, methodical and thor-
ough as a wrecking crane, went on smashing furniture, throwing
pool balls through windows, and battering the jukebox into silence.
Finally he came round to me sitting there still, feeling the cold on
my neck from the broken window, sitting and waiting. He came
swinging the fat, knobbed leg of a broken chair, breath heaving,
red-faced, hair wet with spilt beer, eyes wild and unfocused. He
clubbed the table, but I just sat there staring at him. He couldn't
seem to look at me fully but kept staring by me out into the rain.
Finally our eyes locked. He leaned forward on the table and spit,
"You bloody fucking savage! I should smash you!"

"You better do it, Larry. You better do it now." I waited, listening to the rain and his labored breathing.

Then while I waited for the blow to come, something terrible
passed over his face, like the wrinkling of flesh too close to the
flame. A pain danced through my scarred hand, and I gripped the
table so it would not tremble.

He shook his head and thumped the table with the end of the
chair leg. "She was a cunt!" he shouted. "Just a damn cunt!"

Behind me the sound of the rain was cut by a siren. Somebody,
perhaps Tom, had had the sense to call the police. Larry lurched
toward the door. I stood up. I knew the police, once they saw Larry
coming at them, would gun him down. I waited a moment longer,
then took my beer mug and swung it down hard on the back of his
head.

•

Yesterday I brought Renée a paper bag full of fall leaves, the red
and orange maple, the yellow beech. I had just come from visiting
Danny on another ward. He suffered a good concussion but will
be out of the hospital by the end of the week. All Larry needed
was a few stitches and some aspirin. I didn't want to hurt him, just
knock him out. Because of his war record and some connections
with the police, he got out of that bar brawl with only a stiff fine
and a bit of probation. Danny doesn't want to work in the same
crew anymore. I don't blame him.

Renée was sleeping, so I stood quietly by the window looking
out at the lights in the night. I was feeling the presence of my
grandfather tonight, remembering how he would grin and laugh

and even dance when he related to me the adventures of Wakdjunkaga, the Trickster. I had told Renée some of the funnier
episodes, like Trickster and the laxative bulb, where he has to
climb a tree to escape his own excrement and finally falls in. For a
long time I couldn't understand Trickster's character, because he
was both victimizer and victim, both tricking and being tricked.
The one episode that showed this the most, and the one my grandfather loved to tell the most, was the one where Wakdjunkaga
tricked the ducks into dancing. He told them that he had met no
one whom he could sing for, no one who would dance to his songs.
Everyone always recognizes Trickster, but they're always fooled by
him anyway. The ducks had not danced for a very long time, so
they began to dance while Trickster sang. I saw my grandfather
waddling crazily about, doing the dance of the ducks. This was
always my favorite part. My grandfather performing the dance of
the ducks to the songs he sang as the Trickster. After that, everything would change. Trickster would start to wring the ducks'
necks and they would flee, and Trickster would shout like a warrior, "Ha, ha, this is the way a man acts!" My grandfather would
grin and wink, because we all knew there were always tables to be
turned in any Trickster tale. So he would tell how the Trickster
prepared the two ducks that hadn't escaped for roasting in the fire
and said thus to his anus: "Now you, my younger brother, must
keep watch for me while I go to sleep." I could never figure out
why Trickster had to take a nap right then while his dinner was
cooking, but I guess it was part of his foolish nature that always
seemed to balance out the more destructive pranks. It gave the
opportunity for the small foxes to sneak up and try to steal the
meat. Whites always think Indians tell their tales with such dignity,
but my grandfather was always enthusiastic about acting out the
cruder parts of the Trickster stories, waggling his butt and making
farting noises as he told how Trickster's anus expelled gas with a
loud noise at the foxes. The foxes, however, did not run away until
they had eaten all the meat. Trickster, of course, was very angry
when he awoke and found the meat gone. Here my grandfather,
enjoying the role of the clown, would bend over, stick his head
between his legs, and say, as Trickster did to his anus, "Did I not
tell you to watch this fire? You shall remember this! As a punishment for your remissness, I will burn your mouth so that you will
not be able to use it!" Thereupon, the Trickster took a burning

piece of wood and burnt the mouth of his anus. As he applied the fire, he shouted, "Ouch! Ouch! This is too much! I have made my skin smart! Is it not for such things that they call me Trickster? They have indeed talked me into doing this just as if I had been doing something wrong!" My grandfather would always laugh at the end of the story, laugh so hard sometimes that tears would come to his eyes. I told him I thought it was horrible. He laughed and said, "No, it is just the Trickster, and he is to be laughed at." I frowned, not understanding. "Do not frown, my son," he said, "you look just like Trickster's anus." I laugh now at the memory of this, but I was very insulted at the time. I still think the story is horrible, but perhaps someday I will be able to tell it to Renée, and someday perhaps we will be able to laugh at foolish Trickster like my grandfather. That night I felt I knew Trickster better and was even thinking of telling the story to Renée when she awoke. As I was thinking this, I sensed a change in her breathing and was turning toward her even as she was calling my name.

"Ned." The last time I had heard her call me by name was over the telephone, calling for help. I was at her side in an instant. "I'm here," I said.

"Ned, I was sleeping." She sighed, and her bandaged hands reached out slowly as if to touch something to make sure it was real. "I was sleeping, and I had a dream. In the dream, I was standing in a fast mountain stream, letting the current rush between my legs. The sun was in my face. It was warm. The water was cool, soothing. You were there too, crouched on a big rock near the bank, the water surging around it. You were staring into the water, very still, waiting. I wanted to call out to you, wanted you to turn and look at me in the middle of the river. Suddenly your hands darted like lightning into the water and scooped a fish flashing into the sun, holding it an instant thrashing between your hands, as if it would climb the air itself to be free. I felt the fish's shudder through my body and beat at the river with my fists. Then the fish broke away, tumbling wildly in the air and splashing back into the stream. I was glad you had caught it, and I was glad it had got away. I laughed and called to you, laughing. You smacked the water angrily, then looked up at me and laughed too."

She was smiling slightly, and though I had not seen that smile for a long time, I could only frown in return. "Renée," I called, and she turned to look at me. Was she seeing me, or was I still a part of her dream? I could not tell. "Renée," I said, "that wasn't a dream. It really happened. It happened last June. We went fishing one weekend. Don't you remember?"

She sighed and closed her eyes. "No, Ned," she said, shaking her head, "it was a dream I just had." She was still smiling. "It was a wonderful dream."

•

The sun sits red and spent in the gold crown of a distant oak. Larry stands in the crotch of the elm we've been working on all day. Idly he flicks sawdust off one of the stumps. The tree has been reduced to the trunk and, at the top, the ring of sawed stumps that once held aloft the fullness of the tree. Larry stands in the ring, not more than thirty feet off the ground, stands very still at the apex of the vase-like structure of the elm, his rope hanging loosely by his side, no longer any limb left above to tie off on. All we need to do now is drop the trunk. But Larry is still up there, now only a stark silhouette against the pale twilight. It's as if he doesn't want to come down. All day he's been up there, all day whittling away at this tree, yet still he stands atop the column of wood, not moving. I give his climbing rope a small tug. Startled, he reaches out to embrace the tree and jerks his head around to look down at me. It is too dark and he is too far away to see his face clearly, but somehow I know fear is there. He will come down soon. It is getting cold and dark. Perhaps he knows now that some-day soon the tree will no longer hold him in her sure hand, that someday a knot will slip, a rope will break, a limb will swing the wrong way, that soon the tree will have its revenge. Then perhaps I too can say that I had a dream.

The lyric sung by Larry on page 18 is from the song "Ladies Love Outlaws" by Lee Clayton, Resaca Music, BMI, © 1972. Used by permission of the publisher.

JOANNA HIGGINS

The Courtship of Widow Sobcek

(FROM MSS)

WARMED BY HIS feather-tick, John Jielewicz lay in bed and studied
the ceiling. What day was it? Then he knew, and time began once
more. Saturday; overcast and dull. It looked like snow. He got up
quickly, made coffee, and set to work. After washing his cup and
saucer, he mopped the linoleum in the kitchen and bathroom,
dusted the spools of his furniture, and vacuumed the rose-pat-
terned rugs of his living room. Then he rinsed out his opalescent
glass spittoon in the basement. His housecleaning finished for the
week, he filled the bathtub, threw in his long underwear and shirt,
and lowered himself into the hot water. The day was half gone.

Steam clouded the mirror, and late afternoon light illumined
pale swans and lily pads floating on turquoise wallpaper. He considered the week. On Monday he'd spaded the garden, and on
Tuesday he'd chopped wood. He'd worked at Chet's on Wednesday and Thursday, making Polish sausage and pickled bologna.
Then on Friday, but what had he done on Friday? The stoker?
No. The garage? No. The car? The yard? No. What then? How
could he forget in just one day? The stoker? No. The basement,
the stoker, the coal? Yes, the coal! He'd taken the Plymouth to
Townsend's and ordered a ton of coal. Then he'd come home,
checked the coal bin, and swept the basement.

It was good to think of the work ahead. Soon Chet would be
getting big Christmas orders for smoked hams and sausages, and
he would be busy. Years of working with casings in icy water and
handling cold meats had twisted his hands, and they ached with
changes in the weather. He held them beneath the hot water. Next
to his thin legs, as white and veined as church marble, his hands

looked like gnarled stumps. But they were good hands, he thought, hard-working hands. And he'd done his share of work in his time — the lumber camps, the farm, the store. What else was there besides work? People sometimes said: "That John Jielewicz. He sure knows how to work!" That made him pull back his narrow shoulders and walk proudly.

"Pa," his daughter had said on one of her Sunday night visits, "move in with us." Casting her eyes around the big rooms, she'd said, "Why all this work, Pa? You don't need so much work at your age. And for what? Who sees it?"

Removing his pipe, he'd said, "I see it." Then he'd leaned over his chair to spit into the spittoon, defying all the ranch houses on the south side of town.

The bath water was getting tepid and uncomfortable; he added more hot water, soaped himself with a bar of Fels Naptha, and ducked his head twice under the water. Then he soaped the underwear and the shirt, rinsed them, and pulled the plug.

Later, dressed in clean clothes, his hair parted in the center and combed flat down like feathers, he cleaned the tub and hung his washing on a line running between plum trees in back. Then it was time for confession.

Driving to church in his Plymouth, he took stock. Anger? Yes. Cursing? Yes. Lying? No, never. Any of the others? For years he'd confessed his sins to Monsignor Gapzinski, and the old priest knew him by name. "John," he'd said once, before giving the absolution, "you're a strong, good man, but think about Our Lord's words, 'Everyone who exalts himself shall be humbled.' " Later, in a dim pew, he'd made his penance of one rosary but hadn't bothered about the words. When he'd finished the last decade of the rosary and blessed himself, he rose and walked proudly past lines of people still waiting to confess.

That night, the lines seemed much slower. After a long wait, he finally entered the coffin-like box, and when the panel slid open before his eyes, began his confession in Polish. But an unfamiliar voice interrupted and asked if he could speak English.

Startled, he asked, "Where is Monsignor?"

"He's ill," the unfamiliar voice whispered. "Please pray for him. I'm Father Jim, and I'll be filling in for a while."

How could it be? he wondered. Monsignor sick? Such a good man, too. The unfamiliar voice again interrupted, asking him to begin his confession in English, if he could.

"I was angry this week," he said. "I cursed." He stopped and waited for the priest's response. His eyes adjusting to the darkness, he could just make out a black crucifix and a hearing aid device on the wall before him.

After some time, the priest said, "And is that all?" When he didn't speak, the priest went into a lengthy sermon. His voice rising above a whisper, he talked of flames of love and flames of anger; he talked of charity and God's love. The words ran together, and, unable to keep up with their flow, he lost interest and thought instead of what he would do after Mass the next day. The Lord's Day was not for work, he knew, but a little raking couldn't be called work. He'd raked his own leaves several times, but leaves from neighbors' yards were always blowing into his. He would do a little raking; then maybe he would put another coat of varnish on the woodwork in the archway. He liked wood to be shiny.

The priest broke into his reverie. "And do you understand the nature of your penance, then?"

"Excuse me?" he said in Polish.

"English, please," the priest said loudly.

"I'm sorry. I don't hear you."

The priest raised his voice even more. "Instead of regular penance, which implies punishment," he said, "I would like you to try thinking — all this coming week — of God's love for you. Whenever you can, think of His goodness and of the goodness of life. Do this when you feel anger or when you wish to curse. Do you understand?"

Astonished and confused, he couldn't speak.

"Good," said the priest, after a moment. He gave the absolution, the Latin rushing like water.

Then the small wooden panel slid shut, and he was finished. Outside the confessional, he thought people stared at him; he lowered his eyes. Lights burned only near the confessional, and farther up the nave he could kneel in half-light. He took his usual pew and out of habit began his rosary. But blessing himself with the metallic cross, he suddenly remembered that it wasn't his penance. What was it, then? Something about love when he felt like cursing. No, that wasn't it. It was something about God and love, flames and cursing. He couldn't get it right. Now how do you like that? he said to himself, feeling anger grow. To make matters worse, his stomach started acting up, burning and heaving. He turned around to survey the waiting lines. People were standing as if frozen in the aisles. He looked to the front of the church; the statues, in shadow, seemed miles away. The sanctuary lamp burned red. He was angry now and unsettled; he didn't feel like a new man. It was the priest's fault. The priest had ruined it, and he wouldn't be able to receive Communion tomorrow. I'm not about to stand in line all over again, he told himself. I might as well work tomorrow, then, and be hanged for it.

After a supper of lard on bread, cold sausage, and coffee diluted with milk, he rocked in his dimly lit living room. Smoking his pipe and spitting into the clean spittoon, he mulled over the priest's words — the few he remembered. They seemed like clues or pieces of a puzzle, and he wished he'd listened better. Flames, he said to himself. Flames and love, whatever that meant. Well, he knew about flames, that's for sure. As if it happened the day before, he saw his white-eyed team of horses rearing up against a sky black as hell with smoke. Half-mad himself, he'd fought the crazed beasts to a standstill while Masha got things into the wagon. He knew about flames. But flames and love and how it tied together with cursing, he couldn't figure out.

Cursing, he thought. Now there was his failing. He'd never forgotten the time a storm caught him plowing. The steel-blue sky cracked apart in a dozen places, and the horses lunged, toppling the plow. Straddling a furrow of stony earth, he'd cursed the lightning and the horses, the plow and the field. He'd called on a hundred demons. It seemed he could touch one of the bolts, so close they came, snaking into the earth. The air stank with sulfur. He got the plow unhitched and ran with the horses while rain made rivers of the furrows. In the house Masha, pale as death, was running from room to room, dipping her fingers in a jar of holy water and sprinkling the walls, the floors, the babies. Still cursing, he'd stood dripping wet in the kitchen, while rain blew in the open windows and glasses rattled in the cupboards. Masha had run into the kitchen and sprinkled water on him. Just then a stream of light poured in one window and out the other, burning the very air. It had snaked across the entire kitchen, missing them by inches. Masha, her hand held out as if paralyzed, water still dripping from her fingers, had only said, "See, John? See what your cursing brings?" For a long time after that, he hadn't dared to curse.

How could anything like that be connected with love? he wondered. The new priest must be a little touched. Masha had been a little touched, too. She'd been a good woman, a good worker, but too holy. Once, she came back from the village and went straight into the parlor without saying a word. There, she lit a candle before the statue of the Virgin and then sat, still as a stone, before that little flame. He'd called her and had even asked if she was sick. But there she sat, pale as death. She wouldn't answer him; she wouldn't even look at him. She held a rosary in her lap, but her fingers didn't move over the beads. The parlor grew darker and colder as the day lost its light, and the candle burned more brightly in that dimness. It cast shadows over the Virgin's mantle, and it seemed the figure was moving. Frightened, he left her alone in the room. Finally, long after the candle had guttered out, Masha appeared in the kitchen. He was making pancakes, and flour dusted the planks under the table.

"John," she said, scared as a child. "I seen her."

"Who?"

"The Virgin."

"No."

"Oh yes. On the timber cut going to the church."

He was quiet, afraid of what more she might say.

"She was so bright, I fell down and covered my face. I cried because she was so beautiful, so beautiful."

He hadn't liked it one bit. People would say she was touched, and it wouldn't look good. But he'd been surprised when just the opposite happened. People started saying she was a saint. That made him proud of her even though he didn't think she was a saint. She was just a woman. Couldn't they see that?

As he smoked and waited for bedtime, he looked around the room. His oval wedding picture, his plant in the alcove, his clock, all were sunk in shadow. Shadows blurred the shape of his wife's rocker at the end of the double living room. Sometimes, depending on the play of shadows, it seemed the rocker moved, as if brushed by a wind. "Sleep, Masha, sleep," he would say then. When the clock on the closed gramophone struck ten times, he rapped his pipe against the spittoon and abandoned the living room to darkness. His back resting on a pad of sheepskin, his thin body covered by a heavy feather-tick, he too slept. Outside, the underwear stiffened and moved on the line like a ghost in a frost-blasted garden.

•

That night he slept badly, and all the next day unfinished business plagued him. At Mass he'd sat in the pew, like a bump on a log, he thought, while everybody else went to Communion. By the time his daughter came for her visit, his stomach was good and sour.

"So, Pa," she said. "What did you do today?" She wore a Sunday dress too tight about the waist.

"Do?" he said irritably. One leg made a sharp angle over the hassock. "There's always something to do around here." The smell of fresh varnish still hung in the air.

"Pa, come live with us. We'd like you to." She motioned at the lofty ceilings, the corners. "There's just too much work here."

She's lying, he thought. How could they want him? His stomach turned, and a sour liquid rose in his throat.

"Son of a bitch!" he said in Polish. "I need my powders." He left her alone in the living room.

When he returned from the bathroom, she said, "Pa, go see a doctor with that stomach of yours. 'Powders'! What are these 'powders' you get at Wiesneski's? Go see a real doctor."

In one sharp Polish sentence he cast all doctors into the flames of hell. Then he took his pipe and calmly rocked while his daughter struggled into her coat.

"At least," she said, standing, "why not sell and get something smaller, maybe closer to us?"

"Bah," he said, and spat into the spittoon.

Then she was gone, and he heard her old Hudson start up in the driveway. In the quiet he smoked and rocked and studied his plant. Masha was the one who could grow plants, he thought. She could make sticks grow, while he had to fight the damned soil for each and every potato. He'd been waiting for a long time now for those bright blue and orange flowers promised in the catalogue. It'll be a cold day in hell, he thought. Behind the plant, the radiators hissed. It's too damned dry in here, he decided, and went to the kitchen for water.

After watering the plant and filling the cake pans set on the radiators for humidity, he had time for another smoke. Letting his thoughts go where they would, he remembered old Mr. Smigelski. Once Mrs. Raniszewski had said after church, "Merry Christmas, Mr. Smigelski!" Bowing, the crazy fool shouted, "Ass to me, ass to you!" How she'd looked when he said that! Every time he saw

Smigelski after church, he was tempted to say, "Ass to me, ass to you, you crazy fool!" He said the words as they were intended: *As to me, as to you.* Now what did that mean? Whatever happens to me, let it happen to you? Or, what you say to me, let me say to you? That must be it. The crazy fool! He laughed just thinking about it.

When the clock chimed ten times, he rapped his pipe on the spittoon and rose from the rocker. Before turning off the floor lamp, he saw that his lace curtains were getting yellow. It was time to take them to the Widow Sobcek.

But he forgot about the curtains during the week; there was too much other work to think about. The stoker clogged somehow, and he had to crawl around in the dust, fixing it. Then four shingles blew off the roof, and he dragged out his wooden ladder from the garage. Extended its full thirty-five feet, it was just long enough to reach the north gable. Up he went, hand over hand, with shingles, hammer, and nails in cloth bag at his side. The ladder was springy; wind puffed his jacket and blew in his face. If it should slip, he thought, imagining the old ladder sliding sideways across the clapboard, sending him and his damned shingles all to hell. But it didn't slip, and he finished the job. Only when he was back down on the frozen ground did he feel his legs trembling. Dragging the ladder back into the garage, he was proud of himself. It'd been a job worth doing.

On Saturday, he remembered the curtains. After his housecleaning and his bath, he pulled a straight-back chair to the radiators. Standing on the chair, he freed the curtain rods, pulled off the stiff panels, and let them fall into a wicker basket. "Damn it to hell," he said at the dust. "Pfoo!" He got down and surveyed the bare windows. They looked empty, like Mrs. Kranak's windows during Lent. She took down her curtains on Ash Wednesday and didn't put them back up until Holy Saturday. Her empty, dark windows reminded him of something; he wasn't sure just what, but it wasn't good. How could she stand it all those weeks? On Easter Sunday he was relieved to see her white curtains against the wavering panes of glass. Looking at his own windows, he saw he would have to wash them on Monday. The stained-glass pieces at the top were dusty and dull; the windowpanes were streaked and murky. Before leaving for the Widow's, he had to wash dust from his hands.

Turning his green Plymouth off First Avenue, he drove into a neighborhood of plain houses, fenced gardens, and small yards. No stained glass in the windows; no fancy fretwork on the gables. All was simple and neat and stark in the late afternoon light. The bare yards had a wintry look, and children in winter jackets and caps played in old piles of leaves.

He drove slowly over broken concrete, conscious of his sour stomach. It was churning and heaving. That morning he'd put a spoonful of butter into his coffee and taken an extra measure of the powders, but nothing did the trick. He had a sudden thought, as jarring as a glimpse of a snake disappearing in a rockpile. *What if this is some great sickness?* The thought shook him, but gripping the steering wheel he told himself: *No, by God. Not yet. Not John Jielewicz!*

Scowling, he parked his Plymouth on gravel in front of the Widow's house. The streets had no curbs in her neighborhood. His scowl deepened when he recognized, parked just ahead, the shiny beast of a car that always reminded him of a hearse. It belonged to Mrs. Stanley, a divorced woman with black hair and red fingernails. *"Czarownica!"* he said, lifting his basket from the back seat. She was a proud, mean witch, and it bothered him to think the Widow washed the woman's curtains. He would never do that.

There was room for only one at a time on the narrow sidewalk, and he had to wait for Mrs. Stanley to pass. She carried white curtains over one arm, a white veil over the black fur of her coat. As she passed, hairs on the coat rose, like a dog's, and caught the light. He scowled, but she ignored him. His stomach heaved and fluttered.

Waiting on the porch, he looked over the Widow's yard. Bare maple limbs interlocked above raked grass, and mounds of leaves were heaped over the garden. Low gray clouds in the west reflected pale colors. Earlier every day now, he said to himself, thinking of the sunset.

A small woman wearing a bib apron over a flower-print dress opened the door. "Mr. Jielewicz," she said, "good to see you." She held the door for him, then closed it. Inside, she wiped steam from her glasses. "How are you?"

He set his basket near a drying frame holding a stretched curtain and thought of the black coat and of his stomach. "I'm no good," he said. "No damned good." He looked around the small kitchen. As always, the Widow's linoleum was polished, and the windows were steamed by washing and cooking. In one window she had hung three glass shelves of African violets, and he could see, behind the purple flowers, a gloomy December sky. "I will sit awhile and rest," he told her.

"That's good," she said. "Sit. I will rest, too." But holding the back of a kitchen chair for support, she made her way to the stove. There, a bowl and plate had been warming, and she poured *kvass* and cut two pieces of bread from a loaf cooling on the cupboard.

Slowly, she moved between stove and table, carrying the bowl before her like an offering. She made a second trip for the plate of bread and a spoon. "Eat, Mr. Jielewicz," she said. "Eat and feel better."

He stirred the rich brown soup, with its raisins and prunes and *kloski* like small clouds. When did he last have *kvass* like that? he wondered. Steam rose from the bowl. Masha, he thought. Masha had made *kvass* like that. Ten years in March, then. Taking a blue handkerchief from his pocket, he wiped his brow and very quickly his eyes. When he finished the soup, he looked up. The Widow was watching him.

"It's good," he said. "It settled my stomach."

"Have more," she said. Both hands on the arms of her chair, she slowly lifted herself up. Her legs were wrapped in layers of support stockings, as thick as children's winter leggings.

"Sit," he said, getting up. "I can wait on myself."

While he finished the second bowl of *kvass*, the Widow began attaching a curtain to a drying frame, carefully inserting small pins through the lace to preserve its design.

"Do you get tired doing that every day?" he asked.

"Oh," she said, "yes and no. Some days, when my legs hurt, yes. Today, no." Then she gathered a curtain from the basket and, holding up one end, let it fall between them. "Each so different, so beautiful," she said, "that I don't get so tired."

Through the white lace he saw a young girl. Like . . . but he blocked the thought. Startled, he felt blood rush to his face. Then she let the curtain fall into the basket, and the Widow Sobcek appeared again, gray hair and glasses, the housedress and thick stockings.

Behind the African violets, the sky was growing darker; it was time to leave. He sighed as he put four dollar bills on the oilcloth. She took two of the bills, tucked them into her apron pocket, then pushed the remaining bills toward him. "Take," she said, as she always did when he overpaid. "Take. I don't need."

Driving from the Widow's in the December dusk, he saw that it would snow. All was still and cold and gray. In time for evening confession, he drove down side streets and took stock. Anger? Yes. When? He remembered: that fool of a priest, the penance left undone. Now what? The Plymouth slowed and came to a stop in the middle of a block. He would get worked up, he thought, going back to that priest. He waited for his stomach to start acting up, but it was strangely quiet. Should he go home or should he try it again? On the windshield flakes of snow appeared, hanging there like the Widow's white lace. *So beautiful,* she'd said. He thought of the priest's words — the clues he'd tried to figure out. The Plymouth began to roll forward. He turned on the windshield wipers, and the stone-gray road appeared under the headlights. At the intersection of First and Maple, he turned right, toward the church.

•

It was nearly a year later when his daughter said, on a Sunday evening, "Oh, Pa, everyone's talking about you. It's awful."

He heard sleet at the windowpanes, a low whispering sound. He leaned over his chair and spat into the spittoon. He drew on his pipe before speaking. Then he said, *"Plotka!"*

"No," she said. "Not gossip. They're right to talk. It's crazy, that's what it is. Here you are running over there every week with curtains! Everyone's laughing, but I don't think it's so funny. I think it's . . ."

"Not every week."

"No, but you know what I mean. Every month, then. Just as bad. Don't look at me like that. I'm not the one to blame. People are saying a lot of things. They're saying that . . . that you don't know what you're doing. Oh, Pa!"

He thought over the words. Well, maybe it was crazy. What would she think if he told her about the lace? Ever since the Widow held the lace curtain in the air between them, he'd been seeing lace everywhere. When he cleaned out the stoker, the clinkers looked like lace. So did the ice when he chopped it off the sidewalks. Everywhere lace! At first it'd bothered him and he worried, but then he got used to the idea and began to look at things to see how close they came to the Widow's lace. He was surprised. Sugar in the sugarbowl, the stars at night, even the thorny hedge at his property line. One day while cutting the grass, he saw light coming through little openings in the hedge, and right away he thought: *Lace!* Shadows of tree limbs on grass, car tracks on snow, birds flying through the air — all reminded him of lace. So did the feathery tops of new carrots and even the rougher edges of cabbage and potato plants. It *was* crazy! One day he made a list of all the things that reminded him of the lace curtain, and he was astounded to find over fifty items. He put the list away in his safe, but added to it every week. Crazy? Well, what of it? He wanted to laugh. Lace everywhere! He would make a joke, and she would laugh, too. "Ass to me, ass to you," he said, thinking of Mr. Smigelski. He laughed, showing brown stubs of teeth.

But she was alarmed, and her eyes flew from him to the oval wedding picture to the alcove. "Oh, Pa," she said, "cut out this silliness! Act your age."

The problem was, he thought, he didn't feel his age; he wanted to be foolish. "If I acted my age," he said, "I'd be dead!" He laughed. At the rate he was going, he would probably find lace in the grave as well!

"Pa," she said thoughtfully, "what did you do with your plant?" She was looking at the empty space in the alcove where his plant on its pedestal had been for years.

The alcove looked larger, he thought, without the plant, and the curtains showed better. Should he tell her? It was last Holy Thursday, he remembered, when he'd taken the plant to the Widow's. How she'd laughed when she opened the door. "There's a plant growing out of your head, Mr. Jielewicz," she'd said. He must have looked foolish, with those big gray-green leaves, like rabbit ears, hiding his face.

"Now what are you smiling about?" his daughter was saying. "You won't tell me where you took the plant, but I know! I thought I saw it at the Widow's when I took my curtains there, and I was right. Only I didn't know it could have such nice flowers. Think what you're doing, Pa. Think of Mama, for heaven's sake." She blew her nose in a Kleenex. "Oh dear," she said, putting the wad of tissue in her purse. "I have to get home. John has a cold, and I'm getting it. One thing after another. If you moved in with us, like we wanted you to, none of this would be happening." She got her arms into heavy coatsleeves.

How old was she now? he wondered, studying his daughter. She didn't look like the little girl who'd tangled rolls of string at the store and drew pictures on pink butcher paper. He looked to the wedding picture on the shadowy wall. They'd stood so still, so straight, facing the big camera: Masha, young, thin, unsmiling; himself solemn as a minister and thin as a rail in his new suit.

Standing and buttoning her coat, she said, "For heaven's sake, Pa, at your age, you don't want to be marrying again."

So, he thought. *So.* He saw the Widow in her housedress and felt slippers. A poor woman. He thought of his old safe in his bedroom closet, hidden behind his black suits. His name was printed in gold letters over the combination, but the light in the closet was too dim for it to show. When he opened his safe to get money or to add to his list, he had to use a flashlight. Then he thought: John. Who is John? That is my name. He remembered. John was his grandson, a boy he seldom saw, a little boy — small and pale and weak. He wondered why his daughter always left the boy at home when she visited. Not seeing the husband didn't bother him, but he would like to see the boy now and then. He looked at Masha's rocker, but it was still. I should marry again, he thought, and leave them nothing. His stomach began a faint stir. The *plotki!* He drew in on the pipe and exhaled a great cloud of smoke. That's what they're worried about. She's speaking for the others. He thought of his two sons and daughter who lived in other states and only visited at Christmas. Then they talked about the bad roads and how the town was going to the dogs. He should marry! The idea was pleasing; how they would worry then! But something intervened. He saw the Widow's rough hand pushing the dollar bills toward him. *Take,* she'd said. *Take. I don't need.*

His daughter tied a wool kerchief under her chin, and slipped on gloves. "Well, I'm going, Pa," she said. "Don't forget about dinner at our house next week. You said you would come."

She's tired, he thought. He saw her small house on its barren lot — all clutter and light. No comfortable shadows or large rooms. He didn't like going there. But there was something he wanted to do. What was it? The oilcloth. Yes, what else? The dollar bills. Yes. "Wait," he told his daughter. "Wait just a minute."

He left her in the living room as the clock was striking nine-thirty, and returned several minutes later. Dangling car keys from a gloved hand, she stood near Masha's rocker. "You know, Pa, we still have to talk over this other thing."

"Never mind that," he said. "Give this to the boy. Give this to John."

Startled, she took the unsealed envelope and with gloved hands opened it. "Pa!" she said, as she lifted out a thick packet of bills. "What is this craziness? What's the matter with you!" She tried to push the envelope and bills into his hands, but he stepped back.

"Take," he said. "It's for the boy. For school. For anything."

"Oh, Pa!"

In a moment he was encircling her heavy bulk with his bony arms.

"Never mind," he said. "Never mind."

Only when she moved back, wiping her eyes, did he notice the bunch of lace at her neck. Gathered with a black velvet ribbon, it fanned out like the top of a carrot.

•

Holding a bag of salt in one hand, he let go of the ice-coated porch rail, and his feet took to the sky. That's how he explained it to his daughter at the hospital.

"I saw every kind of star," he told her.

"Never mind stars," she said. "You could have broken your back. Then what?"

But he was too tired to answer; his eyelids shut of their own accord, and he saw stars whirling about his head. He dozed. When he opened his eyes, she was still there.

"I'm going home," he said.

"You can't! What do you want to do, Pa? Fall again?"

He wanted to tell her they had no right keeping him in the hospital when he wanted to go home, but the words wouldn't come. Instead, he dozed and saw a big black hearse slowly backing up to an open door. He was on a cart, rolling toward the car's dark cave. Terrified, he opened his eyes.

"I'm going home," he said, struggling to rise. "I have . . . things to do."

She was beside the bed, holding him back. "Pa! You're not supposed to move. Your ribs are all cracked. Look, here's your lunch. And the nurse!"

"Well, Mr. Jielewicz," the nurse said. "Full of pep, are you? The doctor was right. They don't make 'em like you anymore!"

"I hope not," Eleanor said to herself, but he heard.

It seemed his hair was standing up like a shock of hay, so he brushed at it with a stiff, bandaged hand. Shame, shame, he thought, to be lying here like a baby while strangers walked around the bed looking at him. A young girl wearing a dress of pink stripes swung a narrow table over the bed and set a tray of food on it. He looked at the colors: green, yellow, brown, something red on the side. It looked like his workbench in the basement, where he cleaned his paintbrushes.

"I'm not eating," he said. "I'm going home." He closed his eyes.

"Pa!"

"Don't worry, Mrs. Kirchner," he heard the nurse say. "If he won't eat now, he'll be good and hungry later."

His eyes still closed, he saw himself getting up, putting on his underwear, pants, and shirt, starting the Plymouth and driving home. Then he would . . . But what day was it? Was it still Wednesday?

"What day is it?" he asked his daughter, as if from a great distance.

"What did you say, Pa? I can't hear you."

"Day," he said. "What day?"

"Day? Oh! It's Saturday."

Saturday! He struggled to put the week back together. On Monday he had . . . but he couldn't remember that far back. Tuesday, then. On Tuesday he . . . he worked at Chet's. That's right. It was raining when he drove home. Then it got cold. The next day everything was ice. The trees, the bushes, and the utility wires. The steps and the side of the house. Sunlight was everywhere. Icy tree limbs shone like glass against the blue sky. So bright. So, so bright. He dozed again.

When he awoke, the Widow was there, placing a bowl of *kvass* on the table where the tray of food had been.

"I see in the paper about your fall, so I come," she said. "Eat, Mr. Jielewicz. Eat and feel better."

Was he dreaming? But no, steam rose like incense from the bowl, and he could smell the rich soup. His eyes burned. Suddenly he remembered what he'd seen just before the dark. Sunlight on polished steps. And near the edge, where icicles dripped from the roof, designs as fine as flowers. *Lace.* Then his legs flew from under him, and pellets of salt rose in the air like confetti.

•

One week later, he awoke from a nap and knew it was long after lunchtime. A tray of cold food sat on the bedtable. The Widow hadn't come; something was wrong. All that week she'd come, bringing him good food: *kvass* and ham, chicken and dumplings, *pierogi* and apple pie. He watched the doorway and imagined her walking in, wearing the *baboushka* and long gray coat, the galoshes. The doorway remained empty.

That Monday the doctor had checked him and said he could go home if he promised to be careful. He'd thought a bit and asked the doctor if he could perhaps stay a day or two longer. "Why?" the doctor wanted to know. Then he'd lied. "A little pain yet," he'd said, avoiding the doctor's eyes.

"What time is it?" he asked the girl in pink stripes who brought him a glass of juice.

She looked at her wristwatch. "Three-thirty," she said. "Why? Expecting company?" She laughed, straightened the blankets, then took away the untouched food.

He waited, every minute expecting the Widow to appear in her *baboushka*, coat, and galoshes. The curtain soon made a long shadow on his bed, and then he knew she wouldn't come. It was too late. He was wide awake now; something nagged him. What was it? The Widow shuffling into the room. Yes. What else? Her long gray coat and the heavy boots. Yes. And? Then he knew. Dear God, he said to himself, let me burn forever in hell if I have done a bad thing!

He swung his legs out from under the sheet and blanket; when his bare feet touched the cold tile, he was chilled. He stood, feeling sore all over, but he walked to the closet and found his clothing. He recognized the shirt; he'd been wearing it when he fell. It was so long ago, he thought. He undid the white hospital gown and let it fall to the floor. Then he pulled his underwear up over the bandages. He dressed quickly. Hurry, hurry, hurry, he said to himself, tangling his shoelaces. He looked at the other bed, prepared to lie, but his roommate slept, tubes feeding his arms.

At the doorway he waited for the corridor to clear. He saw nurses talking together at the desk near the elevator; pretending he was just a visitor, he walked to the elevator and turned his back to them. Doors mysteriously opened, and he stepped into the bright cubicle. Free, he thought, pressing buttons. Down, down he went, his heart pounding and his stomach fluttering.

In the mild air outside, he saw a taxi waiting, as if for him. A taxi! He'd never hired a taxi. Did he have any money? Dear God!

He rifled his pockets and found two dollar bills in his pants. Waving the bills in the air, he pounded on the window, startling the driver. He shouted the Widow's address.

The driver got out and walked around the car to open the back door. "Well, hop in, then," he said.

Holding his side, he climbed into the back seat. Hurry, hurry, hurry, he said to himself.

"Nice day," the driver said, starting up a loud clock on the dashboard. "Looks like spring will get here yet."

They were off. He looked out the window and saw puddles of water in the gutters and black-crusted snowbanks in yards. Already the grass seemed green where snow had melted. Hurry, hurry, hurry, he said to himself.

When the driver came to open the door for him, the clock on the dashboard had stopped ticking. "That'll be one dollar and fifty cents."

"Take," he said, thrusting the bills at the man. He rushed up the narrow walk.

At the Widow's door he knocked, but there was no answer. He tried the door, and it opened. Stepping inside, he heard her voice coming from the living room. She was lying like a fallen bird, her legs covered with a thick woolen blanket. What had he done! Dear God in heaven, he said to himself, strike me dead. Bury me in ashes!

"Mr. Jielewicz!" she said. "What are you doing here?"

His side ached, and he couldn't find breath to speak. Finally, he was able to say, "What is the matter, little lady?"

"Oh," she said, "my legs got tired. Not so bad, but everyone wants clean curtains for Easter, and I can't walk so good now." She sat up and turned on a table light. "Mrs. Stanley came today and says she needs her curtains no later than tomorrow. Now, no curtains."

That witch, he thought, seeing the woman in her black coat. What does she need with clean curtains! Under his bandages everything hurt and burned.

"Tomorrow, I will be better," the Widow said, as if she believed it.

He looked at the thick stockings and the felt slippers and knew what he'd done. Dear God in heaven! She'd walked to the hospital all those days.

"Where are the curtains?"

"Oh no, Mr. Jielewicz. You can't do them!"

"Tell me how."

•

In a room off the kitchen he knelt, ignoring a great pain in his side, and plunged his bandaged hands into a washtub of hot water. Steam rose when he lifted a curtain into the air. Water poured off the material, and light from the setting sun made rainbows all over the soapy lace. "Dear God!" he cried, seeing once again the Widow's face behind the veil. In his joy, he nearly upset the tub.

WILLIAM HAUPTMAN

Good Rockin' Tonight

(FROM PLAYBOY)

THE YEAR ELVIS DIED was a strange year, and I remember it not only because of what happened to my brother, Bubba, but because that was the year we had our first transsexual here in north Texas. Bobby Joe Pitts, who worked for Builders' Supply, told the wife and kids he still loved them, but he couldn't stand it any longer: He'd always felt like a woman in a man's body and wanted to go to Houston for a sex-change operation.

He'd been saving money for years in a secret account and was all ready to go through with it. But the doctor in Houston was cautious. He told Bobby Joe he should try wearing women's clothes for six months before the operation, since there would be no going back. So Bobby Joe came to our church, First Methodist, looking something like Mary Tyler Moore. His family took it hard. The preacher suggested, after the services, that he go to the Unitarian church instead, where they took homosexuals and drug addicts. Bobby Joe stormed out, saying we were hypocrites and had no spirit of Christian love.

The first nice day rolled around, he was out at Skyline Country Club, just like every other year, for his eighteen holes of Saturday-morning golf. Harley Otis told me when I walked into the locker room. Said Bobby Joe expected to play in the club tournament, but against the women. Harley was disgusted. "I guess it had to happen here," he said, snorting and throwing his shoes all the way across the room, where they hit the big picture of Arnold Palmer on the locker-room wall.

I felt sorry for Bobby Joe and went out to where he was teeing off alone. He said he was no different from that doctor who became a lady tennis pro. "They're just threatened," he said primly. About that time, Harley drove past in his electric cart and shouted out, asking Bobby Joe if he was for the E.R.A. Bobby Joe shot him the finger.

That night I sat on my patio, drinking Jack Daniel's and looking up at the stars. Through the sliding glass doors, I could see my wife watching her favorite program. Hell, I could see Bobby Joe's point of view. I might like being a woman myself if I looked like Mary Tyler Moore. Trouble was, I wouldn't; and neither would Bobby Joe. I doubted any amount of plastic surgery could do the trick. My wife, alone there in the den, laughed at something on television, and I felt like a ghost. I decided the world was changing so fast nobody could keep up with it.

I'm a doctor myself, obstetrics and gynecology, and I've got a little office across the street from the hospital. Who should come see me the next day but my old high school sweetheart, Nadine MacAfee, whom I'd seen no more than two or three times in all the years since graduation. But my heart still stopped when I saw her there in the reception room.

In my office, she told me she'd like to get off the pill and try some other form of contraception. She dropped hints about her loneliness and talked nostalgically about the days when we'd gone steady; and I soon realized she was looking for romance. I was so nervous I thought I was going to stammer for the first time in years, and resorted to a trick the speech therapist had taught me: flipping my pencil up and catching it, not thinking too much about what I was saying.

"Look, Nadine," I said finally, "if it's all the same, I'd rather not examine you. But I can recommend another doctor."

"That's all right, Ross," she said. "I understand."

She had once been so shy, and this was a pretty bold thing for her to do. But I had never gone all the way with Nadine in high school and I wasn't about to now. I wanted to keep her the way she was in my memory — full of innocence and mystery. So I took out the bottle I keep in my desk drawer, we had a drink, and I got her talking about her kids, my pencil flipping just like old Johnny Carson's.

When I showed her out, my brother, Bubba, who was a big wheel with the Prudential Insurance Company, was sitting in the reception room with a long face on. When I asked him what was wrong, he told me Elvis had died and we had to celebrate his passing away. "The King is gone," he said, "and nobody will ever replace him." I sent the rest of my patients home.

I hadn't known Elvis was so important to my brother, but then I really didn't know Bubba anymore. We played golf now and then, but our wives hated each other, which seems to be the rule, not the exception; so we never saw each other socially, not at all.

We drove out to a bar in the new shopping mall, where neither of us had ever been. Thank God It's Friday's it was called, and I think it was supposed to look like Greenwich Village.

"What the hell has happened here?" my brother said.

"How do you mean, Bubba?"

"What's happened to this town? Why is everyone pretending they're in New York City?"

"I don't know, Bubba; I guess it's television."

To me, the whole shopping mall was a depressing place. Nobody had been able to rest until we got one, just like every other town. There must have been a thousand editorials in the paper about it. On the way in, we'd passed droves of sad-looking teenagers hanging out around the fountain, and I'd thought how much happier we looked out at the Pioneer Drive-In, in our cars. But everyone was proud of the mall as they could be, and who was wrong, them or me?

Harley Otis was there, right in the thick of it, wearing polyester pants, white loafers with gold chains, a leather jacket, and a Dacron shirt with the collar spread out on his shoulders. There was also a little gold chain around his neck.

"Who you tryin' to look like, Harley?" my brother asked. "The Six Million Dollar Man?"

Harley took it as a compliment and started telling us how he'd just gotten back from a Successful Life course in Dallas where he'd learned the importance of a Positive Mental Attitude. "You've got to set goals for yourself," he said.

"What's your goal, Harley?"

"Right now, I'm buckin' for president of Kiwanis. But my immediate goal is to get into Tina Eubank's pants."

I looked over and there was Tina, twice divorced, standing by the jukebox. It didn't look like he'd have too much trouble. "Y'all have a nice day," Harley said, and slid toward her.

Then we drove out the Fort Worth Highway, my brother talking about everything he hated, from women's lib to *People* magazine. I hadn't seen him like this for years. There had been a time, when I was in med school and my brother driving a truck, when he developed all sorts of theories about why this country was going to pieces. He also claimed to have seen UFOs and talked to them on his CB. I finally diagnosed the problem when I discovered he was taking "L.A. turnarounds" — those biphetamine capsules truckers use on long hauls. Once he started working for the Prudential, he settled down and that side of him disappeared.

But now he was driving too fast and talking crazy, like he used to; looking around at everything and not liking what he saw. Just then, I heard a siren and saw flashing blue lights, and a highway-patrol car pulled us over.

It was Floyd Beer, whom I hadn't seen in maybe fifteen years. "Could I see your operator's license?" he asked, all business, holding his metal clipboard.

"It's Bubba Moody, Floyd."

"You were exceeding a posted speed limit of fifty-five miles per hour, and it looks to me like you got alcoholic beverages in the car."

"Floyd, don't you remember? We took shop together?"

"Yeah, I remember. But shitfire, Bubba, you were driving like a bat."

"Floyd, Elvis died today."

"I heard."

"My brother and I are drinking to his memory. Don't give me the cold shoulder, Floyd. Have a drink with us and let's remember all the good and bad old days."

"Well, I do get off duty in half an hour," Floyd said, looking across the car at me and grinning. "That really you, Ross?"

•

Then the three of us went out to the old colored man's place. It was my brother's idea. You could have knocked me over with a stick when I saw it was still there, the little red-brick building with the sign that said HOT PIT COOKED BAR-B-QUE.

The old colored man himself, who was coffee-colored and had a pencil mustache (Fats Domino, we had called him), opened the counterweighted lid of the stove. Inside was at least a chine of beef. He cut off slabs and put them on bread. Then he added half a green onion and a wedge of longhorn cheese and wrapped it all in butcher paper.

We carried out sandwiches to a table, and the other customers, all colored (black, I corrected myself), sort of looked at us without looking at us, for Floyd still wore his highway-patrol uniform; then got up and left, dropping their trash in the garbage can on the way out.

"See, big brother?" Bubba said. "The past is still here, all around us."

I couldn't take my eyes off my sandwich. It sat there on the tabletop, which was bare except for a Louisiana Hot Sauce bottle full of toothpicks. Grease spotted the butcher paper. I took a bite and it ran down my chin. Lord, it was good.

Bubba returned from the cooler with three bottles of Royal Crown Cola, the old-style bottles with the yellow pyramids on them. "Look at that," he said softly, staring at his bottle. "Would you look at that?" Then he drank it.

"What are you up for, Floyd?" he said.

"My wife's going to be wondering where I am," Floyd said, and when Bubba gave him a sour look, added, "Shitfire, Bubba, there's a good program on tonight. About Vince Lombardi."

I nodded. "My wife's not home. Tonight's her yoga class. Y'all could come over and watch it." What was I saying "y'all" for? I hadn't said "y'all" in years.

"What's so important about Vince Lombardi?" Bubba said. "You never knew him. A night like this comes once in a lifetime, and tonight the three of us are going to the Cotton Bowling Palace."

So we drove on down to the long, low building on Holiday Creek, full of the odor of paste wax and the thunder of balls; and the same people were there who had always been there, roughnecks and refinery workers and railroad brakemen. I was clumsy at first, dropping the ball on the lane with a thud; but Bubba was greasing them in right off. We didn't bother to keep score. None of us could remember how. We just bowled, and I relaxed, for by now the evening was lost, anyway, watching Bubba cut up, bowling like Don Carter, and so forth. He could always impersonate anyone he wanted. Mom said his version of me was deadly. When he came over and dropped down beside me in one of the green-plastic chairs, I felt a stab of brotherhood and socked him on the arm, the way I would have in the old days.

"Hey, Bubba," I said. "You old son of a bitch."

"You're not sorry you're not home watching the life of old Vince Lombardi?"

"No, Bubba. I genuinely enjoyed this night."

"Life is a road."

"Yes, Bubba. Life is a road." I waited for him to finish, so drunk the bowling balls sounded like they were rolling through my head.

"Once I thought I knew who I was and where I was going. I could see the road ahead. But I lost my way."

Floyd was out on the lane, yelling. A pin had fallen outside the gate, and when nobody appeared to help, he walked up the lane, slipping and falling down, and got it himself. People were laughing at him.

"There was only one person of our time who never stopped. Who became the person he dreamed of becoming."

"Who's that?"

"Elvis," my brother said.

Do you know what he did then? He stepped up to the booth where you got your shoes and where they called your number when your lane was ready. He grabbed the microphone away from the fat lady who was sitting there and sang "Love Me Tender" to her. It started as a joke, but this was the day Elvis had died, and when he finished, the place was dead quiet. Then everyone applauded and started shouting, "More, more," and I was shouting, too. And he did sound exactly like Elvis, although I never thought he looked like him at all. I thought he looked more like Conway Twitty.

•

One year later to the day, I was riding down Highway 281 in a white Cadillac Eldorado. The oil-well pumping jacks nodded in the fields, the blacktop shimmered in the heat, and in the front seat was my brother Bubba, wearing a white jump suit with silver studs, his hair dyed black. The sign on the side of the car read:

EL TEX AS

BUBBA MOODY KING OF ROCK AND ROLL

NORTH TEXAS' OWN ELVIS

Floyd Beer was driving, wearing Las Vegas shades and the Robert Hall suit Bubba had bought him at the Hub Clothing Store.

Bubba had done better than I would have believed, perfecting his act at Kiwanis and Rotary dances. He'd also done benefits for the crippled and retarded children, which people liked, and borrowed enough money to lease this Eldorado just like the one Elvis

had. Now we were on our way to the first stop on Bubba's summer
tour, which was to end at Six Flags Over Texas. There was to be a
convention of Elvis Presley impersonators, and Bubba intended to
prove he was the best in the world.

"This is the life, isn't it?" he said, looking back at me and grinning. "Man, sometimes I feel so good I've got to go out and take a
walk through K Mart to bring myself down."

We stopped at the Cow Lot in Nocona, where Bubba bought a
pair of ostrich-hide boots and gave the owner an eight-by-ten au-
tographed glossy photo, which he thumbtacked on the wall next to
the photos of Willie Nelson, Arthur Godfrey, Howard Hughes,
and all the other celebrities who, down through the years, had
bought Nocona boots.

When we got back in the car, Bubba said, "Floyd, I think I'm
going to ask you to dye your hair red so I can call you Red West."
That was Elvis's bodyguard. Bubba really wanted to make the act
authentic.

We came to a billboard that said we were eight miles from De-
catur, home of Dico Sausage, and showed a pair of rolling dice.
"Pull over, Floyd," Bubba said.

He struck a karate pose in front of the billboard and Floyd took
his picture with the Polaroid Swinger. I was getting back in the car
when I heard a buzz just like an electric alarm clock going off.

"Christ, Bubba, what the hell you doing?" Floyd said. Bubba had
picked up a baby rattlesnake out of the ditch and was making like
he was going to kiss it, holding it inches away from his lips.

"Get a picture, get a picture," he shouted, laughing like an idiot.

We drove on through more north Texas and finally into Deca-
tur, where a banner across the street proclaimed Bubba's show.
"The King is here," my brother said.

Floyd parked and we walked into the high school, across the
street from the red-granite courthouse. The band was already setting up. Down in the dressing room, Bubba put on his make-up
and I sat on a box of textbooks in the corner and watched. Already
you could hear people filling the auditorium upstairs. "Sounds like
a good crowd," Bubba said, gluing on his fake sideburns.

Then a local disc jockey appeared with a tape recorder and Miss
Billie Tucker, president of Bubba's north Texas fan club. She'd
brought along a list she'd compiled of characteristics Bubba and
Elvis had in common. The disc jockey held up his microphone and
she read it, perspiration on her upper lip.

"Both Elvis and Bubba are Capricorns," she said. "Both were truck drivers, both stationed with the Army in Germany, and both were devoted to their mothers. Both are overweight, both like Cadillac Eldorados, and both like to stay up all night. Both have fantastic sex appeal . . ."

Good Lord, I thought. These people are serious.

Upstairs, I found myself in an ordinary high school auditorium. There were flags of the United States and Texas on either side of the stage. The ceiling was high, yellowish globes shedding down a dim light. Probably the Pledge of Allegiance had been said here thousands of times. Tonight it was full of more middle-aged women than I'd ever seen in one place, and the clicking of high heels and pocketbooks was a constant roar.

Then the house lights went down and it got dead silent. The curtain rose in the darkness and a spotlight stabbed down and my brother leaped into it. He tore into "Heartbreak Hotel" like a man possessed. My brother, who had been good, had gotten better. Maybe he really was the best. He had all the moves down, and from this distance it made no difference at all that he wasn't a carbon copy of Elvis.

He sang "Blue Suede Shoes" and "Don't Be Cruel" and "Jailhouse Rock" and spoke of the series of miracles that had brought Elvis to the top in so short a time. He said Elvis had loved black music and made a plea for integration and sang "In the Ghetto." All this time, he was throwing scarves into the audience and women were fighting for them. Then he said, "There's been a great loss of faith in this country. Maybe it was Nixon, maybe Vietnam. I voted for Nixon, but he betrayed us. He thought he could get away with fooling us rednecks." He looked around, his face incandescent in the spotlight. "That's right. I'm a redneck. So are you. And so was Elvis. We're the people who kept the faith."

There was more, but I don't really remember all he said; and he didn't write it down, he spoke right from the heart. He asked for a moment of silence for the boys who had died in Vietnam, and sang "How Great Thou Art." Then he ripped right into "Hound Dog" and disappeared without an encore. The lights came up and we were back in that shabby little auditorium with flags on either side of the stage.

The audience went wild, like they'd just woke up, and I ran downstairs to Bubba's dressing room, where you could hear them stomping on the floor overhead.

Then Floyd said, "Here come the autograph hounds," and opened the door and they poured in. Bubba signed his own glossies as fast as they could shove them at him, and pretty soon a woman grabbed his gold chain and tore it right off his neck.

"We'd better get out of here, Bubba," Floyd said, and we shoved through the crowd. But they had our way blocked and we had to detour into the girls' rest room. Bubba was still laughing, but to tell the truth I was scared. We climbed out the window and ran across the parking lot, where someone from the band was waiting in the Eldorado. We all piled in and drove off, a crowd of women following us all the way to the corner.

"They shoulda had cops there," Bubba said after a while. "I told them we'd need cops. Floyd, you'd better start packing a rod. You're gonna need it if there's any more crowd scenes like this."

•

At Six Flags, Bubba demolished the other Elvis impersonators. What surprised me was how many there were. They came in all shapes and sizes, and one had come from as far away as Nebraska. There was only one who was serious competition: Claude Thibodeaux, from New Iberia, Louisiana, who billed himself as the Cajun Elvis. He had flash, but nobody could beat Bubba for sheer impact.

Right after his performance, Bubba was approached by someone who wanted to manage him. Elvis Presley's manager, as everyone knows, was Colonel Tom Parker. This was Bud Parker, late a colonel in the U.S. Air Force. The coincidence tickled them both. He promised Bubba in one year he'd be playing Caesar's Palace in Las Vegas.

I was packing my suitcase when Bubba came into my room and said, "Big brother, you and me are going to Houston."

"What for?"

"Looka here at this telegram."

The telegram was from Nancy Jo Miller, who'd been Bubba's high school love. She was married now and lived in Houston. She said she'd read about his act, congratulated him, and hoped they could get together sometime.

Sometimes my brother dumfounded me. But I couldn't say no, and anyway, he was paying for the tickets. So instead of going home, we flew to Houston on Trans Texas, got a rented car and a room at the Holiday Inn.

Nancy Jo lived in a $200,000 brick colonial on the edge of Houston, with pine trees growing in the front yard. Bubba had this idea he wanted to drop in and surprise her, so we didn't phone ahead. He slipped on his shades and I rang the doorbell. I felt sorry for Bubba: He was as nervous as a kid on his first date.

Just for a moment I saw Nancy Jo as she really was, a little faded around the eyes and mouth. But the years had been good to her. I suppose you could say she resembled Angie Dickinson — which, in a way, was a hell of a lot better than she'd looked in high school.

"Oh, my Lord," she said, when she saw Bubba in his white Elvis jump suit, and gave a short, embarrassed laugh that was cut off as if by a knife. Then she said, "I'll make y'all bloody marys," and disappeared into the kitchen.

"This was a mistake," Bubba said. He was trembling so hard I had to hold him up.

Nancy Jo came back and we sat in the tiny front room with the big picture window, which I knew was almost never used except for guests. What with the baby grand piano and the big sofa and the glass-topped coffee table, there was hardly room for the three of us; but from the first, I don't even think they knew I was there. They were totally absorbed in each other. She poured out the story of all that had happened since they'd seen each other last, and I stared at the celery stalk in my bloody mary and tried not to listen.

Nancy Jo had intended to marry Bubba, but he had to do his Army service, and there seemed to be all the time in the world; so she went to Dallas and enrolled in stewardess school. She pictured herself wearing that cute uniform and doing favors for the passengers, bringing them pillows and playing with their kids.

She lived with some other stews on Gaston Avenue, and there were some pretty wild parties; but Nancy Jo locked herself in her room and did crossword puzzles and wrote love letters to Bubba.

It was the airplane that did her in. The other stews hung out in the galley, where you could meet pro-football players and rich oilmen. Nancy Jo didn't want a rich oilman: She was going to have Bubba. So she fought it.

But the airplane was the most boring place in the world. The kids were snotty and their parents were cross and didn't appreciate the favors you did for them. There was nothing to do but look out the window, and when you did, what did you see? Clouds.

In the end, she went to the galley, which was like a nickel-plated singles bar, so tiny you couldn't turn around without bumping into some horny guy. There she met Calvin Sloate, a corporate lawyer for Texaco; and they drank Scotch out of tiny bottles while the galley roared like a sea shell, rocking slightly in the rough air 20,000 feet over Indianapolis.

"I'm sorry, Bubba," she said. "But you were going to be in the Army for another year and that seemed like forever. I had to get off that airplane." So she had married Calvin, and now seventeen years had flashed by like nothing at all.

"We've got a condo in Vero," she said, "and one in Aspen, and last year we went skiing at Sundance and Lisa had her picture taken with Robert Redford."

"Lisa?" Bubba asked in a flat voice.

"My daughter," she said, showing us another picture. "That's her with her Arabian stallion. She loves horses."

She showed us the rest of the house. We stood for a moment at the door of Calvin's study, like visitors at a museum looking into one of those rooms closed off with a velvet rope. Calvin had a collection of beer cans, one from every country in the world; a pair of expensive shotguns; and a lamp shade made of *Playboy* centerfolds. I had already noticed his radar-equipped bass boat in the driveway.

In the bedroom, she slid back the closet door and showed us her $500 Italian shoes. Bubba just looked at her and said, "You know you broke my heart, don't you?"

"Oh, Bubba, don't say that. It sounds so horrible. And, anyway, how could I know you cared that much? Look here."

She took from under her costly shoes the old high school yearbook; and there, on the same page, were their pictures. Their faces were soft and unformed but shining with a sort of light. Bubba had a flattop with "fenders" — long on the sides and short on the top. Over his face he had written, in blue ballpoint pen: "Had a lot of good times with you and hope to see more of you next year. Bubba."

"Couldn't you have said more than that?" she asked, tears in her eyes. "How was I to know I was so important to you?"

"In those days," Bubba said, "you won the game of love by pretending you didn't care. Yeah, that's all we thought love was, a game. But it turned out to be a more serious game than we thought."

At this point I left the room, phoned a cab, and went back to the

Holiday Inn. I don't think they missed me. It rained, and there I spent the rest of the afternoon watching *Return to Earth*, a TV movie about the life of an astronaut, and drinking Jack Daniel's. Later, Bubba came back. "Well, big brother," he said, "it's all settled. She's leaving her husband and I'm leaving my wife, and everything's going to be like it was." He'd been walking around in the rain and his clothes were soaked.

But I was skeptical that Bubba could so easily turn back the clock. Now that he'd become a star, he thought anything was possible. To me, he was like that astronaut who'd achieved his boyhood dream and went to the moon; but sooner or later, he had to come back down to earth and be an ordinary person like the rest of us. On the plane home, Bubba turned to me and said, "Big brother, I'm going to tell you something. You're the only one who'll understand."

"Yes, Bubba?"

"My whole life, I've felt like I was in the wrong body or something. But when I'm Elvis . . . I got it right. I'm the person I should have been, the person I've always known I could be."

Now it struck me that this was what Bobby Joe Pitts, the would-be transsexual, had said. Like Bubba, he only felt like himself when he was somebody else.

"Do you know what I'm saying?" Bubba whispered, holding my shoulder in an iron grip.

Yes, I knew. At the best moments of my life — when I hit a good golf shot or had a woman I adored — I felt like someone else. A version of me, maybe, but a version that was to Ross Moody what a Cadillac Eldorado was to a Ford Pinto. I doubted you could totally become that perfect version of yourself. Bubba felt that way now, but he could not be El Tex As for the rest of his life.

But that was the happiest I ever saw Bubba. On this flight, we had, instead of a stewardess, a male flight attendant. Ordinarily, Bubba would have made some sarcastic comment; but on that day, he seemed at peace with himself. I slept most of the way, but once I woke up. Bubba, in the hollow roar of the cabin, was looking through the porthole and smiling down at the dark world below.

•

When he broke the news to his wife, Jan, she knew just how to take it: like Jill Clayburgh in that movie about the New York woman, nodding, her eyes closed, finishing his sentences for him.

"And so," he said, "I am going to —"

"Move out. All right, buster, go ahead. Do yourself a big favor."

They were standing in the den, and she poked through the big glass bowl on top of the television set full of matchbooks from every restaurant they'd ever been to.

"You'd just better get yourself a good lawyer," she told him.

The strange thing, he said, was that she seemed almost glad. Here it was, the crisis predicted so often. Now she would learn to think of herself and be happy (like Rhoda once she got rid of that slob, Joe), maybe even write a book. The possibilities were endless.

"There is one more thing," Bubba said. "Here is a list of our close friends whom I do not want you to sleep with, as they would be laughing at me behind my back."

"Thank you," she said. "I know just what to do with it."

She slept with the first one, Bubba's boss at the Prudential, that very night; and spent the rest of the week working her way down the list.

Nancy Jo also left Calvin Sloate but, on the advice of a girlfriend, went to a therapist, and the first thing he did was tell her not to make any more sudden moves.

She phoned Bubba and said, "I'm living in an apartment complex with plastic ivy on the walls. There's nobody here but kids; and my lawyer says I won't get any kind of settlement, since I moved out. Bubba, I'm having second thoughts."

So Bubba sped down to Houston, even though he was starting another tour in a few days. Nancy Jo wouldn't see him right away: She had to look through her appointment book and set a date. When they finally got together, all she would do was talk for hours. She had a whole new vocabulary and she wouldn't drink bloody marys anymore, just white wine and something called Amaretto, which Bubba said tasted like Log Cabin syrup.

She was changing, slipping away; but Bubba was desperate to prove he could accept her under any conditions. He went to see her therapist himself and even took her to a Woody Allen movie.

•

I didn't see Bubba for months. At the end of his tour, he phoned from Abilene and asked if I'd come down. I found him that night at the Cross Plains Motel, a real dump.

His appearance shocked me: He'd gained maybe forty pounds. He said, "Did you bring your little black bag?"

"Yeah. What for?"

"You got any speed in it?"

I was offended and told him to forget it. He said it was hard for him to keep his weight down, being on the road and all and eating nothing but junk food. But I wouldn't be talked into it. Then I went right into the john and flushed all my pills down the toilet. When I came back out, Bubba was talking to Floyd, who had his hair dyed red. I sat down and noticed my chair had a Rocking R brand on the arm. It was Roy Rogers furniture, probably bought for some kid thirty years ago, and it had ended up here in this terrible motel. For the first time, I glimpsed the sadness of being on the road singers talk about, and thought it was getting to Bubba.

Floyd said he had a girl for Bubba. "Tell her I'll meet her in one hour," Bubba said. "The usual conditions."

The conditions under which Bubba met his fans were these: They had to be between the ages of thirty-five and forty-five, they had to provide their own car, and they had to park on a dirt road on the edge of town. When Bubba appeared in the Eldorado, they flashed their lights if it was safe. Then Bubba parked and came ahead on foot, bringing his own bottle.

I thought this was a foolish, adolescent thing to do, and told him so.

"You know, big brother," he said, "I feel sorry for you. You been fooling around with women's private parts for so long you've forgotten what they're for."

Like everything Bubba said, there was some truth to this. In my years as a gynecologist, I'd examined most of the girls I'd worshiped in high school, and it meant less than nothing to me. It made me wonder about my choice of profession.

"When are you playing Las Vegas?" I asked him.

"Colonel Parker says I'm not ready for Vegas. I need one more thing to put me over the top — plastic surgery, so I'm identical to Elvis. Course, there'll be no goin' back — but it's worth it if it gets me to Caesar's Palace."

"No," I said. "No, Bubba. You can't do that."

"Why not?"

I couldn't exactly say, but I was thinking: If he loses his face, he loses himself.

"Bobby Joe Pitts decided not to," I said.

"Bobby Joe Pitts?"

"You know. The plastic surgeon told him he should try living like a woman. Well, he joined a women's group, and now he's changed his mind. He says he thought men were boring, but women have the most boring conversations in the world."

This got my brother furious. "Are you comparing me to some miserable little pervert? Christ, Bobby Joe . . . why, he wore a brassiere under his football jersey the whole senior year. And we thought he was joking!"

"Will Nancy Jo love you if you don't have your own face?"

He took a pistol out of the desk drawer, a Colt Python, and spun it around his finger and said, "Nancy Jo doesn't know what she wants. Last time I talked to her, she said she wanted space. I said, 'Hell, you can have all the space you want, once we're married.' "

He aimed the pistol at the television screen, where Elvis was singing to Ann-Margret. It was a reshowing of *Viva Las Vegas* on cable TV.

"His voice sorta went to pieces, didn't it?" Bubba said. "Frankly, I think I'm better now than he ever was."

"Bubba, put down that gun."

"Come on," he said. "I'm going to get some nooky."

So Floyd drove us out to the edge of town, where we parked on a dirt road and could see ahead, dimly, the outline of another car.

"She's not flashing her lights," Floyd said. "It must not be safe yet."

I rolled down the window. There was a full moon that night and I thought I could hear the distant yip of coyotes.

When I mentioned it, Floyd said, "Ain't no more coyotes in this county. Farmers wiped them out with traps and poisoned bait."

Still, I thought I could hear them, as I had on so many nights when we'd driven out on Red River Road.

"Do you have to do this, Bubba? What about Nancy Jo?"

"A man's got to get his satisfaction. And if you can't be near the one you love, love the one you're near."

The headlights of the other car flashed.

Bubba opened the door.

"Don't go, Bubba."

"You know, big brother," he said, "you ought to come with me. It would do you good to see how those ladies give me all that good X-rated sex they been holding out on their husbands all these years." He came around and opened my door. "Just stand outside and listen. She won't mind. Thrill to the days of yesteryear, big brother. Come along with me and I'll show you how good that low-rent lovin' can still be."

And, God help me, I did. My heart was pounding, but I stepped out of the car and followed my brother down that road in the moonlight.

"You know, Bubba, you are a devil. You have the damnedest way of getting people to do what you want."

"Don't I know it?"

"You were right about me being a gynecologist and all. Somehow, I lost interest in women. It just slipped away from me like everything else."

"The things closest to you go first," he said. "They slip away so softly you don't notice. You wake up one morning the stranger in a strange land."

"You're right," I said. "But women are . . . everything."

"Yeah, verily, good buddy."

"Sex may be the secret of American life. In fact, I see now . . ."

But I don't know what I saw, for what happened next drove everything out of my head. The headlights of the car came on, blinding us, and we heard a male voice say, "Try to screw my wife, will you, you sons of bitches! I'll kill you!" Then a shotgun went off and I heard the shot rip through the air right over our heads. The car was rolling toward us and Bubba and I were running back down the road.

"The fence, big brother," Bubba shouted, "hit for the fence." And I dove under it, the barbed wire tearing the coat right off my back. Then we were stumbling through the prickly pear, the shotgun still going off and one pellet stinging the back of my neck like a yellow jacket.

Bubba grabbed me and threw me down. The car stopped and a spotlight probed around until it found us. Bubba leaped up, his fists balled, a foolhardy, magnificent sight. I thought: This is the end of your life, Ross.

Then we heard Floyd laughing and barking like a dog. "Come out, come out, wherever you are, Elvis."

It was all a big joke.

Bubba picked up a clod and threw it at the car, but Floyd only laughed harder. The band had been in on it — I could hear them laughing, too. My face was scratched and my palms were full of cactus thorns, and I could feel cold air on my back where my jacket had been ripped off.

Bubba climbed over the fence and threw himself at Floyd. They circled in the headlights, Bubba throwing wild punches and Floyd dodging them, shouting, "Shitfire and save matches, Bubba. Can't you take a joke?"

"Joke! We coulda been hurt running around in that goddamned cactus patch."

"Oh, hell, you're just pissed off 'cause we pulled that same trick on you in high school. I never thought you'd be stupid enough to fall for it twice."

That stopped Bubba. "All right," he said. "So I did. But this time it wasn't funny. We're grown men now, not high school kids."

Floyd kept laughing.

"All right, Floyd, you're fired. That's right. I'm giving you notice."

Somebody from the band stepped forward and said he thought Bubba was being too harsh, and Bubba fired him, too. He looked around and said, "Anybody else?"

Then everybody said it was fine with them; they were getting fed up with Bubba, anyway. There were some bitter words. It ended up with us going back to the motel and them going off to a honky-tonk to get drunk.

On the way back, Bubba began wondering where he was going to get another band. His troubles were multiplying and he said, "Maybe I should just shoot myself."

"Don't talk that way, Bubba."

At the motel, the television was still on, nothing showing on the screen now but snow. I went into the bathroom, threw my torn jacket in the trash can, and started putting iodine on the scratches on my face. The shot lifted me right off the floor.

He was sitting on the bed, holding the pistol. The television was exploded, a bullet through the picture tube. "I always wanted to know how he felt when he did that," Bubba said. "Now I know."

•

Things went downhill fast after that. My brother never found another band. The bookings dried up and Colonel Parker lost interest. The IRS was now investigating Bubba's income taxes, and, in the middle of it all, he got a Dear John letter from Nancy Jo saying she'd fallen in love with her psychiatrist.

He went down to Houston with the idea of confronting her but, instead, went to Calvin Sloate's house. Calvin himself answered the door and Bubba said, "I'm the son of a bitch who ran off with your wife."

"I know," Calvin said. "You're Bubba Moody. Come on in and let's let it all hang out."

Bubba, feeling numb all over, walked into Lisa's room. She was lying on her bed under a John Travolta poster.

"Your mother doesn't love me anymore," he said.

"I know. I think she's making a big mistake."

"You're the closest thing to her, the way she once was," Bubba said. "You're beautiful."

"Thanks, Bubba. I like your looks, too."

"Will you marry me?"

"Are you serious?"

"Dead serious," he said, and kissed her on her teen-age lips.

When he turned around, Calvin was standing in the door.

•

Bubba phoned from Houston and said he'd been shot in the leg. It was nothing serious — Calvin had used a .22 target pistol. Before I left, I went over to tell Jan, who'd just gotten back from a trip to Las Vegas with Harley Otis. When I got there, she was gluing silver dollars to the top of the coffee table.

"Look here at all the money I won," she said. "Seems like my luck just won't quit."

When she heard about Bubba, she said, "That's his problem. All that's behind me now. I'm starting over."

She disappeared into the kitchen and I was left alone with the television. Tom Snyder was interviewing a judge in California who'd started divorcing fifty people in a group. There were no lawyers required, he just asked everyone if they had irreconcilable differences. When they said they did, he pronounced them divorced and they headed for the door. The men moved slowly, but the women were smiling and hopeful, and I thought how much better women seemed to adjust to modern life. "So would you say this is . . . the coming thing?" Tom Snyder asked, and the judge said it was.

"Notice anything different?" she said, coming back into the room.

"No. Is your hair shorter?"

She told me she'd had silicone injections. "Come on, Ross, you know my breasts always drooped."

"No, Jan. I've never noticed."

She put down her glass of white wine and lay on the floor. "See? They're nice and hard. They're the same standing up or laying down. They're just like doorknobs."

"I honestly can't tell the difference, Jan."

She leaned so close I could feel her breath on my cheek. "Go ahead and put your hand on them. I don't mind. Feel the difference for yourself."

I excused myself and drove home, the whole side of my face burning like I'd stood too close to a hot stove.

•

So Bubba never got his plastic surgery or a trip to Las Vegas (although his wife did). He ended up driving a truck again, but to me he seemed happier, and I found I enjoyed knowing him more than I had since we were kids. He still, however, had his problems with the IRS, and one night, in the dead of that winter, he tapped on my patio doors. We sat outside, in the darkness, while my wife watched *Family Feud*. (She seemed to draw strength from that program: She never missed it.)

"The government lawyers are coming Monday," Bubba said, "and I'm liable to do a couple of years in prison."

I told him I'd lend him money, but he said after the divorce he couldn't face going to court again.

"Let's take one last ride out Red River Road," he said, "in case I never see it again."

So we took a six-pack and drove out and parked on the edge of town, where the pumping jacks rose and fell in the fields on either side.

"You know," he said, "Elvis himself couldn't make it today. Everything today glorifies the loser, the person who can't help himself. Someone like me doesn't stand a chance. Yeah, it's the decade of the loser; and it's the losers who did me in. Come on, big brother, let's go ride those pumping jacks."

So we did. He could always talk me into anything. He sat on one end and I on the other, hanging on for dear life, and we rose and fell like two kids on a gigantic seesaw.

"Well, if that's the way this country's going to be," he shouted over the roar of the diesel, "they can have it. I want no part of it. I'll go right on, trying to do the impossible. Look, big brother," he said, reaching over his head as the pumping jack rose, "I can touch the moon."

Then he fell off. I thought he was dead. But he groaned and threw up in the weeds, and I cleaned him off as best I could.

"We'd better go home, Bubba," I said.

"He never died," Bubba said. "Not really."

"He did die, Bubba. Of a heart attack. We've all got to get older and die."

"No, big brother. I'll let you in on a secret. You and I are going to be the first people in history who don't."

•

The men from the IRS came on Monday, but Bubba was gone. Floyd, who was now back with the highway patrol, found his truck parked by the side of the road near Electra. There'd been lots of UFO sightings the night before. A farmer near Bowie found his cows dead, emptied out; nothing left of them but horns, hooves, and hide, and not a drop of blood on the ground, either. The lights of Bubba's truck were still on, and his CB radio, the key turned to SEND. Floyd found one footprint in the sandy soil just the other side of the fence, apparently headed for a strange depression in the ground, where all the grass was dead. It made the front page of the papers, and the sermon that Sunday was "A Close Encounter with Your God."

•

Then things got more or less back to normal here in north Texas. Bobby Joe Pitts started a marriage-counseling service. He saw himself as someone who'd known the problem from both sides, a sort of Kissinger in the war between the sexes. Harley Otis got a divorce and married Jan, but it wasn't long before she showed up at Stolen Hours, a new bar for housewives where they could drink all afternoon, watch the soaps, and perhaps have a casual affair. Floyd forgot his grudge against Bubba and we spent several nights talking about all that had happened. "I'll tell you one thing," he said. "Your brother was the most remarkable person ever born around here."

In October, I finally made love to Nadine MacAfee. But we both discovered that what we had looked forward to for so long took only moments to do, and, naturally, this was a disappointment. We parted friends, but it confirmed my idea that the past is a closed book: You don't tamper with it.

But that night I couldn't sleep, and long after they played the national anthem on television, and showed the airplane and the prayer, I was still pacing the floor and feeling like a ghost. Then the phone rang.

"Hello, big brother."

For a moment, I couldn't see or speak. "I just wanted to let you know," Bubba said, "that I was still on the planet Earth. In fact, I'm in Globe, Arizona."

"It's good to hear your voice, Bubba."

"It's good to hear yours. Hey, this is great country out here. Leaving that town was the best thing I ever did." He told me he was working as a disc jockey, but he had big plans: There was an old, abandoned drive-in out on the edge of town, and he was going to renovate it and call it Bubba's Fifties Burger.

"You know," he said. "Carhops on roller skates, neon lights, and, on the jukebox, some of that great old rock 'n' roll."

"Better keep a low profile, Bubba. You're still a wanted man."

"Don't worry about that," he said. "The road's right out my back door. And if I have to split, well, that won't be so bad, either. If there's a prettier sight than an American blacktop road goin' nowhere in the moonlight, I don't know what it is."

There was a click, then nothing but echoes along one thousand miles of telephone cable.

Well, goddamn. I took three or four shots of Jack Daniel's and did a sort of dance out there on my patio, hopping around under the stars. Then I got in the car to go tell Floyd the good news: that the King was still with us.

FRED LICHT

Shelter the Pilgrim

(FROM THE HUDSON REVIEW)

To MY GRANDFATHER, who was very much a ghetto Jew, charity was one of the exigencies of life. You breathed. You ate. You gave. Steadily and without having to think about it, my grandfather went every week to visit a hospital run by the Orthodox community, bringing with him cigarettes, fruit, newspapers, and a bit of money.

To my parents, who prided themselves on being "advanced Jews" and brought us up to think of Grandfather as honorable but picturesque, charity was a duty one performed at a distance. They wrote two checks, one at Passover, the other at New Year, and received, in return, a form letter of thanks from the agency that received their donation.

To me, to my brother, and to my sister, charity is an equivocal institution designed to keep the poor in their place. We have read Marx and we have read Freud and we can quote chapter and verse about charity as a form of social bribery and self-delusion for the abreaction of social and personal guilt feelings. We still write and send off checks at regular intervals, but we do so with a good deal of self-irony, as if indulging a quaint but not too harmful superstition. We clearly know that charity is patronizing and shameful and the ugly fruit of uglier injustice. But we are somewhat dissatisfied with our knowledge. We have come to be understanding of our parents and have come to venerate our grandfather and his bag full of cigarettes and oranges with which he set out every Friday after lunch. But we also suspect that we don't know what any of them was all about.

It has always been difficult to think about these things, but my brother and my sister and I are convinced that it is the only thing that we ought to think about, because if we could come out in the clear in this one simple matter, we could make our peace with all the rest.

•

When the affairs of my father's firm required our moving from Paris to Berlin in 1937, my mother, for all her being "advanced," nevertheless felt that inviting the rabbi over in order to make a donation was as much part of settling into a new home as unpacking the suitcases and spreading the carpets.

The rabbi arrived thoroughly unsettled by the phenomenon of a Jewish family moving *to* Germany in those days of flight and panic. He harangued my parents on the irresponsibility of taking the family into the heart of a dangerous storm but accepted the customary check for the charities of his congregation. Mother, always anxious to win her children over to the outdoor life we despised, asked him whether there was an outing club or sports association in which she might enroll her three children. Patiently, as if speaking to a child, the rabbi explained to her that the community was in chaos and disintegration. Those who had not yet fled took every care to dissociate themselves from anything Jewish in the hope of passing unmolested. For burials, for Bar Mitzvahs, and for the High Holidays, he had to hunt and cajole among the remnants of a once-proud community sufficient attendance to constitute a *minyan*, the ritual quorum without which services could not take place.

My mother objected that there must be some sort of activity in which her children could contribute so that they would not feel totally disconnected from the kind of religious community that the whole family had always known.

The rabbi, a rather unprepossessing person, as I remember him, with pudgy hands and tiny, perfectly round and staring eyes, thought awhile and then nodded. There was always something to be done, but he doubted that we would want to do it. The implication that we were too spoiled and too stupid to understand the situation in which we found ourselves stung us all to the quick, and even before he told us what it was he had in mind, we were determined to say yes just to have the pleasure of proving him wrong.

There was, it appeared, a home for retarded orphans still being operated by the community. Most of the healthy orphans had been resettled with the help of Dutch and American and English congregations, but, as was only logical, nobody wanted to take in mentally crippled children. There had been fairly generous contributions to keep the institute in Berlin running smoothly, but there was no getting around the fact that they were being abandoned. Among these children there were quite a few who weren't absolutely hopeless. They could dress themselves and do some rudimentary reading and writing. The aunts and cousins who had placed them in the institution had, for the most part, emigrated, and the children were growing more and more despondent as their former contacts with the outside world dwindled to nothing. The nurses hardly dared take them out for walks anymore because there had been violent incidents. Now that Sunday visits to distant relatives had stopped, these children were limited to their dormitory and to the narrow asphalt yard in which they played. For the utterly benighted children it didn't matter, of course, but for the others . . . In short, would we consider inviting one of these children to our house for weekend visits so that he could have a bit of family life and affection and normal childhood play? It would make an enormous difference.

We children were aghast at the notion, and with the healthy brutality of childhood hoped fervently that Mother, who usually objected to our bringing school friends home because they upset her tidy householder's routine, would refuse. We felt absolutely betrayed when, without so much as glancing in our direction, she said that she would be delighted to receive one of these children for weekends. Two days later the rabbi phoned to tell her that the boy he had selected was called Ernst, that he was fourteen years old, my age, of impeccable cleanliness, and that even though he had the mind of a six-year-old he would amaze us all by a curious gift he had of doing the most astonishingly complicated mathematical and algebraic problems in his head within seconds.

We children had decided beforehand that the one closest in age to the impending guest would bear the brunt of the visit while the others would help out now and then. Ernst, therefore, fell to my lot, and since I didn't have much faith in my sister's and brother's loyalty in this matter, I didn't look forward to Friday. The mathematical quirk of our imbecile guest was a personal offense. Arithmetic was my weakest subject, and I toiled over my homework in daily bitterness and frustration while my teacher kept repeating that if only I could understand the mathematical discipline of mind all the rest would come by itself. To have an idiot crassly expose my weakness enraged me, and I went into a wild tantrum when my mother told me on Friday that I was to fetch Ernst from his institution after school. Parental orders went unquestioned in our fairly authoritarian household. But at this I balked. I would go accompanied by my older sister and by my younger brother or I simply would not go. My mother found the scene I made unreasonable, but felt, on the whole, that my request, though silly, was acceptable. At school's end, therefore, I found Edith and Jonathan waiting for me, looking sulky and keeping a glacial silence. It was a drizzly day toward the end of September, and the orphanage in Moabit was accessible from our school only by a complicated trip that required changing from the underground to a bus and then to yet another bus. I tried to make up for the discomfort that I had imposed on them by offering to buy hot chocolate at the corner Conditorei. Jonathan, who was always straightforward, refused outright. Edith, who was sneaky, accepted the bribe; but after she had greedily finished her hot chocolate, she still refused to speak to me.

It wasn't till we were on the last bus, driving through Moabit, that we drew together again. Moabit is an immense and squalid slum utterly without color or the kind of devil-may-care arrogance that makes the slums of Latin countries less dispiriting. None of us had ever seen such wretchedness before. We were too young to put it into words, but involuntarily and silently we put by our squabble and stood abashed at its triviality. We had suddenly come up against the extent of our good fortune, which had spoiled us and which we took for granted.

The institution, when we finally found it after losing the way several times in the mirror-maze of block after block of uniformity and wretchedness, turned out to be a low barracks, sooty and forlorn. The roof had been mended here and there with tarpaper and wooden laths; the brick wall that ran clear around it bore patches of torn advertisements and was topped by a grim run of broken glass. We were not allowed inside but had to wait in the porter's lodge, which was foul with rancid smells and the fumes of a potbellied stove. The porter stared at us with unconcealed hatred while we shifted from one foot to the other, avoided each others' eyes, and felt by turns vaguely guilt-stricken and aggressively arrogant. The door opened and an elderly lady in a white smock entered, resolutely holding on to a recalcitrant boy with a sullen and peevish look on his round and somewhat beefy face. He was taller than I and bigger, but in a bloated, unhealthy way. It occurred to me that if it should come to a fight, I would win without any great effort.

Meanwhile, with the kind of mechanical cheerfulness that scorns to hide its artificiality, the woman in the white smock was making the introductions.

"Don't they look nice, your new friends? You must be Edith, of course, and which one of you young men is Jonathan and who is Henry? Oh, good! Now off with the lot of you before it gets dark. And remember — be back on Sunday not later than six. Come on now, Ernst," she cajoled in the same artificially patient tone. "Come on, there's no reason to be shy! You'll have a marvelous time."

But Ernst seemed unwilling to budge. I was in an ecstasy of embarrassment and paralyzed with a surge of compassion such as I had never felt before. Jonathan, by my side, was also stricken; of that I felt sure without even looking up. Strangely it was Edith who saved the situation. As long as Ernst remained a weekend guest in our house, I never failed to be amazed at Edith's quick and effective sympathy for him coupled with absolutely cool detachment. Like an efficient but somewhat distraught mother helping her little daughter with her knitting, Edith would step in whenever Ernst and I reached an impasse, set things straight, and hand him back to me while she went quickly on her way. Now, rudely and nonchalantly ignoring the nurse, she broke in with one of those algebraic problems that always made me go clammy and weak inside.

"Ernst, if one car starting out here travels at fifty kilometers an hour and another car starts from the same point seven hours later but travels at sixty kilometers an hour, when will the second car overtake the first car?"

"After three hours and ten minutes," Ernst said, just as you or I might say "good morning" without the slightest hesitation and without a trace of triumph. Though he towered over her, he took Edith's hand as children do at street crossings and without a backward glance turned to leave the porter's lodge. Jonathan and I followed, perplexed beyond the ability to think over what had happened.

Outside, Edith resolutely put Ernst's hand in mine.

"You're going to be Henry's friend from now on," she said.

Ernst looked at her, impassive and stolid, and then looked at me. Unable to fathom what went on in Ernst's round head, I simply stared back, not daring to venture so much as a smile. Then he nodded. His hand, which had lain in mine like a passive object, closed around mine with a firm grip and he nodded again. Edith, Jonathan, and I were seized by the same panic. If we let one minute go by, we would never find the way back to where we belonged. Like children under a spell, we would be doomed to wander about in these gray and rank streets forever. Breaking into a run and dragging a puzzled Ernst with us, we made for the bus stop and did not relax till the familiar lights of the Westend gathered about us once again.

•

At home we were surprised when Mother gave Ernst a very summary and hasty reception. Jonathan and Edith disappeared under spurious pretexts, leaving me to show Ernst my room, which he was to share with me. I expected him to be pleased. It was a large and comfortable room filled with the oddments that I had collected over the years: a small mineral collection begun and then abandoned; stamps that I had kept at with slightly greater constancy; all sorts of sports gear; a Tahitian xylophone; books ranging from the *Iliad* to cowboy tales; a modest collection of records; and a hand-cranked Victrola. Not knowing quite what to do, I put on a record. But Ernst didn't respond one way or the other. He sat in an uncomfortable armchair by the side of his bed and stared at me, patient but obviously expectant, quite oblivious of the Victrola.

"Would you like to play a game?" I asked, wondering secretly what sort of games one could possibly play with Ernst.

His expression didn't change, and for an instant I thought he was deaf. Finally, unable to support his steadfast stare any longer, I got out a piece of paper and tried ticktacktoe. He didn't know the game, and I tried to explain it to him. It is difficult to explain very simple matters when one is fourteen, and I was clumsy and self-conscious as I went about the business of *x*'s and *o*'s and how one had to try to line them up. Ernst followed me very seriously and we tried our hand at the game for a few turns. But just as I finally thought that he understood the game, he unaccountably lost interest. Again he looked at me expectantly. It was many weeks before I realized that his stare was really blank and not at all

expectant. He was quite content to sit and watch me even if I did
nothing more interesting than read a book. Once I discovered this
quirk, things got easier for me, but at that moment I was near the
end of my tether.

With the piece of paper between us and a pencil at hand, I
decided to try another game: the one in which each participant
draws part of an image, folding the paper in such a way as to hide
everything but the bottom lines before handing the paper over to
the next player. The point of the game is the incongruous, fantastic picture that appears when the paper is unfolded. I remember
being fascinated by the game when I was in kindergarten, and
thought it would do beautifully for Ernst. He seemed to understand my instructions quite easily this time and turned out to be a
very meticulous, painstaking draftsman. I was delighted to have
hit on something that made time pass so agreeably.

"All right now," I said when we had reached the bottom of the
page and it was time to unfold the paper, "let's see what sort of
monster we have got here."

Of its sort, the picture was a tremendous success. My sloppy
sketches contrasted vividly with Ernst's precise and sober render-
ing of faces, bodies, and landscape. He looked at the page for a
long time and seemed to grow perplexed at first and downright
angry afterward.

"Don't you think it's funny?"

He shook his head stubbornly and handed the page back to me
visibly agitated, as if he had been tricked in some way and could
see no justification for the deception that had been practiced on
him. But by then it was time to go into the living room, where
Edith and Mother lighted the Sabbath candles. Ernst was very
proud of being given a cap to wear while the prayers were said but
didn't seem to have any interest at all in the little ceremony. He
kept fingering his hat and later asked whether he could keep it on
during dinner.

"Just like in a synagogue," he kept repeating cheerfully.

"Do you often go to synagogue?" Mother asked, and Ernst nodded and laughed.

"I like going to synagogue." Abruptly he started to mutter a few
prayers in Hebrew that he had contrived to learn by heart. But
when we complimented him on knowing them so well, he was
surprised and started to stare again.

At dinner he behaved better than we could have foreseen. He

was clumsy with the silver, holding knife and fork at the very base of the handle, and he sometimes lost track of how much he had in his mouth and stuffed himself, but there was a great attention to detail that bore out the rabbi's assertion that he was very tidy and clean. Once when he broke his roll a few crumbs scattered on the floor, and he simply couldn't go on eating without first getting up, from his chair and squatting on the floor till he had picked up every tiniest speck. He particularly loved apples and had a way of peeling them in a continuous spiral that pleased him immensely. Father asked him whether he would mind peeling an apple for each one of us, and Ernst beamed with gratification. It took almost half an hour before we each had an apple, but because of Father's inspiration we all got up from the table feeling that dinner had been a great success.

Going to bed was what I dreaded most. I hadn't had a chance to get used to my manhood yet, and all the family teased me about being exaggeratedly shy. It was excruciating for me to be seen in my pajamas or my underwear, and now I would have to undress with an utter stranger in my room. For his part, Ernst had no qualms at all. With the careful, studied tidiness that marked all his gestures, he slowly got undressed while I sat on the edge of my bed wondering where I could hide and envying Ernst for his nonchalance. As in a trance, I watched him take off his sweater, then his shirt, his trousers, and his socks. His skin was very white and fine, rather like a baby's; and when he finally stood naked by the side of his bed, I saw that there wasn't the vaguest sign of that change which bedeviled most of my waking and almost all my sleeping hours. The sight of Ernst grown to the full height of a man but childish in every other way overwhelmed me with a sudden shameful but irrepressible wave of physical disgust. I couldn't get myself to undress in front of him. Mumbling some stupid words meant for an excuse, I grabbed my pajamas, my robe, and disappeared into the bathroom.

Returning, I found that Ernst had already turned out the light in my room. I was used to reading in bed before falling asleep; but out of a sense of hospitality I didn't want to turn the light on again even though I could tell from his breathing that Ernst was still awake. I lay in the dark, wondering how I was going to live through the rest of the weekend, when suddenly his voice broke in on me. He sounded strangely shy and hesitant and like a child that wants something but doesn't know what he wants or how to go about getting it.

"Henry? Please ask me a question, Henry."

"All right. Here's a question: What do you want to do tomorrow?" I spoke more brusquely than I had intended. There was a silence. Then:

"Not that kind of a question," Ernst said timidly and obviously close to tears. "*My* kind of a question." He was almost whispering now. As so often in my encounters with Ernst, I felt deeply ashamed and consequently vengeful.

"What's your kind of question?"

"You know — my kind of question. The kind I'm good at."

"All right. But I'm not good at asking them."

"When were you born?"

"On February twelfth, nineteen twenty-two."

"Now ask me what day of the week it was."

"All right, Ernst — what day of the week was it?"

"A Saturday. And now ask me what day of the week it will be in the year two thousand and twelve."

"Why don't you just tell me," I said, exasperated.

"Ask me. Please!"

"On what day of the week will my birthday fall in the year two thousand and twelve?"

"Wednesday," he sighed happily. "Thank you, Henry. Thank you for asking me."

•

Saturday passed easily enough. Ernst liked to stay in bed in the morning, and I sneaked from my room, dressed, had breakfast, and sought refuge with Jonathan. It was eleven before Ernst finally got up, and since it took him a long time to take his bath and get dressed, the morning was gone without my having to do anything at all. Lunch passed off easily, too. We were all a bit apprehensive about whether Ernst would want to peel apples for all of us, but he seemed to have forgotten his triumph of the previous evening. Jonathan promised to take care of Ernst till three, when I was to take him to the movies. I had looked forward to having an hour off, but when I entered my room alone, I found that I wasn't really in the mood for anything much and just moved about restlessly till it was time to go.

Ernst didn't have any preference where movies were concerned and followed me with great docility to a film about car racing. On subsequent visits our Saturday afternoon at the movies was repeated religiously. In time, I took him to every conceivable kind of film but could never quite make out which sort of movie he liked best. Now and then, especially during sequences that played on a ship or at the beach, he would talk to himself, saying how pretty it was, but he never seemed to disapprove of anything. Murder mysteries that frightened me to death and love scenes that I thought contemptible went past him without eliciting visible signs of displeasure. And, strangely enough, he always managed to understand the plot when we talked about the movie on the way home, even though he could never follow the thread when I tried to tell him of some incident that had happened to me or some story a friend had related to me. Maybe the acting out of the story made it easier for him to grasp the situation, while episodes that consisted only of words confused him. I don't know about such things.

•

If Saturday had been a success, Sunday was a despondent failure. We let him sleep again as long as he wanted to, but when he did get up he was nervous and hurried and got everything wrong, and I had to make him undress again and turn his clothes right side out. At lunch he choked on his food; and after the meal, it was obvious that he was already thinking of having to go back to his institution. He just sat there, fidgeting, unable to do anything, just waiting to get it over with. On the bus he hardly spoke a word and kept looking out of the window. He was breathing hard, the window fogged up, and he wiped the pane with his hand, getting himself all smudgy.

"Why don't you stop wiping the window?" I suddenly said irritably.

He folded his hands in his lap, looking at them with distaste but obviously imposing his best behavior on himself in order to please me. At the porter's lodge I tried to shake hands with him, but he refused because his hands were so dirty.

"I'll be here on Friday again."

"I don't think you will come."

"Yes I will. Of course I will. Why do you say that I won't?"

He was silent, looked down, and then turned from me and went through the yard to the barracks at the far end.

After such a gloomy farewell, I expected him to be cheerfully surprised when I came to fetch him on the following Friday. But it was as if he had forgotten all about me in the intervening time, and it was several hours before we were on familiar terms again. The third week he expected me, and even though I always resented the duty my parents had imposed on me, I grew used to it. In a way I managed to get a certain amount of prestige out of the situation vis-à-vis my school friends. It got around that I played nursemaid to Ernst on weekends, and gradually some of my more inquisitive friends asked to see him. On these occasions I would sometimes be extra kind to him to impress my friends with my philanthropic tendencies. Just as inexplicably I would sometimes show off before my school friends by being deliberately cruel to Ernst to show my comrades that I had trained him to loyalty as one might train a dog. And either way, Ernst was happy. He clearly regarded these friends who came and went as ephemeral creatures of no account, while he was part of the family.

"I'm staying here," he would irrelevantly and abruptly tell these friends at odd moments of the afternoon. "And you have to go home."

He quite willingly put up with my willfulness, as if realizing that both my exaggerated kindness and my equally artificial brutality to him were put on only for my friends and had no meaning as far as he was concerned. Once I pushed him so far that we came to blows. My impression that he represented no physical threat to me proved to be quite mistaken. When we began to fight, he was caught off guard. He hadn't noticed my mounting irritation when he remained good-natured and oblivious to the taunts that I flung at him to show my friend that I was like a ringmaster with a beast. Taken by surprise, he fought back with far more energy than I expected, and he easily could have got the better of me. But suddenly he stopped fighting and went limp. Looking at me and at my friend he laughed an odd laugh that was cut short in his throat. I managed to free myself and pushed him away so that he staggered against the wall. My friend, awkwardly ashamed for me and of the spectacle I had put on for his entertainment, said he had to go home.

•

In November my class went on a school trip, and to my surprise and also to my disappointment Ernst gave no sign of sadness when I told him that I would not be back to fetch him next weekend. In

December the whole family was to go to the mountains for a skiing vacation, and Mother decided that we would celebrate Chanukah a little early so that Ernst would be able to be with us for the festivities and for the presents. Edith had knitted him socks. I gave him a little box with minerals that glowed in the dark, Jonathan got him some sweets of which he was especially fond, and my parents bought him a handsome winter coat. Ernst was beside himself with joy. He was allowed to light the candles, and even though you're only supposed to light two candles on the first day of Chanukah, he asked to be allowed to light all eight and stood over the Menorah in beatific enchantment, torn between looking at the presents and the glow of the chased silver candleholder.

He had never been demonstrative of his affections. Probably hugging and kissing is something that has to be learned in the cradle and, being an orphan, Ernst had never learned it. Now, not knowing how to find release for all the pent-up happiness, he ran from me to Mother, from Mother to Edith, and back to me and to Jonathan. He stood in front of us, tense and tremulous, not knowing what to say or do, and when one of us asked him whether he was happy, he went visibly rigid with the effort of trying to tell us just how happy he was. It was Edith who again saved the situation by kissing him soundly on both cheeks. Ernst gave a deep sigh after that and went off to sit in a corner with his presents. The minerals he took to bed with him that night, and there was a soft, steady glow by his bedside when we turned out the lights. In January, when I fetched him home on our first Friday back in Berlin, he seemed to have forgotten Chanukah altogether — or at least he didn't talk about it. We picked up our routine again, with Saturday movies and a walk to a good pastry shop on the Oliva Platz after supper for sweets gluttonously stuffed with whipped cream. He became so much a member of the household that we no longer made special efforts to amuse him. Often I would go out on Saturday mornings with friends and leave him at home all by himself. He didn't mind in the least but played with my things or else went into the kitchen to help peel potatoes for the pommes frites he adored and always got at lunchtime.

•

That every farewell brings with it a premonition of death, of the ultimate farewell, is known to all. Even children have sufficient experience of that numb, wordless sensation of grief that comes with good-byes, a grief that is diluted but never quite dissipated by time and that surges to the surface ever more strongly each time a new turning in our lives tears us from old customs and friendships. But I believe that there is something more important involved than the mere premonition of death. I believe that there is in our good-byes also a prophecy of the manner and the worthiness of our dying. Are we able to part with friends and with life with conscious dignity, or with a hasty nervousness, anxious to get it over with? When we come to partings, are we baffled and confused or can we look steadfastly at what we can't understand and accept it nevertheless? We inevitably show color at such moments, and what really frightens us is the foreknowledge that we will do no better when the final parting comes. Such moments mark us for life.

I don't precisely know when my parents decided that their moving to Berlin in such times and under such circumstances had been an unjustifiable mistake. Or else — my parents have always avoided the subject — they had come to Berlin with a specific purpose in mind and, having achieved it, they naturally decided to go home to Paris again. In any case, we children were told late in April. The school year came to an end in mid-June, and shortly after that we would leave. There remained the business of Ernst.

Mother was of the opinion that it would be best not to tell him anything. What was the use of burdening him and spoiling the weekends that remained? For all we knew, his mind was incapable of taking in recurring events. He might miss me for a few minutes when one fine Friday I didn't show up in the porter's lodge to take him home with me, but his sense of time was confused in any case. He might not even realize that it was Friday. Father and Edith were against such a plan. Secretly I agreed with them, although Mother's idea suited me better, for I recoiled at the very idea of having to tell Ernst that we were leaving for good. We finally arrived at a compromise. Father was to call the doctor who ran the institution (nominally, at least: I don't believe he ever looked in more than fifteen minutes once or twice a week) to put the case before him. The doctor decided that we must tell him and that it would be best to tell him a little bit ahead of time so that he would have a chance to get used to the idea. I know nothing of the clinical side of Ernst's case and cannot tell whether the doctor's advice was sound. But in mid-May, just after Sunday lunch, when Ernst and

I were about to get ready for going back to the orphanage, I steeled myself and took the leap.

"Ernst, I have to tell you something that makes me sad, and I'm afraid that it might make you sad, too. But pretty soon all of us, Edith and Jonathan and I and my parents, will be leaving to go to Paris."

He looked blank, with his head tilted a little to one side, an attitude he sometimes took when he feared being scolded.

"Paris is very far away. Look, let me show you."

I took out my atlas and showed him where Berlin was and where Paris was and how far it was from one city to the other. But I got tangled in trying to explain the map scale to him and that a tiny millimeter on the map was much, much longer than the trip from the orphanage to our home. I suddenly had the feeling that he could understand if he wanted to — we had managed to get more difficult concepts through to him — but that he simply didn't want to understand what I was saying. I grew curt and told him that sometime in June we would go away and that was that. I gave him his jacket and put my jacket on and headed for the front door.

Outside, of course, I repented having been so short and took his arm as we went off to the bus station.

"You see, we have to go to Paris. That's where all our family is. My grandfather and my cousins and aunts. They all live there and we have to go live with them."

He nodded.

"But we won't leave right away. We'll see each other plenty of times before we leave."

He nodded again but I could tell that he had fallen into that obstinate silence that was his only weapon against a treacherous world. Those silences were uncanny; you felt that he would endure martyrdom rather than make a sound.

On the Friday after that, I had some business to attend to at home before going off to the orphanage for Ernst. The weather had turned warm, sultry almost, but strong gusts of moist wind blew through the streets, and gray clouds, bloated with rain, hung heavy and low above the roofs. By the time I got to the orphanage it was getting dark, but I had telephoned ahead to say that I would be late and didn't feel that I need hurry. At the porter's lodge, I sent word, as usual, for Ernst to come and meet me. Even though I am inquisitive by nature, I had never entered the institution, though I had been asked to do so quite often by the nurse who accompanied Ernst to the lodge every time that I called.

I was prepared to wait, as usual, for Ernst. He was slow about getting himself together to go out. But within minutes of my arrival, the woman in the white smock crossed the courtyard alone.

"Maybe he doesn't feel well . . . I don't know what it is, but he doesn't want to come today."

"If he is sick you could have told me when I telephoned."

"Well, I didn't know at the time. But he went to bed. I think he must feel sick. The doctor comes tomorrow in any case. We'll see what he says."

"Does he have a fever?"

"No. I took his temperature first thing. That's why I think we can wait till the doctor comes tomorrow. If you'll call around eleven . . ."

Instinct — or is that just a better word for cowardice? — told me to let it go at that. But I rallied and asked her whether I might come in and see him for a while.

"Of course. Please. I am sure your visit will do Ernst good."

She led me through the asphalted court into a long corridor bleak with peeling paint. Ernst shared a room with four other boys, and two of them were in the room with him when I entered. They were mongoloids and grinned at me ingratiatingly, their heads swaying back and forth. The nurse trooped them out but they went unwillingly.

Only one bulb lighted the room from the center of the ceiling. Through the tall windows the evening looked dark and inhospitable, the color of a dark bruise.

"Ernst? What's the matter? Don't you feel well?" I suddenly cursed myself. The artificiality of my tone made everything inside me shrink with a pang of shame. Why had I come?

"I don't know," Ernst said. His voice was surprisingly even. "Turn the light off, please."

The room was dark now, and I took a chair near his bed. Having started, I vaguely felt that I must go on. I don't know why. But I suppose we all want things to be orderly and tidy. When life frays and threatens to be inconclusive, we try out of sheer selfishness to mend things that can't be mended.

"Won't you come home with me? Edith has a surprise for you."

He got up — I could hardly see him, it was so dark — and rummaged under his bedstead for a bit. Then he got back under the covers. In his hands he held the fluorescent minerals I had given him and they shed a soft glow. He didn't cry. My throat tightened with tears and I was sure that from one moment to the next Ernst too would begin to weep. But he didn't. Maybe he felt too sad for the kind of easy tears that were swelling behind my eyes, or maybe he didn't feel anything at all.

We sat in silence for a long time. Then suddenly as if inspired he clambered out of his bed again, cumbersomely impeded by the minerals he held aloft. Gingerly and with great affection he placed the glowing rocks and pebbles on the floor before me and looked up at me invitingly, as if he expected me to take part in some ritual that would make everything all right. He had some important idea in the back of his mind connected with the radiant stones I had given him. I racked my brain, seized by a sudden panic because I felt quite clearly that I, too, knew what the ritual was — but this knowledge lay just beyond the reach of memory. For a frantic, paralyzing moment I knew how narrow are the limits of the human mind.

Like an animal I was hard up against the electrified wire that circled my little field. I could either break through the imposed limit by risking the shock or I could retreat. For an instant I thought that I might evade the issue yet by deflecting Ernst's grave and expectant stare by throwing him another algebraic puzzle. But no algebraic problem rose to the surface of my mind. It was for me to find what x was worth — I had been given all the data that the equation demanded. With a little effort I could capture the unknown quantity.

Ernst continued to look at me as if what he expected me to do was the most natural thing in the world. The diffuse, tender glow of the mysterious little stones was matched only by the steadfastness of his inviting smile. Then, slowly, only the light of the minerals remained hanging between us as the light of his face subsided under ashen disappointment.

He climbed back into bed then, leaving the little heap of minerals at my feet. Turning on his side he looked unblinkingly at me, with every meaning, intent, or feeling totally extinguished from his eyes.

I stayed a few minutes and then cleared my throat to say good-bye as normally as I could. But my voice didn't quite obey me and the words were left hanging more as if they were a question, a question apprehensive of inducing silence. Then I swiftly left the room, crossed the courtyard at a run, and caught the bus two blocks down the street. I met all my mother's efforts to make another try the next day, and then again the next week, with a steadfast refusal. Adolescent brutality? Fear of hurting Ernst some more? Cowardice? Good sense? It's too long ago for me to tell. But I suppose that it was a bit of each.

We returned to Paris and resumed the life that had been so unpleasantly interrupted. We were still there in 1940 when Paris fell. Six months later — I was nineteen then — my father managed, by means I'll never know, to arrange a complicated plan first to get us out of Paris, then to obtain false papers for us in Marseilles, and finally to bring us across the Pyrenees to the relative safety of Spain.

At first my father insisted that Grandfather come with us. But the old man refused. He insisted that he would only be a hindrance, and he produced any number of Talmudic quotations that spoke of the necessity of preserving young life even if it is at the cost of the old. Besides, he wanted to be buried by the side of his wife and nothing would stir him from his decision. Late in January we were to leave Paris by a night train. On the evening of our flight, Mother made a light supper that we carried in bowls to Grandfather's house. We sat about in silence after dinner till it was time to go. Then, with tranquil deliberation and with unanswerable assurance, Grandfather blessed us one after the other, putting his hands on our heads and speaking a steady prayer over each of us.

During the past two or three years I had grown temperamentally and intellectually into antireligious attitudes. But even I felt incontrovertibly that this man had the power to bless. I felt at peace but I also felt frightened at losing some small detail, because I wanted to remember everything about that moment. It would have to last me to my dying day. Never again would I meet a man who could take the full force of benediction onto himself.

Having given us his blessing, Grandfather stepped back from where we were standing and dismissed us with a nod. It was he who was voluntarily going from us, even though to others it might look as if we were abandoning him in our flight.

Then we slipped away and found . . . well, safety. Survival. Call it what you will.

As for Ernst and Grandfather, details hardly matter. They died

and they died alone. But to the end each had retained the power
to relinquish what had been his, to say farewell on his own terms.
I, on the other hand, have still not learned to say good-bye — nor
has anyone else I know. My brother, my sister, and I, left ponder-
ing the quick and cheerful way Ernst had with his algebraic equations, are resigned to the fact that the puzzle we shall face during
our last moments will be the very one we've never been able to
solve.

MARY ROBISON

Coach

(FROM THE NEW YORKER)

THE AUGUST TWO-A-DAY practice sessions were just sixty-seven days away, Coach calculated. He was drying breakfast dishes. He swabbed a coffee cup and made himself listen to his wife, Sherry, who was across the kitchen, sponging the stove's burner coils.

"I know I'm no Renoir, but I have so much damn fun trying, and this little studio, that one room, we can afford," Sherry said. "I could get out of your way by going there, and get you and Daphne out of my way. No offense."

"I'm thinking," Coach said.

Sherry coasted from appliance to appliance. She swiped the face of the oven clock with her sponge. "You're thinking too slow," she said. "Your reporter's coming at nine, and it's way after eight. Should I give them a deposit on the studio, or not? Yes or no?"

Coach was staring at the sink, at a thread of water that came from one of the taps. He thought of a lake place where they used to go, in Pennsylvania. He saw green water being thickly sliced by a power boat — the boat towing Sherry, who was blonde and laughing on her skis, her back rounded and strong, her suit shining red.

"Of course, of course. Give them the money," he said.

Their daughter, Daphne, wandered into the kitchen. She was a dark-haired girl, lazy-looking, fifteen; her eyes lost behind her bangs. She drew open the enormous refrigerator door.

"Don't lean on that," her mother said.

"And what are you after?" Coach asked.

"Food, mainly," Daphne said.

Coach's wife went away, to the little sun patio off the kitchen. He pushed the glass door after her, and it smacked shut.

"Eat and run," he said to Daphne. "I've got a reporter coming in short order. Get dressed." He spoke firmly, but in the smaller voice he always used for his child.

"Yes, sir," Daphne said. She opened the freezer compartment and ducked to let its gate pass over her head. "Looks bad. Nothing in here but Eggos," she said.

"Have Eggos. I did. Just hustle up," Coach said.

"Can't I be here for this guy?" Daphne said.

"Who guy? The reporter? Uh-uh. He's just from the college, Daph. Coming to see if the new freshman coach has two heads or none."

"Hey, lookit," Daphne said. She blew a breath in front of the freezer compartment and it made a short jet of mist.

Coach remembered a fall night, a Friday game night long ago, when he had put Daphne on the playing field. It was during the pregame ceremonies before his unbeaten squad had taken on Ignatius South High. Parents' Night. He had laced shoulder pads on Daphne, and draped the trainer's gag jersey — No. ½ — over her, and placed Tim . . . Tim Somebody's enormous helmet over her eight-year-old head. She was lost in the get-up — a small pile of equipment out on the fifty, from which warm wisps of air trailed now and then.

She had applauded when the loudspeaker announced her name, and the PA voice, garbled by amplification and echo, rang out, "Daughter of our coach Harry Noonan and his lovely wife: Number One-Half — Daphne Noonan!"

She had stood transfixed in the bath of floodlights as the players and their folks walked by when they were introduced — the players grim in their war gear, the parents looking tiny and apologetic in everyday clothes. The co-captain of the team, awesome in his pads and cleats and steaming from warm-up running, had playfully palmed Daphne's big helmet and twisted it sideways.

From behind, Coach had heard a great "Haaa!" from the home stands as Daphne turned in circles, trying to right the helmet. Her left eye had twinkled out through one earhole, Coach remembered. "God, that's funny," the crowd said. And "Coach's kid."

On the sun porch now, his wife was doing a set of tennis exercises. Framed by the glass doors, she twisted her torso from one side to the other between Coach and the morning sunlight. Through the loose weave of her caftan, he could make out the white image left by her swimsuit.

"I knew you wouldn't let me," Daphne said. She had poured a glass of chocolate milk. She pulled open a chilled banana. "I bet Mom gets to be here."

"Daph, this isn't a big deal. We've been through it all before," Coach said.

"Not for a college paper," Daphne said. "Wait a minute, I'll be right back." She left the kitchen.

"I'll hold my breath and count the heartbeats," Coach said.

They were new to the little town, new to Ohio. Coach was assuming charge of the freshman squad; it was a league where freshmen weren't eligible for the varsity. He had taken the job not sure if it was a step up for him or a risky career move. The money was so-so. But he wanted the college setting for his family — especially for Daphne. She had seemed to begin to lose interest in the small celebrity they achieved in high school towns. She looked bored at the Noonans' Sunday spaghetti dinners for standout players. She had stopped fetching plates of food for the boys, some of whom were still game-sore. She had even stopped wearing the charm bracelet her parents had put together for her — a silver bracelet with a tiny megaphone, the numerals 68 (a league-championship year), and, of course, a miniature football.

Coach took a seat at the kitchen table. He ate grapes from a bowl. He spilled bottled wheat germ into his palm. On the table were four chunky ring binders, their black Leatherette covers printed with the college seal, which still looked strange to him. They were his playbooks, and he was having trouble getting the tactics of the new system into his head. "Will you turn off the radio?" he yelled.

The bleat from Daphne's upstairs bedroom ceased. A minute later, she was back down in the kitchen. She had a cardboard folder and some textbooks with her. "Later on, would you look at this stuff and help me?" she asked Coach. "Can you do these?"

He glanced over one of her papers. It was penciled with algebra equations, smutty with erasures and scribbled-out parts. "I'd have to see the book, but no anyway. Not now, not later. I don't want to and I don't have time."

"Just great," Daphne said. "And Mrs. Math Genius told me 'Do it yourself.' Well, I can't."

"Your mother and I got our algebra homework done already, Daph. We turned ours in. That was in 1956. She got an A and I got a C."

"Mom!" Daphne called, pushing aside the glass door.

"Forget it, if it's the homework you want," Sherry said.

"Don't give in to her," Coach said. "I know you. The last time, you did everything but go there and take the tests for her, and she still flunked. This is summer school, and she's on her own."

"But I can't do it," Daphne said.

"Besides, I've got my own homework," Coach said, and frowned at his playbooks.

•

Toby, the boy sent from *The Rooter* to interview Coach, was un-shaven and bleary-eyed. He wore a rumpled cerise polo shirt and faded jeans. He asked his questions wearily, dragging his words. Twice he yawned during Coach's answers. He took no notes.

"You getting this, now?" Coach said at last.

"Oh, yeah, it's writing itself. I'm a pro," Toby said, and Coach was not certain if the boy was kidding. "So you've been here just a little while then. Lucky you," Toby said. "Less than a month."

"Is that like a question? It *seems* less than a month — less than a week. Seems like a day and a half," Coach said. For the interview, he had put on white sports slacks and a maroon pullover with a gold collar — the school's colors. He had bought the pullover at Campus World. The clothes had a snug fit that flattered Coach and showed off his straight stomach and heavy shoulders. He and Toby were on either end of the sofa, in the living room.

"And you bought this house — right?" Toby said. He stood up. "Well, believe it or not, I've got enough for a couple sticks," he said. "That's two columns, among us press men. If you're going to be home tomorrow, there's a girl who'll come and take your picture. Marcia. She's a drag, I warn you."

"One thing about this town, there aren't any damn sidewalks and the cars don't give you much room if you're jogging," Coach said, getting up too.

"When I'm hitching, I wear a safety orange poncho and carry a red flag and paint a big X on my back," Toby said. "Of course, I realize I'm just making a better target for the speeders."

"I run down at the track now. It's a great facility, comparable to a Big Ten's. I like the layout," Coach said.

"O.K., but the interview's over," Toby said.

"Well, I came from high schools, remember. In Indiana and Pennsylvania — good schools with good budgets, but high schools nonetheless."

"Yeah, I got where you're coming from," Toby said.

"Did you need to know what courses I'll be handling? Fall quarter, they've got me lined up for two. 'The Atlantic World' and 'Colloquium on European Industrial Development,' I think it is. Before, I always taught world history. P.O.D. once or twice."

"That 381 you're going to teach is a gut course. It always has been, in case no one's informed you. It's what we call 'lunch,'" Toby said.

"It's in the nature of a refresher course," Coach said.

Daphne suddenly came into the room from the long hall. Her dark hair was brushed and lifting with static. Her eyes seemed larger than usual to Coach, and a little sooty around the lashes.

"You're just leaving, aren't you, Buster?" Coach said to her.

"Retrieving a pencil," Daphne said.

"Is your name really Buster?" Toby asked.

"Get your pencil and scoot. This is Toby, here. Toby, this is Daphne," Coach said.

"Nice to meet you," Daphne said. She slid into a deep chair at the far corner of the living room.

"Can she hear us over in that county?" Toby said. "Do you read me?" he shouted.

Daphne smiled. Coach saw bangs and her very white teeth. "Come on, Daph, hit the trail," he said.

"I've got a joke for her first," Toby said. "What's green and moves very fast?"

"Frog in a blender," Daphne said. "Dad? Some friends asked me to go swimming with them at the Natatorium. May I?"

"You must see the Nat. It's the best thing," Toby said.

"What about your class, though? She's in make-up school here, Toby, catching up on some algebra that didn't take the first time around."

Toby wrinkled his nose at Daphne. "Algebra? Blah! At first, I thought you meant make-up school. Like lipstick and rouge."

"I wish," Daphne said. She slipped her left foot from her leather sandal and casually stroked the toes.

"She's a nut for swimming," Coach said.

"You'll be *so* bored here," Toby said to her. "Most nights, your options are ordering a pizza or slashing your wrists. Those are the choices of what there is to do."

"Yes, sure," she said, disbelievingly.

"Take it from Toby," he said, waving good-bye.

Coach let Toby out through the front door and watched until he was down the street.

"He was nice," Daphne said.

"Aw, Daph. That's what you say about everybody. There's a lot better things you could say — more on-the-beam things."

"I guess you're mad," she said.

Coach went to the kitchen, back to his playbooks.

Daphne came after him. "Aren't you?" she said.

"I guess you thought he was cute," Coach said. He flipped through some mimeographed pages, turning them on the notebook's silver rings. "I don't mean to shock you about it, but you'd be wasting your time there. You'd be trying to start a fire with a limp wet match."

Daphne stared at her father. "That's sick!" she said.

"I'm not criticizing him for it. I'm just telling you," Coach said.

●

"This is completely wrong," Coach said sadly. He read further. "Oh, no," he said. He drowned the newspaper in his bath water and flung the wet pages over into a corner.

His wife handed him a dry copy, one of the ten or twelve *Rooter*s Daphne had brought home. Sherry was sitting parallel to Coach on the edge of the tub, with her back braced against the tiled wall. "Oh, cheer up," she said. "Probably nobody reads a free newspaper."

Coach folded the dry new *Rooter* into an oblong around Toby's article. "O.K., I wasn't head coach at Elmgrove, and I sure wasn't Phi Beta Kappa. Ugly, ugly picture," Coach said.

"Your head looks huge."

"You were never at Mount Holyoke. Where did he get that one? I didn't bitch about the sidewalks this much."

"You didn't? That's almost too bad. I thought it was the best part of the article," Sherry said.

Coach slipped deeper into the warm water, until it came up to his chin. He kept the newspaper aloft. "Oh, come on, give me some credit here!" he cried. "Don't they have any supervision over in Journalism? I don't see how he could get away with this. It's an unbelievably sloppy job."

"It's just a dinky article in a handout paper, Coach," Sherry said. "What do you care? It wouldn't matter if he said we were a bright-orange family with scales."

"He didn't think of that or he would have. This breaks my heart," Coach said.

"Daph liked it," Sherry said.

Coach wearily chopped at the bath water with the side of his hand. "They read this in the football office. I'll spend my first year here explaining how none of it's true."

"Lie," his wife advised him. "Who'll know?"

"And sure Daphne liked it. She was called 'pretty' or whatever. The pretty Noonan daughter who'll be attending Flippo High School in the fall," Coach said.

" 'Petite,' actually. 'The petite brunette,' " Sherry corrected.

"Daphne's not that small," Coach said.

"I just think the person who's going to come out of this looking bad is that reporter, finally," Sherry said.

"I could kill him," Coach said. "Then he'd look bad."

•

Now Coach had a little more than a month before the start of the two-a-days. He was seated awkwardly on an iron stool at a white table on the patio of the Dairy Frost. Daphne was beside him, fighting the early-evening heat for her mocha-fudge ice cream cone. She tilted her head at the cone, lapping at it.

"You aren't saying anything," Coach said.

"Wait," Daphne said. She worked on the cone.

"I've been waiting."

"If you two want to separate, it's none of my business," she said.

Out in the parking lot, a new powder-blue Pontiac turned off the highway, glided easily onto the gravel, and took the parking slot by the door. The boy in the driver's seat looked familiar to Coach. Good-looking shoulders. The couple in the back — the boy's parents, Coach thought — were both talking at once.

"Have I been wasting my breath for nothing?" Coach said. "*Not* a separation. Not anything like it."

"All right, *not*," Daphne said. She stopped her attack on the cone long enough to watch the Pontiac boy step out. A blob of ice cream streamed between her knuckles and down the inside of her wrist.

"You're losing it, Champ," Coach said.

Daphne dabbed around the cone and her hand, making repairs.

"Hell, real trouble — your father wouldn't tell you about at a Dairy Frost," Coach said. "This apartment your mom found is like an office or something. A place for her to go and get away every now and then. That kid's in my backfield. What the *hell's* his name?"

They watched as the young man took orders from his parents, then came into the Dairy Frost. He looked both wider and taller than the other patrons — out of their scale. His rump and haunches were thick with muscle.

"Bobby Stark!" Coach said, and smiled very quickly at the Pontiac. He turned back to his daughter.

"She wants to get away from us," Daphne said.

"Definitely not. She gave me a list, is how this started. She's got things she wants to do, and you with your school problems and me with the team, we're too much for her. She could spend her whole day on us, if you think about it, and never have a second for herself. If you think about it fairly, you'll see."

"That guy looks dumb. One of the truly dumb," Daphne said.

"My halfback? He's not. He was his class salutatorian," Coach said.

"He doesn't know *you*."

"Just embarrassed. Can't we stick to the point, Daphne?"

She gave a sigh and marched over to a trash can to deposit her slumping cone. She washed up after at a child's drinking fountain. When she came back to the table, Coach had finished his Brown Cow, but he kept the plastic spoon in his mouth.

"What was on this list of Mom's?" Daphne asked.

"Adult stuff, Daphne."

"Just give me one example," she said.

Coach removed the spoon and cracked it in half.

"Dad!" Daphne said.

"I always do that. Your mother's list is for five years. In that time, she wants to be living differently. She wants to be speaking French, regularly. She wants to follow up on her printmaking, and we both know she's got talent there, with her lithographs and all."

"This is adult stuff?" Daphne said.

Coach raised a hand to Bobby Stark. Stark had three malt cups in a cardboard carrier and he was moving toward his car. "Hey, those all for you?" Coach said cheerfully.

"I still got a month to get fat, Coach. Then you'll have five months to beat it off me."

Some of the people at the tables around Coach's lit up with smiles at the conversation. Stark's parents were grinning.

"Every hit of that junk takes a second off your time in the forty," Coach said.

Stark pretended to hide the malteds behind his arm. He was blushing.

"Duh," Daphne said in a hoarse voice. "Which way to duh door, Coach?"

"He can hear you," Coach said.

"Duh, kin I have a candy bar, Coach?" she said. "Kin I? Kin I?"

They watched Stark get into the Pontiac. He slammed the door and threw Daphne a wink so dazzling that she went silent.

•

Coach was in the basement laundry room, with both his arms hugging a bundle of jogging clothes. He was waiting for Sherry to unload her clothes from the washer.

"The Dallas Cowboys are soaking their players in a sense-deprivation tub of warm salt water," she said.

"We know," Coach said.

"If Dallas is doing it, I just thought you might like to consider it."

"We have. Hustle up a little with your stuff," Coach said.

"It's like my apartment," Sherry said. "A place apart."

Coach cut her off. "Don't go on about how much you love your apartment."

"I wasn't," Sherry said. She slung her wet slacks and blouses into the dryer.

Coach had two weeks before the start of the heavy practices. His team would have him then, he knew, almost straight through to the Christmas holidays. "You already spend all your time there," he said.

A little later, Coach and his wife were on the side patio together, sharing a Tab. They could hear the hum and tick of the dryer indoors.

"You know what's odd? Daphne's popularity here," Sherry said. "I don't mean it's *odd*." She was taking sun on her back, adding to her tan.

"No, that isn't new. She's always done terrific with people," Coach said.

"Your people, though. These are hers," Sherry said. "The phone hardly ever stops."

"Well, she's out of math trouble, I guess," Coach said. "And you have your apartment hideout, and you're adjusted here. Now, if only I can have the season I want."

"I love it with her and that reporter," Sherry said.

Daphne had become tight friends with Toby after she telephoned her gratitude for what he had written about her in *The Rooter*.

"Yeah, they're like sisters," Coach said.

"You're still bitter?"

"I'm really not," Coach said. "I live one careful day at a time now. No looking back for a second. Fear motivates me."

"You're fearful," Sherry said.

"Shaking with it," Coach said.

•

It was eight days before the two-a-day practice sessions would begin. The sky was colorless and glazed, like milk glass. When Coach flicked a glance at the sun, his eyes ached as if he were seeing molten steel. He had run some wind sprints on the stadium field, and now he was doing an easy lap on the track. A stopwatch on a noose of ribbon swung against his chest. He cut through the goal posts and trotted for the sidelines, where he had dumped his clipboard and a towel.

Bobby Stark came out from under the stands. His football shoes were laced together and draped around his neck. He was in cutoff shorts and a midriff-cut T-shirt. He walked gingerly in white wool socks. "Did everybody go, or am I the first one here?" he called to Coach.

" 'Bout a half hour," Coach said, heaving.

Stark sat down to untangle his shoes, and Coach, sweating, stood over him. Coach spat. He folded his arms in a way that pushed out his muscles. He sniffed to clear his lungs, twisting his whole nose and mouth to one side. "You know, Stark, I heard you were salutatorian for your class," he said.

"High school," the boy said. He grinned up at Coach, an eye pinched against the glare.

"That counts, believe me. Maybe we can use you to help some of our slower players along — some of the linemen."

"What do you mean — tutor?" Stark said.

"Naw. Teach them to eat without biting off their fingers. How to tie a necktie. Teach them some of your style," Coach said, and Stark bobbed his head.

Stark settled the fit of his right shoe. He said, "But there aren't really any dumb ones on the squad, because they just flunk out here. Recruiters won't touch them in this league."

Coach planted his feet on either side of a furrow of lime-eaten grass. Above the open end of the stadium, the enormous library building was shimmering and uncertain behind sheets of heat that rose from the empty parking area.

Stark got up and watched his shoes as he jogged in place. He danced twenty yards down the field, loped back. Other players were arriving for the informal session. Coach meant to time them in the mile and in some dashes.

Stark looked jittery. He walked in semicircles, crowding Coach.

"You worried about something?" Coach asked him. "Girl problems? You pull a muscle already?"

Stark glanced quickly around them. He said, "I've lived all my life two doors down from Coach Burton's house. My mom and Burton's wife are the best of friends, so I always know what's really going on. You probably know about it already anyway. Do you?"

"What the hell are you talking about, Stark?"

"Oh, so you don't. Typical. Burton's leaving, see, like the end of this year. His wife wants him out real bad, and the alumni want him out, because they're tired of losing seasons. They're tired of finishing third in the league, at best. Everybody says he should go to Athletic Director, instead. So what I heard was that you were brought in because of it, and if we do well this season — because people think you're a winner and pretty young — like, *you'll* be our varsity coach next year."

"That's conjecture," Coach said. But his voice sounded strange to him.

"We could go through four years together. I respect Coach Burton, but I don't see why in four years *we'd* ever have to lose a single game," Stark said. He took a stance, his body pushing forward.

"Ho!" Coach barked, and Stark lunged out.

"See me after this practice!" Coach called to him.

•

It was three o'clock, still hot. Coach was going along a sidewalk with Stark, who was balanced on a racing bike, moving just enough to keep the machine upright.

"Three things," Coach said. "I've seen all the game films from last year, and I came here personally and witnessed the Tech game. No one lost because of the coaching. A coach can work miracles with a good team, but he's helpless if his folks don't want it bad enough. That's the worst thing about running a team — you can't climb down into your people's hearts and change them."

Some college girls in a large car passed and shrieked and whistled at Bobby Stark. "Lifeguards at the pool," he explained.

"I don't know if Burton's leaving or not, but if his wife wants him to, he'll probably go," Coach said. "If you're ever thinking about a career in coaching someday, Bob, think about that. Your family's either with you or you've had it. You drag them all over hell — one town to another — and bury them, and whether you stay anywhere or not depends on a bunch of *kids*, really. I swear, I'd give up a leg for a chance to get in a game myself — just one play, with what I now know."

"I wish you could," Stark said. He swerved his bike's front tire and let it plunk off the curb into a crosswalk. He stood on the pedals for the jolt of the rear tire.

"The last thing is, don't mention the varsity-coach thing to anybody, and I mean anybody. Do you read me?" Coach said.

Stark nodded. They went on a block, and he said, "I turn here. You going to tell your beautiful daughter about it?"

"My daughter. You want a kitten? Because when I tell her, she's going to have kittens," Coach said.

•

No one was home. A plastic-ladybug magnet held a note to the face of the refrigerator. The note read, "Noonan, I'm at my place. Daph's with Toby K. somewhere, fooling around. Be good now. Sherry Baby."

"Dope," Coach said, smiling. He felt very good.

He took a beer upstairs and drank it while he showered. He cinched on a pair of sweat pants and went back down and fetched another beer. He watched some of a baseball game on cable television. He thought over the things he had told Bobby Stark.

"Boy, is that true!" Coach said, and then wasn't sure why he had said it.

He frowned, remembering that in his second year of college, the only year he had been on the varsity team, he had proved an indifferent player. "Not now," he whispered. He squeezed his beer can out of shape and stood it on top of the TV.

There was a thump over his head. The ceiling creaked. Someone had come home while he was in the shower. He took the stairs in three leaps and strode into the bedroom, saying, "Sherry?"

The dark figure in the room surprised him. "Hey!" he yelled.

Daphne was dancing in front of the full-length mirror on Sherry's closet door. She had improvised a look — sweeping her hair over her right ear and stretching the neck of her shirt until her right shoulder was bared. A fast Commodores song thumped from her transistor radio.

"Nothing," she said.

"You're not home. Aren't you with Whoosis? You're supposed to be out. You are *beet* red," Coach said.

Daphne lowered her head and squared her shirt, which bagged around her small torso. "O.K., Dad," she said.

"No, but how did your audience like the show? I bet they loved it," Coach said. He smiled at himself in the mirror. "I'm just kidding you. You looked great."

"Come *on,* Dad," Daphne said, and tried to pass.

He chimed in with the radio song. He shuffled his feet. "Hey, Daph. You know what time it is?"

"Let me out, please," she said.

"It's Monkey time!" Coach did a jerky turn, keeping in the way of the exit door. "Do the Shing-a-Ling. Do the Daphne." He rolled his shoulder vampishly. He kissed his own hand. He sang along.

"Thanks a lot," Daphne said. She gave up trying to get around him. She leaned over and snapped off the radio. "You've got to use a mirror, so you don't look stupid on the dance floor. Everybody does," she said.

"I really was kidding you. Seriously. I know dancing is important," Coach said.

"May I go now? I've got algebra," Daphne said. She brought her hair from behind her ear, which was burning pink.

"Before that, you have to hear the news," Coach said. "Here's a news bulletin, flash extra."

"You're drunk. You and Mom are going to live in different cities. Somebody shot somebody," Daphne said.

"No, this is good news. There's a chance I'll be head coach here, of the varsity. The varsity coach. Me." Coach pointed to his chest.

"Let me out, please," Daphne said.

Coach let her pass. He followed her down the thin hallway to her bedroom. "More money. I'll even be on TV. I'll have my own local show on Sundays. And I'll get written up in the press all the time, by real reporters. Daphne?"

She closed her door, and, from the sound, Coach thought she must have leaned against it.

"What's going on? Tell me, why am I standing here yelling at wood?" he said.

•

By dusk, Coach was drunk at the kitchen table. He was enjoying the largeness of the room, and he was making out a roster for his dream team. He had put the best kids from his fifteen years of coaching in the positions they had played for him. He was puzzling over the tight-end spot. "Jim Wyckoff or Jerry Kinney? Kinney got that tryout with the Broncos later," he said out loud. He penciled "Kinney" onto his diagram.

He heard Daphne on the stairs, and it occurred to him to clear the beer cans from the table. Instead, he snapped open a fresh can. "Daphne?" he said.

"Wait a second. What?" she said from the living room.

"Just wondered who else was alive besides me. I know your mom's still out."

Daphne entered the kitchen.

"You're sorry you were rude before?" Coach said. "That's O.K., Daph, just forget it."

Daphne made the slightest nod. "You *drank* all those?" she said.

"Hold still. What've you got on?" Coach asked. He hauled his whole chair about so he could see Daphne, who had gone behind him.

"Two, four, five," Daphne said, counting the cans. She wore one of the fan shirts that Coach had seen on a few summer coeds. On the front of the shirt, against a maroon field, were the golden letters GO. Across the back was GRIFFINS!

"Now you're talking," Coach said.

"It was free. This guy I met — well, these two guys, really, who

work at Campus World gave it to me. But I don't know, I thought
I'd wear it. I wanted you to see that I care if you get that big job. I
do care. I want to stay here. Do you think we can? Do your people
look any good for this year?"

"Winners," Coach said.

"Yeah, but you always say that," Daphne said.

Coach skidded his chair forward. "Have a beer. Sit down and let
me show you on paper the material they've given me to work with."

Daphne took the can Coach offered, sipped at it, shook her
head, and said, "Ooh, it burns. No wonder people burp."

"These guys are fast and big, for once. I'm not overestimating
them, either. I've seen what I've seen," Coach said.

A car swept into the drive, and then its engine noise filled the
garage. Coach and Daphne were quiet until Sherry bustled down
the short hall that connected the garage with the kitchen.

"Really late, sorry, sorry," she said.

"It's a party, I warn you," Coach said to her.

"So I noticed." Sherry was carrying a grocery sack, not very full.
There were bright streaks of paint on her brown arms. Daphne
got up and plucked a bag of Oreo cookies from the groceries.

"Shoot me one of those," Coach said.

"Any beer left for me?" Sherry said. "I want to drown my disappointment. I can't paint."

"You can paint," Coach said.

"Ugh. My ocean today looked like wavy cement. My rocks looked
like big dirty marshmallows." She put her sack down on the
kitchen counter.

"Tell Dad he's got to do well so we can stay here," Daphne said
to her mother.

Coach said, "Man, Daphne! I hope somebody finds your 'off'
switch." He told his wife, "Plant your behind in that chair, Picasso.
Let me tell you how we're moving up in the world."

"Every August," Sherry said, "Coach wants us to get packed up
for a trip to the moon."

CHARLES JOHNSON

Exchange Value

(FROM CHOICE)

ME AND MY BROTHER Loftis came in by the old lady's window. There was some kinda boobytrap — boxes of broken glass — that shoulda warned us Miss Bailey wasn't the easy mark we made her to be. She had been living alone for twenty years in 4-B down the hall from Loftis and me, long before our folks died — a hincty, half-bald West Indian woman with a craglike face, who kept her door barricaded, shutters closed, and wore the same sorrylooking outfit — black wingtip shoes, cropfingered gloves in winter, and a man's floppy hat — like maybe she dressed half-asleep or in a dark attic. Loftis, he figured Miss Bailey had some grandtheft dough stashed inside, jim, or leastways a shoebox full of money, cause she never spent a nickel on herself, not even for food, and only left her place at night.

Anyway, we figured Miss Bailey was gone. Her mailbox be full, and Pookie White, who run the Thirty-ninth Street Creole restaurant, he say she ain't dropped by in days to collect the handouts he give her so she can get by. So here's me and Loftis, tipping around Miss Bailey's blackdark kitchen. The floor be littered with fruitrinds, roaches, old food furred with blue mold. Her dirty dishes be stacked in a sink spidered with cracks, and it looks like the old lady been living, lately, on Ritz crackers and Department of Agriculture (Welfare Office) peanut butter. Her toilet be stopped up, too, and, on the bathroom floor, there's five Maxwell House coffee cans full of shit. Me, I was closing her bathroom door when I whiffed this evil smell so bad, so thick, I could hardly breathe, and what breath I drew was horrible, like a solid thing in my throatpipes, like soup. "Cooter," Loftis whisper, low, across the room,

"you smell that?" He went right on sniffing it, like people do for
some reason when something be smelling stanky, then took out his
headrag and held it over his mouth. "That's the awfulest stink I
ever smelled!" Then, head low, he slipped his long self into the
livingroom. Me, I stayed by the window, gulping air, and do you
know why?

You oughta know, up front, that I ain't too good at this gangster
stuff, and I had a real bad feeling about Miss Bailey from the get-
go. Mama used to say it was Loftis, not me, who'd go places — I
see her standing at the sideboard by the sink now, big as a Frigi-
daire, white with flour to her elbows, a washtowel over her shoulder, while we ate a breakfast of cornbread and syrup. He
graduated fifth at DuSable High School, had two gigs, and, like
Papa, he be always wanting the things white people had out in
Hyde Park, where Mama did daywork. Loftis, he the kinda brother
who buys *Esquire*, sews Hart, Schaffner and Marx labels in Robert
Hall suits, talks properlike, packs his hair with Murrays, and took
classes in politics and stuff at the Black People's Topographical
Library in the late 1960s; who, at thirty, makes his bed military
style, reads *Black Scholar* on the bus he takes to the plant, and,
come hell or high water, plans to make a Big Score. Loftis, he say
I'm bout as useful on a hustle — or when it comes to getting ahead
— as a headcold, and he say he has to count my legs sometimes to
be sure I ain't a mule, seeing how, for all my eighteen years, I can't
keep no job and sorta stay close to home, watching TV or reading
World's Finest comic books, or maybe just laying dead, listening to
music, imagining I see faces or foreign places in water stains on
the wallpaper, cause somedays when I remember Papa, then
Mama killing theyselves for chump change — a pitiful li'l bowl of
porridge — I get to thinking that even if I ain't had all I wanted,
maybe I've had, you know, all I'm ever gonna get.

"Cooter," Loftis say from the livingroom. "You best get in here
quick."

Loftis, he'd switched on Miss Bailey's sulfurcolored livingroom
lights, so for a second I couldn't see and started coughing — the
smell be so powerful it hit my nostrils like coke — and when my
eyes cleared, shapes evolved from the light, and I thought for an
instant like I'd slipped in space. I seen why Loftis called me, and
went back two steps. See, 4-B is so small, if you ring Miss Bailey's
doorbell the toilet'd flush. But her livingroom, webbed in dust, be

filled to the max with dollars of all denominations, stacks of stock in General Motors, Gulf Oil, and 3M Corporation in old White Owl cigar boxes, battered purses, or bound in pink rubber bands. It be like the kind of cubbyhole kids play in, but filled with . . . *things* — everything — like a world within the world, you take it from me, so like picturebook scenes of plentifulness you could seal yourself off in here and settle forever. Loftis and me both drew breath suddenly. There be unopened cases of Jack Daniel's, three safes cemented to the floor, hundreds of matchbooks, unworn clothes, a zinc laundry tub, dozens of wedding rings, rubbish, World War II magazines, a carton of one hundred canned sardines, mink stoles, old rags, a birdcage, a bucket of silver dollars, thousands of books, paintings, quarters in tobacco cans, two pianos, glass jars of pennies, a set of bagpipes, an almost complete Model A Ford dappled with rust, and, I swear, three sections of a dead tree.

"Godamighty damn!" My head be light; I sat on an upended peachcrate and picked me up a bottle of Jack Daniel's.

"Don't you touch *any*thing!" Loftis, he panting a little; he slap both hands on a table. "Not until we inventory this stuff."

"Inventory? Aw Lord, Loftis," I say, "something ain't *right* about this stash. There could be a curse on it . . ."

"Boy, sometimes you act weakminded."

"For real, Loftis, I got a feeling . . ."

Loftis, he shucked off his shoes and sat down heavily on the lumpy arm of a stuffed chair. "Don't say *any*thing." He chewed his knuckles, and for the first time Loftis looked like he didn't know his next move. "Let me think, okay?" He squeezed his nose in a way he has when thinking hard, sighed, then stood up, and say, "There's something you better see in that bedroom yonder. Cover up your mouth."

"Loftis, I ain't going in there."

He look at me right funny then. "She's a miser, that's all. She saves things."

"But a tree?" I say. "Loftis, a *tree* ain't normal!"

"Cooter, I ain't gonna tell you twice."

Like always, I followed Loftis, who swung his flashlight from the plant — he a nightwatchman — into Miss Bailey's bedroom, but me, I'm thinking how trippy this thing is getting, remembering how, last year, when I had a paper route, the old lady, with her

queer crablike walk, pulled my coat for some change in the hallway, and when I give her a handful of dimes, she say in her old
Inner Sanctum voice, "Thank you, Co-o-oter," then gulped the
coins down like aspirin, no lie, and scurried off like a hunchback.
Me, I wanted no parts of this squirrelly old broad, but Loftis, he
holding my wrist now, beaming his light onto a low bed. The room
had a funny, museumlike smell. Real sour. It was full of dirty
laundry. And I be sure the old lady's stuff had a terrible string
attached when Loftis, looking away, lifted her bedsheets and a
knot of black flies rose. I stepped back and held my breath. Miss
Bailey be in her long-sleeved flannel nightgown, bloated, like she'd
been inflated by a tire pump, her crazy putty face bald with rot,
flyblown, her fingers big as bananas. Her wristwatch be ticking
softly beside a stump of half-eaten bread. Above the bed, her wall
had roaches squashed in little circles of bloodstain. Maggots clus-
tered in her eyes, her ears, and one fistsized rat rattled in her flesh.
My eyes snapped shut. My knees failed, then I did a Hollywood
faint. When I surfaced, Loftis, he be sitting beside me in the livingroom, where he'd drug me, reading a wrinkled, yellow article from
the Chicago *Daily Defender.*

"Listen to this," Loftis say. " 'Elnora Bailey, forty-five, a Negro
housemaid in the Highland Park home of Henry Conners, is the
beneficiary of her employer's will. An old American family, the
Connerses arrived in this country on the *Providence,* shortly after
the voyage of the *Mayflower.* The family flourished in the early
days of the 1900s! . . ." He went on, getting breath. " 'A distinguished and wealthy industrialist, without heirs or a wife, Conners
willed his entire estate to Miss Bailey of 3347 N. Clark Street for
her twenty years of service to his family' . . ." Loftis, he give that
Geoffrey Holder laugh of his, low and deep, then it eased up his
throat until it hit a high note and tipped his head back onto his
shoulders. "Cooter, that was before we was born! Miss Bailey kept
this in the Bible next to her bed."

Standing, I braced myself with one hand against the wall. "She
didn't earn it?"

"Naw." Loftis, he folded the paper — "Not one penny" — and
stuffed it in his shirt pocket. His jaw looked tight as a horseshoe.
"Way *I* see it," he say, "this was her one shot in a lifetime to be
rich, but, being country, she had backward ways and blew it."
Rubbing his hands, he stood up to survey the livingroom. "Some-

body's gonna find Miss Bailey soon, but if we stay on the case —
Cooter, don't you square up on me now — we can tote everything
to our place before daybreak. Best we start with the big stuff."

"But why didn't she *use* it, huh? Tell me that?"

Loftis, he don't pay me no mind. When he gets an idea in his
head, you can't dig it out with a chisel. How long it took me and
Loftis to inventory, then haul Miss Bailey's queer old stuff to our
crib, I can't say, but that decrepit old ninnyhammer's hoard come
to $879,543 in cash money, thirty-two bank books (some deposits
be only $5), and me, I wasn't sure I was dreaming or what, but I
suddenly flashed on this feeling, once we left her flat, that all the
fears Loftis and me had about the future be gone, cause Miss
Bailey's property was the past — the power of that fellah Henry
Conners trapped like a bottle spirit, which we could live off, so it
was the future, too, pure potential: can *do.* Loftis got to talking on
about how that piano we pushed home be equal to a thousand
bills, jim, which equals, say, a bad TEAC A-3340 tape deck, or a
down payment on a deuce-and-a-quarter. Its value be (Loftis say)
that of a universal standard of measure, relational, unreal as number, so that tape deck could turn, magically, into two gold lamé
suits, a trip to Tijuana, or twenty-five rimjobs from a ho — we had
$879,543 worth of wishes, if you can deal with that. Be like Miss
Bailey's stuff is raw energy, and Loftis and me, like wizards, can
transform her stuff into anything else at will. All we had to do, it
seemed to me, was decide exactly what to exchange it for.

While Loftis studied this over (he looked funny, like a potato
trying to say something, after the inventory, and sat, real quiet, in
the kitchen), I filled my pockets with fifties, grabbed me a cab
downtown to grease, yum, at one of them high-hat restaurants in
the Loop . . . But then I thought better of it, you know, like I'd be
out of place — just another jig putting on airs — and scarfed instead at a ribjoint till both my eyes bubbled. This fat lady making
fishburgers in the back favored an old hardleg babysitter I once
had, a Mrs. Paine who made me eat ochre, and I wanted so bad to
say, "Loftis and me Got Ovuh," but I couldn't put that in the wind,
could I, so I hatted up. Then I copped a boss silk necktie, cashmere
socks, and a whistle-slick maxie leather jacket on State Street, took
cabs *every*where, but when I got home that evening a funny, Pan-
doralike feeling hit me. I took off the jacket, boxed it — it looked
so trifling in the hallway's weak light — and, tired, turned my key

in the door. I couldn't get in. Loftis, he'd changed the lock and, when he finally let me in, looking vaguer, crabby, like something out of the Book of Revelations, I seen this elaborate boobytrapped tunnel of cardboard and razor blades behind him, with a two-foot space just big enough for him or me to crawl through. That wasn't all. Two bags of trash from the furnace room be sitting inside the door. Loftis, he give my leather jacket this evil look, hauled me inside, and hit me upside the head.

"How much this thing set us back?"

"Two fifty." My jaws be tight; I toss him my receipt. "You want me to take it back? Maybe I can get something else . . ."

Loftis, he say, not to me, but to the receipt, "Remember the time Mama give me that ring we had in the family for fifty years? And I took it to Merchandise Mart and sold it for a few pieces of candy?" He hitched his chair forward, and sat with his elbows on his knees. "That's what you did, Cooter. You crawled into a Clark bar." He commence to rip up my receipt, then picked up his flashlight and keys. "The instant you buy something you *lose* the power to buy something." He button up his coat with holes in the elbows, showing his blue shirt, then turned round at the tunnel to say: "Don't touch Miss Bailey's money, or drink her splo, or do *any*thing until I get back."

"Where you going?"

"To work. It's Wednesday, ain't it?"

"You going to work?"

"Yeah."

"You got to go *really?* Loftis," I say, "what you brang them bags of trash in here for?"

"It ain't trash!" He cut his eyes at me. "There's good clothes in there. Mr. Peterson tossed them out, he don't care, but I saw some use in them, that's all."

"Loftis . . ."

"Yeah?"

"What we gonna do with all this money?"

Loftis pressed his fingers to his eyelids, and for a second he look caged, or like somebody'd kicked him in his stomach. Then he cut me some slack: "Let me think on it tonight — it don't pay to rush — then we can TCB, okay?"

Five hours after Loftis leave for work, that old blister Mr. Peterson, our landlord, he come collecting rent, find Miss Bailey's body in apartment 4-B, and phoned the Fire Department. Me, I be folding my new jacket in tissue paper to keep it fresh, adding the box to Miss Bailey's unsunned treasures, when two paramedics squeezed her on a long stretcher through a crowd in the hallway. See, I had to pin her from the stairhead, looking down one last time at this dizzy old lady, and I seen something in her face, like maybe she'd been poor as Job's turkey for thirty years, suffering that special Negro fear of using up what little we get in this life — Loftis, he call that entropy — believing in her belly, and for all her faith, jim, there just ain't no more coming tomorrow from grace, or the Lord, or from her own labor, like she can't kill nothing, and won't nothing die . . . so when Conners will her his wealth, it put her through changes, she be spellbound, possessed by the promise of life, panicky about depletion, and locked now in the past cause *every* purchase, you know, has to be a poor buy: a loss of life. Me, I wasn't worried none. Loftis, he got a brain trained by years of talking trash with people in Frog Hudson's Barber Shop on Thirty-fifth Street. By morning, I knew, he'd have some kinda wheeze worked out.

But Loftis, he don't come home. Me, I got plenty worried. I listen to the hi-fi all day Thursday, only pawing outside to peep down the stairs, like that'd make Loftis come sooner. So Thursday go by; and come Friday the head's out of kilter — first there's an ogrelike belch from the toiletbowl, then water bursts from the bathroom into the kitchen — and me, I can't call the super (How do I explain the tunnel?), so I gave up and quit bailing. But on Sat'day, I could smell greens cooking next door. Twice I almost opened Miss Bailey's sardines, even though starving be less an evil than eating up our stash, but I waited till it was dark and, light-headed with hunger, I stepped outside to Pookie White's, lay a hardluck story on him, and Pookie, he give me some jambalaya and gumbo. Back home in the livingroom, fingerfeeding myself, barricaded in by all that hope made material, the Kid felt like a king in his countingroom, or God in February, the month before He made the world (Mama's saying), and I copped some z's in an armchair till I heard the door move on its hinges, then bumping in the tunnel, and a heavyfooted walk thumped into the bedroom.

"Loftis?" I rubbed my eyes. "You back?" It be Sunday morning. Six-thirty sharp. Darkness dissolved slowly into the strangeness of twilight, with the rays of sunlight flaring at exactly the same angle they fall each night, as if the hour be an island, a moment, outside time. Me, I'm afraid Loftis gonna fuss bout my not straightening up, letting things go. I went into the bathroom, poured water in the one-spigot washstand — brown rust come bursting out in flakes — and rinsed my face. "Loftis, you supposed to be home four days ago. Hey," I say, toweling my face, "you okay, brah?" How come he don't answer me? Wiping my hands on the seat of my trousers, I tipped into Loftis's room. He sleeping with his mouth open. His legs be drawn up, both fists clenched between his knees. He'd kicked his blanket on the floor. In his sleep, Loftis laughed, or moaned, it be hard to tell. His eyelids, not quite shut, show slits of white. I decided to wait till Loftis wake up for his decision, but turning, I seen his watch, keys, and what looked in the first stain of sunlight to be a carefully wrapped piece of newspaper on his nightstand. The sun surged up in a bright shimmer, focusing the bedroom slowly like solution do a photographic image in the developer. And then something so freakish went down I ain't sure it took place. Fumblefingered, I unfolded the paper and inside be a blemished penny. It be like somebody hit me hard between the shoulderblades. Taped on the penny be a slip of paper, and on the paper be the note, "Found while walking down Devon Avenue." I hear Loftis mumble like he trapped in a nightmare. "Hold tight," I whisper, "it's all right." Me, I wanted to tell Loftis how Miss Bailey looked four days ago, that maybe it didn't have to be like that for us — did it? — because we could change. Couldn't we? Me, I pull his packed sheets over him, wrap up the penny, and, when I locate Miss Bailey's glass jar in the livingroom, put it away carefully, for now, with the rest of our things.

NICHOLSON BAKER

K. 590

(FROM THE LITTLE MAGAZINE)

THE FOUNTAINBLUE HOTEL and Apartments distinguished itself from the rest of the apartment courts in Isla Vista — a town composed almost entirely of students at UC Santa Barbara — by the fact that it had housed the San Francisco 49ers during their summer training the year before. The team had practiced on the enormous brown field nearby (brown except for several lush spots of bright green, where the recessed water sprinklers leaked continuously); but apparently they had also rehearsed at least some of their plays in their rooms at the Fountainblue, for after they had left (in two air-conditioned buses), Mrs. Warner, the manager, found many enigmatic dents and lesions in the walls, which seemed to have been created by blunt instruments such as shoulder pads or elbows. Six doorknobs had been twisted out of their sockets. Whenever Mrs. Warner thought of her ruined doorknobs she shook her head at the callous forces of destruction in the world.

The Fountainblue was also notable in that it actually had a blue fountain. It adjoined the kidney-shaped pool in the courtyard: hexagonal, with four artificial rocks of cast concrete spray-painted silver submerged around the pump, and a sprig of plastic seaweed bobbing on the surface. The inside of the fountain was painted an intense, Pacific Pool Supplies blue. It was very impressive when turned on, but Mrs. Warner, economical about electricity, saved it for special occasions — as when she was showing around prospective tenants, or when she felt depressed and needed something beautiful to soothe her. The water, when the fountain was on, made a lovely sound that recalled the short chirps of hundreds of small birds.

Mrs. Warner had already finished vacuuming the gold carpeting in the lobby, and was now going over the turquoise indoor/outdoor carpeting around the pool. She had chosen all the Fountainblue carpeting herself, as well as a good deal of the furniture. The apartment desk chairs, for example, had off-white textured vinyl pads and a cluster of artificial rubies inset into the backs. But the carpeting, her pride and joy when it had first been installed, was now a source of deep distress, for ever since the oil spill it had been accumulating hundreds, perhaps thousands, of ineradicable tar spots. Mrs. Warner had put a sign at the entrance, CHECK YOUR FEET FOR TAR! with a rag and some kerosene, but it had failed to generate interest.

The situation was at its most serious in the Refreshment Room, for which she had chosen pink shag carpeting to go with the purple Moorish-style trim. Chunks of tar had imbedded themselves among the shag fibers like ticks, feeding on the pinkness. Seeing her carpeting grow ugly day by day filled Mrs. Warner with a sense of tragedy.

But on that particular summer morning, right there in the Refreshment Room along with the pink shag, the Moorish trim, and the wood-grained vending machines, a *string quartet*, of all things, was rehearsing Mozart's K. 590 in four of the ruby-studded chairs. K. 590 is the third quartet dedicated to King Frederick William II, and the last Mozart composed (1790, or 179 years before the oil spill): a witty work with spots of great lyric beauty. The quartet was, still is, in F major, whereas Mrs. Warner's vacuum cleaner played a steady B-natural with occasional rises in frequency when she pressed the wand hard into the poolside carpeting. This creates for us, in the position of hearing both, a harmonic tension that must be resolved. The young Mozart himself once got out of bed to resolve a similar interval when someone had played it on the piano, or so the story goes. The musicians were working on the first movement. Suddenly the first violinist stopped playing and waved his bow.

"Hold it, hold it. Stop," he said, and the music trailed off near the end of the development section. The vacuum cleaner was faintly audible. "We're getting really harsh-sounding here, I think. It needs to stay more light, more calm. Especially you, Steve" —

looking at the second violinist — "I think it should be more . . .
joyful, more joyful at that spot near G."

"More joyful," said the second violinist irritably. "I felt joyful.
That's an incredibly hard passage to play joyfully, you know."

"I agree, though," said the cellist. "We'll hold back there, then
you kind of sing that run, *deedledeedledeedledeedle-dah poof!*" He
waved his fingers like cilia in the air. "Just super light, super clean."

"Fine," said the second violinist. "I'm going to be super light and
more joyful the next time through, as simple as that." He pulled a
loose hair from his bow, frowning. The cellist shrugged.

"I had an idea about that section," said the violist. "Eight after
G, where it modulates, wouldn't it be effective if we got a little
calando just before it picks up again?"

"Ah, *calando* schmalando," said the second violinist. "I doubt
Mozart even knew that word."

"A *calando* sounds good to me," said the cellist.

"O.K., look," said the first violinist, marking his part. "Why don't
we do that whole section. We'll try Myron's mysterioso idea, and
we'll try in general to keep it less agitated-feeling."

"And I'm going to be deeply joyous," said the second violinist.

The first violinist made an upbeat with the neck of his violin and
they started. The second violinist, who was wearing sandals,
clenched his toes to the rhythm. By some freak the pink shag
carpeting and Moorish trim made for nearly perfect acoustics. The
quartet played well: They frowned, they swayed with the phrase
in their ruby-studded chairs, their fingers, fantastically bent,
moved like the jointed legs of large arachnids over the strings.
While they were playing a man walked in for a pack of cigarettes.
His flip-flops made an interesting sequence of peeling and slapping sounds against his heels. The violist got distracted and missed
an entrance.

"Boy," said the second violinist, "I'll tell you right now, if we play
it like that at the Coleman Competition there will be zero chance
of us winning anything." There was a silence. Mrs. Warner's vacuum cleaner was faintly audible.

"David, is there any other place we could rehearse?" asked the
cellist. "I think this environment is getting us down."

The first violinist took his instrument from under his neck.
"There's the laundry room, but (a) there's too much noise from
the washers and (b) the humidity would ruin the instruments. Case

closed." He began inspecting his left index finger, pressing it tenderly with his right thumb.

"How's your callus doing?" the cellist asked.

"Professor Belanyi said to file it down, so I just took a nail file and zapped the hard part off." He extended the finger. There was a yellowish area on the end that had been flattened by a file. "It hurts when I start playing, but then the skin warms up and it gets flexible."

The cellist said, "You know that Miriam's callus on her middle finger split once just before a concert, and she had to play the whole Lalo concerto with a Band-Aid on?"

"Can we rehearse?" said the violist. The pitch of the vacuum cleaner rose suddenly, perhaps an obstruction, then resolved to tonic.

"The thing is," said the first violinist, "we're all trying too hard with this movement. We're playing it *agitato* when what we need is to be more relaxed, sunny, sprightly. You know?"

"Joyous," said the second violinist. "You've made that clear."

The first violinist counted off a slightly faster tempo and they started playing. Identical moments of great lyrical beauty transpired, but a little faster. They were already into the recapitulation when two girls walked in with towels around their necks. One was carrying an orange Frisbee. The cellist got to a difficult chromatic section and played it perfectly, bunching his mouth and flaring his nostrils, although he wasn't aware of this. One of the girls stuck a coin in the cold-drink machine. It made a series of complex clicks and scraping sounds, then came to rest. Another coin was introduced: more clicks and scrapes, slightly varied. The first violinist played a cascade of descending thirds in G minor. *Sprite* was pushed. There was a loud click followed by distant thunder: The pop can rocked once, then lay tranquil in the orifice. The violist answered the violinist with more descending thirds, in C major. The other girl invested in a Tab and a Mars Bar. The music sounded really nice, so they both stopped to listen. The quartet passed the double bar, and the first violin and cello had a witty interchange moving to tonic that was abruptly punctuated by two sharp hisses, followed by sounds of tearing metal. Both girls put their pull tabs on the first joint of their middle fingers. They leaned against the large window, through which the pool was partly visible, sipping waves of carbonated beverage and listening to the music. The movement ended and the quartet was all smiles.

"Hey, that was beautiful that time!" said the cellist.

"And we kept right on it at the *deedledeedledee* section," said the violist. "I really think the bouncier tempo helped it."

"That sounded really nice," said one of the girls. The first violinist looked over his shoulder and said thanks.

"We were supposed to be rehearsing in this joker's apartment," said the cellist, pointing to the first violinist. "But his roommate decided to get sick this morning."

"Oh," said the girl. No one could think of anything else to say. There was a scream and a splash from the pool. The vacuum cleaner had been turned off.

The violist began tuning. "Why don't we work a little on the second movement, since the first seems to be jelling pretty well, and then call it a day."

The other three players tuned, and then they started the second movement. One of the girls began eating her Mars Bar. She heard the repeating chords of the accompaniment over the wet, seaside sounds of chewy caramel. The other girl smiled and tapped the orange Frisbee lightly against her thigh. Complex polyrhythms.

Just then the door opened and Mrs. Warner came in, holding her vacuum cleaner. She meant to vacuum the pink shag carpeting, for you have to keep things looking as nice as you can, even though its complex geography of tar spots never failed to depress her. But here was a string quartet playing nice, calm, graceful music in the Refreshment Room. The two barefoot girls from 178 already listening. She stood still for a moment. The door hissed shut behind her and tapped her lightly on the elbow. All four of them were weaving the sounds together like that, so light, so joyful; it was just right for the Moorish trim, it made the shag beautiful again, newly pink. She was filled with a complicated emotion and sat down to listen in a chair near a decorator trash can, holding her vacuum cleaner by the handle in the manner of a cello. Very lovely music, she thought. But why don't they seem to be enjoying it?

She watched the players bob and sway. She noticed the cellist's sharp endpin, putting a hole in her carpeting. This pained her, but then everything is compromise and where are you going to find perfect beauty except in front of the blue Fountainblue fountain? The first violinist came to a melody that reminded her of singers on old 78 records, very nice, pressing his fingers into the strings and rapidly shaking his left hand.

"Hey!" interrupted the second violinist, getting angry all of a sudden. "David! Stop! I hate it when you turn on that fast machine vibrato: *eh-eh-eh-eh-eh-eh-eh*. No one else in this quartet uses Fritz Kreisler vibrato!"

"Well, goddamnit!" said the first violinist, getting angry back. "That's my conception of the melody!"

"Let's try to be rational," said the violist.

"And anyway you haven't been marvelously in tune today, Steve, or very easy to rehearse with," said the first violinist.

"How can I be in tune when you're laying on that Fritz Kreisler vibrato right next to me?"

The two girls gave each other a surprised look. The one with the Frisbee said, "Sorry to interrupt your little argument, but I'm a waitress at Borsodi's Coffee Emporium, down there two blocks?"

The first violinist turned around and nodded yes.

"Well, I'm a waitress there, and we have a classical music night every Wednesday, and I know Mr. Borsodi would really love it if you guys came and played because it sounds really nice."

"How much?" said the second violinist.

"Ignore him," said the cellist.

"Well, I mean it's not really paying, it's just for people who want to play, *you* know," said the girl.

"I'm through with freebie charity engagements!" said the second violinist, clutching his violin by the neck. "We've got one of the finest quartets you're likely to hear in a long time, and we certainly aren't going to sweat out Mozart for a bunch of mellow organic-food people sitting around drinking Arabian coffee."

"He's like this," said the cellist. "Doesn't really mean it."

"No, I'm dead serious," said the second violinist. "This is the kind of crap that ticks me off. I'm sitting here trying to play Köchel 590 staring at a row of vending machines. It's pathetic."

"So that's why we want to win the competition, Steve," said the cellist, to placate.

The girls smiled at each other and shrugged. But Mrs. Warner, still sitting quietly next to the trash can, was saddened that four young men who played such nice music together could get along so poorly. Not only that, but when the violist took his instrument from under his chin she noticed a large pink callus where the chin rest rubbed against the jawbone, built up over years of practice. Ugliness.

"Come on, Steve, everybody," the violist said. "Let's calm down and rehearse. I don't have much time, and we keep getting distracted."

They started from C, reluctant at first, then wholly committed. Mrs. Warner closed her eyes. Without the sight of the cellist grimacing and flaring his nostrils the music was much better. It was so graceful. She thought of her daughter before she went off to school, when she was still doing her baton twirling, and could toss it high in the air where it glittered in the sun and then catch it deftly behind her sequined back. She sat, smiling slightly, eyes closed.

While the quartet played, one of the girls noticed a deposit of tar on the smooth curve of her arch. Frowning, she picked up her foot and examined the thick black spot. She attempted to dislodge it by picking at it with her pop-can tab. Mrs. Warner opened her eyes. The girl's back was to her, and she watched in horror as the pop-can tab scraped off a large shaving of tar that fell on the carpeting.

The quartet continued playing. Mrs. Warner jumped up. Here was one of her tenants participating in the destruction of her carpeting right in front of her eyes, yet if she cried out, if she seized her by the shoulders and shook her, if she yelled at her about the callous forces of destruction in the world, the music would stop, and the four young men would think of Mrs. Warner as a callous force of destruction herself. The girl lowered her foot. Mrs. Warner felt such outrage and hurt that she left the Refreshment Room quickly, wheeling her Hoover behind.

She walked past the pool, shaking her head. She needed something beautiful to soothe her, so she put the vacuum cleaner away, went into the office, and flipped the switch that said FOUNTAIN in turquoise Dymo labeling tape. From the pump surrounded by the silver-painted rocks there rose four trembling silver plumes of water that began interlacing in complex trajectories of great formal beauty. The plastic seaweed bobbed hypnotically on the water. Mrs. Warner sighed and sat down in the office with the door open so she could see and hear the fountain yet remain in the shade. All tar spots dissolved from the world. The watery noise of hundreds

of small birds drowned out any Mozart that might have been audible from the Refreshment Room. The pump motor, by pure
coincidence, hummed a slightly sharp B-natural.

Twenty minutes later the two girls left the Refreshment Room,
squinting and laughing, along with the four musicians, each of
whom held an instrument case in one hand and a soft drink in the
other. The second violinist noticed the fountain and stopped in his
tracks.

"Oh lordy," he said. "What have we here? What an amazingly
tacky fountain!"

"I know, I know," said the first violinist ruefully. "It was hard to
take at first. But actually now I kind of like it. It's got its own
integrity."

"California's poisoning your blood is what's happening," said the
violist.

"Are we going to Borsodi's for coffee, or are we not going to
Borsodi's for coffee?" said the cellist.

"Come on," said the girl with the Frisbee.

"Fine," said the second violinist. "We'll go to Borsodi's for coffee.
Anyplace is better than this shrine to chintz."

As they left, the hum of the pump motor stopped, stunned, and
the four weaving plumes of water slowly dropped back to pool
level.

•

Later that day came night, twinkling oil derricks and all. The only
light in the Refreshment Room glowed from the vending machines, and the four ruby-studded chairs were lost in shadow. But
on the enormous field carpeted with greenish-brown turf where
the 49ers had practiced the summer before, fifty recessed water
sprinklers abruptly poked their heads above the grass, and plume
after plume, fountain after fountain sprouted and rose up over
the playing field, triumphantly vindicating the Fountainblue. The
sound of the rushing water made a gentle, distant white noise in
the air.

JOYCE RENWICK

The Dolphin Story

(FROM CHOICE)

DICRAN STOOD ON the porch, the mug of hot, strong tea in his hands, and watched the choppy black water before him. The stars were still out. A cold March land wind, carrying the familiar smells of garlic and sweet tea, whipped through the ancient town at his back. The smells seeped from the kitchens, the samovars of Kobuleti, this Black Sea fishing town that had been the home of his family for centuries. A bell clanged, but the call to the boats had not yet sounded. This morning, as he watched the rising tide, he knew the fishing would not be good. He knew they should already be moving out to the fishing grounds, and he was angry again at the fools of the Fishing Collective who knew nothing of the sea. They knew politics, that was all — not the tides, the seasons, the directions of the wind.

The samovar was still boiling in the house behind him. Someone would find it. He had passed through the dark house, hitting a chair leg with his boot, stopping only long enough in the kitchen to open the small paper sack, spoon the dry, black tea into a pot and wait until it was drinkable. When he had entered the room he'd noticed a flicker from the charcoal fire under the samovar, still warm from the night before. Mr. Noblakoff had been up late playing his balalaika, and Dicran had not slept well, hearing the laughing and singing rising from below. While he waited impatiently for the tea to steep, he'd felt around on the dark shelf for a mug. He'd poured the black tea carefully before coming out on the porch, trying to be quiet to avoid meeting anyone in the kitchen, though it would be unusual for any of the others to be up before the sun.

Although the house had once been his, he didn't associate with the other roomers. Now only a few things were left of the old life. Perhaps he still had Lizaveta's nest of dolls, he wasn't sure. The dim lantern hung on a post outside the house, and in his room under the bed he kept the handmade chessboard that had been his father's.

At last the call to the boat — a horn blared from the pier below him — and then a half-dozen progressively fainter sounds came out of the darkness down the coast. No doubt Captain Yorkovitya enjoyed sounding the call with the other captains of the Fishing Collective. Once, with a wave of his arm, he'd told Dicran that each morning he imagined he was an ancient seaman, blowing a conch-shell horn, calling to the argonauts to sail over these same waters.

Fool, Dicran had thought, and he had turned away and looked down at his feet, wondering if the line was from one of the Captain's speeches. It had the ring of preparation, repetition. It was probably part of one of his speeches for the Collective — no, not serious enough for that — for the café late at night, then, when everyone was drunk after a long dinner. He had heard that the Captain never ate at the café — he ate at home with his fat wife and all their children — but he would come in later when the fishermen were drunk, stand on a chair and test his speeches, bowing and smiling to their applause. Dicran was sure it was the speeches that had won him his position. The Captain was a small man, extremely careful of his clothes and mustache, unlike most of the men. Dicran supposed he had sea experience, though it seemed that without warning he was suddenly Captain. Although Dicran rarely went to the meetings, he'd always thought his friend Ivan would be appointed. He had taught Ivan all he knew.

The horn sounded again and voices rose from the dock below. Dicran spilled his cold tea over the railing, flung open the door to the kitchen, and tossed the mug into the house. It landed on something soft. No matter. He pulled on his knitted cap, yanked his collar up around his ears, and swung down the yielding steps to the pier.

Ivan was pulling the nets down from the pilings where they had been hung last night to dry. His light hair curled up around his cap and his nose made a shadow across his cheek in the lantern light.

"Hey, Dicran, smile," he said in greeting.

Dicran nodded but didn't smile. "Too early. Mr. Noblakoff played his damn balalaika again half the night."

"Ah." Ivan, still smiling, looked down at the net. He pulled at the cork floats, and then stooped to pick up a suspicious-looking one. It crumbled in his hand.

Dicran took his place beside Ivan. Pulling the net section by section between his extended arms, he spread the jute, testing for weak spots, looking for tears. They had used the same nets for as long as he could remember, repairing, renewing them until they were not the original nets at all but a patchwork, from the sweet-smelling new rope to the musty gray of the oldest sections. He pulled a fold open before him and turned it toward the lantern light. Was this a portion his father had mended or a section his grandfather had made? He couldn't tell.

Ivan was bent over the net. He replaced the float and then rose to help Dicran, as the rest of the men dragged the last of the nets on board. Ivan cast off the lines. He threw them to Dicran, who caught the lines in midair and coiled them like fat snakes on the deck. After the first few coughs of the engine, the fishing boat rattled in idle.

The tide was rising rapidly. Pulled on board by one of the crew, Ivan turned to talk to the man as Captain Yorkovitya came running down the pier. No one offered the Captain a hand — he didn't seem to need one — and he leaped into the boat just as it cleared the dock. The small man nodded and saluted one and then another of the men. He stroked down his mustache and muttered, "Morning, comrades, morning," as he stepped over feet and sprawled legs on the way to the pilothouse.

One of the younger crewmen, sitting with his friends at the stern, shouted to Dicran, asking why he had missed last night's meeting. As the young man waited for a reply, some of the others stopped to listen.

"The nets needed mending," Dicran shouted above the drone of the engines. He turned so the man would not question him further.

Ivan had been sitting with the group of younger men. He rose to his feet and joined Dicran at the bow. "Will the weather break today?" he asked, wiping his hands on his slicker.

Dicran looked at the gray clouds hugging the early morning moon and shook his head. The wind seemed to sit heavily on his shoulders. After circling the Red Sea, sweeping over Iran and the yellow hills of Turkey, it now blew its stale breath at their backs. Dicran knew these winds as he knew the sturgeon and herring. He could point out the winds and weather as he could point to the slick of the fishes' feeding spots even in murky water, not needing to rely on the gulls to signal their presence.

"Overcast and cold. The fishing won't be good," he said.

Ivan studied the sky for a moment, then rejoined the small group of men at the stern. The young men were lively, passing a flask, laughing at a skinny boy doing a jig on the deck, hands in pockets, boot laces flying. The older men sat apart, against the gunnel on overturned boxes and bait pails. They'd be telling the old stories again. The few oldest men sat quietly, leather-skinned and red-cheeked, bundled against the cold, their ropy brown hands clasping their knees.

He remembered how his father had looked — mornings going out to the fishing grounds, and evenings in the flickering light of the lantern. Each night after mending the nets, they had played chess in the old house. When his father died, Dicran had abandoned the nets for long walks. One night he'd discovered the chess games in the park.

He supposed the old man had taught him, almost wordlessly, about the winds, the fish. He never mentioned his father to the others. The prejudice against the man had been maintained — like the nets — in additions and repairs until there was nothing more of the original than a remembered grudge. Years ago the old man had spoken strongly against the Revolution; he had wanted no more killing. Dicran did not remember standing on the shore as a child watching the dock burn, although his father had told him he had been there and both of them had escaped unharmed before the flames blocked their exit. Someone had told him his father had shouted over and over to Lizaveta to jump. Dicran's sister had been playing at the end of the dock as they mended nets, unaware of the person with a torch in the skiff below her. She had cried, then screamed, but wouldn't jump off the high dock into the water. Dicran didn't remember any of it. He had watched the old man become quiet, mending nets in the evening, weaving his convictions into a web of silence floating noiseless as nets in the sea.

He moved further forward in the bow and watched pink caps form on the water as the moon disappeared and the sun crept over the horizon. Ivan left the stern, slapping one of the crewmen on the back as he rose, and joined Dicran.

"Smile, Dicran, the nets are almost out." Ivan leaned against the gunnel. His yellow slicker contrasted with the damp, dark wood behind him.

"Smile?" Dicran looked at him. "I know your smiles, Ivan. You think the whole world's been drinking with Yolana." He took a tobacco pouch from his pocket and offered it. Ivan shook his head.

It was getting light, the rising sun making a path in front of them. Dicran knew soon it would be his turn to work, to find the school, pull the purse line, haul in the encircling net over and over again until the hull, full of fish, settled low in the water. In front of them gulls swooped at the debris on the water — a tree branch, strange out so far, and a few weathered boards, half submerged. Looking at the debris as they steered around it, he remembered something he had once seen in a book, a sketch showing the feeding cycle of the oceans, and he imagined, deep below the green limb and the rotting wood they had passed, small particles of life being carried in poorly filtered light toward the jellyfish that would engulf them. He saw oysters closing their ruffled shells, except for one, a pearly eye open to innumerable species of fish swimming into the dark caves of larger and larger mouths, moving in his mind, from small to large, large to small, like the legless wooden dolls of his sister's childhood, arms and smiles painted on, one within the other, enameled, bright-colored, smaller and smaller until he remembered she had picked out a doll smaller than her thumb, and she had squealed with pleasure at the toy he had given her.

Years later, Moira had squealed too with pleasure at this doll, or perhaps in pleasure with him when she had seen the child's things the day she visited him in the old house by the pier. They had had tea that day, and she had insisted on making it. He had complained about the leaves she never seemed to be able to strain completely from the tea. He had wanted it pure, clear yellow, and she had been unable after three pots to please him, or keep her patience. Although she was the only woman he had allowed himself to love, he had demanded perfection and it had been too much for her. Memories can be perfect, she had told him, never people. He did not remember it clearly. Moira — had she too been lost in the fire? No, that fire had been of a different kind, but she was gone and just as well extinguished from him now as if she had been on that flaming dock with his sister.

"Dicran."

Ivan was beside him. He had forgotten.

"Dicran." Ivan was smiling, his eyes slits on his large face. "You should have heard the Captain's speech at the meeting last night." Ivan wiped the back of his hand across his mouth to cover his smile.

Dicran watched him.

Ivan laughed. "Coming out we were talking about it. The speech was the funniest in a long time, one of the Captain's best. You should have seen his face, his gestures." The winch screeched behind them, peeling out the net.

"In the middle of the meeting he stood up on his chair and everyone —"

"I've heard enough of them," Dicran interrupted.

The nets out, conversations died away and it was quiet except for the screeching gulls and the water slapping at the hull. Dicran pulled on his pipe. The sturgeon were there, let the nets do their work. He would wait. He knew this was a lie, the nets didn't work at all, it was the action of men, the laying out and pulling in that produced the catch. Without the lines, the winches, the sweat, the nets would do nothing more than float away with the tide, imprisoning, entangling without purpose.

He sat back against the dark bulkhead, the chill wind still pressing against his cheeks. Even though the sun had risen, it had not gotten much warmer. He brought out his worn pouch and worked cold fingers into the tobacco, pushing the dry apple slice aside and filling the bowl with the black pungent shreds. He looked over the water. At some distance he thought he saw the silver back of a dolphin.

He strained to see, thinking it might be one of the group they usually saw playing in the evening as they were coming in with the catch. Ever since he was a boy he had imagined they called to him, a high, soft sound through their blowholes. He leaned forward, seeing one dorsal fin and then another coming up fast. He moved closer to the rail and then called to Ivan, who looked up drowsily and then made his way through the men to the ladder.

"At least twenty of them," Dicran said as Ivan pulled himself up beside him.

Ivan looked over the water. "Maybe thirty."

Dicran heard the rest of the crew moving and talking behind them. They too were leaning over the side to watch the school of dolphins approaching the boat. They all knew dolphins meant good luck and fair weather. Perhaps their fishing would be good today after all.

Ivan was shaking his head and smiling. He clapped Dicran on the shoulder. "The crew's making more noise than the women who wait at night for the boats to come in."

Dicran looked at him. "Women, that's all you think about."

"Not women now. Listen to the crew, the dolphins," Ivan said, smiling and leaning over the gunnel.

Dicran grunted.

The dolphins seemed to be coming at them from all directions, crowding around the boat, jumping and calling, squealing and clicking, grunting and sculling, moving to the north and back again. Their sounds were high-pitched, hysterical. They seemed to have forgotten those manlike sounds, those smiles and hellos the men knew so well.

Some of the crewmen moved to the bow with Dicran and Ivan. They laughed and shouted above the sounds of the dolphins swimming below them in sleek-bodied frenzy, the water splashing in the men's faces as the dolphins jumped high above the surface and plunged deep again. Dicran had never seen a school of dolphins this close before, never before felt from them this urgency. Seeing other fishing boats in the distance, he wondered why the dolphins were circling their boat, jumping, splashing, inundating them with bursting, pulsating sound. There was no doubt they were begging the men to follow.

Dicran put down his pipe as he noticed one of the dolphins backwatering and looking directly at him. It was larger than the others, almost completely out of the water, resting on its churning tail. The dolphin looked at him directly, the eyes wide and circled in black, the gaze not the dead stare of a blind man but the look of something seeing and perceiving. Dicran felt momentarily frightened.

Shaking his head, he patted at his jacket until he found the breast pocket, where he deposited his cold pipe. He backed up against the bulkhead, not looking at the dolphin, trying not to listen to his whistle, a piercing falsetto, unlike the others. He watched Ivan go down to the aft deck, watched him pointing to

the water and turning his head this way and that as he talked to
the rest of the men.

Captain Yorkovitya burst out of the pilothouse, pulling on his
windbreaker. The shrill sounds of the dolphins, overriding the
men's excited talk, was confusing, deafening. Dicran couldn't hear
what Ivan was saying. He watched his friend talk seriously to the
Captain. He shook his head and pointed alternately at the water,
the net, the dolphins. Soon the Captain, too, was shaking his head
affirmatively. The Captain, Dicran thought, is a man easily per-
suaded. He must think he is going to benefit from this, although
Dicran could not imagine at the moment what the benefit would
be.

He slid down the ladder and joined the group around Ivan and
the Captain. As soon as he arrived he was sorry; he recognized a
look on the Captain's face that always preceded a speech.

"Comrades," the Captain began, surveying the crewmen, who
were gathered around him, talking among themselves. He
dumped a bait pail over, then stood on it. "Comrades," he shouted.
He raised an arm to gain their attention.

Dicran groaned. Ivan smiled and put a finger to his lips.

"Often," the Captain exclaimed, "we find we must deviate from
the line of duty to answer the call of a greater duty."

The men were standing in small groups with their arms folded,
solemn looks on their faces. When the Captain looked away they
rolled their eyes at their companions.

The Captain swung his arm toward the dolphins who were circling the boat. "Today this greater duty is upon us." His face was
somber as he lowered his arm and then raised his hand over his
heart. Dicran looked at his boots.

The Captain pointed to the dolphins and then panned the
group for their reactions. Satisfied with their serious expressions,
he continued. "You might ask, can we take time to follow the call
of these intelligent beings? Can we waste the Collective's time to
pursue an unknown mission we are being so persuasively called to
accomplish? I say this —" he turned to look at Dicran — "this is
our universal duty: to repay these dolphins, who through the ages
have been the friends of men." He took a deep breath. "They are
not harnessed by man, nor are they beaten down nor domesticated, no, they roam free in the great sea, playing and loving; it is
their life."

"Playing and loving," Dicran heard Ivan whisper to the squint-

eyed man at his right, "I like that." The man burst into a laugh,
then quickly shielded his face with his hand. They composed themselves and looked back at the Captain, who was still speaking and
swinging his arms in grandiose gestures, to the concealed amusement of the men. Dicran stepped back from the group.

"But sometimes," the Captain was saying, "the dolphins find
they have need of us. They do not ask often; they do not expect
gratitude for the numerous friendly acts of the past." The Captain
looked at Ivan and smiled. "Remember the dolphin who carried
the boy to school over the Bosphorus. The dolphin died when he
discovered the boy drowned."

A tall man at the front leaned over to say something to his
shorter companion. The Captain continued, "Remember the dolphins who guided to shore the horses pushed overboard from
sinking ships; dolphins who supported unconscious sailors to the
safety of other islands; dolphins who herd mullets to shore as
Mauritian fishermen beat the water with clubs . . ."

"Of course they aren't dumb," Dicran mumbled as he moved up
beside Ivan. "We all know this."

Ivan, still watching the Captain, put a hand on Dicran's arm and
whispered, "He's enjoying himself, watch."

The Captain was swaying as he spoke. "There are times when
we must put business aside and lift the standard of universality."
He lifted an imaginary standard high above his head. "Life is dull
enough without ignoring dolphins."

There was silence, and then someone or something whistled
from the back of the crowd. Another whistle rose here, and then
there, until the whole crew was whistling and stomping their boots
on the deck, cheering the Captain, who smiled broadly at his men.
One man began a Georgian dance. He fell over almost before he
began — pushed by his laughing companions. The Captain
watched from atop his bait pail. Dicran, parallel to the Captain,
leaned against the side of the boat. He cleared his throat and
looked at the Captain's shoe for a long time before he turned and
spat in the water.

Dicran tried to speak over the noisy crew. He wondered why he
was the only one who was concerned about their fishing. As he
watched the Captain move the bait pail out of the way, he thought
of dolphin fish. Not these large intelligent mammals who were
circling their boat now, but the blunt-nosed fish that hide under

floating debris and, when caught, flash rainbows of yellow, purple, and blue. After a few minutes in the air they become gray and soft, and if the cook's silver spoon turns black in the pan, they're quickly thrown back to sea. "We should leave them to their own lives," Dicran shouted over the noise of the crew and the squealing dolphins. "The fishing hasn't been good. There's sturgeon out there. We'll never meet our quota." No one seemed to hear him.

Some of the men were leaning over the side, trying to touch the dolphins for good luck; someone was passing a flask, and one man — really no more than a boy — was doing back flips, landing with a thud each time on the deck. Two of the men were clumsily pulling Captain Yorkovitya with them to the stern.

Ivan remained behind. He put his hand on Dicran's back and spoke softly. "Dicran, join us — here, have a drink." He offered him his flask.

Dicran shook his head. "No."

"All right, all right." Ivan moved closer. "For the women who loved you." Ivan smiled.

"What women?" Dicran pulled his collar up around his neck.

"Moira did once." Ivan smiled again.

"You're never serious." Dicran scowled and slapped his leg, then pulled out his pipe. He watched the water churning with dolphins.

"The largest dolphin," Ivan continued, "listened to his whistle — can you ignore that?"

"Yes." Dicran dug into his pocket for his pouch.

Ivan pounded his fist on the gunnel. "We should follow them. Where's your sense of adventure?"

"Where's your sense of duty? We have a quota."

"Quota —" Ivan laughed. "You heard the Captain."

Dicran looked over the water. He saw a dolphin flipping like a silver coin on the horizon. The son of Poseidon, he thought. As he looked, more dolphins were appearing, coming over the horizon like a silver horde. He saw not porpoises, not the wheel-like rolls of the puffing pigs, but the high-jumping movements of dolphins. Their slender bodies flashing, their flukes twisting above the surface, they cavorted, calling to him. Once he had heard that, years ago, a hundred thousand dolphins had gathered at one time around a ship, their numbers increasing, their pulsing sonar calling more and more of their kind. A hundred thousand dolphins — their sounds deafening the men on the ship who wandered lost at sea until the dolphins realized they had confounded them. The dolphins had gathered and, pressing their smiling beaks against the ship, pushed it to shore. He didn't believe it. Yet now, seeing the hordes coming, he wanted to believe. But perhaps it was not hordes, perhaps it was only one more dolphin he saw, and then another and another, and he imagined hordes.

Ivan clapped Dicran on the arm, slid down the ladder and joined the others at the stern who were busy pulling in the net.

The crewmen quickly sorted the catch and, leaving the trash fish to the gulls, followed the dolphins northward. The sun was high now, but the air was cool. The engines sputtered. Dicran took off his jacket and opened his collar. There was little wind, surprising on a March day, no more breeze than that made by the movement of the boat, and no sounds except for the entreaties of the dolphins who swam ahead, crisscrossing their bow. Above them, stillness, as if a portion of the wind was holding its breath until they passed. There were no turbulent winds from Siberia, not the cold anticyclone common this time of year, only an almost imperceptible breeze from the west. To Dicran it smelled of the foehn wind, warm from the mountains of the Crimea. Moira had been born there. "No matter," he said aloud. She had not stayed.

Dicran was still standing at the gunnel when Ivan came back. "We'll follow the dolphins," he said breathlessly, his face flushed. "The men agreed — if there's anything to be done" — he took a breath — "Dicran, you and I will do it."

"Anything to be done," Dicran repeated, shaking his head. "Ivan, what's this foolishness?"

"Foolishness." Ivan grinned as he sat down against the pilothouse and dug his hands deep into the pockets of his slicker.

The dolphins led them steadily northward, along the coast. Ivan scanned the shoreline. "Look, we must be nearing Sochi. Haven't you ever gone to one of the sanitariums for vacation, Dicran? A twenty-eight-day cure —"

Dicran quickly broke in. "I don't need a cure," he said, "I'm never ill." He looked down at his dark hands resting on the gunnel and watched the water parting easily before their bow.

They followed the dolphins. Dicran watched them rub against each other as they swam, seeming to touch shoulders, to comfort each other as they called back and forth. Each seemed to have a characteristic sound, a signature whistle. It was something he had never noticed before. He remembered his father had always spoken of dolphins with respect; he had never completely understood why. One summer when a boy, while aimlessly combing the beach, he had found a dolphin — eyes filmed over — purple and stinking in the sun. He wanted to touch it but hadn't dared. He had wondered at this dolphin lying so close to the pier, so close to the leaning porch of his father's house. He had told his father of the discovery, hoping for an explanation, but the old man only looked out to sea, his mouth moving as if speaking to himself. He remembered at the time thinking about his mother, who had died a long time before — he remembered now only the printed kerchief she wore — but his father had acted as if he had forgotten Dicran was there. After a few minutes of silence Dicran left, deciding to walk up the hill to the old town. At the square he watched the village boys play lapta on the cobblestones.

They were in the shallows now. The shore was rocky at the base of the mountains that rose in front of them. The sun was high overhead. The wind had picked up and it was cool and biting now at midday. In the creaking vessel Dicran was grateful for the channel markers, grateful for the bell buoy he could hear clanging ahead. As they neared it, the dolphins began to swim faster before them, whistling to each other. Although the buoy was still at some distance, Dicran could see it swaying, the sunlight reflecting off its surface. The dolphins were circling the buoy, circling and calling back to them on the fishing boat. Someone passed Dicran a pair of battered binoculars. Now he could see why they had been called. A dolphin calf was tangled in a net, caught in the arms of the bell buoy. The other dolphins were anxiously churning a path from the buoy to the boat.

"Ivan, look at this," Dicran shouted over the dolphins' whistles, and he waved the binoculars. "We'll use the lifeboat."

Ivan looked at him strangely, took the binoculars, and then lurched ahead to grab the oars from the overhead in the pilothouse. As Dicran followed, he heard a loud discussion coming from the stern. One of the new crewmen was saying he, not Dicran, should go out in the lifeboat. Dicran didn't even go to the Collective meetings. When the voices got loud, Captain Yorkovitya demanded silence. He listened quietly, smoothing his mustache, as Ivan reminded the crew that they had earlier agreed that Dicran was not only his partner but also the best seaman.

Dicran unlashed one of the lifeboats, ignoring the discussion, and set the boat swinging on the davits. Somewhat grudgingly, the others pushed the lifeboat outside the hull and, after Dicran and Ivan climbed in, lowered it into the choppy water. Dicran and Ivan watched from the rocking boat as the engines were reversed and the fishing boat noisily backed off to deeper water. The dolphins began to circle the lifeboat.

Dicran settled himself in the bow. "Row, Ivan," he told his friend. "I'm the water man." He looked at the bleak sky and could not say whether it was gray or blue. The clouds were huddled on the horizon like dirty sheep from the steppes.

Ivan fit the oars into the locks and moved his feet to the sides of the boat to avoid the water in the bottom. He pulled on the oars, his back to the buoy. He pulled with all of his body, and Dicran noted that he seemed to be smiling at the effort, enjoying the strain on his muscles.

The jumping dolphins were swamping their boat. The wind seemed colder, stronger, close to the water, and a fine spray blew in their faces. Dicran found a rusty can under his seat and began bailing, all the while talking to the large dolphin swimming beside the boat. He watched the creature's eye, circled in black, appearing, disappearing, as he rode the water beside them. "Easy now, old man, easy now," Dicran said as he watched the dolphin swim close and then plunge beneath the boat. Two other dolphins circled them, grunting and chirping. Ivan rowed steadily toward the buoy. When they were clearly out of hearing distance of the fishing boat Ivan stopped.

"I thought you were going to spit on the Captain's shoe after that speech." He looked at Dicran with a half smile on his wide face.

Dicran laughed. "I thought of it," he said as he dumped the water from the bailing can over the side.

Ivan looked at him steadily. "I know you did."

"He was so busy swinging his arms and jumping up and down he never would have noticed." Dicran scraped the can along the bottom of the boat.

Ivan leaned toward him. "The men wouldn't have said a word" — he leaned back — "though the new man might." He pulled a flask from his hip pocket.

"They're sheep in a fishing boat," Dicran said as he continued to bail. Ivan took a drink from the flask and then offered it to Dicran. Dicran shook his head.

"Why don't you relax sometime?" Ivan asked as he put the flask back in his pocket and then pulled on the oars. He leaned so far back he almost hit the seat behind him.

"Why?" Dicran asked. "We're following the dolphins. You wanted this. We're soaked from their splashing." He dipped the rusty can into the water at his feet.

Ivan shook his head and pulled on the oars. Dicran turned and stared at something behind them, the bailing can still in his hand.

Another lifeboat was zigzagging toward them through the school of dolphins, and in it, rowing furiously, was Captain Yorkovitya. Dicran turned away.

Ivan waved and looked back at Dicran. "Ah ho — he must be sweating even in this cold. Didn't think he could miss this." Ivan laughed. "Just watch, it'll soon be his story. He needs a new speech." Ivan pulled on the oars, not waiting for the Captain.

The sky was brighter now, the water slate-colored. As they reached the buoy the dolphins stopped their high-pitched whistling and became ominously mute. Looking closely, Dicran could see the small dolphin was caught in a purse seine that was wedged between the rusted arms of the buoy. The calf looked uneasy; he probably had never seen a man before. Dicran watched the circling dorsal fins and realized that he, too, had an uncomfortable feeling in his stomach. The sun was hot, the air cold. The wind was blowing stronger from the northeast, and their boat rocked as Ivan tried to steady it with the oars. He looked at Dicran.

"Are you going in?"

"No other way." Dicran struggled with his boots, watching the rocking bell buoy. "He's wedged in tight."

At that moment the other lifeboat pulled alongside. The Captain started to speak. Dicran ignored him and eased himself over the side. In the rocky shoals the water was dark gray and choppy. Dicran had forgotten the shock of seawater in March. He treaded water for a few minutes and then began to swim toward the buoy. Thrashing, fighting the water and his clothes, he made his way between the gliding dolphins. His wool shirt tugged at him, pulling him down. He should have taken it off with his boots. Treading water, he unbuttoned it, shuddering as he wrung it above his head and then threw it to Ivan. Just short of Ivan's grasp, it sunk below the surface. Ivan sat down again, shaking his head, and pulled an oar to keep the boat turned so he could see the buoy. In the other lifeboat the Captain struggled with the oars. He was saying something Dicran couldn't hear.

Swimming was somewhat easier without his shirt. Dicran reached the buoy and held on with one hand. The small dolphin's eyes were half hidden by the net. It was twisted over his head, wrapping him tightly against the buoy, his blowhole barely above the lapping water; the dolphin was lucky he hadn't drowned. Seeing the dented buoy, Dicran knew the dolphins had spent a long time pushing it, butting it, trying to free the calf, before they had called on them.

He examined the net, pulling at it to test its strength. It was newly mended, the firm new rope spliced and tied carefully. Whoever had mended it knew what he was doing.

Suddenly two of the dolphins raised themselves to their full height, backwatering and whistling shrilly. Ivan pulled his boat closer. "The dolphins are impatient," he called.

Dicran looked in all directions to see if there was something else that might be alarming the dolphins. The cold water splashed at his chest. He saw and heard nothing but the men in the lifeboats, the dolphins themselves and, beyond that, the faintly squalling cloud of gulls gliding and dipping over the fishing boat rocking in the distance. He turned back to the buoy and pulled violently at the net, holding on with one hand and working with the other.

"Use your knife," Captain Yorkovitya shouted from his lifeboat.

What, no speech? Dicran thought as he struggled with the net a few minutes longer. "I will untangle it," he yelled back.

Dicran's hands were red from the frigid water, the knuckles raw from repeated scraping against the rough jute. His efforts, the wind, the choppy sea, all kept the buoy rocking. The calf was making soft, frightened noises, and one dolphin, perhaps the mother, kept coming over to nudge at him. She'd circle, look at Dicran and then pass close to the calf, making a shrill sound like crying. Another dolphin, maybe a nursemaid, clicked loudly and rubbed against her each time she left the baby. Dicran decided the small dolphin was a newborn; there were no marks on his smooth gray skin.

"Use your knife," the Captain shouted again.

Dicran looked at Ivan, who was pulling impatiently at the oars, not looking at the man in the boat beside his.

"No," Dicran replied breathlessly, "a good net." He noticed an outer ring of dolphins circling beyond the lifeboats. A shark screen, he thought.

As he worked, Dicran tried to be gentle, although his large hands were numb and clumsy with cold. The calf was quiet, the frigid water sharp as a scythe cutting his legs at the thighs. He couldn't feel his legs below mid-thigh, and he began to wonder if they had dropped off his body like icicles off a roof.

The Captain's voice, despite all his speech making, wasn't strong, and he had difficulty projecting it over the insistent cries of the dolphins.

"Watch the baby," Ivan shouted over the Captain. "What's a net?"

Dicran didn't look up as he continued to tug at the purse seine, moving aside the white marker floats and pulling at the wet knots that seemed to get tighter the longer he worked at them. A dolphin swam close, looking at Dicran quizzically. It circled nearer and nearer, finally rubbing its smooth side against him. Dicran pulled away in surprise.

The Captain put down his oars and gingerly stood up in his rocking boat. The sun was bright behind his back; the cool wind flapped his large windbreaker at his sides. "Gods harness dolphins to chariots, not buoys," the Captain yelled.

He's acting again, Dicran thought. "Ivan." Dicran motioned to his friend and ignored the Captain. "Ivan," he shouted, "I can't do it. The cold."

As he spoke he hung onto the buoy, moving his legs to keep the circulation going even though he could not feel them anymore. It seemed to get suddenly colder. Dicran looked up to see a cloud had momentarily covered the sun. The sky was chalky gray with clouds, now dark gray, massing in the east. He hung on the buoy by his elbow and lowered his head to blow into his hands. He rubbed them together as best he could while the rusted bell clanged rhythmically in his ear. He had not noticed the bell before, hanging above his head.

"Try again," shouted the Captain, who was leaning down, holding on to the side of Ivan's boat to stabilize his own. He stood up again and shouted, "Dolphins are reincarnations of the Pharaoh's men, lost when the Red Sea parted."

Dicran was hanging on the buoy and moving an arm in large fanning motions, trying to keep warm. In the bottom of a swell, he couldn't see the fishing boat, and for a moment wondered if the crew had drunkenly mutinied and left them behind. He stretched his neck trying to see the cloud of gulls above the boat, feeling he had to at least keep them in sight. He moved his dead legs to be sure they had not fallen off frozen into the net, and spread his fingers, seeing for the first time they were bleeding, but unable to feel the sting of the abrasions.

He turned back to the small dolphin and saw it was looking at him, an eye visible through the net. As he watched, he thought he saw one eye slowly close and then open again.

"Ivan," Dicran shouted to his friend, "he winked."

"Foolishness," Ivan shouted back. "Dolphins can't wink."

"Use your teeth," yelled the Captain. "He will drown. He will starve. Dolphins nurse under water."

Dicran tried again, pulling at the net with all his strength, though the tingling and then the numbness that had begun at his fingertips had now gone up his fingers and palms to his wrists. His hands seemed no longer connected to his arms. Breaking a few strands of the jute with his teeth, he heard a tearing sound from below, but he soon realized this method would be too slow. The small dolphin was showing signs of exhaustion. His chirps were weaker, and, Dicran thought, a film was beginning to form over his eye. Dicran tried again to untangle the net, his fingers stiff as if they belonged to someone else, the water slapping his face.

"Use your knife," the Captain shouted, leaning toward him over the hull of Ivan's rocking boat. The sky turned dark again as the mass of gray clouds obscured the sun.

Hoarsely, Dicran called back as he yanked at the net, "A net lasts for years."

"A dolphin lives thirty," the Captain shouted through the wind.

The bell clanged over Dicran's head. "The net is —" Dicran began, and then stopped in midsentence. He thought of plankton floating toward the clear danger of jellyfish, and other mouths opening and eating, chewing and spewing out into the sea. He thought of his sister playing with the nest of dolls and finding the smallest one, of the pot of camomile tea, the yellow debris floating on top in the hands of the woman who would not stay, his father meticulously mending nets beside him in the flickering lantern light, the old man's mouth moving in the darkness, saying nothing. And then he heard again the cries of the dolphins and felt the sleek bodies gliding around him, appealing with blunt noses, fins without usable fingers, all emotion without the capability to act skillfully, decisively, finally.

Dicran tore at the knife case at his belt. "You're right, you're right," he shouted.

At this the dolphins, who had been keeping back from the buoy, moved in close and began swimming around and around him, noisily grunting and squealing, whistling to each other and churning up a wake that washed over his head and tore him off the buoy. He surfaced, sputtering. He wiped an arm across his face and then dove beneath the water. Two of the dolphins followed him, and although he could see nothing in the darkness, he felt their presence. They called to each other; he had forgotten the creatures could make as much noise below the surface as above it. One swam closely by him. He was overwhelmed by its size. It was as long as he was tall. He felt its power, yet it glided by him without ruffling the water. Breathless, he surfaced. There was no sound from the calf. He felt something wet on his face. He pulled the seaweed away, the knife still in his hand.

"The baby's not moving," Ivan shouted over the choppy water.

Frantically, Dicran sawed through the net and cut the baby free. "He's all right," Dicran called hoarsely. The young dolphin didn't move. "You're free." He slapped the dolphin calf on the side and gently pushed him clear of the net.

An explosion of activity seized the dolphins. Two swam on either side of the calf and carried him along with the raw energy of their thrust. The others charged around Dicran, smiling and squealing and churning up the water. He locked his elbow around the arm of the buoy as the water sloshed over his head. His teeth chattering, he no longer felt his forearms or legs. The air was filled with grunts and chirps, barks and whistles. Finally, the dolphins quieted and Ivan rowed in close to the buoy to pull Dicran on board. "It was a fine rescue," Ivan said, grinning as he leaned over, grabbed Dicran's belt and pulled him into the boat.

Captain Yorkovitya rowed up beside them. The oars floated in their locks as he struggled to take off his windbreaker. "Here — take my jacket," he said as he handed it to Dicran, who accepted it without comment, pulling it around his naked chest. Ivan tossed him his flask and Dicran took a long swig, his hands shaking so violently he could hardly keep the flask at his mouth.

The Captain watched them for a minute. Then, saluting Dicran, he pushed off against the side of their boat and rowed his own in a zigzagged course toward the fishing boat. Not far from them, the dolphins were gathered around the calf.

Ivan let the Captain outdistance them as he rowed toward the waiting boat. He looked at Dicran somberly as the other man shivered and held the Captain's jacket close around him. As Ivan rowed, Dicran sat at the bow, hunched over, his legs and hands still numb, unfeeling. The wind blew colder. Soon they reached the fishing boat, and from the way the men were noisily celebrating, it was obvious the Captain had already given his speech.

The men clasped Ivan's arm and pumped Dicran's hand as they helped them on board. Dicran was surprised when the Captain appeared and offered him a mug of brandy. The raw liquid tore at his throat. Numb, he thought of changing his clothes, thought of moving below, as the Captain came around again, cradling the bottle of brandy to his chest, the label facing outward. The oily, gold Serbian Plum Brandy was supposed to be the best. Perhaps he should sip it. Ah, yes, he accepted some more. It tingled on his tongue and burned his throat.

"A fine brandy, Captain," he said.

He went below to put on dry clothes. When he got back on deck, he was feeling warmer, the brandy mug empty in his hand, the Captain's windbreaker again around his shoulders. He went forward and found to his surprise the dolphins massed at their bow. Watching the calf, he remembered the net they had left tangled in the buoy. They should have retrieved it, he thought, he could have mended it.

Dicran went up by the pilothouse to smoke, and Ivan sprung up the ladder to join him.

"Hey, Dicran —" Ivan seemed restless. "A vodka tonight, for the dolphins?" Dicran didn't answer. "Have supper with us in the café," Ivan urged him. "Tell the story, Yolana will enjoy it."

Dicran said no, looking over the water. "Not tonight." He puffed on his pipe and looked at the sky washed pink with late afternoon.

"What are you doing tonight?" Ivan moved against the bulkhead. The dolphins had broken formation and were crisscrossing their bow.

"You forget," Dicran said impatiently, "the tournament at the park." He moved his pipe to the other side of his mouth. "Tonight I'll watch."

"Ah, yes," Ivan said as he turned toward shore, "the chess match."

Dicran looked at his pipe and then knocked it against the side of the boat. He stood silent for a few minutes. He could hear the dolphins playing in their wake, their high, soft sounds above the squall of the gulls and the wash of the water against the hull.

Dicran grabbed Ivan and turned him by the shoulders. Roughly, he kissed one blond, bristly cheek and then the other.

Ivan was wide-eyed. "You're crazy, Dicran."

"Not so crazy. We'll drink tonight."

The dolphins' sleek bodies cut through the wake. When they reached a certain spot on the water they stopped and rose on their tails. Seeing this, Ivan swung into the pilothouse. The engines stopped. The dolphins were backwatering, emitting a chorus of sound. Further out, dolphins in a ring were flipping like coins on the horizon.

The crewmen were suddenly stretching, awake, looking up, asking what was going on, talking among themselves.

Ivan called from the pilothouse. "We're there."

Dicran turned toward his voice. "Where?"

"Where the dolphins first met us. We're at the same latitude, the same longitude," Ivan shouted. "Dicran, look." He leaned out the window of the pilothouse and alternately beckoned to Dicran and pointed to shore. "Look at the coastline. Look how the sun dips over the mountains." He pointed to the sky. "Look at the gulls, they're the same."

Dicran looked at the sky, the coastline. "You're right," he said smiling. "Everything — even the gulls — the same."

LISSA McLAUGHLIN

The Continental Heart

(FROM THE MASSACHUSETTS REVIEW)

SHE TOOK UP TRAVELING because it frightened her to stay long in one place.

Oh come on, her friends said. It's got to be more complicated than that. So she agreed with them, laughing, Oh yes. It's not just that.

She said, Oh yes, it's a whole lot of things.

She packs everything so carefully the customs men have to apologize. Madam, it is form. Chunky carry-on, the dresses look exactly like her, elegant, in the suitcase. She digs in it for them. Profuse apologies.

Underwear. Insinuated in a bag of plastic, the kind you'd buy goldfish in.

The waiter startles her by offering her water.

Tall bag of slimness for her shoes.

She insists everyone be quiet. Quiet! she raps on the wall of the next train compartment, they're having some sort of party. Please, be quiet! She squeezes her forehead, leaves it between her fingers as the trees open, revealing a view of water.

This time, the man looks at her tape recorder.

You must have to listen a lot.

Yes, all the time, it's as if I just have to use my ears, and I'm in.

If she doesn't press too hard, the latch of the suitcase might open without a fight. Otherwise it jams, she has to straddle it. She puts her legs on each side. Sweat unlatches her, pore by pore. She pounds it with both fists, her chin lowered to the leather.

What if she can't get in?

The train rocks. In the hall a woman startles her. Advancing, in a burst of English, her face black with blood, the curtains swaying, puts her hands out, Don't touch me!

She looks for the conductor. The woman is shouting. Her own head fills with something like water, she doesn't dwell on the fact she speaks several languages with unquestionable fluency or that her travel copy is set instantly into expensive paper by a well-considered magazine. The conductor's face is like a doorway into which she can hurry for safety. Oh please hurry! She's having some sort of attack —

She goes into her compartment. The curtain is rotating in circles. She puts her arms on the chair arms. Recognition throbs in her like an attack.

The language she writes in is English, sometimes she shatters a nail on the typewriter keys, bent toward them.

She tries her tape recorder, on, off, her hand trembles with the thought of the woman who was stupid, she decides. "An angel," the tourist guide fumbled for his own face, clapped his head. He wanted to touch her instead, but she put her eye on her watch and let him take her around by the entrance to the tomb. He kept looking back at her. Procured especially like some special food. Dull seal-like head. She looked from him to the walls. The tomb usually opened for art devotees and his black feet sullen on the steps. As they went down the grooved steps, Nowhere? she said loudly, he had said such tombs existed nowhere else. Then he was up against her, rotating his hand. She wanted to say Fuck you, but, his lips raised, he instantly pointed to various places on the wall, forgetting about her. At one point she uttered such a sound of frustration with her tape recorder he looked at her, laughed, and, with his long hand, slapped the wall. He caressed it.

She opens her eyes. There in front of her EAT DRINK. She raises her leg. Light moves over it. They have pulled into a city. The stern train bearing down, the curtain straightening.

She must bear her own irritation, all these uneducated people. In their strange, curled shoes. Whose language no one else knows, because they keep it to themselves.

Self-conscious about her large, ineffective bones. Once in a Bulgarian city she tried to lift an old man who had fallen straight down into the street, but a couple rushed up, Do you want to kill him? Embarrassed, his arm folding in two places as it fell, she let go. But he had opened his eyes, blinking them. She looked around quickly, but no one had seen. The old man was lying still. Terrified, she abandoned the couple, young and blond with the sun crushed in their shirts and their arms around each other. The old man already lifting his eyes to the police, opening and closing his mouth.

She has a habit of crying out multisyllabic things in her sleep. The hotel management is pretty used to this. They send a sleepy clerk up. Are you in there? Her eyes fly open. In her dream a huge wave of water lazily followed the child, the two men, down the hillside. It covered them while she shouted their names. She wakes up. Are you in there? Yes, her hand over her mouth, she's forgotten what they look like.

She tolerates her ineffective bones. She knows how to get a foreign doctor, if the lumps show up. She has seen the X rays of herself, knows the exact lay of the ribs, the large fingers inserted in her chest. She can tell you where the breast will erupt into cysts, the kind that move if you push on them, near the nipple. All kinds of trouble starts right here, she tells herself trying to laugh, tapping her skin over hot coffee. She is shaking so hard some of the coffee sloshes inside her robe and leaves a long red mark. The doctor will ask about it later. She rubs herself, rueful, because it's so appropriate. She knows how to call a doctor and get his reassurance. Put money in or dial first or talk to the operator according to who, in this country, is available. The tape recorder slides around in her purse, contriving to help her forget herself. The doctor will talk to you now. She knows how scornful his face can look in the mirror, fitting his cool hands at arm's length. His white cuffs. She stares at a row of instruments, not yet disarranged. Flinches to see her own face in the mirror.

The hotel staff manages to bang loudly enough. The side that produces all the trouble. Shouting Thank you, wondering as the covers slide over her why her breath makes her thank it, why he used to wake her with one finger and make her thank him.

Looking back from the motorcruiser she wonders why she takes such an interest in these particular things. The wind blindly disturbing the leaves. The trees dwindling where the boat slips off the shore. Placed to look Jamesian. But as the boat moves, off center, she thinks of Hemingway. She catches herself throwing things in the water, bits of her notebook that stand up, white. Distracted.

The page eats anything, eats anything she puts in its damn

mouth, healthy or not. She's been drinking. Slapping the yellow copy back, she breaks the pencil in two, puts it gently beside the pen, the doctor has given her a mild antidepressant.

The porpoises live under the rocks. She rubs her eyes, Private Life of Porpoises Strung Along the Shore, holds her notebook over her forehead. Updating a shoreline she's stared at time and time again, it's gotten too familiar, like the Americans who frequent this shore with their prissy shoes. The natives become mere bits of bushes, unaccented in their private lives. The porpoises rise, rush back and forth, black and concentric. Some soil falls noisily away under her feet and she makes a sharp motion with her hand. She stands close to the hot scent of rosemary and it cuts off her wind, under the crumbling edge of the cliff a few black-skirted women probe the green surf, the perfect roll of the water irritates their hands. The sea is like an eye something's got into, the women scornfully point at it. No longer amusing. The sun blazes and the women lift their arms not to her but to the suddenly indifferent sky.

Is it a clinical problem, she wonders, that I don't care where I go, that I spread my legs to keep the interest of my damn lap?

She used to wonder if she should change her lovers. You simplify, which means you often lie. He pressed his fist to the table.

Yes, it's true. As usual he was right.

Should she change him for someone else? Edit?

But that's her damn job. A little girl, she put coins in the bus while her grandfather stood beside her, helping her try to understand what made the bus go. Somewhere under them the little disks rolled along and pushed something. The old man was in business. How does it go? she said to his hand. Oh, money and other things, he said, tapping her hair, smiling down.

In Brussels a man gets up, walks to a piano. She sits still. In the concert hall she touches her chest. It's wonderful, that brush with his enormous hands. Maybe she could go see him. Then she thinks about the piano, how sudden its enormous silence. The blind pianist fallen forward.

Her editor laughingly warns her. Neither the water nor the wine is potable there, Don't expect much. He lifts his drink. They toast each other and she pretends to be serious, tells him she expects to be thirsty.

She laughs. A severance of respect, she is remembering the generous lies of her lovers, their promises they would want her always, that their violent wants had flowered wildly on top of her. Her hand comes out from under her in the hotel bed. A kind of residence. In the woman's aching face, lashing in the hall, a long stretch of caution absolutely disarranged, like the guides and their ferocious attention to telling her nothing important. Now the gulls stall over the undrinkable water and she watches them reflecting sourly on themselves, the sea so baroque it must be shared, given credibility, the view patted with the hands.

She wants to tape-record the sea so she stands near the rocks, holds the recorder under her arm and buttons her coat to her chin. The wind whips her hair out. Then she sees how the wind holds on to the light and begins tugging it down below the horizon, down under the rocks, only the end closer to her glistens and she wants to remember it, scared not to. She snaps the player on in her hand. Later there will be only the sound of the sea, too loud, indistinct. She will frown, helpless. Crackling, dry, pervading everything.

The tape comes round to the piano. He looked at her. You simplify everything.

She was angry, It's only a small machine. Defending her technology.

You've used it to compare us. You've got us both on it now, don't you? So you don't have to decide.

She was listening, waiting to say, It's you who simplifies. But too fast for her, he leaned toward her. So what do you want me to agree with?

What, she doesn't know. She's in a new town, has her notes on the tape, the voice of the guide in his small green coat. This one talked rapidly like an elf. Here she can eat everything, the town is small but pompous.

The wind blows off the water, making her head pound. She puts her head to her glass, the water is like nothing she's ever tasted before, realizing the fact she can drink it startles her. She sits still. The wind lifts her hair off her shoulders.

The window heats up her arms. Someone to talk to. Bizarre, withdrawn, the engine in its movements pushes her head to one side. A kind of lever, like a lover's hand, a blackened coin dropped into a slot.

Sometimes the pressure wakens like a seismic shock. Fallen side-

ways in the seat she wakes up, there's sweat on her arm. Gulps
water. Through it impurities dreamily fall. She doesn't care, drinking greedily. The portion of her life that sets her against herself,
her sturdy system inviting danger.

They're inside her now, like the works of a bus, the swollen
nodes. The husband's sweet, puzzled face slowly lifted free of the
skin. Then the unsweet, suspicious face of that first dazzled lover.
Smashed. Then all the others till the most recent, circling around
laughter of her son in bed, his arms hot and throwing off sparks,
his voice shrill with fever. The tree trunk tilted outside his window,
with the furzy, ear-lobe shape she points out to him, the bole she
says is just like his ear to calm her panic, seeing his red face. In
what school are you now? she asks later. Suddenly she wants to put
her finger on something so desperately but her steps have sealed
her in. Who can she steal from but herself? Where is the ladder
she can lean against his window? She comes out of a movie, Oh,
the sexual thundering, she laughs, but she is stopping in the
square, standing still, the buildings shrink the light. Something
she's never acquitted herself of. The green square with the traffic
where she told her son he must escape himself perfectly. Running
from him across the light.

She has a dry throat from going so long in this unfamiliar sun.
Drinks from a tall, strange glass.

There it is in the magazine, in the airport. She wrote it to be
funny. Now something makes her bend it back, sharply, stop half
through. She dumps the slick pages in the garbage, they make her
eyes hurt. With much groaning and screeching, the continents
were flung apart, had been all one large piece no one cared too
much about. Only separated, plants started poking up on them.
They'd slid out on the undrinkable water. They flowered, allowed
to. The jury of time indifferent, showered the shapeless mud constantly, where the real estate of Florida made its thick roots. Planes
already stirring in the bellies of the biggest animals.

She wants to laugh, her ignorance of science. But has also told
her own story too clearly. Suddenly, dreads the bright type of the
by-line.

Listen! she urges a friend later. Handing her a drink, he's annoyed by her cheerfulness.

Beneath which there is some restlessness. The tape recorder is
on. A sound goes out. As if he could remember for her the exact

details of that moment, the sightless pianist sitting in his chair, the piano pursued by his minute hands stretching, covering the keys, his preoccupation with the sound, the expensiveness of it bending him flat. Looking up, the friend realizes as she drinks the stiff drink he's made her, she feels for it with her lips. Looks at him. Tests him.

Her feeling, sipping the tepid water, that the musician's memory has come up to shake the water in the glass. She is a woman who feels some massive shift that makes her groan. What is her job now? She feels officious, laughing. Somewhere there must wait to be discovered every species of reason. Why people wait. Why, though she drinks, she wants to drink more. The sounds in the next car her fingers are listening to so exactly now. They are minute. As if listening to another continent.

ROBERTA GUPTA

The Café de Paris

(FROM MSS)

PSST! I SAY! You with the Afgha and bemused eyes! Yes, you on the edge of the group, looking over your shoulder. Over here! I'm in the doorway — the dark gentleman behind the magazine racks . . .

Ah, how do you do? Pardon me, accosting you like this, but you look a little lost. May I offer my services? I have time to kill and you seem lonely. Visitor, are you? Tourist? I thought so. It's the season.

Well, what do you think of London? Disappointing city, eh? But why ask, you won't admit it. Few tourists will. It's a matter of pride with all of you. You don't care to acknowledge squandered money, wasted time (lost dreams?), so you put on a good face and say, "Everything's fine. Great little city."

Let me tell you the tourist's problem. It's the age-old dilemma of the stranger, the alien. None of you knows where to go. London has moved underground, like a wounded animal (a lady of the night), and none of you knows where to find her.

I watch you scurry from one attraction to the next, like children at a fairground, and my heart goes out to you. I was once a stranger in this city.

Like a burnoosed Moroccan sidling at the mouth of a dark, secretive alley I want to beckon you, say, "Dear tourists, follow me! I will show you such delights, such rarities as will pop the eyes of the folks back home in Tokyo, Arkansas, Saudi! I will give you your heart's desire — temporarily — for a small fee."

But generally I am too busy, too caught up in my own pursuits to get involved with people. However, I like your face, and you find me in a rare mood — the mood to befriend you — take you on a small tour of London, one or two special places. How does that strike you?

You seem reluctant. Worried about your wallet, your camera, your integrity? Come, come, they don't interest me. I'm a man of means. Your companion is all I want to be. Take courage, dear tourist — leave the group and follow me.

And the first stop is Piccadilly Circus. We shall not move far from its environs. My tour takes place within a bow shot of Lord Eros.

Ha, Eros, greetings! If ever disappointment was personified — deified — there he stands, my friend. Look at him! The god of love! He has his roots in Ancient Greece. Homer knew him, and English bards through the ages have sung his praise — love, love, love. Well, I ask you, what is he? A naked boy, tarnished and rusty. Of all the indignities, they have placed a fancy hat on the head that tops the naked, unformed body. He stands above a disused fountain — a well run dry — there's an analogy for you! He aims his deadly dart at a hoarding, a neon sign that flashes GUINNESS IS GOOD FOR YOU. Well, we know he's blind. He's also worn out — an atrocity — the city council should remove him.

But it's not Eros I've brought you to see. I merely wish to locate you, give you a landmark to return to, should you lose yourself wandering at my heels.

Here it is, almost at the corner — the crossroads, you might say — a small, narrow doorway. So inconspicuous you'd have passed it, wouldn't you? Even though that little neon sign winking over the doorway tells you this is the Café de Paris.

Let's go in! What, you don't fancy it? It looks a trifle seedy? You don't care for the looks of the patrons? One fault of tourists is that they always judge by appearance. Come along, you're safe with me.

See that lady with the orange pompadour? See how one kohl-rimmed eye winks at you? See how her plump hand reaches out through the semicircle in the grille? Just slip your five crowns into her palm and she will give you a ticket — your passport to a night of bliss at the Café de Paris.

Ah, I thought you'd come round. Isn't the scent of evil hard to resist! Her perfume? I think she calls it *Joie de Nuit*. Overpowering? Yes, but her name is Celia. She has to live up to it. If you'd like an

introduction — Not your type? Well, the night is young. We'll find
something more to your taste, whatever it may be.

Now we go down these three marble steps to the foyer — notice
the red carpet — the royal treatment. A little worn, a little threadbare? But think of the feet that have walked it!

How do you like the mirrors? Notice the frames — the cross-
work, the flowers, the intertwined leaves — someone fashioned
them lovingly. The gilt is peeling? Not what they were, I daresay,
but that's part of the atmosphere here. This place is old. Older
than St. Paul's, in some ways.

Observe the wallpaper. A nice thought, a rather apt motif!
Naked baby angels. See how they recline on gold-ribbon clouds,
chubby, dimpled arms stretched invitingly, the hair, the eyes of
young girls — the essence of the Café de Paris!

Well, I see you're charmed, but let's walk through to the balcony.
There's a bar. You indulge, I hope? See how we go in a circle?
Everything is circular here.

We'll sit where we can look down at the dance floor and also
have a view of the door. Now, what'll you have? Brandy's my drink.
The same? Two brandies, my good fellow! Hold on, make those
doubles, if you please. My friend and I have some time to kill.

So say, dear tourist, what do you think of the Café? Not much,
your face tells me. Well, she isn't awake yet. Wait till the girls come
in! But I see you're eyeing the ladies — the two at the bar. Which
do you fancy? The blonde in the fishnet stockings, or the brunette
with the rose in her hair? Past it? Them, or you? But I see you're
a man of my own inclination. We'll leave those two for the young
bucks with more appetite than taste. We'll wait till the girls come
in.

Ah, you've seen it! Finally! I wondered when you'd notice. That,
my friend, is the pride — the ladies excepted — of the Café de
Paris. What a wonder it is. Gaze upon it! A great, glittering orb
suspended from the center of the ceiling by a thread of silver —
hanging by a mere thread, it seems — devilish clever! See how
every inch of its circumference is mirrored — there must be a
thousand minute, perfect mirrors there. I exaggerate? Maybe.
Beauty, perfection, drive me to hyperbole. I'm a romantic at heart.
And when the lights dim the orb comes to life, it spins, slowly at
first, then faster and faster in time to the music, shooting colors,
flashing lights, round and round it goes, and the dancers, looking

up, see themselves a thousand times — all right, a hundred — minute, perfect figures of light and glorious color, whirling in the ball, mirrored in eternity. Ah, the brandies — and the musicians! Do you want to dance? The blonde is showing some interest. Personally, I don't care for the waltz. Later on we'll have their more exotic fare — the rumba, the tango — and the cha-cha-cha, my specialty. I come early to warm up, watch for the girls as they trickle in around eleven or so. Long-haired angels with lost eyes. Wonderful! Why do they come? Dear tourist — they come for *us* — the men in their prime!

And although I'm no cad, I'll tell you (confidentially) that the number of angels I've taken home with me over the years exceeds a century. You look amazed, spill your brandy. (Have another.) Is it so hard to believe when you look at me? I'm different, you must admit. Striking in any crowd, but a knockout in the group we have here. They're all Englishmen, you know. But you knew that — unmistakable — the rumpled suits, the mouse-brown hair, stooped shoulders — rheumatism is rampant in this climate — not to mention influenza. Look at their eyes, perpetually watered, the influenza virus has sucked all the colour out, all the verve, all the *joie de vivre*. Now look at me! Bronzed skin (that's natural), jet-black hair, dark eyes — smouldering, they've been called — even hypnotic (she was a lovely little girl) — and my body — you can see the shape I'm in. Constant exercise of a particularly regenerating kind. There's no denying it, women go for me. They fall. It's my single greatest headache. I'm romantic, y'see. Did I say that? Well, it's true. I'd love 'em all — all the time — if there were enough of me. But there's only so much one man can do — and don't get me wrong — I'm never in danger of losing my perspective — or rarely. Which puts me in mind of a curious incident — a personal experience, to be candid — that still puzzles me. We have an hour to kill. Let me tell you a story. Oh, come now, don't be unsociable — forget your watch, forget time — tonight the drinks are on me.

It began right here in the Café, as most of my stories do, on a Saturday night about the same time of year — spring, isn't it? Blasted British weather. One loses track of the seasons. I was sitting at this very table — or anyway, one just like it — commanding a view of the door. I was watching for the girls to come in. (I notice you look at me oddly each time I mention the girls. Yes, I see what you see. Most of the women here are — mature, shall we say?

Average age thirty-five to forty? You'd put it higher, would you? Really? And the men the same? But my dear fellow, you can't compare in that way. A man comes into his prime at forty, and if he's careful it lasts beyond sixty. A woman now is over the hill at thirty. But the girls to whom I refer — the bright-haired angels of nineteen or so — they come later, as I said. Celia brings 'em in. She's an expert persuader. She stands in the doorway and whispers to them as they wander down Shaftesbury Avenue — the lost angels of the night gathered in by Celia promising them a heavenly time — indispensable Celia!)

I am sitting with my brandy and my friend Michael — he was an habitué this time last year — and, as usual, I am pulling his leg about my success with the girls versus his lack of it. But he doesn't like it a bit, apparently. They can't take a joke, these Englishmen — they're as bad as the Germans. Oh, I say, sorry! You're not? I could have sworn you said — no harm done, then. Anyway, Michael says, "My dear chap, I must protest. You have the advantage. You were born in the Orient" — this is his way of reminding me; can't forget they once had an empire — "you have this Kama Sutra in your veins — your looks — your aroma — You attract a certain *type* of female, naturally."

And I want to say, "My *dear* chap!" Yes, I want to catch him by his Oxford blue tie, pull his pale English face up to mine, and say, "Old chum, what absolute nonsense you talk — every time you open your public-school mouth I'm awed by the volumes of rubbish you churn out." But I don't say or do any of that. We're all civilized here. A terribly civilized nation. I don't even complain he's got my country of origin wrong — I'm from — well, never mind, to them it's all the same once you've crossed the sea. But I will tell you this — help you place me — my father was an ambassador while his managed a bank on some high street, though he *says* "in high finance." I've been to more public schools in more countries than he could count on the fingers of his two hands.

What I do say, leaning back in my chair, lowering my lids languorously (this maddens him) is, "Michael, a woman is like an instrument — a sensitive, finely tuned, highly crafted instrument. The music she produces depends upon who plays. You are looking, Michael, at a master musician."

His thin nostrils tighten, a white spot appears on the tip of his nose, his fingers close into his palms. I have hit home. I always do.

I beg your pardon? Dear tourist, you spoke? What do you lack? What can I get you? Oh, you wonder where the girls come in! Right here!

I turn my head from Michael and see them. There are four in a group, and pretty as a bouquet! But friends are hard to separate and you'd never get four of one mind, so, regretfully, I let them go. Then comes one alone, and she's lovely. My type to a T. Tall, slender (but not too), golden hair as fine as a baby's, and not much more than that herself, I'd swear. She's dressed in a wisp of something transparent, and shiny stockings, high heels. What I could teach her. But even as I rise she smiles past me, waves to someone behind. I turn and there's this old roué at the bar, adjusting his tie, grinning foolishly. I know him, and I know his concern for his heart — its functions, not its emotions — but he has money. And if that's all she's interested in, I have no use for her. I turn away disdainfully. But her perfume as she brushes me, and Michael's sneering comment, "Missed that one, old boy!" affect my sang-froid. In fact, my mood changes. I turn nasty, glare at the staircase as though to consume with fire from my eyes the next one who appears there.

She comes. It couldn't be worse. She's not my type at all. Not one I would choose in a million years. No, no, she's too dark, too thin, she looks undernourished. She's so dark she may even be foreign!

However, it is well past eleven. I see Celia close the grille. There will be no more to choose from. I have to make a quick decision, and I decide that since it's Saturday night and I don't care to go home alone she'll have to do — for one night. I get up. "Excuse me, Michael," I say. Michael looks across the well of the balcony to where she stands, curls his lip, says, "You must be kidding, old man!"

I go toward her, but there's no spring in my step, no roguish glint in my eye, no charming smile, none of my customary Saturday night animation. Almost, I walk past her, go home. But it *is* Saturday night. So I stop in front of her, look up to where she hovers on the top step, say, "Hullo there! I'd love to dance with you." She flinches, bites her lip, as if I'm an apparition; looks at me as though I were holding a knife in my hand.

"Dance," I repeat, very distinctly, with my hands behind my back. "Would you care to dance?"

She draws in her breath, prepares to speak, but the effort, apparently, is too much. She simply grasps the stair rail and nods her (dark) head. I hold out my hand to help her down the steps — not a gesture of old-world courtesy — on the contrary, it seems she will never get down them without aid. I wonder, is she consumptive? Is that a contagious disease? But it's too late to back out, we are on the staircase, going down.

The band is between numbers and the dancers are standing around. I lead her into a space, we look at each other. Her face, as a matter of face, is quite passable — she has large eyes — if only there were more of her like that. She has, too, a very disconcerting way of staring at me, as though I were a reincarnation from a previous life. Jack the Ripper, perhaps? And, funny thing, I also feel as if we've met before. But that's impossible. She's not my type!

When the music begins (it's "Autumn Leaves," a song I abhor) she seems to swoon in my arms. No resilience here, I think, no endurance. She'll not stay the course. My heart sinks, I support her around the floor. I know I have to converse, turn on the charm, if I am to persuade her to leave with me in ten minutes or so, but I lack incentive to move my lips, form words. I decide I should settle this health business, at any rate. It bothers me.

"How are you feeling tonight?" I say, to her hair. She startles, as though I had suggested something obscene. "I don't wish to be personal," I continue, "but there's something wrong, isn't there? Can I help in any way?"

Then she speaks. "I'm sorry if I seem unfriendly —"

"Not at all! Not at all!"

Over her shoulder I see the baby blonde whisk by in the arms of her old benefactor. Her skirt twitches up and I have a glimpse of smooth (virgin?) thigh. Something catches in the pit of my stomach, I miss what my partner has said.

"I beg your pardon?" I force back my eyes, my attention, fix them like steel.

"It's silly, I know. He was just a friend."

"Who was?" I ask, politely.

"Gareth, the boy I'm telling you about."

"Oh, just a friend, was he?" and slowly I am filled with horror by what I hear — not the words she speaks — I hardly listen to those — her accent — it's atrocious! It's not English at all! What is it? I've heard it before, but, for the moment, can't place it. It's not common in the places *I* frequent.

"And so he had a perfect right to leave," she is saying, "I don't deny that. It's my fault, not his —" and now she has found her tongue I see I am to be subjected to an unintelligible monologue on the rights of this person called — Gareth?

"I let myself get too fond of him. I'm like that," she says.

"I'm sure you have a very warm nature," I say, watching the blonde, her way of pretending to listen to what her partner says; her way of glancing sideways around the floor. Perhaps there *is* still a chance? Perhaps I gave up too soon? I try to meet her eyes over the dark head of the girl in my arms.

"Yes, I do," she says, as though I had offered her something. "I love people very easily."

"You should watch that!" I say sharply. Love is a word I'm not partial to on the lips of women. It is a word they usually employ as a euphemism, I have found.

"I know," she says. "It really wasn't fair of me to love him when he made it clear from the start —"

The blonde meets my eyes. I raise my eyebrows, smile faintly. She gives me a long, appraising look — I think she is going to smile — she flicks her head away, gives the dazzling smile to her old beau. "Bitch!" I think.

"I'm really not blaming him," the other girl, the one I'm stuck with, starts to tell me, but I'm sick of this. "Look," I say, "you're obviously very upset. Surely you don't feel like being in a place like this?"

"I just came out to get away." She looks at me with eyes that seem naked — no guile, no defence — I can't take it. Her eyes depress me.

"Would you like to go round the corner to Maxime's?" I say. "It's quiet, relaxing, soothing — we can talk better there. And you can eat!"

A small smile lights her face suddenly, evokes a reluctant response on mine. I take her arm. "Come," I say.

But as I lead her out into the street (nodding to Celia who lifts one arched eyebrow, then shrugs — there's nothing she hasn't seen) I am disturbed by the ease with which I have drawn her — no effort, no persuasion, she simply comes — it's like leading a lamb to the slaughter, catching a child with sweets. I don't like how it makes me feel. If I had charmed her, if she had shown some resistance — a challenge to overcome! But nothing of the sort. It's like picking up money in the road. One pockets it, of course, but not without vague stirrings of guilt. It was dropped in the street, is ownerless, but not actually yours all the same.

"What's your name?" I say, as we walk down cold, drizzling, littered Shaftesbury Avenue, the theatre crowds coming out. She tells me it's Gwyn, brief, ugly, tuneless. But then I hit upon something romantic, something to maneuver us onto the right track (I'm not, you understand, having romantic feelings toward her — not at all — it's done as much for my sake as hers). "Not short for Guinevere by any chance?" I ask, my eyes soft, voice whimsical, reminding myself this girl is my last hope (God help me) tonight.

"Gwyneira," she corrects me, without a smile.

"Gwyneira!" I repeat, mispronouncing it. "What kind of barbaric name is that?"

"Welsh," she says, "it's a Welsh name."

And it all falls into place! I'm a person who relies a lot on instinct, and it hardly ever fails. My immediate antipathy to her, I now see, went far deeper than her dark hair, her emaciated body. That instant distaste was a warning from my instinct, which I should have heeded. I hate the Welsh! They're worse, far worse, than the English, or the Germans — oh, I say, sorry! Oh, that's right, you're *not*!

Well, the other two races are, at least, civilized. The Welsh are animals, like all the Celts. The English were right to build fortresses, barriers — the mistake was pulling them down. Now they swarm over the border in the belly of the Green Dragon every time their outlandish national game is played here. Welshmen are drunken braggarts and brawlers (look at their one major poet), and look how they treat their women. But the women are worse! They have an atonement complex. They believe they have to atone for their men — atone for the sins of the world — and that, I think, is what I have roped in here. An atoner — a girl with a bundle of guilt on her most inadequate shoulders — what fun will that be? Like seducing a nun. I am stirred. For the first time since seeing her, genuinely stirred. She has grown up in the wilds, amongst wild men. What I can teach her! Yes, I'm faintly interested now.

"Was this person — this, er, Gareth — he was Welsh too, I assume?"

"Oh, yes, we practically grew up together."

Ah, how boring! There is certainly potential here.

We arrive at Maxime's. Maxime's! Another word for elegance, luxury, plenitude, dreams! Maxime's is a glimpse of exotica, a whisper of the Orient, right in the heart of shabby, worn-out Soho. Maxime's surprises you, catches your imagination — like an orchid in the lapel of an old whore. And its mystery, its allure, flow into the street from its wide-open doors, beguiling you, drawing you in, like a charming face at the window of a house of ill fame. Who can pass Maxime's!

We walk through the green and gilt doors. A silent old man — in his eyes all the wisdom that once was China's; his lined face, yellowed moustache, long, dark robe, hands folded into the sleeves, head courteously inclined — harks back to a younger, higher age, golden Byzantium!

"Welcome," his sleeves motion, and we follow him into the deep-carpeted, dimly lit foyer. On the walls red and green dragons curl their proud tails, breathe fire. Unobtrusive, white-coated waiters slide by the dragons, moving between kitchen and dining rooms like the ministering slaves of Byzantium. Everything is unobtrusive here. The atmosphere of Maxime's is pervasive, elusive as the aura of a fascinating woman long dead or mythical — Helen, Lucrezia, Frances the Jacobean witch — you think what might have been were it not for that barrier we call time. Ah, dear tourist, what might have been! *That* is the essence of Maxime's!

I look at her face to see what she feels. She feels scared! So I take her by the arm — it's like catching air, she doesn't eat, this girl — and we go up the stairs. The staircase is wide, carpeted like the foyer, lit by small, porcelain, hand-painted bracket lamps. A dragon stretches his tail the entire length of the wall; massive, green, indestructible strength. His fiery head meets you at the top. I feel her flinch, and I smile. A nervous little girl — easily frightened. I don't mind that.

And an interesting thing, my friend — Maxime's was constructed along the same lines as the Café here. A balcony, tables placed around it, and the diners look down the deep well — there are three tiers — to a grey, white, and black mosaic dance floor. Another little, intimate dance floor!

We sit at one of the candlelit tables. Immediately a waiter appears, out of the mouth of the dragon it seems. I consult the menu. She sits primly, hands folded in her lap, a schoolgirl out with Uncle

— alas for her, no uncle, I. Her eyes flit nervously, taking in the decor, the diners, the waiter. The waiter smiles at her pityingly. I am annoyed. I'm used to admiration for my women, not sympathy. I order curtly, ask for wine.

"So, Gwyn," I say, sitting back, drumming my fingers on the tablecloth. She reaches into her bag, brings out a cigarette, lights it, and coughs. I think of consumption again.

"You're not sick, are you?" I ask, casually.

"Oh, no," she says, "just —" She shrugs, draws on the cigarette. I look over the balcony, scanning the tables, the dance floor. There is nothing about this girl that attracts me, and I ask myself, What is my purpose here? What do I hope to achieve, get out of this? Still, it's only one night — and I'm doing her a favor first — she needs the meal.

The wine, the food, arrive. We have not spoken again. The waiter serves us in silence, glancing under his lashes at Gwyn, as if he would communicate something; God knows what it could be. The food served, the waiter hovers. I wave my hand, dismiss him. "Eat," I tell her, and she says, "I can't."

I am angry. I point my fork at her, say, "I've bought you a meal, so eat it." She looks scared — a premonition — looks around (for whom? for what?), meets only blank, disinterested faces, picks up her fork and begins.

"I don't mean to be rude," she says.

"Stop apologizing," I reply.

She looks at me with the fork halfway to her mouth, her shoulders lift slightly. "It's just that — I don't know how to behave now. I've lost something."

"Just eat," I say, but after a minute I ask her, "What? What have you lost?"

She puts down her fork, folds her hands behind her plate (like one saying grace), looks at me as if she were waiting for just this question. "When he left me — when someone leaves like that — you lose the point — there's no point, suddenly."

"I don't know what you're talking about," I say. Her face in the candlelight is pale, grave, like a wax effigy in a church alcove. It discomforts me. I'd like to leave.

"Love," she says, "I'm talking about love."

"I've never been in love," I tell her, and turn my attention to the meal.

But she seems to think I have asked for further explanation. "You see," she says, playing with her fork (this annoys me), "being in love is like walking a line —" She looks up at me, an embarrassed little smile. My face is impassive. "That sounds risky, doesn't it? It *is* — but at least I felt I was walking *to* somewhere — there was some goal, some point at the end of the line — now it's over."

"You fell off the line!" I say, raising my glass to her. She is supposed to laugh, but the hand holding the fork quivers, she looks down, a quaint falling movement of the eyelids, as though they suddenly became too heavy for her face, which *is* small — fragile like the rest of her. I wonder how such creatures survive in this world — how they draw sustenance. But apparently she doesn't, and will soon be snuffed out.

"Eat!" I say.

"I'm sorry—I really can't." She puts down her fork.

"Then drink your wine."

She does, and I play with my glass, wonder what to say to her. I can think of nothing so I say, quite brashly, "Would you like to come home with me?" I am brash simply because I don't care one way or the other. If she were to walk out, offended, it would be a relief. I feel like the burdened Saint Christopher I have seen around the necks of seamen (except I'm no saint, of course).

But she says, "Yes."

I signal the waiter. "Let's go, then," I say, with no feeling of conquest.

Outside it is very cold, late. We hurry to the tube station, catch the last train, mainly drunks, down-and-outs, crazies, a few lovers. The lights in the carriage are harsh, striking the haggard faces like the strobes of an ambulance; persons-to-be-identified in a mortuary. I hate the last tube, but I ride it from necessity.

She sits very close to me on the lumpy cushioned seat. The cushions are thick with dust and stains; impossible to guess what colour they once were. A mad old drunk leers at her with one eye — the other is matted shut — she stares down at the littered floor, presses her arm against me. I look out of the window. A row of expressionless, yellow faces look back at me — people on their way to a penal camp, the gallows. A whim. They are merely the homeless riding the Circle.

At Earl's Court I nudge her, get up. We walk out of the deserted station into dark, empty streets. She walks very close to me. Our footsteps echo. I don't touch her although I believe she wants me to take her arm, put my arm around her. She's scared! She doesn't know where she's going — but neither do I, with her.

"How do you suppose they got like that?" she says suddenly.

"Who?" I say.

"Those people on the train. They have nowhere to go."

"They didn't provide for themselves properly," I say, thinking of my own investments; my mother's legacy — dwindling now, but still adequate. My parents, thank God, were aware of material necessity and taught it to me.

"In what way?" she says, and her question startles me. Her voice, her paleness, her frail shape are ghostlike in the dark, silent street.

"I only know of one way," I say. She says, "I don't know of any — for sure."

My house — my flat, that is — is just two streets from the station. I hear the trains all night. It's a dark street that I live on; Victorian houses, a small rectangle of grass running down the center of the two blocks, seats, trees. In the daytime old people, unemployed foreigners, sit there, read newspapers, feed the birds. It was once a wealthy neighbourhood, has gone downhill. I have a large flat at very reasonable rates.

I let us into the house, lead her up the pitch-black stairs. I must hold her hand now, and in the darkness I feel I am leading a wraith. I shudder — distaste. My instinct tells me, get rid of her — but it's too late.

My flat is at the top, and as we draw near my spirits improve; I feel some pleasure, no small pride. Wait till she sees! I unlock the door, go in, turn on the light, beckon to her where she waits, hands clasped, in the hall. She is wearing a white dress, I notice for the first time.

"Come in, please."

She gasps, as I had anticipated. "Well," I say, closing the door, "what do you think? You like it?"

"It's —" she says, but clearly she doesn't know what to say. Quite unexpected in this part of London (and to a girl like this), so much luxury, lavishness, such unique taste. I rub my hands, smile. "Sit down," I say, "I'll bring drinks."

As I cross the room to the kitchen I turn on the stereo; Italian songs, crooning, romantic, *Amore, scusami*. I put brandy, wine, two glasses on a tray, come back. She is still standing near the door, staring.

"Well?" I say. "Well?" I put down the tray on the carved brass table in front of the Oriental sofa bed that is covered with a gold damask spread, red and black velvet cushions. I pour drinks, wine for her, brandy for me, and look around myself. My room, no matter how dejected London makes me feel (and it *does* depress me, sometimes — the infernal weather!), never fails to cheer me. Twenty years of care, taste, love (I use the word in context here) have gone into this room, and a stranger feels it immediately. This is a room you enter once in a lifetime, and they know it, my girls.

All the furniture is low, rich, Oriental — carved tables, some brass, some teak; low sofas spread with damask; a damask wall-hanging behind the bed — golden tigers with eyes like gems. On every table are treasures, objets d'art from the four corners of the world, each one reflects my refined personality, my unique preferences — figures carved in porcelain, marble, sandalwood — the beauty of the female body, the virility of the male; the wonder, the mystery of exotic love, captured forever in ivory, ebony, alabaster.

"Come and sit down," I say, taking off my coat, moving toward the bed. She is staring at a batik on the opposite wall; the god Krishna entwined with Radha, an amazing feat of both artistic achievement and sexual.

"Come," I say, but instead she goes slowly across the room to my bookshelves, stands with her back to me, reading the titles. "Boccaccio," she says, "the Marquis de Sade" — she turns quickly; dark, frightened eyes. I shrug, sip brandy. "I have certain tastes —" I smile suavely.

She looks toward the door and I move, place myself between her and it. She turns back to the shelves. "What are these?"

I come up behind her, look at her narrow shoulders, her small frame — a too-strong grasp might break it — sip my brandy. She is looking at my bird collection.

"Birds from foreign countries," I say. "Beautiful, exotic birds such as you'll never see in London."

She stares at the small, bright, stuffed creatures in the glass domes; puts her fingers against her mouth.

"Beautiful, aren't they?" I say.

She turns from the birds, looks around the room. "It's — it's like a museum!" she says, her eyes huge. I smile at her awkwardness. "It's a treasure-house, my dear. Do you know Keats's poem "Ode to a Grecian Urn"? Do you know that one? 'A thing of beauty is a joy forever,' " I tell her, "according to the poet, and I agree. But the only way to retain, capture beauty, is to fix it."

She thinks about this, looking at each object in the room. "I'm not sure —" she says.

"About what?" I ask her, tipping back on my heels, holding the glass lightly, raising my eyebrows at her, amused, confident.

"I'm not sure your concept of beauty is correct."

I feel a spark of anger, but control it. What does she know? Consider her background, her age, her experience with — I forget his name. Besides, the brandy has warmed, mellowed me. I even feel the beginning of a very slight attraction, so I say, "Look, make yourself comfortable" — I gesture with my glass toward the sofa bed. "Take off your shoes, drink some wine, listen to the music, relax. I'll just be a minute."

I cross to my dressing room. At the door I turn, say to her, "Please relax. You've been through a difficult time. I'm sure you're very confused." Her eyes cloud over. I smile to myself, go in, close the door.

While I am changing it occurs to me that she might decide to leave. My room may have been too much for her. It has affected her differently from my other girls. They were all city girls with — young though they were — a certain chic. And the thought of finding her gone, finding myself with nothing to look forward to on a Saturday night, greatly increases her attraction. I hurry out of my shirt, into my black velvet, gold-embroidered smoking jacket. When I come back she is sitting on the edge of the bed, holding her glass in both hands, staring at her feet. She has taken off her shoes.

She looks up at me, is surprised by my appearance. (I am sure what's-his-name's style of dress, his method of seduction, are a world away from mine — he, a subhuman Welshman, I, a man of the world.) I smile, turn off the main light, put on a little red-shaded lamp near the bed. The damask glows like liquid gold, the tigers' eyes leap to life. She puts her hand over her mouth, giggles. She really *is* very nervous. I pour myself another brandy and sit down beside her.

"Where did you get all these things?" she asks me.

I shrug. "From all the countries of the world. I've been to every one of 'em — almost."

She looks impressed, takes a cigarette from her bag, draws a hand-painted Chinese dish toward her.

"Not that!" I say sharply, go into the kitchen, bring her the glass ashtray I keep for guests.

"You're very particular," she says.

"Yes," I say, looking at her, "usually."

She draws on the cigarette twice, sips the wine. I try to set my mind to seducing her but something — Firstly, my attraction, now that I see she is staying, really *is* very lukewarm. But there's something else. Is it the ghost of her runaway lover hovering over us? No, I could soon oust him. I look at her closely. Her dark hair, in the lamplight, is very fine, soft as a bird's wing. Her face is pale as one of my ivory statues, delicate as porcelain. Her body — rounded shoulders wilting from lack of strength — I can't actually *see* her bones protrude, but I know they do, just under the thin material of her dress. There is something about her that prevents my making the usual advances. I suppose it is merely that I don't like breakable girls.

"How did you come to travel so much?" she asks me.

We sit side by side on the bed like brother and sister, or friends.

"As a child I travelled with my parents," I say, looking into my brandy. "My father—my father was an ambassador for many years."

"Really!" She turns her large eyes on me, looks doubtful.

"How did you end up in London?" she tests me.

"I got tired of my work," I say, "and London seemed impersonal — and far away."

Normally, I do not encourage questions, conversation from my girls. *Normally*, by this time on a Saturday night my relationship with my female companion has progressed beyond words. But this is a unique situation, and to prevent her from asking, "Far away from where?" (or what?), I say, "I was a merchant seaman for a while."

"Oh, that's strange," she says.

"May I ask why?" My voice is cool. She makes an apologetic gesture with her cigarette. I watch the ash on the end, look pointedly toward the ashtray I have provided for her.

"You don't look like one," she says.

"I may not be built like a bull," I snap, thinking of her Welshman, "but I assure you, I'm as strong as the next man."

"You look delicate," she says.

I make a derisive sound, frown at my brandy, drink some. As I said, what does she know? I could not have lived the life I have if I were delicate.

"And also," she says, "I thought ambassadors' sons — well, I didn't think they became merchant seamen."

"Ambassadors' sons may become whatever they please," I say, "and, anyway, I broke with my family before that."

"Oh, I'm sorry," she says, and looks it.

"Don't be," I say, pouring more wine, brandy. "It was a relief for everyone."

"I shouldn't be so inquisitive."

"No," I say, handing her the glass, "you shouldn't. Curiosity ruins friendship."

She looks at me a long moment but finds nothing in my face, bends her head to light another cigarette. I get up, sighing, go to my mahogany roll-top desk, take a bundle of joss sticks from the drawer, place some in the incense burner and light them. The room is filled with scents of rose, jasmine, lavender.

"My smoking bothers you," she says. I shrug. If that were all!

"Thinking about what you said —"

"What was that?" I say. I don't go back to sit with her. I feel restless — not my usual Saturday night mood at all — I wander about the room, fingering my treasures, rearranging some.

"That curiosity ruins friendship. Perhaps that was part of it, with Gareth."

Ah, yes, Gareth — that's his name!

"I like to know where I stand with people," she says, "but perhaps one expects too much. One should allow for differences, I suppose."

"Yes, quite," I say shortly. She's obsessed with this Gareth, and it doesn't improve my frame of mind — or the state of my body.

"What's the matter?" she says, watching me finger a statue. I see what I am doing, put my Venus down abruptly.

"Look," I say, turning on her, "don't you know that one doesn't discuss past affairs with — with a new — a potential — It just isn't done!"

"I didn't know you were thinking of me in that way," she says simply. She puts out her cigarette, sets down her glass, folds her hands in her lap — a girl ready for her first communion, only it isn't, obviously.

I clench my fists, stride over to stand in front of her. She looks up at me, quite calm.

"Exactly what do you expect?" I ask her.

She raises her shoulders. "Nothing."

"Why did you come home with me?"

"I felt lonely," she says, "and so did you. I thought we'd talk, and maybe —" I burst out laughing. "Me?" I say, pointing at my chest. "*Me*, lonely? That's very funny."

She looks round the room, back to me. "Why don't you sit down?" she says quietly, and I do, because all this is exhausting.

"If you want to make love —" she begins, and I glare at her, totally put off. I can't stand women who throw themselves at me. As I said, a challenge, a little resistance, mystery.

"I haven't the least inclination," I say, and she looks relieved. "Then may I have something to eat?"

"You should have eaten your dinner," I tell her, "but come into the kitchen."

She sits on a stool at my table while I bring things from the fridge, make sandwiches. She smokes, and she talks. It's Gareth again. I am too discouraged, worn out, to stop her. I think that after the sandwiches she can do what she likes, I'm going to sleep. The fact is — to be blunt — I am not stirred by her, and this Saturday is a write-off. I've accepted it.

"You see," she says, watching me cut bread, "I believe in commitment, don't you? I believe a relationship involves commitment."

"No, I don't believe that," I say, slicing ham, cheese.

"Neither did Gareth, I realize, but he didn't say so. You're more honest than he was."

"I daresay." I think, Welshmen! I think, why did I bring her here? Instinct, I think, always trust instinct!

"Actually," she says, reaching out for a piece of cheese, "he wasn't very honest at all. Actually," she stares at the cheese, "I think he used me."

I look at her, think of something, say, "Go on." I wave the knife carelessly. "Talk about it if you want."

"It helps," she says. I watch her eat. She has small, white teeth — a small creature. Something catches me. I sip brandy, go on with the sandwiches.

"Your kitchen is quite different from — that other room." Her eyes take in everything; the bright enamel cooking pots hanging on the wall, the plants in the window, the scrubbed counters, shining stove. "You like to cook, don't you?"

"Why not?" I say. "It's useful to know how, when one —"

"Lives alone?" She stares at me.

"That's how I like it," I say. I bring two plates, pass her one, sit down across the table.

She picks up a sandwich. "But since we broke up — since he *left* me — I've been wondering."

"What?" I say irritably. I find it annoying, her habit of assuming I keep track of all she has said.

"If I was right — about commitment in a relationship."

"You weren't," I say.

"I should have left him free."

"It doesn't make much difference, does it?" I sigh, "since he went, in any case. It wouldn't have mattered, either way."

"Well, you know," she says, "I've thought about that, too. Some people can't make commitments. Maybe they're afraid — been hurt, do you think?" She puts down her sandwich, presses her hands to her chin. "I'm afraid that will happen to me."

I stop eating, put my hand over my mouth, look at her. She smiles at me. "That's why I talk so much."

"Sometimes," I say, not smiling back, "people simply prefer to be independent — as you just said, free. One can't make a commitment and stay free."

"I'm not sure one can't," she tells me.

I find I'm not hungry. I get up, take my plate to the sink, rinse it. "I'm going to bed," I say. "Good-night."

"What about me?" she says, and I say, "You do what you like. You're welcome to stay — there's room enough — and I suppose you'll have to, since you won't get home tonight. But don't worry," I add, my hand on the doorknob, "I won't harm you."

"I know you won't," she says, smiling.

I go into my dressing room, put on my maroon silk pyjamas, get into the sofa bed, turn off the light, lie in the darkness watching the light under the kitchen door. I hear her strike a match, think of fires. In the dark room my alabaster, ivory figures gleam like small ghosts. A train passes. The boat-trains go past here; Dover, Calais, points of embarkation for foreign places — Europe, the Near, the Far East. The train whistles. I know I can't sleep.

She turns off the light, comes out of the kitchen. I don't hear her cross the room. She lies down beside me.

"Do you mind?"

I say, "No. Did you put out your cigarette?"

In the darkness she laughs. In the black room full of small ghosts she reaches out, puts her hand on my arm. Her touch shocks me. Her hand is warm, and not at all weak. Her fingers, curling around me, ask a response. I turn to her, she moves closer, into the space of my arm.

"Do you know," she whispers, "that you frightened me, at first?"

"Yet you came with me."

"Because I didn't know what else to do — and it didn't seem to matter much."

"And now I *don't* frighten you?"

"Not at all."

"Good," I say, "then we can go to sleep."

She does, very quickly, but I stay awake through two more trains, see the room streaked with grey light. She is lying in my arm, her body against me, and I don't want her at all, but I don't mind that she is there as the trains whistle past, the dawn comes.

When I wake rain is beating on the windows, and she is gone. I sit up. The dull light makes my room look pale, overcrowded, and empty. "Gwyn," I say, and from the kitchen she calls, "Making breakfast. It's my turn."

I smile, shake my head. As if I could be rid of her that easily! She comes to the kitchen door in her creased white dress, a frying pan in her hand. "Eggs," she says, holding it out to me, "but I'm not good at it." I laugh, go toward her.

She stays with me that Sunday. It rains all day, and we don't go out. We listen to music, and we talk — she does, mostly. Toward midafternoon I make love to her. Perhaps to stop her talk, close her eyes, I don't remember, but I recall that it was good for a first time, and considering that she inhibited me from my usual variations, techniques — not that she said anything — my conviction of her fragility, I suppose.

When it is getting dark outside the window and I reach across her to turn on the lamp, she says, "I should go."

"Why?" I say, surprising myself.

She is surprised too. "Don't you want me to?"

Very quickly I tell her to please herself, but I say there is a very good Indian restaurant down the road where I usually eat Sunday evenings, and she might like to try it with me. She says, "I have to go to work in the morning, but I could catch the first tube."

You wonder, my friend, dear tourist, why I hang on to this girl after all I have said about my criterion of beauty being blonde, shapely — of my aversion to her type, hatred for her nation. I wondered myself, but I think on that Sunday it was three things: Firstly, she had not been at all bad in the lovemaking, not gauche or awkward as she was in other things (I think, especially, of her eternal questioning); secondly, she hadn't mentioned her ex-lover, her Gareth, all day; and thirdly, there was a week to get through until Saturday. At the time I thought it reasonable to keep her a week.

In the restaurant, seated at a snug corner table, drinking tea, watching the rain pelt the pavements, the miserable people under umbrellas; feeling warm and protected by the pungent aromas, the hot food, the wine, the attentive waiters, I find *myself* becoming talkative. I tell her about some of my experiences as a seaman, describe some of the places I have seen, and she is a delighted listener. I tell her of the Street of Cages in Bombay, how beautiful, how lost the women are; I describe the marketplaces of North Africa where one may buy anything, even a child. I describe the exciting shapes of countries as one approaches them from the sea; tell her of the deserts, the jungles, empty spaces in their interiors.

"Why did you go so far from home in the first place?" she asks me. "To get away," I say, and she puts her hand on my arm, says, "I see." I stop, but she presses my arm, says, "Go on. I like to listen. I like you to talk to me." And if she weren't Welsh, and didn't smoke, I believe I would actually like her.

And I think, when you've made love with someone there's a kind of kinship — though I've never thought this before. And you know, although there are several baby blondes in the place I hardly notice them. I notice, but nothing more. I'm too busy talking. It's a strange but not unpleasant evening.

We walk home. It is raining harder than ever and her dress is soaked. She takes it off and I make love to her again — even put in a few variations — which she likes.

"Did Gareth do any of that?" I say afterwards. She says, leaning on her elbow on the pillow, smiling down at me, "I think he lacked imagination. There was a lot he lacked, when I think of it," and I like the tone she assumes.

Next morning she is gone, and I remember she had to catch the first tube, go to work. Well, I think, that's that. I tidy the flat, dust my treasures, open all the windows to clear the air of smoke. The rain has stopped, a watery sun shines, the park looks green. I prepare couscous for dinner, go out for a walk. I believe I walked half across London that day. I think I went into the National Gallery, looked at the pictures. I think I looked at *Hero and Leander*. Yes, I remember, I walked down Piccadilly, stood across the road from the Café. But it was closed, of course, and didn't look the same, none of the magic, the promise it holds after dark.

I came home around six, exhausted, put the couscous on to heat. I don't remember at all what I was thinking, except, maybe, that I had walked from Earl's Court to Earl's Court again. I put on some music, am dropping off to sleep when the doorbell rings, and there she is, in black stockings, tweed jumper, hair pulled back, a big, black briefcase under her frail arm.

"What are you?" I ask, incredulous.

"A schoolteacher," she says, coming in, "and I've come straight from school — brought all my marking with me." She throws the case onto my velvet chair, scratching the velvet.

"Charming," I say. "I suppose you haven't eaten?"

"Oh — no."

After the couscous we sit at the kitchen table. She piles up exercise books, takes a red pen and begins to make checks, crosses. I sit opposite her with my brandy.

"Can you talk while you do that?"

"I *want* to talk to you," she says, clicking her tongue, shaking her head at a child's mistake. "I've been thinking some more about commitment — on the train going home, and coming here."

I groan.

"I was thinking," she says, making a cross against childish handwriting, putting in a correction, "it's not something one can demand, but it's not something one can run away from, either. I demanded it — Gareth ran away from it" — Gareth again! — "both of us were wrong."

"Very likely," I say. "It sounds like a very misguided affair from the beginning. Welsh people should avoid Welsh people, as should everyone else." I try to make light of it, but she persists. "What do *you* think?" she asks, pointing at me with her pen. I have a vision of her in the classroom, tyrannizing children with her "What do you thinks?"

"I don't think in terms of commitment," I say. "As I told you, I prefer to be independent — keep to myself."

She looks at me, is going to say something, says something else instead. I know because her expression changes.

"Why do you hate the Welsh?"

"Do you really want to know?"

"Yes."

I set down my glass, lean toward her. "Because they're an uncouth nation — they have no refinement — no culture, no art."

She smiles at me, not hurt. "Do you like the English?"

"Not much, but they're not as bad as the Welsh."

"Maybe," she says, making checks, crosses, "maybe you persuade yourself you hate people as a defence — especially people who appear to have characteristics that might threaten you." She glances up at me, looks down again.

I pick up my glass too quickly, spilling brandy. "Would you care to explain that?" I say, very coldly. I am controlling anger. She has no right! I met her only the day before yesterday.

"People think of the Welsh as passionate, impetuous, emotional —"

"Lacking self-control — uncivilized," I finish for her.

"Exactly," she says, intent on her books, "uncivilized — not hiding emotions!"

"Look," I say, "have you come here just to mark books, or was there something else?"

She closes the book, caps the pen. "We can make love if you like."

"It would be better than have you lecture me," I say, and, as we walk into the other room, I add, "You're certainly different from my first impression."

"So are you."

"I don't see that," I say.

•

She comes every day that week, stays every night, and I discover she has other exasperating habits, besides her nonstop talking, questioning. For example: I like to go to sleep after lovemaking, but she keeps me awake, stroking my hair, whispering to me. The first time she does this I tell her, "Don't stroke me. I'm not a child," but she pays no attention, and I have to put up with it.

Another thing she does is lead me into saying things I never intended — personal things — things one doesn't normally tell. One night we are lying together listening to the trains and she is

talking about her mother, in terms of her mother's commitment
— "to her family," she says, "to all of us children. She cooked,
cleaned, washed for us; took us on outings to the park, the sea;
read to us, loved us — everything was for us."

"She sounds wonderful," I say. My voice sounds nasty, as though
I don't mean it.

"Yes, wonderful," she says, stroking my hair, "but was it right?
What I mean is, she made no commitment to herself."

"She did," I say. "She committed herself to look after you."

"Yes," she insists, "but what was it in the end, for her? What did
she get out of it, really? All this worries me. I feel as if my mother
only had half a life. That's terrible!" Her voice, in the darkness,
sounds as though she will soon cry, and I stroke her back, only to
avoid this embarrassment.

"And the same with Gareth," she says suddenly, as if a light has
come on inside her head. "The same with me!"

I'm not sure what she means. I say, "Well, my mother wasn't at
all like yours. She had a very *full* life. She committed herself to life,
you might say."

"Tell me about her," she says, calmer, quietly. I think of my
mother for the first time in an age. You see, don't you, what this
girl is doing to me?

"She was very beautiful," I say, "and, as an ambassador's wife,
very busy indeed. Always travelling, entertaining — a *very* full
life."

"What about you?" she asks. Her voice, very small, is like a match
struck in the dark room.

"Me? Well, at first I went along with her — with them — of
course. I could tell you about Christmas celebrations in ten different countries —"

"Tell me."

"— if I remembered any of them."

"It's funny," she says, "when you think about your childhood,
the things you remember are not the things that seemed important
at the time. I mean, I can hardly remember my first day at school,
can you?"

"Oh, yes," I say. "I remember as though it were yesterday."

"Tell me."

I am going to say no — after all, why drag up the past? — but
one of her thin hands is stroking my hair, the other clasps my own,
presses my fingers, and it is dark. I think, well, why not?

"I was five," I say, "and going away to school — boarding school. I remember my mother came to the station with me, put me on the train, care of the guard. There were lots of boys, and lots of mothers, a lot of kissing and crying going on — so embarrassing, little boys and their mothers. But my mother wasn't like that. She knew that tears, recriminations, are pointless — you do what you must. I think, even at five, I knew that too. We were an ambassador's family." I stop. "Go on," she whispers. "What did your mother do? What did she say?"

"She looked so lovely that morning — it was January — we lived in Geneva then. There was snow everywhere, and she was wearing a coat that had a big collar of silver fur. I remember the collar because it set off her dark hair, and because, when she bent down, put her hand on my head, I put my face into the fur and it was like a great warm wrap coming round me, shutting out the snow, the train, the boys and their mothers. I wanted to stay there forever, her hand on my head, her perfume, all that soft, silver fur —"

"Like Kaye and the Snow Queen," she says.

"What?" I say, the image fading.

"Oh, just a story my mother used to tell us. What happened then?"

"Then," I say, "my mother held me in front of her, told me about being brave, being good, being a credit to my father and her. She explained how things had to be a certain way in an ambassador's family. Then she said she'd see me in June, kissed me (I think) and went away."

She is silent a long time, although her hands communicate with me. At last she says, "What did you think? How did you feel?"

"I don't remember," I say, and then, "probably I thought that, like she said, that was how things had to be. Yes, probably that's what I decided. What stands out in your mind, about your childhood?" I ask, only because I want to change the subject. Recalling the snow-banked station, the grey Swiss train — the steps to the carriages were high, I remember — makes my mind, my body cold.

"Like I said," she begins, "it isn't big things. All the major incidents, going to school the first time, my first dance, going to college — all those things seem to merge into —"

"Into what?"

"Well, what I really remember clearly are things like coming into the house on a cold day, after school or playing outside, and my mother making supper, setting the table, the house full of good smells because she has been baking. I remember the way she looks glad to see me, tells me to call my brothers because it's getting dark outside.

"I remember the stories, all of us sitting around her, my eldest brother saying, 'I'm not listening tonight. I'm too old for stories about giants and witches and fairies.' And my mother just smiling, saying, 'I hope you'll never be too old for that!' And his coming, after all, to sit with us, and listening as hard as we. But once I remember —" She holds my hand tighter. "Yes?" I prompt.

"Once — one day toward winter — I'm sitting by the fire, in my mother's chair, with one of her books — it has lots of pictures — and she is washing clothes in a big, wooden tub by the window, scrubbing them on a board. The noise of the scrubbing is like a tune in my head, but it stops suddenly. I look up and she is staring out of the window. 'Look, Gwyn,' she says, 'all the birds are flying away.' I don't know why I remember that especially," she says.

"What about your father?" I ask her. "You never mention him."

"My father," she says, "was a coal miner, and a dreamer. Those are difficult things to reconcile, but he managed it after a fashion. He managed it over beers at the Miners' Club, giving his pals his dreams in return for beer. My father," she says in a tight voice, "didn't exist, except in dreams."

"We come from very different backgrounds," I tell her.

"Yes," she agrees, "but does it matter? It's the same in the end, isn't it? What we want, what we need — what we give each other."

"I'm not a giver," I warn her, "I'm a collector — as you see."

And all this talking has made me want her. "I want to make love to you," I say. "That's the first time you've admitted it," she says, and I think she is smiling at me. As I take off her clothes, feel her warm body, I say, "There is a train that goes right across Russia, from Moscow to the Black Sea."

"Is there?" She reaches her arm up behind my head to draw me closer to her.

"You are on it for days. It becomes like your home, almost. You get to know the guards, the passengers, the dining-car attendants. Everyone greets you when you go in to meals. You play chess with an old man who becomes your favorite uncle; flirt with a girl who becomes your wife. Then, you reach your destination."

"Take me on that train!" she says, and I catch her mood, say, "I will! We'll have long breakfasts, long dinners, as the steppes slide past the windows. We'll wave to peasants, cossacks on horseback. We'll play endless games of chess, you can smoke endless cigarettes —" She laughs. "And at night," I say, bringing her body against mine, "I'll wrap you in furs to keep out the Russian cold — the fur of wolves, white bears —"

"And then we'll reach our destination," she says, and stops my talk by kissing me.

•

On Friday evening when she comes she asks to see a photo of my mother. I say I don't have one, but she tells me, "You must have." So I look, and find it, at the back of the roll-top desk, amongst bundles of old letters. It is shabby, creased, but one can see her plainly enough. It was taken at Beirut airport — the plane is in the background. She is waving — to me, perhaps. Gwyn smoothes out the creases, studies my mother's face. "Why," she says, "your mother looks like me!"

I laugh, and she looks embarrassed. "Oh, she's very beautiful," she says quickly. "I didn't mean that. She's the same physical type, that's what I mean."

I look at the photograph over her shoulder, though I hadn't intended it.

"Small, dark, thin," she says.

"Fragile," I say, "I believe that's the term. Breakable," I say.

"What happened to her?" she asks me.

"She was handled by too many people," I tell her. "She was broken, finally." I laugh, take the photo from her, push it back into the desk. "Though whether by my father, or some other person, I don't know. I never knew her that well." I close the desk, stand with my back to Gwyn. She says nothing, and so, after a moment, I turn to face her, my hands on my hips. "I've had enough of this, actually," I tell her. "All these long, vague talks about parents, lovers, commitments — what do they resolve, in the end? Tomorrow," I say, not giving her a chance to answer, "is Saturday. I can't see you."

"All right," she says, lighting a cigarette. "Do you want to see me again?"

"I really don't think there's much point," I say. "We're not — We're too different."

She smiles at me brightly. "Well, if this is our last talk, may I tell you my conclusions?"

"On commitments?" I smile, in spite of myself. "Since it's the last time I shall hear it, go ahead."

"I think," she says, assuming her serious, schoolteacher's face, "that it's two things, basically. First, commitment to oneself — to one's beliefs — ideals, if you like —" She pauses, searches my face for my reaction. My face gives nothing away. "Go on," I tell her.

"Not only that, but one must decide, if possible, what one is going to do for oneself — a kind of fulfillment that does not depend on other people." She pauses. "Continue," I say.

"And when one has sorted that out, one can, I believe, make commitments to others — to family, friends" — she hesitates — "lovers. One really can't without the first step — oh, and there's a third thing!"

"Yes?"

"Which I learned from Gareth — and from you."

"Me? What did you learn from me?"

"That it doesn't need to be reciprocal — it can be, and probably that's wonderful — but it doesn't have to be."

"How do you mean?" I walk to the table, pour some brandy, hold up the wine bottle, she shakes her head. I look at Radha and Krishna, committed to a very difficult, problem-fraught relationship — a mortal and a deity!

"I mean," she says, "that the happiness one gets from other people should come from making commitments, not demanding them. I believe it can, if everything else is intact."

"If everything else is intact," I repeat. I look at the joy on the face of Radha. When I turn back Gwyn is standing up.

"You're going?"

"I can still catch the last train."

"I'll walk to the station with you," I say, but she shakes her head. "Don't bother. I've liked it," she says, smiling. "Thank you."

"Thank *you*," I reciprocate, half expecting her to shake my hand. "Take care," she says, opens the door, and is gone.

"Gwyn," I say, to the closed door.

I think about going after her, but realize in time the complications that would involve for an independent person like myself. Instead I cross to the window, watch her walk down the street. She walks firmly enough. I wonder why I thought her frail. Appearances. How they deceive!

I don't sleep well that night — or, at least, I dream — of trains, the Circle line, the train to the Black Sea; faces on trains; the Green Dragon; my mother boarding a plane for the Orient; Maxime's, a flying Maxime's, "all aboard for a journey to the past. One-way ticket holders only, please!" The Café de Paris hurtling through London; the stewardesses are all blonde, the pilot is Celia, and her face cracks into a malicious, mindless grin. The blonde stewardesses scream — the passenger next to me — she is dark — cries, "Jump! Jump for your life! Throw yourself to the sea!"

I wake in a sweat, with travelling, getting out, on my mind. As I make breakfast, tidy the flat, I decide I've seen enough of London, London enough of me. Twenty years! I can't believe it. If ever the time was ripe — Yes, I'll move on. I'll sell my things, I decide, impetuous, most unlike me. I'll get up enough money for a long trip. I may go back to sea. But, it *is* Saturday, and I can't leave at once. I have to make plans, decide on a destination. I think, once more — just once more, for old time's sake — to the Café de Paris.

I dress up, drink more brandy than usual, get myself a little drunk for the occasion, and set off for the farewell scene.

But on my way, on the tube, watching the blank faces of the Saturday night crowds, I decide no, I am not going in. Best a clean break, now I've made up my mind. I will simply walk past, on the other side of the road; salute her, because she has meant something to me.

So I get off the tube at Piccadilly, follow the crowds up into the night, stop at the bar of the Regent's Palace for a couple more brandies — amazing how nervous I feel! — then down Shaftesbury Avenue, and when I come directly opposite the Café I stop, press my fingers to my lips, address her:

"Hey there, old Café, old friend! Procuress of young virgins, old whore of mine! We've lain together too long, my love," I tell the winking, beckoning neon sign. "There isn't a trick either of us can pull the other doesn't anticipate. It's time to kiss and say goodbye!"

But as I turn to go back, the lighted doorway, the glimpse of marble, red carpet, arrests me. There's life in her yet, I think. She may not be what she was, but she's seductive still. So I turn back, and I say, "Don't worry, sweetheart, you're not past it yet. Older women have something — a certain look, a knowledge — young girls simply don't have. Don't you worry," I say, "there's many a young buck will pass between your doors before you close them finally." She winks at me.

I start to leave again, but I think, "Perhaps Gwyn is in there," and I'd like to say good-bye to her, too. I didn't say it properly, last night. I cross the road, salute Celia, go in.

"You're late," Michael tells me. "You missed the girls coming in."

I shrug, order brandy.

"I see you soon tired of your little mouse," he says.

"What?" I lift my head sharply.

Michael sneers at me. "She was here, looking around. For you?"

"Where is she?" I say, leaning toward him.

He looks surprised. "Well, she left — as I say, you're late. There are others, though. What do you say to that pair over by the stage? Not bad. Shall we make up a foursome tonight?"

"Go ahead," I tell him, "I'm not in the mood."

He raises his eyebrows. "What did she do to you," he says nastily, "the little mouse?"

I don't answer him. I finish my brandy quickly and, lightheaded now, go down to the dance floor. I look among the dancers in case Michael is mistaken and she is still there. But she's not. I look up at the orb, catch myself in it, a single figure among the couples; a hundred, no, I swear, a thousand of me; tiny, perfect creatures of light and glorious colour, standing quite still, looking up to eternity.

I turn and I leave. I swear, as I say good-night to Celia (who looks only faintly surprised), that I will not come back; not to the Café, not to Maxime's, not to London.

Ah, dear tourist, you fidget, you fret, glance at your watch. Almost eleven, is it? Well, sit, sit, the girls will soon come in, and my tale's almost finished. "Why, then," you must be asking yourself, "is he still hanging about, one year later, if he made that decision a year ago?" My friend, you are young! Old habits die hard; old places, old friends, lay claims on us. Commitment, my friend! And, I must admit, since it seems I am telling all, I must admit it did occur to me she might come here again. But, as you see, she didn't — and so, I *am* going soon. Don't look like that. I am! I'll get up one fine morning, and go. I feel it! Why, I felt it as a sign, an omen, when I befriended you earlier this evening. I've never done that before — never just walked up to someone and offered my friendship, just like that.

You *must* go? Why? The night is young, and I really feel like talking. Ah, quite, you're a tourist. You have to make an early start. So have I, for all I know! I've been selling my treasures, bit by bit, now that the legacy's finally gone. When the last one is sold — *that's* when I'll go! There, I've decided — you helped me to it. Yes, you did! You're my first commitment in years, if you don't count — but you can't count a week's acquaintance! Only I don't dismiss it, either. She touched me — reached out and touched me in the dark — that girl.

Well, well, all right, go if you must. I raise my glass, salute you. No, we shan't meet again. I won't be here next time. So, *arrivederci, bon voyage,* good luck! Remember that in old, disappointing London I was the stranger who befriended you, showed you sights you might never have seen. Remember me!

ALVIN GREENBERG

The Power of Language Is Such That Even a Single Word Taken Truly to Heart Can Change Everything

(FROM STORYQUARTERLY)

I

NO ONE LEFT ON the island any longer except me and the feral pigs, so you can imagine my surprise when I was out walking the main road down the center of the island this morning and found the word LOVE written in the dirt. I would not have thought the pigs were familiar with such a word, let alone able to spell it correctly. The letters, gouged deep in the sandy roadbed and stretching large, from one side of the road to the other, looked at first like the usual markings left by the pigs in their regular foraging as they root up the earth for mast, which was why I failed to notice anything out of the ordinary right off and simply kept on along my morning stroll. I must have gone on another hundred yards or so before I suddenly realized I had seen something quite remarkable. I quickly retraced my steps.

By the time I got back to the house, quite certain after a careful examination of the markings in the road that I had indeed seen what I had seen, it occurred to me that there were, of course, at least two other possible explanations for this phenomenon. But I was positive, first of all, that there had not been, for some months now, another human being on the island besides myself. There had never been many of us here to begin with, a few visitors like myself, come to work in the big house for the sake of the privacy this island retreat offered, and a dozen or so permanent residents, the ones who made it possible for the rest of us to stay and work here. And the visitors, myself excepted, had all been whisked away to the mainland by boat within days of the time it was realized that the island was adrift and moving slowly away from the Georgia coast and out into the Atlantic. I had some difficulty convincing them to let me stay on, but, after all, there was no immediate danger apparent — the island was merely drifting, not sinking, if anything it seemed to have become lighter for having forsaken its roots and to have risen another foot or so above sea level — and other boats would soon be departing and I did have some small influence here.

The permanent residents, naturally, stayed on somewhat longer. This was where their homes were, after all, where many of them had lived most of their lives. Where would they go now? But soon enough, within days, in fact, as we all began to realize that the island was heading steadily out to sea and that the mainland was falling away on the horizon with surprising rapidity, they too agreed to leave, gathering such possessions as could easily be loaded on the two remaining boats and hurrying to the dock, for it was late afternoon already when the mass decision was made, and many were overtaken by the sudden fear that by sunrise the next day the mainland would be out of sight altogether. It was a reasonable fear, for none of them had ever been out of sight of the mainland before; and it was also reasonable that in their anxiety they should not at first have remembered that I was still on the island. No doubt the minute they realized it, even in the midst of loading the boats, they hurried back to the house; but by then I was gone, safely off by myself wandering about the far end of the island, where they would never have time to search for me before darkness fell. All there was for them to find was my brief note, explaining my decision to remain on the island, inasmuch as such a decision, which was bound to seem a bit bizarre under the circumstances even to the most rational reader, could be explained. I was grateful when I returned to the big house the next morning — and the mainland was indeed no longer visible by then — to find that they had at least left my belongings, for I could see that someone had begun to pack my suitcase and then abandoned that task, unfinished, in the middle of the room. I also appreciated the note the Director had left, promising to return for me in a day or so, when I had had more time to reconsider my foolhardy decision. It is to his credit that he did indeed come back the following day, and that Coast Guard helicopters searched the island every few days for a couple of weeks after that, but thanks to his warning I had found myself a secure hiding place by then.

So I was quite certain that there was not another human being on the island who could have written that word. I had soon gone through all the same homes of the permanent residents and assured myself that no one had remained behind, though I was pleased to see that they had left their pantries well stocked. It is possible, of course, that someone else has arrived on the island since those days of exodus, but why would I not have seen such a person by now? Surely whoever it was would have come to the main house by now, in search of food — for I soon moved all the supplies to the big pantry here — or shelter from the frequent rain. Surely I would have seen such a new visitor by now, even someone washed ashore from a shipwreck or someone who had put into one of the coves in a small boat, for I wander the island from end to end, walk the beaches, explore all its inner recesses, and I have never yet seen another footprint but my own. And this is no place for small boats any longer, for the island rides the high seas now.

No, there is no one else but me on this island now, of that I am quite sure, and I confine my writing to these sheets of white paper and I do my writing solely on this small portable typewriter that I brought with me. And if I were to take to scrawling letters in the sand, I do not think I would have written what I found written there. But it did occur to me, of course, that there was another possible explanation: namely, that the combination of those four letters in the sand, into that one word, was fortuitous, a chance conglomeration of accidental lines gouged in the road by the pigs in their ordinary search for food, as meaningless as any of the irregular markings they leave scattered across the forest floor, however many of them seem vaguely to resemble an X or a T or a V or an L. All through the daylight hours the pigs course the island, pushing their snouts through the sandy soil in their hunger for roots and acorns, and, as many pigs as there are here, for they breed freely, untroubled by natural enemies and held in check only by the island's limited food supply, it was inevitable that some of their scratchings in the earth should, purely by chance, look not unlike some of the scratchings we humans make.

Still, the firmness and clarity of those letters seems very convincing to me, the O in particular, nearly perfect in its roundness and therefore most unlikely to be merely the chance by-product of the search for food. And the E, what about the E, could you really expect a complex letter like that E to occur just by accident? And then of course the biggest question of all, the question of the whole word itself, what were the odds on that? There is, of course, the old gang-of-monkeys explanation, and I suppose that cannot entirely be put aside. But as I recall, the monkeys in that theory are always given typewriters to work on; they do not actually have to make the letters, only to strike the keys and let the words take their accidental shapes, to let some of the ready-made letters fall by chance into the patterns we call words, as eventually some would do. That is just a matter of statistics, I think, just a matter of statistical theory, in fact, but what has happened here is not theory at all; it is not statistics, there was no bunch of non-word conglomerations of letters, false starts as it were, with here or there an actual word occurring in their midst; here there was just a single word, just a single reality: LOVE.

II

I am fairly certain that I know now which pig is teaching them to write. Twice already, in the week since I first saw that word in the road, I have come across sizable groups of pigs engaged in what appear to be very unusual activities, for pigs at least, and one sow seemed to be the focus of their attention on both these occasions. The first time was the very next day after I had spotted that word. I had gone down the main road where I had seen it, late in the morning again, wanting another look at the word because in the course of thinking about it and trying to set down these few words of my own about it when I came back to the house the previous day, it had all begun to seem very unreal. It was no surprise to me, however, to find that no trace of the word remained. I seemed to remember that once, when I awoke in the middle of the night, I had heard it raining, and that alone would have been enough to wipe any sign of the previous day's activity from the sandy roadway. Yes, I am certain it must have rained the night before. I do not believe, though, that I would have found the word there even if I had returned at once, that very afternoon I discovered it. No, I think the pigs would have been back there before me, rooting up the evidence of their literacy as effectively as they rooted up nuts and mold, scattering with their tiny, sharp hooves the message they had written in the sand. For subsequent events have led me to conclude that the pigs do not want me to know that they are learning to read and write.

But I do know. When I passed the spot where they had left their word on the road the day before and found nothing remained, I kept on along the road for another mile or so, watching the road for signs, certain that sooner or later I would find another confirmation of my remarkable discovery of the preceeding day. Then I turned off on a seldom-used side road, overgrown with young palmettos and crisscrossed by the rotting trunks of fallen palms. Soon the road passed into a heavy stand of thick-trunked live oaks, some of the oldest on the island, I believe, some of them perhaps several hundred years old, possibly dating back to a time before there were even pigs on the island. It was there that I saw them, grouped in a clearing in the midst of the giant oaks and partially concealed from view by the heavy, gray-green curtains of Spanish moss that hung from the branches of the oaks. Even hidden as they were, however, so that I could not count them, I realized that I saw there more pigs by far than I had ever seen gathered in one place at one time on this island. Normally, I never saw more than a few at one time, or at the most a sow with half a dozen piglets nosing about in the underbrush in her vicinity, and maybe one or two other adult pigs nearby. But here there must have been several dozen, and they were not feeding; they were, so far as I could tell, simply standing there. Not for long, of course. I had stepped off the road and hidden myself behind a tree the moment I spotted them, but it was a young red pine, not really thick enough in the trunk to conceal me well, and no doubt the pigs had heard me coming. It would not surprise me to learn that they had a lookout posted back up the road. So they quickly broke ranks and scattered, as they always did when I came upon them, squealing away into the underbrush.

But not before I noticed a number of things in that strange, brief moment of silence, beginning with the fact that they were not feeding, that I had never seen even a small group of pigs just standing there like that. In addition, it seemed, though I could not tell for certain because of the trees and hanging moss that interrupted my view, that they were not just randomly standing, but that they were gathered in some kind of order. The group consisted of an inordinate number of young ones. Oh, there are always plenty of piglets on the island, two or three or even half a dozen to a sow, but here I think the ratio must have been more on the order of ten to one. Yes, I thought at once, get them started young, that's always the best way. And they were so attentive, at least for that moment before they broke ranks and scattered in all directions, that it was some time before I realized that I had been watching them so closely that I had almost missed seeing what their attention was focused on. But I had not missed her. I might have seen her only at the last moment and out of the corner of my eye; but so striking was her presence that long after they had all gone, when I had come out from behind the small pine to stand in the middle of the road and think about all I had just witnessed, I retained a clear and vivid image of her.

Not only did her height make her stand out above all the others gathered before her, but it suddenly occurred to me that I had also seen something even more unusual. For in the few seconds I had had to observe her, I had seen her take a step or two forward, and as she did so, the pig standing in front of her backed away. And I realized that never in my life, either here among the wild pigs on this island or among domestic pigs, had I ever seen a pig back up. It is simply a thing that pigs do not do, nor do most other animals, so far as I know. You can train a horse or a dog, or even a bear, to backstep, of course, but they do not do it naturally. They will sidestep, they will turn about and move away, but no, they do not back up. And yet that was just what I had seen: a pig backing up.

The presence of that regal-looking sow would have done it, of course, if anything would. She was by far the tallest pig I had seen on my several visits to the island, and she was a solid, gleaming, unblemished black, of a purity that was rare, if not hitherto unknown, among the island pigs, for their ancestry was almost as diverse as that of the American population itself. They had been brought to the island in all the wide variety of breeds that can be imagined — by French settlers and African slaves, by Spanish and

English colonists, by privateers of various nationalities, by a long
succession of determined but ill-fated pig raisers from the mainland; and it is even possible that an indigenous variety of wild boar
flourished on the island long before the Europeans arrived. But
that makes little difference now when they have all gone back to
the wild, have had the run of the island for centuries, in fact, and
bred and interbred and filled the island to the limits of the pig
population. Here and there, of course, you can see the markings
of some recognizable breed — the sharply ridged spine reminis-
cent of the razorback, or the wide black belly band of the Poland
China, or the long tusks of the wild boar — but always those traits
are so intermixed with others that the island appears a veritable
melting pot for pigs. It is possible that they know many languages,
not just English.

The second time I came across them in the midst of their studies
was on a little beach not more than a couple hundred yards from
the house. We were all so startled by meeting — I at finding them
busy at their lessons so close to the house and they, no doubt, at
my venturing out of the house so early in the morning, which was
only the product of the several sleepless nights that had followed
my previous encounter with them in the forest — that for a long
time, it may have been a full minute, none of us moved. The pigs
turned, en masse, with one exception, and stared at me as I
emerged through the palmettos onto the white sand. And I, for
my part, had ample time to examine them as they stood there, in
some sort of order, but all with their backs to the sea and facing
the big black sow. She alone, impressive, stolid, undisturbed, did
not turn to look at me, but stood tall and unmoving, and kept her
gaze firmly fixed on her pupils, until at last, with a slight nod of
her head, she dismissed them, and once again they scattered,
squealing wildly as they fled across the road and into the underbrush. As the last of them scampered off the beach, she, their
teacher, their queen, turned about and followed them. She did not
even glance in my direction. She looked once about the beach and
then she turned and walked away.

I hurried at once down to the beach where they had been assembled, but of course there was nothing to be seen. In their milling
about before they stampeded and fled, they had erased all the
signs of their studies, all the words they had painstakingly
scratched out in the sand, and once again I had no more solid

evidence of their work than in the oak grove, where their sudden departure had so churned up the covering of leaves and debris on the forest floor as to effectively erase all traces of their writing. There was nothing left to do but to return to the house, to my own writing, to set down these strange events I have witnessed before they come to seem so unreal that even I cannot believe what I have seen. I kept my eyes on the road all during the short walk back, hoping in vain for some small, further written sign. As a result I came upon the house itself so suddenly that I was quite startled, almost frightened, as if everything had altered and even the house itself, in my brief absence, had made some unexpected move.

III

Until today I was beginning to fear that perhaps I had placed too much importance upon a single word, and that word glimpsed only briefly and by chance, written in the sand and then seen no more. Many weeks have passed since the last time I saw the queen of the pigs guiding her subjects in their studies, though I can well understand how after those two previous encounters they might have found it necessary to remove their classes to farther corners of the island and to keep more careful lookouts posted. Centuries of sharing the island with humans and learning the danger such proximity has posed to their very lives would undoubtedly have bred a certain caution into their behavior. But now that the spring is well advanced and the weather much improved — it has grown so hot for this time of year, in fact, that I feel certain we must be drifting steadily south, into the tropics — I expected to find further signs of their progressing education. Not all over the island, of course, but at least here and there, in some isolated spot where perhaps with the pride of accomplishment some piglet had trotted off refusing to obliterate a word or a phrase transcribed with unprecedented grace and accuracy. That I have not come across any such further evidence — neither a misspelled word left behind in frustration by a struggling young scholar nor a sentence abandoned halfway through by the sudden flight of its writer as I stumbled accidently upon the scene of creation — I can only attribute to the shrewdness of intellect for which pigs have always been known. It makes no difference, of course; the single word is quite enough. Have we not extrapolated enormous dinosaurs from a single bone, whole species from an imprint in the clay, entire civilizations from a potshard?

Still, I always keep my eyes to the ground as I go about the island, so certain am I that further evidence of what I know is happening here will eventually come to my attention. From time to time I stop to pick up and sample the acorns and other nuts I find on the forest floor or beside the road, for I have begun to realize that even the well-stocked pantry that was left to me here will not last indefinitely. The fact is, I am growing quite tired of canned foods. For a while I relished the fresh oysters from the tidal streams. But because the island floats now upon the ocean's surface, rising and falling with the ocean's rhythms, and its tidal streams, having achieved a certain equilibrium, no longer cleanse themselves by emptying and filling twice a day, I cannot trust the oysters. I am glad I have not eaten pork for a long time. The nuts are somewhat bitter, but tasty on the whole. Recently, I have begun to supplement my diet with mushrooms, having found in the extensive library at the big house an excellent, well-illustrated guide.

By mid-morning today I had nearly filled an old coffee can with mushrooms. I am still new to this diet and afraid to eat them in the forest without bringing them back to the house to check them against their pictures and descriptions in the book. I was even wondering, as I straggled along, eyes to the ground, whether the pigs themselves might not benefit from a chance to examine that particular text, and it occurred to me that I might leave it out for their perusal, on the side porch where it would be protected from rain, perhaps along with a number of other books they might find edifying. I was not sure just what, though I felt reasonably certain they might find a dictionary a valuable asset. Perhaps some scientific texts, in the more popularized vein, for I have no evidence on the state of their mathematics. Possibly one of my own books, even if only as a sign of the sort of human who shares this island with them, some indications of the workings of his mind and language, for what could a pig be expected to make of a fiction? Though only time would enable me to discover what really interested them, I was beginning to feel, as I considered how best to make my library available to them, that given sufficient time I might indeed make a considerable contribution to their education.

Just then a sudden flash of light caught my eyes, the glitter of sunlight off the glassy calm of the ocean; I had arrived at the end of this particular road on the southwestern tip of the island — or what had originally been the southwestern tip. I had taken my shirt off some ways back and tied it about my waist, for it was the hottest day I had experienced on the island so far and an almost visible humidity hung heavily in the forest air; my pants were rolled to my knees. I had removed my shoes some time back, not very far from the house, and left them by the side of the road, my socks stuffed inside. I would have kept them on, I suppose, to walk in the forest itself, where the ground was littered with sharp-edged pine cones and broken twigs, but here on the road I enjoyed the feel of the warm sand on my bare feet. I watched the sand sift between my toes as I walked, watched, above all, for any signifi-cant-looking markings along the way, and kept my eyes totally focused on the ground before and around me so that I did not see her till I was almost on top of her.

She stood squarely in the center of the road before me, the glossy black of her skin shimmering as brightly as the sea. Every-thing about her size and stance and posture spoke of authority. She effectively blocked my route home, for on one side the road was bounded by swamp and on the other by a stretch of pine forest that I dared not risk in bare feet. But I did not want to move away from her or try to get around her; in fact, I am not sure that I could have pulled myself away if I had wanted to, so entranced was I by the power of her presence there. She gave an enormous sense of strength as she stood there, motionless, head lowered and eyes, piercing black eyes, fixed directly upon me, not ten feet away. She was assessing me — I am sure that was all there was to it — as I stood there in the middle of the road, clutching my coffee can full of mushrooms, my body gleaming with sweat, my eyes looking back into hers as she held me transfixed. Clearly she knew how to use the moment. I heard an airplane going over, high, high above, just a faint sound trailing across the silence of the island, but I couldn't seem to free myself to raise my head. I heard her make a slight scuffling sound. She was scraping the sand with her left forefoot. Now, I thought, elated, now is the moment! She has something to say to me, something to show me, and now is the time, now she will show me her command of the language. Instead, as I looked at her, as I leaned toward her, waiting, anticipating, she pawed the earth once more with her forefoot, as if to erase the message she had begun, turned about and trotted off. I could see as she moved away from me the powerful thrust of her shoulders and haunches, the imperial determination in her stride; and I could not help admiring the way she had almost spoken to me and then held back at just the last moment, with restraint, as if it were not becoming of her to do so, not just yet anyway. Just before I lost sight of her, she paused in the road and turned and glanced over her shoulder at me. Then she hurried out of sight, off the road, among the young palmettos, and I trotted down the road after her, clutching the can of mushrooms to my chest, my head swaying loosely back and forth as I scanned the ground before me. One day I know that she will come closer again, that she will speak to me.

R. E. SMITH

The Gift Horse's Mouth

(FROM THE TEXAS REVIEW)

"ARE THOSE HAWKS or vultures?"

"I think, honey," Estelle said, "those are vultures. Hawks fly alone."

I'm like a hawk, she thought, coming out here on my own. If Ed wants to come down in two weeks instead of now, fine, he can fly in. But I've had it with Houston, and I'm tired of him talking about nothing but that new building of his, and if I feel like getting some peace and quiet in the country with just Barbie, and I feel like driving, why then that's just what I'll do.

"Rio Ancho thirty-two miles, Jackson's Creek seven," Barbie read.

Estelle had thought Barbie had lost her case of the squirms after they stopped for a hamburger in New Braunfels, but now she was back to reading every sign along the road. She liked best the long, wordy signs for film development, political candidates, and gala country music weekends, which she would try to read completely before the car was past.

Estelle thought again that it was strange to name a town Rio Ancho when it was the Sangre River that cut over the limestone along the west side of town before flowing into a broad pool below the plateau on which the town was set.

"Welcome to Rio Ancho, Guest Ranch Capital of the World, Enjoy Yourself in the Beautiful Texas Hill Country," Barbie read. As they turned onto the main street, Barbie began reeling off "Circle R Trading Post, Horseshoe Bar, James Kelcy, Attorney at Law, NAPA Auto Parts" until the signs came so quickly she gave up and lapsed into silence.

A pickup truck coming toward them suddenly made a U-turn without signaling.

Estelle hit the brakes. Barbie pitched forward but awkwardly braced herself on the dash with her hands. Recovering, Barbie reached across the seat for the horn. Estelle pushed her hand away.

"Stupid old man," Barbie said. "Why don't you honk at him?"

"He may be right," Estelle said. "We're just too used to the big city. We need to calm down a little, get in tune with a slower pace. It's different out here. Besides, I'm kind of used to that. He drives the way my grandfather used to drive."

Estelle had read a condensed version of *Talking to Your Child* in one of her ladies' magazines. She didn't remember the fine points of the article, but she did recall that you don't argue with your child when the child is experiencing emotional difficulties.

"I know you feel frustrated at not being able to honk the horn," Estelle tried, "but we do things differently in the country than we do in town."

The truck turned left, again without signaling.

"He's still a stupid old man."

"I wish you had known my grandfather," Estelle went on. "Maybe you wouldn't feel that way. Some of the best times of my life were when I'd go visit him and Grandma in the summer. He'd take me with him when he went trading for cattle and horses, and he kept a horse for me to ride." Estelle became a little weepy. "In fact, he was killed driving his cattle truck."

"Ninety-seven," Barbie said, reading the time-temperature sign in front of the bank.

They stopped at the grocery store for supplies. Estelle thought it was silly of the cashier to ask for identification when she had been buying things there for years. Besides that, she was wearing her emerald ring, the big one, which should have been proof to anybody that she wasn't going to write a bad check for a few piddling groceries.

After a stop at Jed's Drive-In where Barbie had her Big Red soda, they went past the Watering Hole, now advertising cocktails, the Cedarcrest Nursing Home, and into the hilly country beyond. The Eldorado swooped across the low water bridges where families, most of them Latin, sat on bright-webbed aluminum chairs and splashed in the shallows.

Just as she rounded the bend before their turnoff, she noticed something in the road ahead. She braked and honked. Three vultures took flight with laborious indignity and glided off to wait in the weeds.

"Gross," Barbie said, looking at the armadillo crushed on the pavement.

Topping a small hill on their road, Estelle saw a truck approaching and pulled over as far as she could. The truck stopped, and both waited for the dust to settle a little before lowering their windows.

"Hello, Mr. Wilson," she began.

"Hello, Mrs. Grady," the rancher returned. He lived on the ranch beyond theirs, and for the privilege of running some of his cattle on their land, he kept an eye on their place and looked after their horses when they were gone. "Hot enough for you?" he asked.

"Certainly is warm, isn't it?" she replied. "Are the horses down?"

Wilson nodded.

"How are you getting along?" she asked.

"Can't complain," he said.

After a pause, Estelle said, "I guess we'd better be getting along. We'll see you later."

The electric window sealed out the heat and dust, and they eased down the hill. Off to the left, a deer stand stood like a sentinel tower.

The house was hot and stuffy. Estelle opened the windows and started the air conditioner to drive the heat out. She put the groceries away, turned on the water, made the beds, and then closed the windows, resealing the house.

"Well, what do you want to do?" she asked Barbie as she mixed a big pitcher of iced tea.

"I don't know," Barbie said.

"How about going riding?"

The summer before she had been so enthusiastic about riding they had bought her a horse plus a second one so somebody could ride with her.

"It's too hot."

"How about a walk, then?"

"It's too hot for that, too."

Having driven the entire morning and then some so they could enjoy the ranch, Estelle was irritated at the nebulous refusal to utilize the opportunities.

"How about a swim? That'll cool you off."

"There're snakes down there."

"I know it's different from swimming in a pool like at home," Estelle said, "but it's very safe. Let's go get our suits on."

"All right," Barbie said and heaved herself off the couch.

They drove the half mile to the river, the Eldorado bumping over the road that was little more than two tracks through the grass. One reason Estelle had argued for buying the place was that the river made a big curve as it cut around a bank and provided an ideal swimming hole. Swimming in the clear water, Estelle thought for a moment of shucking her bathing suit. As long as she was out to enjoy nature, why not be totally natural? But then she would have to explain to Barbie why she was running around naked. In the end, she undid the straps on her top when she lay down to soak up the afternoon sun.

As they drove up to the house, she noticed that the horses had come up to the fence. She stopped and they got out to pet them. The bay was the one she usually rode, while Barbie or guests not used to horses rode the old sorrel mare. Both leaned against the fence and stretched out their heads.

Estelle scratched them behind the ears while Barbie climbed onto the top rung of the fence. As Barbie talked "nice horse" language to the animals, Estelle watched a solitary hawk rising above the hilltops in wide circles. She felt cleansed by the river. The warmth of the day radiating from the rocks and earth enveloped her.

She knew how to really enjoy the land, just like that hawk she was watching. Relax and get in tune with what was around you. Don't worry what you look like. Let the days float along. In the house behind her there was no schedule, no calendar crammed with appointments. It was rejuvenating to live without demands, and she always felt more alive and fresh when she returned to Houston.

Barbie's cry jerked her out of her reverie. Barbie looked on the verge of crying and was holding the upper part of her left arm. "She bit me," she said, as if a trusted friend had suddenly hit her.

The mare shook her head slowly from side to side as if denying the accusation, but, prying Barbie's hand away, Estelle saw the large red area and the imprint of the incisors. It looked as if the mare had twisted her head as she nipped, so that the skin was pulled and broken in several spots.

Estelle weighed the seriousness of the wound and decided, "We'd better have the doctor look at it."

Barbie began to cry in earnest. "He'll give me a shot. I know he will."

"He may not. First, let's clean it up."

She drove the fifty yards to the house, where she washed the arm and bandaged it to keep Barbie from massaging dirt into it. Estelle kept her bathing suit on but threw a bright patterned shift over it and ran a comb quickly through her hair. Thank goodness for blow-dry haircuts, she thought; otherwise I'd be a fright.

Estelle drove quickly, but as they passed the city limits the digital clock in the dash indicated that it was well past closing time for offices. The doctor's office was a small brick building off the main street. Thank goodness she was observant and had noticed on an earlier trip, or they'd have had to drive all over town and really be late. As they arrived, a man in boots and checked, jean-cut slacks was coming down the steps. Estelle rushed up while Barbie climbed out of the car.

"Is the doctor still in?" she asked.

"He just left," the man said. He looked in his mid-fifties, but she really couldn't tell with the brim of his western straw pulled low on his forehead. "What's your problem?"

"A horse bit my little girl."

By this time, Barbie had come up, and the man could see her holding her arm. "Let me see," he said, and peeled back the three Band-Aids Estelle had laid over the bite.

"Better go inside," he said, straightening up.

"But you said the doctor wasn't in," Estelle said.

"He's not," the man said, "but as soon as I unlock the door, he will be."

"Oh," said Estelle, but didn't go any further.

The man looked at her tolerantly. "My medical license is on the wall if you'd like to check it against my driver's license," he said.

Estelle smiled her best smile. "Let's just get Barbie fixed up," she said.

The doctor clumped across the waiting room and down the hall, turning on lights as he went. The floor was linoleum tile throughout with nondescript vinyl couches in the waiting room, above one couch a picture of a huge Santa Gertrudis bull. Estelle thought the office looked more like a veterinarian's than an M.D.'s. Still, if anybody was accustomed to treating horsebites a country doctor would be.

•

"Next time a horse does that," he said as he let them out, "you bite it right back."

Barbie grinned. She was feeling like a survived martyr with the gleaming bandage on her arm and the doctor's judgment that she didn't need a shot. She had had a tetanus booster a month before as part of her pre-camp physical. To perk her up further, Estelle took her to the Corral Restaurant to each chalupas. Barbie ordered a hamburger instead.

After Barbie was asleep, Estelle took a walk. The afternoon had upset her, but the night calmed her once more. She walked toward the road until she was well beyond the circle of light cast by the mercury-vapor lamp next to the garage. She could not see another light anywhere. She stood for a while, surveying the isolation, looking at the stars bright in the cloudless, moonless night. A gentle breeze came over the land, scattering the heat of the day. As she returned, skirting the fence, she could hear the horses moving quietly and see their dark shapes outlined against the paler earth.

•

When she woke the next morning, the sky was cloudless still, the sun harsh and bright. Squinting against the brightness, she stopped beating the eggs for omelets and tried to see what was moving in the pasture with the horses. Something or several somethings were on the ground, but she couldn't see clearly because the fence blocked her view.

She put the bowl down and went outside. Before she reached the fence she had an idea of what she would see, but she forced herself on anyway. The bay was grazing calmly off to one side while straight ahead three or four black vultures were walking around the mare stretched on the ground, as if they were appraising merchandise.

She stood at the fence debating what to do. She climbed the fence and picked up a rock as she approached the group. The vultures noted her approach and took to the air in an awkward flapping and fluttering before she was close enough to throw the rock. Once aloft, they glided to landings at a safe distance and turned back to watch.

The mare's eyes were open, her head stretched at the end of her neck as if she were reaching for something. Several flies buzzed around her loose, grizzled lips. Estelle looked at the mare's flanks. They remained sunken. Estelle started to nudge the horse with her foot but drew back. The animal was clearly and indisputably dead.

•

Barbie had been watching her from the den. "What's the matter with Bootsie?" she asked as soon as Estelle was inside.

Let's be honest, Estelle thought. "She's dead," she said.

"Serves her right for biting me," Barbie said. "Are those vultures out there?"

Estelle nodded.

"Gross," Barbie said.

"Let's have some breakfast," Estelle suggested. Whatever the problem, she knew, you do better to face it with a full stomach.

"I don't want any breakfast," Barbie said. "A dead horse and vultures, super gross!"

Estelle managed to coax Barbie into eating a bowl of Count Chocula cereal. As they got into the car and headed back toward town, Barbie said, "One of them's sitting on top of her. And three others are looking."

Estelle didn't look.

•

"Office Hours 1:00–5:00," the sign on the doctor's door said. She could have sworn the sign said something else when they were in the day before. Whoever heard of a doctor who didn't have morning office hours? She opted for staying in town rather than driving out to the ranch and back.

A Tab, a Diet Dr. Pepper, a Diet Pepsi, and a pair of shoes she really didn't want later, they returned to the doctor's office. He came in ten minutes late and began working his way through the pile of folders waiting for him.

"My horse died," Estelle told him as soon as he swept into the examining room.

He looked around the room for a brief moment as if he expected to find something lying on the floor.

"I'm sorry to hear that, ma'am," he said, "but I'm not a vet."

"I mean the horse that bit my daughter died."

"I doubt we have anything to worry about," he said. "You told me it was an old mare. Probably just old age. But we still ought to check to make sure nothing's really wrong."

"How do we do that?"

"Pretty simple," the doctor said. "Just cut off its head and take it or send it to the public health labs."

Estelle pictured the decapitated horse lying in the pasture.

"When could you do that?" she asked.

He looked at her as if she failed to understand what he had just said.

"I mean," she said, "you don't do anything in the mornings, do you? Doctors are used to cutting on things." Even thinking about it she could feel her stomach muscles contract, her throat tighten.

"In the mornings I make rounds of the nursing home and invalids. In the afternoons I have office hours, and in the evenings I drive thirty-five miles to see my patients in the hospital. I don't have time to tend to the people in this town, much less take care of that dead horse. Tell you what, go talk to Clyde Morris. He's the vet. You'll have to see him anyway to get the shipping box and forms. Or hire somebody to do it for you."

At the Rio Ancho Veterinary Clinic, Estelle was met by a German Shorthaired Pointer and a twentyish young woman with a child.

"Clyde's out in the field," the woman said after Estelle asked to see the doctor.

Estelle looked around but didn't see anything but live oaks and cedars around the house. Maybe he farmed a little somewhere. "Could you go out in the field and call him?" she asked.

"I mean," the woman said, "he's out making calls. I can try to raise him on the radio."

Estelle and Barbie followed the woman through a back entryway stacked high with cartons of medicine.

"This is Pig Cutter One calling Pig Cutter Two," the woman intoned into the microphone. "Can you read me?"

How quaint, Estelle thought.

After several tries, a man's voice came over the speaker. "I read you. What do you need?"

"Lady here has an emergency."

"Put her on."

Estelle took the microphone gingerly from the woman. Estelle never used the CB her husband gave her for Christmas because she couldn't stand the static.

"Hello," she said.

"This is Morris," the voice came back. "What do you need?"

She wasn't going to make the same mistake with him that she had made with the doctor. "Our horse bit my little girl," she began.

No reply.

"And then the horse died," she added.

"What's the emergency, then?" the voice asked.

"The horse might have had something wrong with it."

"If it died, I'd say that was a pretty sure bet."

Estelle thought she heard the wife snicker behind her, but she didn't turn to look.

"But I mean something bad." She could not bring herself to say "rabies."

"If you're worried about it being rabid," the vet said, "fill out the forms and ship the head off to Public Health in San Antonio."

"That's my emergency," Estelle said.

"My wife'll give you the forms and the address."

"But I can't cut off the animal's head."

"Neither can I," the voice said.

"But you're a vet."

"That's right, but I'm a vet with a sow that's ready for a Caesarian and a call twenty miles away from a rancher with a sick stud bull. No way I'll be home until after dark. Tomorrow's the same thing. It's no big deal. Just get a sharp knife and have at it."

"But I can't," she protested.

"Try Phil Murphy. He might be willing to do it for you. I have to get back to this pig. I've taken almost too long already."

"Thank you," Estelle said automatically as she handed the microphone back to the wife.

She spent an hour trying to track down Phil Murphy but couldn't find him.

She filled up the car at the filling station she usually patronized, led up to the topic as easily as she could, and asked the owner if he knew anybody who might help her out.

"You do have a problem," he said and called over the boy who worked in the station. In between servicing cars, they conferred for ten minutes, one proposing a name, the other judging the nominee. "I'm sorry," the owner finally reported, "but I can't think of anybody right off who might do that kind of thing."

She stopped at the Watering Hole. She ordered a Coke for Barbie and a light beer for herself. Halfway through the beer she sauntered over to the group of men at a corner table.

They must have been occupying the table for a long time, judging from the piled-up ash trays and how loudly they guffawed at her story of the dead horse.

"Lady," one of them said, "I'd be happy to go out to your place."

"You would?" she said.

"But not for no dead horse."

She stopped short of throwing her beer in his face, whirled, and walked away, feeling their laughter hit her square between the shoulder blades.

On the way home she remembered her neighbor, Mr. Wilson, dependable Mr. Wilson who looked after everything for them.

"He's gone cattle buying," Mrs. Wilson told her. "Making the rounds of the auctions. Won't be back until Thursday."

Dinner was burritos and canned chili microwaved back to life. Barbie took her plate to the TV and watched a rerun of *Gilligan's Island* while she ate. When she brought her plate back, she asked, "Am I going to die?"

"Of course not," Estelle said. "We just want to check and make sure Bootsie wasn't sick when she died."

"Will I have to get lots of shots?"

Where did she pick up all this business about shots? Estelle wondered. "I don't think so," she said.

Barbie showed instant relief. "What happens to the head when they're through with it?"

"I suppose they dispose of it some way or the other."

Barbie clouded up again.

"It's kind of bad," Estelle comforted, still following the article she had read, "thinking about an old friend like Bootsie dying and being worked on in a laboratory."

"It's not that," Barbie said.

"What is it, then?" Estelle asked.

"I wanted to take it to school," Barbie said. "It'd be a lot neater than the bird's nest Billy brought in last week."

Estelle let Barbie stay up later and watch the movie on television, to make up for the problems of the day. In bed, Estelle tried reading. The book's cover pictured a young woman in a pale dress fleeing from a decrepit mansion set on the cliff behind her, but the story didn't hold Estelle's attention. She thought of taking a walk to calm herself, but somehow she didn't want to go outside. She went to the bar and mixed a pitcher of martinis.

Halfway through the pitcher, she hit upon a solution. She would think of it just like packing a suitcase. They would get up, eat, pack to go home, she would pack the horse's head, and they would close up the house and leave.

She drifted off to sleep in the recliner chair. She dreamed she was having an affair with a friend of her husband. He took her to a discreetly located hotel with a luxurious decor. At the door to their room he kissed her passionately, then pushed open the door and swept her inside. In the middle of the king-sized bed was a horse watching Johnny Carson and working a crossword puzzle. "Enjoy your stay," her lover said and left.

She woke up, staggered into the king-sized bed in the master bedroom, and fell asleep.

When she pulled the pillow off her head in the morning, she thought for a moment of ringing for room service instead of going down to breakfast. As the familiar items in the room focused, she remembered where she was. She felt nauseous.

She thought of just leaving, period.

But if anything happened to Barbie, she'd never forgive herself. Her husband would never forgive her. Barbie would never forgive her. Why did that stupid horse have to die?

She showered, dried her hair, and examined her wardrobe, trying to decide what she should wear for cutting off a horse's head. She finally put on a pair of jeans and a bandana blouse.

She did everything neatly and overly precisely. They had breakfast. They packed. She put things in the car.

Opening the knife drawer, she felt like a character in one of her novels presented with a case of dueling pistols and told to choose. Except none of the knives looked very efficient. You would think with all the deer that bunch of boozers slaughtered, they would keep a decent knife in the place, but then they all took their kill to the processing plant in town. The cost made a handy tax write-off, since they donated the meat to the children's home outside of town. She couldn't find a cord long enough to use the electric carving knife. Even though it didn't feel very sharp, she took the biggest one she could find, a butcher knife. She wanted to sharpen it, but the electric can opener with the sharpening attachment was in town. She put on her sunglasses, picking up the packing box in the garage, and started for the pasture.

It was hot already. Around her she could feel the land reflecting the heat it didn't absorb. The sky was cloudless. In the distance, she could see a hawk riding the air currents between two hills. The vultures were riding the dead mare. One was perched on her flank while the others hopped off and on her. As Estelle approached, they turned, one by one, to watch her. Only when she was close enough to see their featherless heads in detail did they begin to move sullenly away from the horse. She beat on the box with the knife and shouted to hurry them away. They sailed off for a short distance to watch her, as if she were auditioning for a part.

The birds had begun working on the mare on the softest part of her body, her anus. They had torn the opening larger and were working down her stomach. Except for her ravished flesh, the mare looked as she had the day before, but stiffer, duller. Her lips were pulled back from the yellow teeth, dried as stone. Her eyes were open and staring, but covered with dust. Ants marched in and out of her nose.

Estelle thought she was going to pass out. She shut her eyes and gripped her stomach until the feeling passed. On second glance, the mare didn't look quite as bad as she had originally. The details seemed to have more distance to them. Estelle looked at the head where she was supposed to cut.

She couldn't do it.

She opened and shut her eyes several times more. The dead body by itself was not so revolting as the thought of touching it. She bent down and touched the neck and drew back immediately, shivering.

She poked the horse's neck again. She shut both eyes and lowered the knife until she felt it touch the horse. She squinted one eye to see where the blade lay.

Keeping her head turned away, she placed the knife behind the curve of the large cheekbone and pulled the knife toward her. Slowly she looked to see the rend in the flesh.

All she could see was a little disturbance in the dust on the horse's neck.

With both eyes open, she pushed the knife back and forth more, bearing down a little. The hair bristled up about the edge of the knife and went flat at one spot. The skin was parting.

She stopped, leaving the knife resting on the horse's neck, and covered her face with her hands.

Where were *they?*

She was not supposed to be out in a rocky pasture, getting her pants filthy dirty, sweating through her blouse, getting sick at her stomach, cutting off the head of a horse that did something as stupid as bite her daughter and then die. She cursed her husband who hadn't accompanied her, cursed the kickers in town, cursed the horse, cursed Barbie for being bitten, cursed the vultures, cursed the pasture, cursed the heat, and cursed the stupid idea of having a place outside of town.

She thought about just leaving and just seeing what would happen. But what kind of a mother would she be if she did that?

Holding her stomach with one hand, she started sawing the knife back and forth again.

If she didn't look at the head and the rest of the body, it was kind of like cutting up a big roast. She put both hands on the knife and bore down.

Except that roasts weren't hairy. And roasts didn't make the sickening popping sounds that the cartilage in the throat did.

She waited for her stomach to calm down again, and attacked furiously. She tired quickly and stopped to catch her breath.

She was almost halfway through, she thought, but she couldn't tell for sure. She stood up to check and noticed that the vultures had eased closer, like spoiled pets who stop for a moment after a reprimand and then begin again. She shouted at them, threw rocks at them, and drove them back a little further.

She touched the horse's head with her foot and shoved. It didn't move very far. She felt her leg muscles pull when she shoved it a second time, but the nose moved out, turning the cut from a slit to an open wedge. The ground underneath was stained with blood and fluids. She retched and found her mouth dry. She was afraid if she ever went back into the house she wouldn't finish the job. She stepped over the neck and resumed cutting.

She worked steadily, brushing the sweat off her forehead with her wrist. It was like stuffing envelopes for the Heart Fund or Muscular Dystrophy or whatever it was she volunteered to work on that year. You were supposed to feel good for helping, for doing your duty, and all it was was boring. Her clothes were already ruined, so she knelt and put her full weight into each downstroke and pulled on the upstrokes.

The knife grated against the neckbones and she stopped. It was like trying to cut a rock. How did she do chicken joints? She either wedged the knife in and twisted or she whammed down with the biggest knife she could find. She tried slipping the knife between two vertebrae, but she couldn't force it.

She beat on the vertebrae, both hands on the knife. Meat scraps flew around her. One landed on her forehead, and she wiped it away, almost poking herelf in the eye in her haste.

She found that she was crying, kneeling on all fours and crying. Then she was hiccuping and retching, and then she was vomiting coffee, eggs, and English muffins, her throat raw and burning.

She spat out the dregs of breakfast and started back toward the house. She washed her mouth out with the hose at the side of the house and marched into the garage. It took her a moment to find the axe, but when she did she yanked it off the floor and started back outside.

Holding the axe across her chest, she put each foot down as if she were stamping on some vile insect. At the horse's head she didn't think about taking a deep breath but did and brought the axe down with all her strength on the neck. She jerked the axe back up, clumsily, both hands on the end of the handle. She swung it in a wide arc, aimed for the same spot, and stepped sideways to brace herself for the blow. Her foot hit her own vomit, slipped, and she fell headlong across the horse's neck, the axe flying out of her hands.

She jumped up, repulsed. Breathing heavily, she spat the dust out of her mouth. She half-walked, half-ran to the axe, picked it up, and slammed it into the horse's neck as soon as she had her footing. Again and again she put all her force into the blows. Some hit the splintering vertebrae, some hit the flesh, splattering it in chunks. Even after the last white cord in the spine had severed, she continued slamming the axehead into the dirt between the severed head and the neck.

She leaned on the axe, panting, wiping the perspiration from her forehead. She let the axe fall and pulled the box over to the disembodied head still staring at the cloudless sky. She considered the problem for a while, then grabbed an ear in each hand. They were fuzzy and stiff. She heaved. The head was much heavier than she had thought it would be. She heaved again, feeling her stomach muscles strain, and lifted the head off the ground. But it wasn't high enough, and she only hit the side of the box, knocking it away.

She heaved a third time, pulling the head up her leg, trying to lift it with her knee. She poised it over the open box and let it drop. She closed the lid and stood up.

She dusted herself off, erasing the line the horse's head had made up her leg. The vultures had eased closer and stood in an ugly and studious circle around her.

She flung rocks at the birds. She grabbed the axe and ran at them, ready to chop off their heads. She raced from one side of the circle to the other, screaming at them. Clumsy and slow as they were, they moved out of range. She threw the axe at one with all her might, but it fell short by a wide margin. She did not bother to retrieve it.

Her back muscles popped as she lifted up the box and started toward the house, staggering from time to time as she stepped on a rock. She put one last effort into the task and worked the box high enough to drop it into the car trunk.

She slammed the lid and sat panting on the bumper. She wiped her brow and flung her hand out, spattering the concrete floor with sweat. When her breathing became more regular, she went inside. She grabbed a can of Pearl Light out of the refrigerator and took a long drink. She shivered with the cold beer and the air-conditioned temperature and told herself she would be better outside until she cooled down.

Sipping the beer, she stood in the shade of the garage, her eyes squinted against the glare and watched another vulture glide to a landing in the pasture. She shivered again, but not with the cold.

It wasn't pretty, she told herself. The land wasn't the least bit pretty. It was hot and hard and life died on it and was eaten by other life. The land would burn your skin, wrinkle your face, and turn your hands into tools. People out here didn't care any more than they did anywhere else. She could break her leg and nobody would know. The house could burn down and no help could save it.

The only things that made you civilized were flush toilets and
electricity. That was all. She followed the power line from the
corner of the house until it disappeared in the cedars along the
road. That one thin wire was the only thing that made the country
livable, cooling the drinks, cooking the food, running the air conditioner, pumping the water.

She saw the wire running on through the cedars to join the other
wires along the highway that ran into the co-op electrical company.
Wires were all along the highways; they traced and followed all
her journeys. They crossed and crowded each other, and she could
follow them all the way to Houston, but Houston was nothing more
than a bigger tangle of wires.

All along, she had been thinking of going the moment she finished her task. Now she found she wanted to stay. One place was
like another. Besides, she had met the country as it was. She had
done what needed to be done. Nobody had helped her. Nobody.
Not her husband, not her child, not her neighbors, not the people
you expected to help you. She was the one who had done the
sickening work. Now she wished she had been braver as she did it.
Surely she could have kept her stomach if she had tried a little
harder.

It would be better to go, though. In another day the corpse
would begin to rot and stink. When they returned there would be
nothing in the pasture but a heap of bones. She would leave a
message for Wilson to take the bay back to his place. Maybe he
could drag the body to the far end of the pasture.

She finished the beer but didn't go back in immediately. She
heard nothing but the wind in the cedars, and liked the sound.

•

"What did you do with Bootsie's head?" Barbie asked as Estelle
passed her on the way to clean up.

"It's in a box in the trunk," she said.

"Gross," Barbie said.

Estelle spun and pointed a finger straight into the child's face.
"I am sick and tired of hearing that word! You say it one more
time and I'm going to slap your face!"

Barbie didn't say anything else until they were on the other side
of Rio Ancho, headed for San Antonio.

"Are we going home?" she asked.

Estelle had thought that after she left the head at the Public

Health Offices she would reward herself with a shopping trip. Somehow, that no longer seemed attractive. Spending money was something anybody could do.

"Yes," she said. "We're going back to Houston."

She wasn't sure what she would find once she returned to Houston, but whatever it was, she felt ready for it.

CHARLES BAXTER

Harmony of the World

(FROM THE MICHIGAN QUARTERLY REVIEW)

I

IN THE SMALL Ohio town where I grew up, many homes had parlors that contained pianos, sideboards, and sofas, heavy objects signifying gentility. These pianos were rarely tuned. They went flat in summer around the Fourth of July, and sharp in winter at Christmas. Ours was a Story and Clark. On its music stand were copies of Stephen Foster and Ethelbert Nevin favorites, along with one Chopin prelude that my mother would practice for twenty minutes every three years. She had no patience, but since she thought Ohio — all of it, every scrap — made sense, she was happy and did not need to practice anything. Happiness is not infectious, but somehow her happiness infected my father, a pharmacist, and then spread through the rest of the household. My whole family was obstinately cheerful. I think of my two sisters, my brother, and my parents as having artificial pasted-on smiles, like circus clowns. They apparently thought cheer and good Christian words were universals, respected everywhere. The pianos were part of this cheer. They played for celebrations and moments of pleasant pain. Or rather someone played them, but not too well, since excellent playing would have been faintly antisocial. "Chopin," my mother said, shaking her head as she stumbled through the prelude. "Why is he famous?"

When I was six, I received my first standing ovation. On the stage of the community auditorium, where the temperature was about ninety-four degrees, sweat fell from my forehead onto the piano keys, making their ivory surfaces slippery. At the conclusion of the piece, when everyone stood up to applaud, I thought they were just being nice. My playing had been mediocre; only my sweating had been extraordinary. Two years later, they stood up again. When I was eleven, they cheered. By that time I was astonishing these small-town audiences with Chopin and Rachmaninoff recital chestnuts. I thought I was a genius, and read biographies of Einstein. Already the townspeople were saying that I was the best thing Parkersville had ever seen, *that I would put the place on the map.* Mothers would send their children by to watch me practice. The kids sat with their mouths open while I polished off another classic.

Like many musicians, I cannot remember ever playing badly, in the sense of not knowing what I was doing. In high school, my identity was being sealed shut: My classmates called me El Señor Longhair, even though I wore a crewcut, this being the 1950s. Whenever the town needed a demonstration of local genius, it called upon me. There were newspaper articles detailing my accomplishments, and I must have heard the phrase "future concert career" at least two hundred times. My parents smiled and smiled as I collected applause. My senior year, I gave a solo recital and was hired for umpteen weddings and funerals. I was good luck. On the Fourth of July the townspeople brought out a piano to the city square so that I could improvise music between explosions at the fireworks display. Just before I left for college, I noticed that our neighbors wanted to come up to me, ostensibly for small talk but actually to touch me.

In college I made a shocking discovery: Other people existed in the world who were as talented as I was. If I sat down to play a Debussy etude, they would sit down and play Beethoven, only louder and faster than I had. I felt their breath on my neck. Apparently there were other small towns. In each of these small towns there was a genius. Perhaps some geniuses were not actually geniuses. I practiced constantly and began to specialize in the non-Germanic piano repertoire. I kept my eye out for students younger than I was, who might have flashier technique. At my senior recital I played Mozart, Chopin, Ravel, and Debussy, with encore pieces by Scriabin and Thomson. I managed to get the audience to stand up for the last time.

I was accepted into a large midwestern music school, famous for its high standards. Once there, I discovered that genius, to say nothing of talent, was a common commodity. Since I was only a middling composer, with no interesting musical ideas as such, I would have to make my career as a performer or teacher. But I didn't want to teach, and as a performer I lacked pizzazz. For the first time, it occurred to me that my life might be evolving into something unpleasant, something with the taste of stale bread.

I was beginning to meet performers with more confidence than I had, young musicians to whom doubt was as alien as proper etiquette. Often these people dressed like tramps, smelled, smoked constantly, were gay or sadistic. Whatever their imbalances, they were not genteel. *They did not represent small towns.* I was struck by their eyes. Their eyes seemed to proclaim, "The universe believes in me. It always has."

My piano teacher was a man I will call Luther Stecker. Every year he taught at the music school for six months. For the following six months he toured. He turned me away from the repertoire with which I was familiar and demanded that I learn several pieces by composers whom I had not often played, including Bach, Brahms, and Liszt. Each one of these composers discovered a weak point in me: I had trouble keeping up the consistent frenzy required by Liszt, the mathematical precision required by Bach, the unpianistic fingerings of Brahms.

I saw Stecker every week. While I played, he would doze off. When he woke, he would mumble some inaudible comment. He also coached a trio I participated in, and he spoke no more audibly then than he did during my private lesson.

I couldn't understand why, apart from his reputation, the school had hired him. Then I learned that in every Stecker student's life, the time came when the Master collected his thoughts, became blunt, and told the student exactly what his future would be. For me, the moment arrived on the third of November, 1966. I was playing sections of the Brahms Paganini Variations, a fiendish piece on which I had spent many hours. When I finished, I saw him sit up.

"Very good," he said, squinting at me. "You have talents."

There was a pause. I waited. "Thank you," I said.

"You have a nice house?" he asked.

"A nice house? No."

"You should get a nice house somewhere," he said, taking his handkerchief out of his pocket and waving it at me. "With windows. Windows with a view."

I didn't like the drift of his remarks. "I can't afford a house," I said.

"You will. A nice house. For you and your family."

I resolved to get to the heart of this. "Professor," I asked, "what did you think of my playing?"

"Excellent," he said. "That piece is very difficult."

"Thank you."

"Yes, technically excellent," he said, and my heart began to pound. "Intelligent phrasing. Not much for me to say. Yes. That piece has many notes," he added, enjoying the non sequitur.

I nodded. "Many notes."

"And you hit all of them accurately. Good pedal and good discipline. I like how you hit the notes."

I was dangling on his string, a little puppet.

"Thousands of notes, I suppose," he said, staring at my forehead, which was beginning to get damp, "and you hit all of them. You only forgot one thing."

"What?"

"The passion!" he roared. "You forgot the passion! You always forget it! Where is it? Did you leave it at home? You never bring it with you! Never! I listen to you and think of a robot playing! A smart robot, but a robot! No passion! Never ever ever!" He stopped shouting long enough to sneeze. "You *should* buy a house. You know why?"

"Why?"

"Because the only way you will ever praise God is with a family, that's why! Not with this piano! You are a fine student," he wound up, "but you make me sick! Why do you make me sick?"

He waited for me to answer.

"Why do you make me sick?" he shouted. "Answer me!"

"How can I possibly answer you?"

"By articulating words in English! Be courageous! Offer a suggestion! Why do you make me sick?"

I waited for a minute, the longest minute my life has seen or will ever see. "Passion," I said at last. "You said there wasn't enough passion. I thought there was. Perhaps not."

He nodded. "No. You are right. No passion. A corruption of music itself. Your playing is too gentle, too much good taste. To play the piano like a genius, you must have a bit of the fanatic. Just a bit. But it is essential. You have stubbornness and talent but no fanaticism. You don't have the salt on the rice. Without salt, the rice is inedible, no matter what its quality otherwise." He stood up. "I tell you this because sooner or later someone else will. You will have a life of disappointments if you stay in music. You may find a teacher who likes you. Good, good. *But you will never be taken up! Never!* You should buy a house, young man. With a beautiful view. Move to it. Don't stay here. You are close to success, but it is the difference between leaping the chasm and falling into it, one inch short. You are an inch short. You could come back for more lessons. You could graduate from here. But if you are truly intelligent, you will say good-bye. Good-bye." He looked down at the floor and did not offer me his hand.

I stood up and walked out of the room.

Becalmed, I drifted down and up the hallways of the building for half an hour. Then a friend of mine, a student of conducting from Bolivia, a Marxist named Juan Valparaiso, approached, and, ignoring my shallow breathing and cold sweat, started talking at once.

"Terrible, furious day!" he said.

"Yes."

"I am conducting *Benvenuto Cellini* overture this morning! All is going well until difficult flute entry. I instruct, with force, flutists. Soon all woodwinds are ignoring me." He raised his eyebrows and stroked his huge gaucho mustache. "Always! Always there are fascists in the woodwinds!"

"Fascists everywhere," I said.

"Horns bad, woodwinds worse. Demands of breath made for insanes. Pedro," he said, "you are appearing irresoluted. Sick?"

"Yes," I nodded. "Sick. I just came from Stecker. My playing makes *him* sick."

"He said that? That you are making him sick?"

"That's right. I play like a robot, he says."

"What will you do?" Juan asked me. "Kill him?"

"No." And then I knew. "I'm leaving the school."

"What? Is impossible!" Tears leaped instantly into Juan's eyes. "Cannot, Pedro. After one whipping? No! Disappointments everywhere here. Also outside in world. Must stick to it." He grabbed me by the shoulders. "Fascists put here on earth to break our hearts! Must live through. You cannot go." He looked around wildly. "Where could you go anyway?"

"I'm not sure," I said. "He said I would never amount to anything. I think he's right. But I could do something else." To prove that I could imagine options, I said, "I could work for a newspaper. You know, music criticism."

"Caterpillars!" Juan shouted, his tears falling onto my shirt. "Failures! Pathetic lives! Cannot, cannot! Who would hire you?"

I couldn't tell him for six months, until I was given a job in Knoxville on a part-time trial basis. But by then I was no longer writing letters to my musician friends. I had become anonymous. I worked in Knoxville for two years, then in Louisville — a great city for music — until I moved here, to this city I shall never name, in the middle of New York State, where I bought a house with a beautiful view.

In my home town, they still wonder what happened to me, but my smiling parents refuse to reveal my whereabouts.

II

Every newspaper has a command structure. Within that command structure, editors assign certain stories, but the writers must be given some freedom to snoop around and discover newsworthy material themselves. In this anonymous city, I was hired to review all the concerts of the symphony orchestra and to provide some hype articles during the week to boost the ticket sales for Friday's program. Since the owner of the paper was on the symphony board of trustees, writing about the orchestra and its programs was necessarily part of good journalistic citizenship. On my own, though, I initiated certain projects, wrote book reviews for the Sunday section, interviewed famous visiting musicians — some of them my ex-classmates — and during the summer I could fill in on all sorts of assignments, as long as I cleared what I did with the feature editor, Morris Cascadilla.

"You're the first serious musician we've ever had on the staff here," he announced to me when I arrived, suspicion and hope fighting for control on his face. "Just remember this: Be clear and concise. Assume they've got intelligence but no information. After that, you're on your own, except you should clear dicey stuff with me. And never forget the Maple Street angle."

The Maple Street angle was Cascadilla's equivalent to the Nixon administration's "How will it play in Peoria?" No matter what subject I wrote about, I was expected to make it relevant to Maple Street, the newspaper's mythical locus of middle-class values. I could write about electronic, aleatory, or post-Boulez music *if* I suggested that the city's daughters might be corrupted by it. Sometimes I found the Maple Street angle, and sometimes I couldn't. When I failed, Cascadilla would call me in, scowl at my copy and mutter, "All the Juilliard graduates in town will love this." Nevertheless, the Maple Street angle was a spiritual exercise in humility, and I did my best to find it week after week.

When I first learned that the orchestra was scheduled to play Paul Hindemith's *Harmony of the World* Symphony, I didn't think of Hindemith, but of Maple Street, that mythically harmonious place where I actually grew up.

III

Working on the paper left me some time for other activities. Unfortunately, there was nothing I knew how to do except play the piano and write reviews.

Certain musicians are very practical. Trumpet players (who love valves) tend to be good mechanics, and I have met a few composers who fly airplanes and can restore automobiles. Most performing violinists and pianists, however, are drained by the demands of their instruments and seldom learn how to do anything besides play. In daily life they are helpless and stricken. In midlife the smart ones force themselves to find hobbies. But the less fortunate come home to solitary apartments without pictures or other decorations, warm up their dinners in silence, read whatever books happen to be on the dinner table, and then go to bed.

I am speaking of myself here, of course. As time passed, and the vacuum of my life made it harder to breathe, I required more work. I fancied I was a tree, putting out additional leaves. I let it be known that I would play as an accompanist for voice students and other recitalists, if their schedules didn't interfere with my commitments for the paper.

One day I received a call at my desk. A quietly controlled female voice asked, "Is this Peter Jenkins?"

"Yes."

"Well," she said, pausing, as if she'd forgotten what she meant to tell me, "this is Karen Jensen. That's almost like Jenkins, isn't it?" I waited. "I'm a singer," she said, after a moment. "A soprano. I've just lost my accompanist and I'm planning on giving a recital in three months. They said you were available. Are you? What do you charge?"

I told her.

"Isn't that kind of steep? That's kind of steep. Well, I suppose . . . I can use somebody else until just before, and then I can use you. They say you're good. And I've read your reviews. I really admire the way you write!"

"Thank you."

"You get so much information into your reviews! Sometimes, when I read you, I imagine what you look like. Sometimes a person can make a mental picture. I just wish the paper would publish a photo or something of you."

"They want to," I said, "but I asked them to please don't."

"Even your voice sounds like your writing!" she said excitedly. "I can see you in front of me now. Can you play Fauré and Schubert? I mean, is there any composer or style you don't like and won't play?"

"No," I said. "I play anything."

"That's *wonderful!*" she said, as if I had confessed to a remarkable tolerance. "Some accompanists are so picky. 'I won't do this, I won't do that.' Well, *one* I know is like that. Anyhow, could we meet soon? Do you sight-read? Can we meet at the music school downtown? In a practice room? When are you free?"

I set up an appointment.

•

She was almost beautiful. Her deep eyes were accented by depressive bowls in quarter-moon shadow under them. Though she was only in her late twenties, she seemed slightly scorched by anxiety. She couldn't keep still. Her hands fluttered as they fixed her hair; she scratched nervously at her cheeks; and her eyes jumped every few seconds. Soon, however, she calmed down and began to look me in the eye, evaluating me. Then *I* turned away.

She wanted to test me out and had brought along her recital numbers, mostly standard fare: a Handel aria, Mozart, Schubert, and Fauré. The last set of songs, *Nine Epitaphs*, by an American composer I had never heard of, Theodore Chanler, was the only novelty.

"Who is this Chanler?" I asked, looking through the sheet music.

"I . . . I found it in the music library," she said. "I looked him up. He was born in Boston and died in 1961. There's a recording by Phyllis Curtin. Virgil Thomson says these are maybe the best American art songs ever written."

"Oh."

"They're kind of, you know, lugubrious. I mean they're all epitaphs written supposedly on tombstones, set to music. They're like portraits. I love them. Is it all right? Do you mind?"

"No, I don't mind."

We started through her program, beginning with Handel's "Un sospiretto d'un labbro pallido" from *Il Pastor fido*. I could immediately see why she was still in central New York State and why she would always be a student. She had a fine voice, clear and distinct, somewhat styled after Victoria de los Angeles (I thought), and her articulation was superb. If these achievements had been the whole story, she might have been a professional. But her pitch wobbled on sustained notes in a maddening way; the effect was not comic and would probably have gone unnoticed by most non-musicians, but to me the result was harrowing. She could sing perfectly for several measures and then she would miss a note by a semi-tone, which drove an invisible fingernail into my scalp. It was as though a gypsy's curse descended every five or six seconds, throwing her off pitch; then she was allowed to be a great singer until the curse descended again. Her loss of pitch was so regularized that I could see it coming and squirmed in anticipation. I felt as though I were in the presence of one of God's more complicated pranks.

Her choice of songs highlighted her failings. Their delicate textures were constantly broken by her lapses. When we arrived at the Chanler pieces, I thought I was accustomed to her, but I found I wasn't. The first song begins with the following verse, written by Walter de la Mare, who had crafted all the poems in archaic epitaph style:

> *Here lyeth our infant, Alice Rodd;*
> *She were so small,*
> *Scarce aught at all,*
> *But a mere breath of Sweetness sent from God.*

The vocal line for "She were so small" consists of four notes, the last two rising a half-step from the two before them. To work, the passage requires a dead-eye accuracy of pitch:

Singing this line, Karen Jensen hit the D-sharp but missed the E and skidded up uncontrollably to F-sharp, which would sound all right to anyone who didn't have the music in front of his nose, as I did. Only a fellow-musician could be offended.

Infuriated, I began to feel that I could *not* participate in a recital with this woman. It would be humiliating to perform such lovely songs in this excruciating manner. I stopped playing, turned to her to tell her that I could not continue after all, and then I saw her bracelet.

I am not, on the whole, especially observant, a failing that probably accounts for my having missed the bracelet when we first met. But I saw it now: five silver canaries dangled down quietly from it, and, as it slipped back and forth, I saw her wrist and what I suddenly realized *would* be there — the parallel lines of her madness, etched in scar tissue.

The epitaphs finished, she asked me to work with her, and I agreed. When we shook hands the canaries shook in tiny vibrations, as if pleased with my dutiful kindness, my charity, toward their mad mistress.

IV

Though Paul Hindemith's reputation once equalled Stravinsky's and Bartók's, it suffered after his death in 1963 an almost complete collapse. Only two of his orchestral works, the *Symphonic Metamorphoses on Themes of Weber* and the *Mathis der Maler* Symphony, are played with any frequency, thanks in part to their use of borrowed tunes. One hears his woodwind quintets and choral pieces now and again, but the works of which he was most proud — the ballet *Nobilissima Visione, Das Marienleben* (a song cycle) and the opera *Die Harmonie der Welt* — have fallen into total obscurity.

The reason for Hindemith's sudden loss of reputation was a mystery to me; I had always considered his craftsmanship if not his inspiration to be first-rate. When I saw that the *Harmony of the World* Symphony, almost never played, would be performed in our anonymous city, I told Cascadilla that I wanted to write a story for that week on how fame was gained and lost in the world of music. He thought that subject might be racy enough to interest the tone-deaf citizens of leafy and peaceful Maple Street, where no one is famous, if I made sure the story contained "the human element."

I read up on Hindemith, played his piano music, and listened to the recordings. I slowly found the music to be technically astute but emotionally arid, as if some problem of purely local interest kept the composer's gaze safely below the horizon. Technocratic and oddly timid, his work reminded me of a model train chugging through a tiny town where only models of people actually lived. In fact, Hindemith did have a lifelong obsession with train sets: In Berlin, his took up three rooms, and the composer wrote elaborate timetables so that the toys wouldn't collide.

But if Hindemith had a technocrat's intelligence, he also believed in the necessity of universal participation in musical activities. Listening was not enough. Even non-musical citizens could learn to sing and play, and he wrote music expressly for this purpose. He seems to have known that passive, drugged listening was a side effect of totalitarian environments and that elitist composers such as Schoenberg were engaged in antisocial Faustian projects that would bewilder and infuriate most audiences, leaving them isolated and thus eager to be drugged by a musical superman.

As the foremost anti-Nietzschean German composer of his day, therefore, Hindemith left Germany when his works could not be performed, thanks to the Third Reich; wrote textbooks with simple exercises; composed a requiem in memory of Franklin Roosevelt, set to words by Walt Whitman; and taught students, not all of them talented, in Ankara, New Haven, and Buffalo ("this caricature of a town"). As he passed through late middle age, he turned to a project he had contemplated all his life, an opera based on the career of the German astronomer Johannes Kepler, author of *De*

Harmonice Mundi. This opera, a summary of Hindemith's ideas, would be called *Harmony of the World.* Hindemith worked out the themes first in a symphony, which bore the same title as the opera, and completed it in 1951. The more I thought about this project, the more it seemed anachronistic. Who believed in world harmony in 1951? Or thereafter? Such a symphony would have to pass beyond technical sophistication into divine inspiration, which Hindemith had never shown any evidence of possessing.

It occured to me that Hindemith's lifelong sanity had perhaps given way in this case, toppled not by despair (as is conventional) but by faith in harmony.

v

For the next rehearsal, I drove to Karen Jensen's apartment, where there was, she said, a piano. I'd become curious about the styles of her insanity: I imagined a hamster cage in the kitchen, a doll-head mobile in the living room, and mottoes written with different colored inks on memo pads tacked up everywhere on the walls.

She greeted me at the door without her bracelet. When I looked at her wrist, she said, "Hmmm. I see that you noticed. A memento of adolescent despair." She sighed. "But it does frighten people off. Once you've tried to do something like that, people don't really trust you. I don't know why exactly. Don't want your blood on their hands or something. Well, come on in."

I was struck first by her forthrightness and second by her tiny apartment. Its style was much like the style in my house. She owned an attractive but worn-down sofa, a sideboard that supported an antique clock, one chair, a glass-top dinner table, and one nondescript poster on the wall. Trying to keep my advantage, I looked hard for telltale signs of insanity but found none. The piano was off in the corner, almost hidden, unlike those in the parlors back home.

"Very nice," I said.

"Well, thanks," she said. "It's not much. I'd like something bigger, but . . . where I work, I'm an administrative assistant, and they don't pay me very much. So that's why I live like a snail here. It's hardly big enough to move around in, right?" She wasn't looking at me. "I mean, I could almost pick it up and carry it away."

I nodded. "You just don't think like a rich person," I said, trying to be hearty. "They like to expand. They need room. Big houses, big cars, fat bodies."

"Oh, I know!" she said, laughing. "My uncle . . . would *you* like to stay for dinner? You look like you need a good meal. I mean, after the rehearsal. You're just skin and bones, Pet — May I call you Peter?"

"Sure." I sat down on the sofa and tried to think up an excuse. "I really can't stay, Miss Jensen. I have another rehearsal to go to later tonight. I wish I could."

"That's not it, is it?" she asked suddenly, looking down at me. "I don't believe you. I bet it's something else. I bet you're afraid of me."

"Why should I be afraid of you?"

She smiled and shrugged. "That's all right. You don't have to say anything. I know how it goes." She laughed once more, faintly. "I never found a man who could handle it. They want to show you *their* scars, you know? They don't want to see any on you, and if they discover any, they just run." She slapped her right hand into her forehead and then ran her fingers through her hair. "Well, shit. I didn't mean to do this *at all!* I mean, I admire you so much and everything, and here I am, running on like this. I guess we should get down to business, right? Since I'm paying you by the hour."

I smiled professionally and went to her piano.

Beneath the high-culture atmosphere that surrounds them, art songs have one subject: love. The permutations of love (lust, solitude, and loss) are present in abundance, of course, but for the most part they are simple vehicles for the expression of that one emotion. I was reminded of this as I played through the piano parts. As much as I concentrated on the music in front of me, I couldn't help but notice that my employer stood next to the piano, singing the words sometimes toward me, sometimes away. She was rather courageously forcing eye contact on me. She kept this up for an hour and a half until we came to the Chanler settings, when at last she turned slightly, singing to the walls.

As before, her voice broke out of control every five seconds, giving isolated words all the wrong shadings. The only way to endure it, I discovered, was to think of her singing as a postmodern phenomenon with its own conventions and rules. As the victim of necessity rather than accident, Karen Jensen was tolerable.

Here sleep I,
Susannah Fry,
No one near me,
No one nigh:
Alone, alone
Under my stone,
Dreaming on,
Still dreaming on:
Grass for my valance
And coverlid,
Dreaming on
As I always did.
"*Weak in the head?*"
Maybe. Who knows?
Susannah Fry
Under the rose.

There she was, facing away from me, burying Susannah Fry, and probably her own past and career into the bargain.

When we were done, she asked, "Sure you won't stay?"

"No, I don't think so."

"You really haven't another engagement, do you?"

"No," I admitted.

"I didn't think so. You were scared of me the moment you walked in the door. You thought I'd be crazy." She waited. "After all, only ugly girls live alone, right? And I'm not ugly."

"No, you aren't," I said. "You're quite attractive."

"Do you think so?" she asked, brightening. "It's so nice to hear that from you, even if you're just paying a compliment. I mean, it still means *something*." Then she surprised me. As I stood in the doorway, she got down on her knees in front of me and bowed her head in the style of one of her songs. "Please stay," she asked. Immediately she stood up and laughed. "But don't feel obliged to."

"Oh, no," I said, returning to her living room. "I've just changed my mind. Dinner sounds like a good idea."

After she had served and we had started to eat, she looked up at me and said, "You know, I'm not completely good." She paused. "At singing."

"What?" I stopped chewing. "Yes, you are. You're all right."

"Don't lie. I know I'm not. You know I'm not. Come on: Let's at least be honest. I think I have certain qualities of musicality, but my pitch is . . . you know. Uneven. You probably think it's awfully vain of me to put on these recitals like this. With nobody but friends and family coming."

"No, I don't."

"Well, I don't care what you say. It's . . . hmm, I don't know. People encourage me. And it's a discipline. Music's finally a discipline that rewards you. Privately, though. Well, that's what my mother says."

Carefully I said, "She may be right."

"Who cares if she is?" she laughed, her mouth full of food. "I enjoy doing it. Like I enjoy doing this. Listen, I don't want to seem forward or anything, but are you married?"

"No."

"I didn't think so." She picked up a string bean and eyed it suspiciously. "Why aren't you? You're not ugly. In fact you're all right looking. You obviously haven't been crazy. Are you gay or something?"

"No."

"No," she agreed, "you don't look gay. You don't even look very happy. You don't look very anything. Why is that?"

"I should be offended by this line of questioning."

"But you're not. You know why? Because I'm interested in you. I hardly know you, but I like you, what I can see. Don't you have any trust?"

"Yes," I said, finally.

"So answer my question. Why don't you look very anything?"

"Do you want to hear what my piano teacher once said?" I asked. "He said I wasn't enough of a fanatic. He said that to be one of the great ones you have to be a tiny bit crazy. Touched. And he said I wasn't. And when he said it, I knew all along he was right. I was waiting for someone to say what I already knew, and he was the one. I was too much a good citizen, he said. I wasn't possessed."

She rose, walked around the table to where I was sitting, and stood in front of me, looking down at my face. I knew that whatever she was going to do had been picked up, in attitude, from one of her songs. She touched the back of my arm with two fingers on her right hand. "Well," she said, "maybe you aren't possessed, but what would you think of me as another possession?"

VI

In 1618 at the age of seventy, Katherine Kepler, the mother of Johannes Kepler, was put on trial for witchcraft. The records indicate that her personality was so deranged, so deeply offensive to all, that if she were alive today she would *still* be called a witch. One of Kepler's biographers, Angus Armitage, notes that she was "evil-tempered" and possessed an interest in unnamed "outlandish things." Her trial lasted, on and off, for three years; by 1621, when she was acquitted, her personality had disintegrated completely. She died the following year.

At the age of six, Kepler's son Frederick died of smallpox. A few months later, Kepler's wife, Barbara, died of typhus. Two other children, Henry and Susanna, had died in infancy.

Like many another of his age, Kepler spent much of his adult life cultivating favor from the nobility. He was habitually penniless and was often reduced, as his correspondence shows, to begging for handouts. He was the victim of religious persecution, though luckier in this regard than some.

After he married for a second time, three more children died in infancy, a statistic that in theory carries less emotional weight than one might think, given the accepted levels of infant mortality for that era.

In 1619, despite the facts cited above, Kepler published *De Harmonice Mundi,* a text in which he set out to establish the correspondence between the laws of harmony and the disposition of planets in motion. In brief, Kepler argued that certain intervals, such as the octave, major and minor sixths, and major and minor thirds, were pleasurable, while other intervals were not. History indicated that mankind had always regarded certain intervals as unpleasant. Feeling that this set of universal tastes pointed to immutable laws, Kepler sought to map out the pleasurable intervals geometrically, and then to transfer that geometrical pattern to the order of the planets. The velocity of the planets, rather than their strict placement, constituted the harmony of the spheres. This velocity provided each planet with a note, what Armitage calls a "term in a mathematically determined relation."

In fact, each planet performed a short musical scale, set down by Kepler in staff notation. The length of the scale depended upon the eccentricity of the orbit; and its limiting notes could generally be shown to form a concord (except for Venus and the Earth with their nearly circular orbits, whose scales were of very constricted range) . . . At the Creation . . . complete concord prevailed and the morning stars sang together.

VII

We began to eat dinner together. Accustomed to solitude, we did not always engage in conversation. I would read the newspaper or ink in letters on my geometrically patterned crossword puzzles at my end of the table, while Karen would read detective novels or *Time* at hers. If she had cooked, I would clear and wash the dishes; if I had cooked, she did the cleaning. Experience and disappointments had made us methodical. She told me that she had once despised structured experiences governed by timetables, but that after several manic-depressive episodes she had learned to love regularity. This regularity included taking lithium at the same time — to the minute — each day.

The season being summer, we would pack towels and swimming suits after dinner and drive out to one of several public beaches, where we would swim until darkness came on. On calm evenings, Karen would drop her finger in the water and watch the waves lap outward. I favored immature splashing, or grabbing her by the arm and whirling her around me until I released her and she would spin back and fall into the water, laughing as she sank. One evening, we found a private beach, two hundred feet of sand all to ourselves, on a lake thirty miles out of town. Framed on both sides by woods and well-hidden from the highway, this beach had the additional advantage of being unpatrolled. We had no bathhouse in which to change, however, so Karen instructed me not to look as she walked about fifty feet away to a spot where she undressed and put on her suit.

Though we had been intimate for at least a week, I had still not seen her naked: Like a good Victorian, she demanded the shades be drawn, the lights out, and the covers pulled discreetly over us. But now, with the same methodical thoroughness, she wanted me to see her, so I looked, despite her warnings. She was bent over, under the tree boughs, the evening light breaking through the leaves and casting broken gold bands on her body. Her arms were delicate, the arms of a schoolgirl, I thought, an impression heightened by the paleness of her skin, but her breasts were full, at first making me think of Rubens's women, then of Renoir's, then of nothing at all. Slowly, knowing I was watching her, she pinned her hair up. Not her breasts or arms, but that expression of vague contentment as she looked out toward the water away from me: *That* made me feel a tingling below my heart, somewhere in an emotional center near my stomach. I wanted to pick her up and carry her somewhere, but with my knees wobbly it was all I could do to make my way over to where she stood and take her in my arms before she cried out. "Jesus," she said, shivering, "you gave me a surprise." I kissed her, waiting for inspiration to direct me on what to do next: Pick her up? Carry her? Make love to her on the sand? Wade into the water with her and swim out to the center of the lake, where we would drown together in a Lawrentian love-grip? But then we broke the kiss; she put on her swimsuit like a good citizen, and we swam for our usual fifteen minutes in silence. Afterward, we changed back into our clothes and drove home, muttering small talk. Behavior inspired by and demonstrating love embarrassed both of us. When I told her that she was beautiful and that I loved her, she patted me on the cheek and said, "Aw, how nice. You always try to say the right thing."

VIII

The Maple Street angle for *Harmony of the World* ran as follows: SYMPHONY OF FAITH IN A FAITHLESS AGE. Hindemith, I said, wished to confound the skeptics by composing a monument of faith. In an age of organized disharmony, of political chaos, he stood at the barricades defending tonality and traditional musical form. I carefully avoided any specific discussion of the musical materials of the symphony, which in the Schott orchestral score looked over-complex and melodically ugly. From what I could tell without hearing the piece, Hindemith had employed stunning technique in order to disguise his lack of inspiration, though I did not say so in print. Instead, I wrote that the symphony's failure to win public support was probably the result of Hindemith's refusal to use musical gimmicks on the one hand and sticky sweet melodies on the other. I wrote that he had not been dismayed by the bad reviews *Harmony of the World* had received, which was untrue. I said he was

a man of integrity. I did not say that men of integrity are often
unable to express joy when the occasion demands. Cascadilla liked
my article. "This guy sounds like me," he said, reading my copy.
"I respect him." The article ran five days before the concert and
was two pages away from the religion-and-faith section. Not long
after, the symphony ticket office called me to say that my piece
had caused a rush of ticket orders from ordinary folk, non-concert
types, who wanted to hear this "religious symphony." The woman
from the business office thanked me for my trouble. "Let's hope
they like it," I said.

"Of course they will," she assured me. "You've told them to."

But they didn't. Despite all the oratory in the symphony, it was
spiritually as dead as a lampshade. I could see why Hindemith had
been shocked by the public reaction. Our audience applauded
politely in discouragement, and then I heard an unusual sound
for this anonymous city: one man, full of fun and conviction,
booing loudly from the balcony. Booing the harmony of the world!
He must be a Satanist! Don't intentions mean anything? So what if
the harmony and joy were all counterfeit? The conductor came
out for a bow, smiled at the booing man, and very soon the applause died away. I left the hall, feeling responsible. Arriving at
the paper, I wrote a review of crushing dullness that reeked of bad
faith. Goddamn Hindemith! Here he was, claiming to have seen
God's workings, and they sounded like the workings of a steam
engine or a trolley car. A fake symphony, with optimism the composer did not feel! I decided (but did not write) that *Harmony of the
World* was just possibly the largest, most misconceived fiasco in
modern music's history. It was a symphony that historically could
not be written, by a man who was constitutionally not equipped to
write it. In my review, I kept a civil pen: I said that the performance lacked "luster," "a certain necessary glow."

IX

"I'm worried about the recital tomorrow."

"Aw, don't worry. Here, kiss me. Right here."

"Aren't you listening? I'm worried."

"I'm singing. You're just accompanying me. Nobody's going to
notice you. Move over a little, would you? Yeah, there. That pillow
was forcing my head against the wall."

"Why aren't you worried?"

"Why should I be worried? I don't want to worry. I want to make love. Isn't that better than worrying?"

"Not if I'm worried."

"People won't notice *you*. By the way, have you noticed that when I kiss you on the stomach, you get goose bumps?"

"Yes. I think you're taking this pretty lightly. I mean, it's almost unprofessional."

"That's because I'm an amateur. A one-hundred-percent amateur. Always and totally. Even at this. But that doesn't mean I don't have my moments. Mmmmmm. That's better."

"I thought it would maybe help. But listen. I'm still worried."

"Uhhhn. Oh, wait a minute. Wait a minute. Oh, I get it."

"What?"

"I get it. You aren't worried about yourself. You're worried about me."

X

Forty people attended her recital, which was sponsored by the city university's music school, in which Karen was a sometime student. Somehow we made our way through the program, but when we came to the Chanler settings I suddenly wanted Karen to sing them perfectly. I wanted an angel to descend and to take away the gypsy's curse. But she sang as she always had — off pitch — and when she came to "Ann Poverty," I found myself in that odd region between rage and pity.

> *Stranger, here lies*
> *Ann Poverty;*
> *Such was her name*
> *And such was she.*
> *May Jesu pity*
> *Poverty.*

But I was losing my capacity for pity.

In the green room, her forty friends came back to congratulate her. I met them. They were all very nice. She smiled and laughed: There would be a party in an hour. Would I go? I declined. When we were alone, I said I was going back to my place.

"Why?" she asked. "Shouldn't you come to my party? You're my lover, after all. That *is* the word."

"Yes. But I don't want to go with you."

"Why?"

"Because of tonight's concert, that's why."

"What about it?"

"It wasn't very good, was it? I mean, it just wasn't."

"I thought it was all right. A few slips. It was pretty much what I was capable of. All those people said they liked it."

"Those people don't matter!" I said, my eyes watering with anger. "Only the music matters. Only the music is betrayed, they aren't. They don't know about pitch, most of them, I mean, Jesus, they aren't genuine musicians, so how would they know? Do you really think what we did tonight was good? It wasn't! It was a travesty! We ruined those songs! How can you stand to do that?"

"I don't ruin them. I sing them adequately. I project feeling. People get pleasure from them. That's enough."

"It's awful," I said, feeling the ecstatic liftoff into rage. "You're so close to being good, but you *aren't* good. Who cares what those ignoramuses think? They don't know what notes you're *supposed* to hit. It's that goddamn slippery pitch of yours. You're killing those songs. You just *drop* them like watermelons on the stage! It makes me sick! I couldn't have gone on for another day listening to you and your warbling! I'd die first."

She looked at me and nodded, her mouth set in a half-moue, half-smile of non-surprise. There may have been tears in her eyes, but I didn't see them. She looked at me as if she were listening hard to a long-distance call. "You're tired of me," she said.

"I'm not tired of you. I'm tired of hearing you sing! Your voice makes my flesh crawl! Do you know why? Can you tell me why you make me sick? Why do you make me sick? Never mind. I'm just glad this is over."

"You don't look glad. You look angry."

"And you look smug. Listen, why don't you go off to your party? Maybe there'll be a talent scout there. Or roses flung riotously at you. But don't give a recital like this again, please, okay? It's a public disgrace. It offends music. It offends *me*."

I turned my back on her and walked out to my car.

XI

After the failure of *Harmony of the World,* Hindemith went on a strenuous tour that included Scandinavia. In Oslo, he was rehearsing the Philharmonic when he blinked his bright blue eyes twice, turned to the concertmaster, and said, "I don't know where I am." They took him away to a hospital; he had suffered a nervous breakdown.

XII

I slept until noon, having nothing to do at the paper and no reason to get up. At last, unable to sleep longer, I rose and walked to the kitchen to make coffee. I then took my cup to the picture window and looked down the hill to the trees of the conservation area, the view Stecker had once told me I should have.

The figure of a woman was hanging from one of the trees, a noose around her neck. I dropped my coffee cup and the hot coffee spilled out over my feet.

I ran out the back door in my pajamas and sprinted painfully down the hill's tall grass toward the tree. I was fifty feet away when I saw that it wasn't Karen, wasn't in fact a woman at all, but an effigy of sorts, with one of Karen's hats, a pillow head, and a dress hanging over a broomstick skeleton. Attached to the effigy was a note:

> In the old days, this might have been me. Not anymore. Still, I thought it'd make you think. And I'm not giving up singing, either. By the way, what your playing lacks is not fanaticism, but concentration. You can't seem to keep your mind on one thing for more than a minute at a time. *I* notice things, too. You aren't the only reviewer around here. Take good care of this doll, okay?
>
> XXXXX,
> Karen

I took the doll up and dropped it in the clothes closet, where it stands to this hour.

Hindemith's biographer, Geoffrey Skelton, writes, "[On the stage] the episodic scenes from Kepler's life fail to achieve immediate dramatic coherence, and the basic theme remains obscure . . ."

She won't of course see me again. She won't talk to me on the phone, and she doesn't answer my letters. I am quite lucidly aware of what I have done. And I go on seeing doubles and reflections and wave motion everywhere. There is symmetry, harmony, after all. I suppose I should have been nice to her. That, too, is a discipline. I always tried to be nice to everyone else.

On his deathbed, Hindemith has Kepler sing:

> *Und muss sehn am End:*
> *Die grosse Harmonie, das ist der Tod.*
> *Absterben ist, sie zu bewirken, not.*
> *Im Leben hat sie keine Statte.*

> Now, at the end, I see it:
> the great harmony: it is death.
> To find it, we must die.
> In life it has no place.

XIII

Hindemith's words may be correct. But Dante says that the residents of limbo, having never been baptized, will not see the face of God. This despite their having committed no sin, no active fault. In their fated locale they sigh, which keeps the air "forever trembling." No harmony for them, these guiltless souls. Through eternity, the residents of limbo — where one can imagine oneself if one cannot stand to imagine any part of hell — experience one of the most shocking of all the emotions that Dante names: "duol senza martíri," grief without torment. These sighs are rather like the sounds one hears drifting from front porches in small towns on soft summer nights.

EDITH MILTON

Coming Over

(FROM THE YALE REVIEW)

BEFORE I EVER GOT on the S.S. *Gripsholm*, I had decided I would be kissed before I got off again. I went about achieving this goal on one of the upper decks, somewhere in the middle of the Atlantic. The mist was so thick that it fell like rain where I sat inside the embrace of a Dutch sailor, embracing, rather to my astonishment, his moist and weaving tongue inside my innocent mouth.

The sound of a tango, to which my sister was undoubtedly dancing with either Mr. Richards or Sergeant Moody, drifted toward us from a lower deck. Mr. Richards and Sergeant Moody danced with delicate nostalgia, as if every step they took reminded them of some moment of their distant youth. They both looked permanently married.

"They're so *middling*," I complained to my sister.

"You're a snob," she said.

She was twenty, as supple and tawny as a barley stalk. She was modeling her character on Douglas Fairbanks, Jr., and her style on Marlene Dietrich. I was fourteen. And I was not so much a snob as impatient at the dullness of the example she set. It seemed unlikely that she was enjoying her tango under the colored lights below. But in the dark, I knew myself, certainly, to be losing control of my enterprise on the boat deck.

That I had had my breasts investigated did not surprise me, since I had been given to understand that that was standard procedure. But a hand was now reaching inside the elastic of my gym knickers. I did not know what to do about this hand, though I found its exploration thoroughly alarming; partly because it called up echoes of half-heard warnings I had never quite understood;

largely because I knew that thick cotton gym knickers were inappropriate attire for what the hand was doing to them. And although a hand could hardly be expected to know that the disgraceful knickers were maroon red with a large thistle embroidered on the side to let anyone who might be interested know what team I was on at school, I blushed with shame at the exorbitance of my own innocence.

The hand tried a new approach, via the thistle, where it paused briefly, tracing the outline with a puzzled finger.

"That'th a thiththle," I gasped, disengaging my mouth, which squelched like a suction cup. "It's my house. I played for Scotland."

I played, I should have told him, for Scotland very badly. And the captain of Thistle had offered several times to swap me to Rose or Daffodil for one of *their* duds. But my Dutch sailor was anyway not listening.

"Baby," he crooned. It seemed to be the only English he knew. But his hand had made headway through the elastic, and at last found home.

•

The war had been over for a year. People were going home. People without a home to go to were going somewhere else, and the American Committee for Jewish Refugees had taken over five of the four-berth cabins in Standard Class for twenty of us who had relatives who were already American citizens. We had been given visas and passage on the *Gripsholm*'s first voyage since her transformation from a hospital ship back to passengers and peace.

The porthole of our cabin was close to the level of the sea. It swung insecurely between the elements, like a drowning man. In its up moments it looked upon nothing but free blue air. But in its down moments it turned toward an obsessive scrutiny of the dark water, which reached up as if it might claim us at any moment.

The porthole did not open easily. It stayed shut even though I tried prying it with a nail file. Under its ambiguous view of the environment there was a tiny sink, and next to the sink there were two minute chairs. The only other furnishings were four storage lockers that pulled out from under the two sets of double-decker bunks. My sister and I had already put our suitcases on the bunks to the right of the entrance and my sister had locked away our only heirlooms, five Swiss watches and our grandmother's diamond ring, when Rosa and Bruna came in.

"Excuse me," Bruna said. "Would you mind very much? We

would like so much if possible two top bunks. If it makes no difference."

They had been in Dachau for several years. They were not sure how many. At night they still woke often, thinking that they were there, and to see another bunk above their own would convince them that their nightmare was not over.

My sister moved her suitcase down at once. "*I* don't care where I sleep," she said.

They were grateful. Would she mind also turning the electric light on and off for them that evening? It was Friday, and they did not want to break the Shabbas.

"All right," my sister said. "But I ought to tell you, I'm Jewish too, you know."

"Orthodox?" Bruna asked. She had the voice of a prompter, inexpressive and very low. None of the things she said seemed quite to belong to her. "I assume from the way you dress that you are Reform."

"How do I dress?" said my sister, alarmed: Dietrich's outfits were certainly not Reform. But she said she would do the lights.

"And about toothbrushes," Rosa added. Though they both spoke English remarkably well, Rosa's was livelier and more fluent than her sister's. She explained that it would not be kosher to use for their toothbrushes the single glass on the little shelf over the sink, if we were to use it too.

"Christ!" said my sister, putting her toothbrush back in her suitcase.

•

We had had a long day. It had begun to rain that morning as we left our hotel. It was still raining on Euston Station as we waited for our train there; and all the way up to Liverpool there was nothing but drizzle. In Liverpool it poured. The middle-aged man who had shared our third-class compartment on the train rushed to raise his umbrella over my sister's head. From the way he looked back at me as I absorbed rain out of range of his umbrella, I was sure he had daughters my age; perhaps even my sister's age, though she had whispered to me that his name was Mr. Richards and that he was divorced.

Clark Gable was divorced. Errol Flynn was divorced. Mr. Richards to me looked married.

Everyone who had been on the boat train arrived together at the boat. There was some trouble at the mouth of the boarding ramp, where two officials checked the papers of those rushing toward shelter out of the rain.

But my sister was looking out to sea. "Jesus," she said. "Did you ever see so many rubbers?"

I had never in fact seen any rubbers at all. When I looked where she pointed toward a scum of white bobbing at the edge of the quay, the vision did not instruct my curiosity. I could see corks and bottles, planks and cardboard boxes, a doll's head floating beside a doll's limbless body, and the drowned corpse of some animal that had once been the size of a small sheep. There was nothing else in the direction my sister pointed to, except that deposit of what looked like laundry foam.

But it seemed to me that the dark mysteries that she saw must be invisible only to an ignorant eye like mine, and that the initiated could certainly sort them out from the other garbage. So I said "Gee, yes," and snickered dutifully.

•

It was still raining when the ship weighed anchor.

"Prosit," said my sister, raising her glass to chaos. Dinner the first night out was a buffet. In Standard Class no one had been assigned tables yet. There were too many people on board. The forks had run out, and the woman next to me was slicing her meat with a spoon. It was announced that the fish mousse was no more, but that the ham salad would be resurrected in the near future. With eight or ten other people, Rosa and Bruna sat apart at the long table where kosher food was expected but not, as yet, forthcoming. In the passage outside, voices were raised over questions of luggage, and people lined up to leave their cash and jewelry at the bursar's office.

We were sitting in a corner with Mr. Richards, and with Sergeant Moody, who shared a cabin with him. After many attempts they had secured a liter of wine from the bar, but the glass of milk I was supposed to be getting had still not appeared. "Yo. Yo," said the steward from whom it had been ordered. He was brilliantly above anything so bland as milk; a long, golden youth, beautifully turned toward cheerfulness, with gentian eyes barely visible under the blond fountain of his forelock. Smiling still in his comfortable surrender to total incomprehension, he rushed off to bring me something, and brought me an empty wine glass. Then he stationed himself behind the roast beef and began carving.

"Moment," he said, slicing furiously. "Moment." A gnarled and ugly boy on crutches was trying simultaneously to hold out his plate for meat and to hold himself steady against the motion of the ship. It lurched, and the slice of beef about to be settled down onto his plate threw itself onto the floor. Our golden steward and the gnarled young cripple looked down upon it ruefully, as if it proclaimed something they would rather have kept to themselves.

For want of milk, Mr. Richards finally poured me some wine.

That night I swam to bed and rocked to sleep in the arms of Neptune and Dionysus. My sister also complained of a strange stomach. And we both forgot that it was the Shabbas, and that Bruna and Rosa were still at large. I was long asleep when a whisper dragged me from the heaving deep where I had lain.

"Please," it said. "The light, please."

Obedient in somnolence, I switched on the light. The room leaped from its darkness, a brilliant green except for Rosa's and Bruna's faces. They were golden, suffused with the light of ineffable joy.

"We listened to music," Rosa said.

"We are learning to dance," said Bruna.

"From Sven," Rosa added. They were trying to speak softly, so as not to wake my sister, perhaps; or, more likely, so as not to wake themselves from this happy dream.

"Sven," said my sister, turning in her bunk. "Handsome Sven the steward in the dining room? The one behind the roast beef? That Sven?"

"He is asking us to teach him English."

"Why would he do that?" said my sister. "He speaks perfect English. *Yo. So. Rossbiff. Sose.* What more does he want?"

"Yes, but when we give him the lessons, he says in exchange he is teaching us to dance. Rosa and I, we never danced in our life."

"Sven the goy," said my sister. "Did you pause to consider that he might be less kosher than my goddamn toothbrush?"

"We smoked a cigarette," Rosa whispered. It was a confession, this time, not a confidence. But my sister had turned her face to the wall, like Nebuchadnezzar, and heard no more.

•

When my Dutch sailor had looked for something in his pocket, I knew, with the sober shock of all epiphanies, that I would at last see a rubber. What he pulled out instead was a package of French cigarettes, of which, swept by disappointment into an easy corruption, I at once accepted one.

The Gauloise proved useful for keeping the sailor at bay. Held at the correct angle, low toward the thigh, it even removed his hand from my secret shame, the gym knickers. But the smoke made me feel strange. As if I had borrowed someone else's body, several sizes too large for me.

In the sharp light hung over the hatchway, the face of the Dutch sailor had taken on a sinister bias. He had a Slavic jaw and small, cruel teeth that I imagined biting into the flesh of babies and other minority victims. He had a pimple under his lower lip, which looked at the same time too distant and too large, like something seen close-up in a movie. He was smiling.

"Komm, komm," he said soothingly, alarming me. He made a comic pantomime of someone puffing inexpertly on a cigarette and choking. Then he took my Gauloise tenderly between forefinger and middle finger, drew it gently from my hand, and threw it into the void, out where the sea would be.

By noon on our second day out I had become accustomed to the swaying of the ship. The other passengers had begun to arrange themselves in the inchoate organization of social intimacies. Table assignments had been posted that morning, and as the news of their appearance spread, people turned their backs on the bright Atlantic sunshine above, to go into the darkness below and discover what place in the Order of Things had been allotted to them.

I looked for a comfortable deck chair in which to read my current volume of Victor Hugo, and took the place next to where Rosa and Bruna lay with their eyes closed, courting a suntan. The gnarled boy who had dropped his meat the night before was trying to make himself agreeable by asking them riddles.

"Es gibt drei Lügnern aus Berlin," he said. "Und der Erste sagt . . ."

Rosa and Bruna, without opening their eyes, said they did not know the answer. I could not blame them for not looking at him. His face was bony and very thin. Poised between crutches it looked like a gargoyle's, ready for mounting.

"Ah, Fraülein," he said, seeing me stare at him. "Vielleicht wissen Sie die Antwort? Es gibt drei Lügnern aus Berlin, ja? Und der Erste sagt . . ."

"I'm sorry," I said. "I don't speak German."

"Ah, please," he said. "I apologize." He seemed delighted to have found someone to speak to. I had discovered from Rosa that his name was Arnold and that he was afflicted with an arthritic disease that had become worse during his five years of hiding from the Germans in a damp Dutch cellar. Rosa said he would die of it soon. "I thought you were one of us brats with the Refugee Committee."

"I am," I said.

"Then you must be from Poland. Or France, perhaps? I speak several languages, whichever you prefer."

"English," I said. "I only speak English."

Several sailors had come up from below. They had bought themselves half-pints of beer at the little bar nearby, and now stood by the ship's railing, their backs to the sea, surveying the inland scenery displayed on deck. Their eyes focused particularly on my sister, who was playing blackjack with the sergeant, and whose pillar of poker chips had grown and spilled in front of her into a flood of red, white, and blue. She was trying to maintain a sporting distance from her own success, I could see, but she grinned in triumph as she swept up the sergeant's last, small, desperate stake.

"That is extremely clever," said Arnold. "For a refugee to speak only English. How did you manage that?"

"I forgot my German," I said, truthfully. Two of the sailors were making mouths at my sister, as if they were whispering suggestions of an unspeakable nature into the air over her head. She failed to notice them. The other two sailors gave her up and turned their attention over a wider range; toward Rosa and Bruna, I saw. Their eyes slid along the two girls as if they were following a tennis match between neck and ankle.

"You forgot your German?" said Arnold.

"I don't like German," I said. "I don't like being German."

"But that's very original," Arnold said. "You don't like it. So you forget it. Did it go away?"

The sailors' attention had moved still further toward the south. One of them noticed me.

"Yes," I said. "Of course it went away. I'm going to America."

With enormous deliberation, the sailor engaged my eye. He was, I saw even then, an amazingly ordinary sort of boy; the sort of pale, blue-eyed, medium-sized boy who fills the schools between Amsterdam and Seattle, between Copenhagen, Glasgow, Toronto, and points west. The species might be indicated on a map by a chain of round-headed, pleasant, brown-haired stick figures circling the globe a little above the fiftieth latitude. He looked very nice, I thought; appetizing. But I knew I would never be able to describe him to anyone in years to come.

Seriously, taking his time to complete the gesture, he winked at me.

"I think," Arnold said, "that you may be just the sort of political analyst who would enjoy solving riddles. In this one, three liars from Berlin are speaking. And the first one says . . ."

The sailors had left. But not before the anomalous boy who had winked at me had also blown me a kiss.

•

The next morning a discussion began among the refugees about where we had spent the war and which of our relatives we were to join in New York. During this conversation Arnold leafed through the notebook in which he worked his mathematical puzzles and chess problems, and became preoccupied with a long equation that I saw took up several pages.

I had begun to feel that the Dutch sailor might be the perfect provider of my first kiss.

•

Not that he seemed in any hurry to volunteer. He kept his distance when he appeared on deck at four bells that afternoon. The next afternoon he came again. On both these occasions he had only one friend with him. Loyal to the established pattern, they leaned against the railing with their backs to the sea, and my sailor carefully smirked and winked at me over the brim of his glass. I construed his grimaces, possibly correctly, as indicating concupiscence. But I noticed that when he looked upon the dashing presence of my sister, which he did long and often, his face became serious and expressed the deep, religious understanding of one who accepts that God may be too busy counting falling sparrows to pay any attention to him.

My sister, for her part, noticed him then no more than she had noticed him the first time. Sergeant Moody had finished with blackjack, probably forever. Forced into a tête-à-tête, she and Mr. Richards had begun to play deck tennis; but after an hour of being humiliated, Mr. Richards retired, not merely from deck tennis but from the deck. My sister was now playing darts with Kurt Weinberg.

She had ripened in the sun to a vibrant ocher. Kurt Weinberg was darker and deeper, the color of treacle. His chest was covered with a mesh of fine gold wire, and his eyes were pale and gray. He did not look married. Nor for that matter did he look divorced. After he won his second game from my sister, I asked him if he had fought in the Underground; and like any man would who has fought in the Underground, he said, "What on earth makes you think so?"

"There are five men," said Arnold, "whom we will naturally call A, B, C, D, and Eric. Each tells either entirely the truth, or equally entirely the untruth." Arnold's world, though full of ambiguities, was also a universe ruthlessly oversimplified. The pinpoint of verity could, by the right procedure, always be found in the midst of an infinity of everything that was not itself. I thought such hopefulness annoying. To me, to find the tiny truth or to define the enormous untruth seemed like two witches' tasks in a fairy tale, equally impossible. I told him so.

"But this is mathematics, not witchcraft," he said. "We are speaking algebraically. A, B, C, and D represent binomial possibilities of *yes* and *no*. They have nothing to do with real life. Eric also has nothing to do with real life, but he is very charming. I introduced him to involve you emotionally in the calculations. I think his hair may sweep down over one eye, and he should be seen almost constantly in profile."

My Dutch sailor, meanwhile, had made his appearance. He seemed bored, and after winking at me twice he began to waggle his ears. He could move them several inches forward and backward.

"The important thing," said Arnold, "from the point of view of solving the riddle, is that A, B, C, D, and Eric each is wearing either a blue dot or red dot on his forehead. Blue for truth, red for lies, naturally. What are you staring at?"

I waved my head, as unobtrusively as I could, toward the sailor, who had managed to get his scalp to join his ear muscles, and was presenting, for my delectation, a cranium in total upheaval.

"You have something wrong with your neck?" Arnold asked.

I hissed at him to look over his left shoulder.

"He has something wrong with his head? Good afternoon, sir," said Arnold. "Is it catching?"

"Hoh?" said the Dutch sailor, staring quite rudely. But in time he realized what he was doing and stopped doing it. He even smiled, a little uncertainly, and held out his hand. Then he had another idea. Conspiratorially, glancing uneasily at me, he bent down to whisper something in Arnold's ear, probably in Dutch. Arnold answered aloud, probably in German. Soon they were talking.

"He wants to know," said Arnold, "whether I have any romantic claims on you. Do I have any romantic claims on you?" After some further talk with the sailor he turned to me again. "He is asking how old you are," Arnold said. "I have so far supposed, from the maturity of your riddle-solving capacity, that you must be at least fifty. But he tells me you do not look at least fifty, and that he is worried about the opinion of his comrades. They take a dark view of the seduction of children, and he wants to know, I suppose, if he seduces you, whether he will be considered perverted. He says I am to ask you if you are sixteen."

I was caught. I wanted to say that certainly I was sixteen. That I was, indeed, seventeen, eighteen; going on twenty. But I had a premonition that such an untruth would lessen me in Arnold's estimation; would in fact turn me into nothing better than one of his riddles' liars.

I compromised. I said I was not yet entirely sixteen. Almost, but not entirely.

"A baby," said my Dutch sailor, when this news was translated to him. But he was grinning enthusiastically, and went into further consultation with Arnold; I assumed, therefore, that almost sixteen was all right.

"He says his name is Renni," Arnold said.

"Tell him my name, too."

"I don't think he cares," Arnold said. "He says could you meet him here for the dance tonight. Could you be here on deck at nine?"

"Sure," I said. "Of course. Yes."

Arnold looked at me for several seconds before he translated this to the Dutch sailor. "Gewiss," he said. "Bestimmt. Ja." It sounded unpleasantly like a political slogan; but my sailor smirked at me, satisfied.

When he had returned below to the crew's quarters, Arnold drew a sigh of contentment. "Back to important things," he said. "You recall the situation: Five characters? Red and blue dots? Then, to go on — A says he can see three red dots and one blue dot. B says he can see three blue dots and one red dot. And Eric says he has seen only his own hair since 1932."

•

A stroke of genius. I had given my Dutch sailor to understand that it was too cold for me up on deck. It was, in fact, too cold for me up on deck. I said "Brrr" and hugged my arms around myself to show him the ineffable sincerity of my feelings.

"Baby, baby," he said. But he also put his pea jacket over my shoulders, which were trembling under the cold hands of fear and dampness. He thumped me kindly on the back for a few moments, but then he had a better idea. Taking my hand, he led me down below, as I had hoped he would. Below, where all the sensible people must be on a wet night.

The little smoking lounge where he brought me was paneled in polished wood. Long carved benches stood around its walls, and in the center there were small round tables surrounded by chairs upholstered in pale green plush. The carpet on the floor was thick, and also pale green. It looked like a very comfortable room to sit in. But there was not another soul sitting there except for the two of us.

•

I had begun to feel afraid much earlier in the evening. Not of the sailor or of the nasty things that it seemed possible he might do to me. It was my own behavior that frightened me. It seemed quite unlike my own behavior. Its unfamiliarity was like seeing another face stare back at me from the mirror. Why, for instance, had I not mentioned to my sister that I was going to the dance? Why had I said nothing when, her honey skin wrapped in white taffeta, her brown feet laced into silver sandals, she had gone into her usual Dietrich routine?

"Here I stand all dressed for the whorehouse," she said. "Care to join me?"

I had decided not to wear one of my own schoolgirl frocks, but to take a dress from my sister's locker. The one I had chosen was dark blue, with little white flowers around the hem, and neither she nor I liked it much. She would certainly have been happy to lend it to me if I had asked her, though she might perhaps have tried to persuade me to borrow instead a black linen sheath that she cherished and that I admired. But I failed to ask her.

It was the night for dressing up. Soon after my sister had left,

Rosa and Bruna came in with new dance gowns that they had
bought at the little shop on B Deck where the First Class passengers got their sunglasses and their tanning oil. Rosa was quick and
exquisite; she animated her yards of yellow organdy like the dark
spirit that moves a thundercloud. Bruna was pale and placid; she
did very little for her layers of pink chiffon. And they did nothing
for her.

"Is it right? Is it fashionable?" Rosa asked me. "We have spent
all our money. Are we pretty?"

They had bought lipsticks to match their dresses. The lipsticks
were made by someone called Max Factor; Rosa said this sounded
to her like a Jewish name, and she thought the lipsticks therefore
were probably kosher. Did I agree that they were probably kosher?

I showed them how my sister put one color of lipstick on top of
another, pink on orange, orange on pink, to give her lips a lumi-
nous glow.

"How wonderful," they breathed, leaning their heads together
toward the little mirror while they tried my sister's method. They
floated out, buoyed with the joy of what they saw in the mirror;
airborne upon the bouffant abomination of their gowns.

After they were gone, I pinned my own hair back into a loose
knot, and, eschewing the lipstick I had urged on Rosa and Bruna,
I powdered my face to an interesting pallor. I looked dramatically
ghastly: Lady Jane Grey on her way to the scaffold, or her ghost
on the way back.

•

In my anxiety not to be late, I was early. My Dutch sailor was not
in sight. Nor was a large part of my sister that Kurt Weinberg was
hiding in his embrace, his black, cable-knit arms encircling her
white taffeta being while his face was buried in the butterscotch
hollow of her shoulder. He looked like Dracula with a sweet tooth.
For a whole hour that afternoon he had defeated her at darts,
until at last he had steered her toward shuffleboard where she
could win. Now he claimed the prize of her victory.

As they waltzed on the slippery square of dance floor in the mist,
I could see, under the colored lights, that she had her eyes closed.
I stayed out in the dark, by the bulwarks, where, even if she
opened her eyes, she would be unlikely to see me. And even if she
saw me, she would be unlikely to recognize me: though I supposed
she might recognize her own dress.

My sailor arrived. He had two red roses for me. I clasped them to the chaste bosom of my stolen dress. He also brought me a tall pink drink that tasted like rotting cherries, and a bracelet made of beads that he tried to thrust upon the arm free of roses. I saw that my sister had left Kurt Weinberg, his prize ungranted, and that Kurt Weinberg was now dancing with someone else. It was Bruna, in fact; she was melting like warm spun sugar into his cool embrace.

And my sister, laughing her Dietrich laugh again, had opened her eyes unusually wide. She was alone with Mr. Richards, but Sergeant Moody had only gone for a fresh liter of wine. I thought she had still not seen me. But when my sailor finally succeeded in twisting the bracelet onto my arm and began to draw me away from the music and dancing, further into the darkness, my sister raised her glass to me in formal, sardonic salute.

•

My state of dishevelment was terminal; the stolen dress lay at half-mast, and various other pieces of clothing unhooked, unrolled, and fell from me in a confusion that I had long since stopped trying to catalogue. My hair had unbound itself, and though I was still in complete possession of my gym knickers, and, incidentally, my virtue, the damn thistle was now patent to anyone who cared to look. In this instance only the Dutch sailor, who gazed slightly ruefully at my transformation from the Martyr Queen to Banquo's ghost.

The sailor had released his grip, along with my stockings, and he seemed uncertain what to do next. He may even have asked me what he ought to do next, but if he did, he certainly got no answer. In the end, *faute de mieux*, what he did was play the piano.

I have no idea what distracted him from what I assumed was his raging lust; possibly the revelation of my thistled knickers; possibly the realization of my extreme youth and disintegration; more probably the fact that it was getting late, or that, lacking any talent for depravity, he was getting bored. The piano, to which he turned from me as I began to reassemble my pieces, was an old upright that stood in one corner of the lounge, and that sounded yearningly after its own lost youth, so that all the melodies put into it came out of it in modes of deep despondency and feebleness. He played "Lili Marlene" three times, and "I'll Be Loving You (Always)" three times. "The Blue Danube" he tried only once.

At eight bells he indicated that it was time for him to return to duty. He walked me as far as the companionway that led to my cabin. Half-teasing, before he left me he kissed my hand. The one with the bracelet on. The one not holding the roses. "Ciao, Baby baby," he said.

•

I pulled my bracelet off with my teeth. And I pulled the porthole open, shattering, with the force of my need to pry it free, Rosa's and Bruna's kosher toothglass on the floor. I threw the bracelet and the roses as far into the Atlantic as I could, and then, behind them, my gym knickers. The honor of Scotland floated out to sea, and sank. But it could be replaced. In my locker I had two other pairs identical to the knickers I had just set adrift.

Rosa had to knock to be let in. I had locked the door. She stood on the other side, diminutive in dampness, her billowing organdy collapsed around her like the wet wings of a bright yellow butterfly.

She climbed to her bunk, and we lay silently, waiting for our sisters to return. Mine came in before I fell asleep, and hit her shin on one of the small chairs and said "Shit." I heard her looking through her locker, checking on our heirloom watches and our grandmother's ring before she got into bed. Bruna was still not there next morning.

•

She was at breakfast, though. Still in her pink dress, sitting next to Kurt Weinberg at the kosher table. They seemed not to be saying anything to each other.

Arnold was also there, drinking coffee. He hardly ever took meals with the rest of us, and I had never seen him at breakfast.

"Joining the peasants?" I asked him.

"Stopping by to see how they all are. How are they all?"

"Some of them look a bit weedy to me," I said, glancing at Bruna.

"How are you?"

"What?" I said. "Fine, I suppose. How should I be?"

"Forgive my asking," Arnold said. "I am merely gathering a little empirical data. One never can tell about peasants." He seemed glad to see me.

•

"A man from Prague is traveling through Germany. He stands at a crossroads," Arnold said. "He wishes to know the way to Frank-

furt. Of the three people from whom he asks directions, one is
from Bremen and always tells the truth. One is from München
and always tells a lie. And one is from Nürnberg and is very unsure
of himself. He alternates between telling the truth and telling a
lie."

He was not well, even by the standards of his sickness. He took
medication that did not go with sunshine, and his days of sitting
on the deck had given him a deep red flush. In patches his skin
was puffed and swollen. He had been confined below, and I spent
hours in his company in the main lounge, where crew members
were not allowed and where therefore my sailor would not find
me.

"Why are there always liars in your riddles?" I asked.

"Liars make riddles possible," Arnold said. "Besides, I put in just
as many people who tell the truth."

"What about the man from Prague?" I said.

"What about him?"

"What is he?"

"A Czechoslovakian," said Arnold.

"I mean, does he tell lies or does he tell the truth? We've no way
of knowing. When he says he wants to go to Frankfurt, why should
we believe him? Perhaps he's only being frivolous when he asks
for directions, in which case you and I are just wasting our time."

Arnold's dark eyes shone at me from his flushed face. "Wonderful," he said. "I can see you are right. The man wants nothing
more than idle chitchat. He is probably trying to hide from his
German friends how much he hates their country and longs to go
back to his own. Shall we have tea?"

By then, even crossing the length of the lounge on his crutches
was an effort for him. I went for tea and a tray of biscuits, and
brought them back to our little table. He poured our cups from
the squat metal pot.

"Why am I so obsessed with riddles?" he said. "Do you know?
Why do *you* think I am so obsessed with riddles?"

We began in time to speak of other things. Among the subjects
we covered that afternoon were the ability to foretell the future
from one's dreams, and the disappearance of the Bengal tiger.
After a while, when it was already well past dinnertime, I asked
him if he would mind if I read him a chapter or two from my
Victor Hugo.

·

Toward the end of the voyage, the atmosphere of the dining room had changed. People I had never seen, Americans given over to *mal de mer,* appeared with pale faces and displayed their dyspepsia publicly, as if to exercise it before it disembarked. Those who had made friends or acquired lovers became jealous of each minute not devoted to their company, and changed seatings and tables so as to be with the beloved. There were no exceptions to this. Kurt Weinberg, for instance, had become irreligious and moved as far away from the kosher table and from Bruna as he could. I discovered that it was not likely, after all, that he had fought in the Underground; he shared his new table with someone he had known since childhood, someone he had grown up with in Winnetka, Illinois.

From his safe distance I caught him now and then looking over his Greek nose and under his golden lashes in Bruna's direction; like me, I suppose, waiting for her to come to a proper realization that she had been seduced and abandoned, and to act accordingly. But she disappointed us both. She ate well and slept soundly. At least she snored. For dinner she put on the dismal pink dress she had bought for the dance, serenely unaware that it had brought her anything but good luck and happy memories for her later years.

It was Rosa, in fact, who did all the complaining, beloved though she was. Golden Sven rushed forward as soon as she came into the dining room. He pulled out her chair for her. He hovered over her with kosher offerings of meat and gravy. As she left the table on our last night aboard, he looked after her, his eyes tragic with parting.

But Rosa was disappointed in him. "He doesn't know to dance," she told me. "The waltz a little. The fox trot bad. And the rumba not. For that I spent money on a new dress?"

On the last night there was a ball in the First Class lounge for the upper classes. We in Standard were excluded, but my sister and Mr. Richards were going anyway. So was Sergeant Moody. And even Rosa and Bruna were thinking of putting their dresses to a final use.

I was going to read to Arnold.

•

He liked the descriptive passages in Hugo: "The grandest productions of architecture are not so much individual as social works, rather the offspring of nations in labor than the inventions of genius."

The dramatic passages, however, puzzled him. "Do you understand that?" he would ask after a particularly Gothic moment that had not seemed to me, really, something that needed to be understood.

Further consideration usually brought me to the conclusion that I understood it well enough. "I think they're all batty," I explained.

"One should read it again," said Arnold. "We are missing something somewhere."

I was on my way to the library, to read it again and find what we were missing, when I passed a line of sailors standing on the companionway. The Dutch sailor was at the end, at the top of the line. They grinned joyfully at my approach, as if this were exactly what they had waited for, catbirds beholding the oncoming cat. One by one they began to whistle. I held my head straight, though my face was burning. It was too late to turn and run.

"Baby baby," said the Dutch sailor between whistles. I wondered what he had said about me to the others. "Baby baby baby."

Under the compulsion of forces too strong for me to resist, I turned on the lot of them, and stuck out my tongue. A deed so craven that I confessed it to no one, ever; not even Arnold.

•

For some reason I thought it was important to see the Statue of Liberty, so I got up at six the next morning in order not to miss it. I spent two hours staring toward America, mistaking one lighthouse after another for the Mother of Exiles. After ten lighthouses had gone by, I gave up and had breakfast.

The dining room was empty. There were only three people at the kosher table. I had almost finished the last crumb of my brioche when my sister tottered in with her eyes half-closed. She said the dance had been a great success. They had been thrown out five times.

I wanted to look at New York, so I left her triumphant and yawning. It had started to rain. The skyline, if there was one, was hidden by the sky, which hung over the city like an executioner's mask. We were surrounded by traffic; tugs, tankers, barges. The noise they made was terrible. Around the shores of one of the nearby islands I could make out a road crawling with giant insects, a species from Brobdingnag.

"Are those cars?" asked Rosa, pointing. She and Bruna had joined us. Arnold stood next to me.

"Luxury tanks," he said. "A new concept in warfare."

We stared at these shores on which we would soon disembark, where things grew beyond any scale that we had ever known before. Out there people we did not remember, who shared our blood, waited to claim us. My sister and I would live near Boston. Rosa and Bruna in New Jersey. Arnold was to die in Chicago. When at last Bedloe's Island came in sight, and the great raised arm of Liberty, in scale with the enormousness of this new land, her torch was lost in the lowering mist.

My sister had given the watches and the ring to Sergeant Moody, who had told her that, as a soldier in uniform, he could get them through customs for her more easily than she could herself. Now she had lost Sergeant Moody and appeared walking back and forth over the deck, looking for him. "Son of a bitch," she said. The strangers on shore who laid claim to us would expect us to arrive complete with those goods of which we were advertised as being in possession. They were the charms for our safety.

We were almost in the harbor. Tugs had taken over our progress and were bringing us in, while in the lounge a mob formed around the immigration officials who had just come on board.

" 'Your tired, your poor, your huddled masses,' " said Arnold, who had looked it up in the library the night before, in preparation for this moment when we passed under Liberty's nose. Her great blank eyes, as blind as Polyphemus's, stared away from our future toward the place from which we had come. "It seems an unnecessarily insulting form of invitation. 'Wretched refuse.' Do you think one should accept it?" His hair was hung with shining beads of water from the rain.

And when it was time to leave, he had some trouble adjusting his crutches so as to take my hand in both his own.

ANNE HOBSON FREEMAN

The Girl Who Was No Kin to the Marshalls

(FROM THE VIRGINIA QUARTERLY REVIEW)

IT BEGAN BACK at her birth, or at least her baptism, when she was named Clare Colston for the mother of her Richmond grandmother. Although this fact endeared her to her relatives in Richmond, it endangered her in Lexington, a dark, alien, and mountainous land ruled by her other grandmother, Margaret Lewis Marshall Marshall. The grandmother for whom Clare's older sister, Maggie, was named.

Every June their parents used to dump the two of them up there while they tootled off for two weeks of vacation — two bleak weeks for Clare, two blissful weeks for her sister, who could do no wrong in Lexington just as surely as Clare could do no right.

If there was one thing in the world that Grandma Marshall could not abide, it was a child who was timid, a child who hid tear-splotched postcards from her mother underneath her pillow, a child who slunk around the halls, jumping back as if she had just seen a snake when her own grandmother happened to walk past her, and, worst of all, perhaps, a child who would come creeping in, in the middle of the night, and tiptoe all the way around the enormous walnut sleigh bed her grandparents slept in to wake up her grand*father*, whispering, "Come help me. Please. I can't make the water stop running in the john."

The madder Grandma got, the more timid Clare got. Finally, one Easter night when they were visiting there, as Clare lay in bed she heard her grandmother saying to her mother downstairs:

"Mark my words. You are making a mistake to let that child grow up sensitive and timid. Which is just plain self-centered, if you ask for my opinion. How can you expect her to develop any backbone?"

Clare's mother murmured something.

Then Grandma's voice, strong and clear again: "Of course she can't help the fact she's so much less attractive than her sister — who has inherited the Marshall coloring . . ." (That meant dark, curly hair. And fair, rosy skin.) "While Clare," she was saying, "is like all of the Colstons" (Clare's father's family) . . ."Blonde and pale and pasty. Every time I look at her I think, That child can *not* be kin to me."

At the breakfast table, during those interminable visits in June, Clare would stare into her plate, the Blue Willow pattern, trying to imagine she was halfway round the world from Lexington and Grandma, standing on that tiny bridge with those tiny Chinese people who, she could tell from a certain apologetic hunch in their posture, were every bit as sensitive and timid as the Colstons. She would stare into her plate so that she wouldn't have to look at all the portraits and the photographs of dark-haired, rosy-skinned, flashing blue-eyed Marshalls, lined up on the walls like an infantry division, backing Grandma up.

Actually, the least ferocious-looking Marshall in the bunch was the old Chief himself, his leathery face webbed with tiny wrinkles. But at least some of them looked like laugh wrinkles. And what she took to be his napkin was tucked into his collar, as if he were expecting to sit down to breakfast, too.

Way down by the sideboard, over Granddaddy's shoulder, there was even more significant visual relief. A steel engraving of Robert E. Lee — full face in his double-buttoned uniform, with soft white hair and beard and eyes that twinkled with a quality she read as sympathy, since he, too, was no kin to the Marshalls.

A slight exaggeration. You would have had to go a long way in Virginia to find a person who was absolutely no kin to the Marshalls. But General Lee was distant kin, at best. As were the poor old Colstons. And heaven knows her grandmother had made it very clear that didn't count.

After they had sat for what seemed several hours at the breakfast table, Grandma would pick up a brass belle (literally, a tiny lady with a clapper under her hoop skirt) and ring for the maid to clear the table.

The maid was a robust, dirty-blonde, pink-kneed girl from Hogback Mountain, with a reputation on the campuses of Washington & Lee and V.M.I. that Clare's high-minded grandmother chose simply to ignore.

Her name, it just so happened, was Virginia. And she would bump open the swinging door with one enormous haunch, turn and glare at Grandma with her freckled arms folded on her bosom, and say, "What d'ya want?"

"You may clear the table now, Virginia," Grandma would answer with a sigh indicating she would never, ever, quite recover from her dislocation from the better-mannered colored maids of Portsmouth and the genteel customs of Tidewater in general, where people drove around in "cyars," and cultivated "gyardens," and sometimes even tried to dignify their "gyarbage."

As they pushed their rickety Victorian chairs back from the table, Grandma would train her steel-blue eyes on Clare and say, "It's time for you to walk your grandfather to V.M.I."

Released, at last, Clare would bound out to the sitting room to fetch his leather pouch and pipe, while he'd unhook his khaki officer's cap from the coat rack in the hall, and off the two of them would go. Never once did she question the necessity of walking her grandfather to work. Or ask why her sister was kept at home with Grandma. All she ever wondered, every now and then, was how Granddaddy got to work when she was gone.

By that time he was treasurer of the Virginia Military Institute, a job his friends and cousins got him in the early 1930s when his small bank, the Bank of Tidewater, in Portsmouth, failed.

As the screen door slammed behind them, she would slip her fingers into her grandfather's rough tobacco-stained hand, and they would cross Washington Street, then step onto the bright white cement walk that ran, like a hem, along the bottom of the lush green lawn of Washington & Lee.

Now Granddaddy was a Marshall, too, of course. He was, in fact, her grandmother's double second cousin. And Clare always assumed, though nobody ever told her, that the main reason Grandma married him was so she wouldn't have to change her maiden name.

But Granddaddy didn't seem like a Marshall. Not Grandma's kind of Marshall, anyway, which Clare came to understand later was a relatively rare kind — a city Marshall, fully urbanized, even worse, Tidewaterized. While Granddaddy was a country Marshall, the more common kind that grew up poor as Job's turkey in Fauquier County right after the Civil War and rode a horse or mule five miles a day to a two-room schoolhouse to acquire a fairly modest education.

Of course she didn't understand these distinctions back in those years when she was eight and nine and ten. All she understood was that if Grandma was a Marshall, then Granddaddy was different, thank the Lord. He seemed to have no standards where people were concerned; liked practically everybody that he ever met. Up to, and including, her.

So she could forget her troubles as she walked along beside him, taking two short steps to every one of his sharp-creased khaki strides, while that huge green hill of Washington & Lee, crowned with white pillared buildings, striped with bright white ribbon walkways, revolved like the canopy of a giant merry-go-round above them.

By the time they had climbed up through the gates of V.M.I. and onto the parade ground she would be giddy with relief, saying absolutely anything that came into her head. But then it would be time for Granddaddy to lean down and give her a whiskery, tobacco-smelling kiss and disappear into one of those crenelated, taffy-colored castles. And there he had to stay till one o'clock, when she could come to fetch him back for lunch and a game of croquet or maybe rummy.

In the meantime there was a whole morning before her. She would turn then and pick her way back along the edge of the parade ground, trying not to notice the bruise-purple mountains hovering above her, like the pictures of the Marshalls at the dining-room table, trying not to wonder what her sister and her grandmother were planning.

Soon after she had dropped back down the cement walkway into Washington & Lee, she would pass Lee Chapel, just about the time the two ladies who worked there would be propping open its bright, white double doors. The wonderful thing was that she didn't have to pay to get into the Lee Chapel and Museum. All she had to do was say, "Major Marshall's grandchild," words that worked exactly like "Open Sesame." Looking back, she suspected that they must have had a policy of free admission for the families of both college faculties. But back then she was convinced that the miracle was rooted in the awesome power of the Marshall name (a power she could borrow now and then and use on innocent out-siders, who didn't understand the paradoxes of genetics, but a power she could obviously never really own).

Though the lady at the table with the tinted postcards was used to her by now, Clare still felt obliged to mumble "Major Marshall's grandchild," and the lady would then press her lips together, nod, and say, "Make yourself at home."

Which is exactly what she did.

Pushing open the inside door she would step into the cool, clean, absolutely empty chapel, with its bright white walls and curving ceiling, its long white wooden benches lined up in review before the platform where General Lee was sleeping on his marble camp bed with his marble army boots (square-toed ones, she noticed, not round-toed like Granddaddy's) sticking out from underneath his too-short marble army blanket.

She remembered best one drizzly morning, the last week of their visit in 1944. She had a book with her that day, *The Adventures of Tom Sawyer,* so she slipped into a pew and read there till her back began to ache. Then she walked up on the stage, through the archway in the center, and plopped down on the floor beside Lee's statue. The light for reading was wonderful back there, coming as it did through a window on the side and reflecting directly off the marble. And she felt so at ease beside that gentle, sleeping man.

As irony would have it — she had even managed one day to get Grandma to admit it — General Lee was better born than the Mar-shalls. So much better that he didn't have to worry about who took after who. She had heard one of the ladies explaining to a tourist that Lee liked all his students, no matter who they were or where they came from. And he liked children, too. She took that to mean all of them, even timid ones who weren't but so attractive.

On a warm day she could sit and read beside him for half an hour maybe. (In those days of World War II and gas rationing, it wasn't very often that a tourist would disturb her.) But on this particular day, the hard chill of the marble floor soon worked through her cotton skirt and underpants, so that she had to stand up, and, rubbing her behind to restore the circulation, clank on down the iron steps to the museum in the basement.

In the hall down there was a photograph of Lee as a civilian in a floppy gray hat, sitting on his horse, Traveller, as relaxed as anybody else would be sitting in an armchair. And since Grandma was making Clare take riding lessons every afternoon, she stopped and studied the photograph a while.

"Now that's what I call horsemanship," said the shorter, fatter museum lady as she passed her standing there.

"What made him so relaxed?" Clare asked.

"Love," the lady said. "Just plain love between a man and animal who'd ridden through so much together. So much dust and rain. And all those muddy, bloody battles. They had learned to communicate like two parts of one body."

Clare couldn't help but notice how loose Lee held his reins. Probably because he didn't even need them. With a slight shift in his weight, or pressure from his leg, he could tell Traveller exactly what he wanted.

After that, Clare wandered down to General Lee's office, which was just as he had left it, the ladies always said, so that visitors could have the feeling that he might be coming back. Maybe that was why Clare could not quite work up the nerve to sit down in his tufted black leather chair and read at his octagon-shaped table.

Instead, she walked on down the hall, took a hard right at the end, and flopped down on her stomach beside the tall glass case that had the skeleton of Traveller inside it. There she set her book down, opened flat, in a rectangle of daylight sifting through a window in the thick white basement wall.

She felt as much at home beside the bones of Traveller as she did upstairs beside the statue of his master. And secretly she longed to break open that case and write her name, Clare Colston, on a chalk-white rib, the way so many students had written theirs before her.

It was curious, really, that she felt so much at home there, when, at that point in her life, the thing that scared her most, next to Grandma, was horses. Live horses, of course. With long, enormous muscles and sweat-soaked, smelly skin. Horses that could bite your fingers off, if you didn't hold your palm perfectly flat when you offered them a carrot. Horses that could get *mad* and lay their ears back flat and give a mean kick sideways, the way her sister's would as he cantered past her and poor old Buck.

Buck was what they gave her at the V.M.I. stables, a swaybacked veteran from the cavalry of World War I (when they were in the midst, of course, of World War II). A sweet-natured, gentle thing. Terrified as she was of all horses in general, she could not help acknowledging that fact about old Buck. And things would have been all right if her grandmother had been content to let her walk and trot and, maybe every now and then, canter. But Grandma was a pusher, bound and determined that each child would go home with a skill she had lacked at the time she was committed to her care. And that third summer of lessons, when Grandma noticed Clare had managed, finally, to learn to walk and trot and canter, she insisted it was time for her to *jump.*

Clare was so alarmed when her grandmother announced the plan at breakfast that she actually talked back to her for once: "Oh, why, Grandma? Why? Can't I just pull Buck over to the side and let Maggie and White Lightning take the jumps?"

"Are you afraid to jump?"

"Yes," she said. "I am."

"Then don't you see? That that's the very reason you have to learn to do it."

No, she didn't see. But she was more afraid of Grandma than she was of jumping. And for that reason she began to jump.

One afternoon of that last week in 1944, a day or two after the rainy morning in Lee Chapel, she was trotting Buck up to a three-foot rail that she had taken fairly easily before. But this time, at the last minute, Buck shifted his footing, and Clare bumped out of the saddle as well as both her stirrups, and took the jump straddling his neck.

As Buck came down to the ground and started cantering around the bend, Clare felt herself falling in that awful stretched-out time of a slow-motion movie. First, she tipped over sideways and began slipping down the horse's side (the side facing the ring, thank heavens, not the stucco wall). Then she found herself hanging with one leg hooked over the horse's neck, the other leg swinging free under his stomach. And her head was down there, too, turned and watching, with a curious detachment, as the back hooves did a fancy dance sideways to avoid stepping on her as she fell.

What she felt a second later, sitting in the dust without a scratch or bruise on her, was not fear but gratitude to Buck.

"Are you hurt?" Grandma called from the bench where she was sitting, her black shoes pressed together, her face crumpled into wrinkles as she looked into the sun.

"No," said Clare, standing up and brushing the dust off the jodhpurs, two sizes too big, they had borrowed from the daughter of a Captain Somebody who taught mathematics.

"Then you know what you have to do now. Don't you?"

"Yes," Clare said, "I have to get back up on Buck. And take the jump again."

During all of this, the corporal in charge of the V.M.I. stables, the person who was meant to be giving them their lessons, had not said a word.

Clare walked over to Buck, who was standing waiting for her with his long reins drooping. First, she ran her hand down his sweat-soaked neck, to thank him. Then she gathered up the reins, stuck her toe in the stirrup, and pulled herself up into the saddle.

The wonder of it was that she still wasn't feeling scared. If anything, she felt apologetic. Because she knew if she'd been riding right, with thighs and knees and calves clinging to Buck's sides, the way that Lee rode Traveller, she would not have lost her balance in the first place.

After they got home and took their baths, Maggie went off to the movies with a girl she knew from camp, leaving Clare to spend the rest of the afternoon alone with Grandma.

As they walked downtown to get some meat for dinner, Clare didn't speak to Grandma, because, as usual, she couldn't think of anything to say. But as her grandmother was pushing open the door into the butcher's shop, she said to Clare out of the blue: "I was proud of you today."

It was as if Grandma had given her a diamond, and Clare took that little piece of praise and turned it over in her mind to get every single glint of glory from it. She felt absolutely radiant with glory as she stood beside the slanted white and glass meat counter, watching the butcher trim the fat from the pork chops, watching Grandma tear a coupon from the perforated sheet in her meat-ration book.

But then, two minutes later, she was in trouble again. Her grandmother had just dropped the pork chops into her string shopping bag and was looking down at her: "What would you like to do now?"

"Oh me. I don't know," Clare said, suddenly impaled on this unexpected question. What was she supposed to say? If she said she wanted to do something Grandma didn't want to do. Oh, dear. What would happen then? "I don't know," she said again.

"How can anybody *not know* what they want to do?"

The finely wrinkled skin on Grandma's neck was getting red.

Which meant, of course, that she was getting mad at her. So Clare looked down at the floor and began to trace an arc in the sawdust with her sandal, trying to keep back the tears she could feel coming on, tears that would make Grandma *furious* at her.

Suddenly she felt her grandmother's fingers lifting up her chin. "Try to think of me." Grandma's bright blue eyes were boring into hers now, so she couldn't look away. "You're not being fair to me. What I want to do is what you want to do. But there's no way I can do it, if you keep on being shy and hiding what you think from me."

So Clare took a deep breath and blurted out, "Can you take me to the library to get another book?"

"Of course I can, but I took you there on Tuesday. You checked out *The Adventures of Tom Sawyer.* I thought at the time it was too advanced for you. Is that the problem? It's too long?"

"I've finished it," Clare said.

"Good for you," Grandma said. And then she let go of Clare's chin, but still looked straight into her eyes and added, "I'll say this for the Colstons. I always did hear that they were smart."

ANNE F. ROSNER

Prize Tomatoes

(FROM TRIQUARTERLY)

ALL RIGHT, EVERYONE at attention. There's been ample time since watering for revival. Beans! Pick up those bottom leaves. New tomato plants, stand up! That's it. Erect stems, leaves perpendicular. Remember, I have plans to enter tomatoes in the county fair this year. So you must work very hard. You all look beautiful. I'm proud of the effort you've all put forth this evening. Thank you and good night.

I'm lingering. Going into the house seems an undeserved sentence. I glance around the familiar landscape. New townhouses loom, a smug wall, to the east. The lights of a new shopping center reflect in the darkening sky. Turning westward, I can see a large field stretching away into a line of trees. When I face this way, the neighborhood of large homes retains its air of remoteness that I loved when our house was first built.

The twilit sky holds me, and I, standing in the purity of the sun's last rays, could be only another briefly drawn streak, like the evening clouds.

A door slams at the house. I know without turning that my daughter, Barbara, will be standing on the porch looking worriedly toward the garden. "Dad." Her voice is carried on the soft air.

I wave, smiling a smile she can't see from the porch. But this casual smile prepares me to walk to the house. Light, light step. Easy, loose gait. The picture of a man returning from engaging in a modest interest. She'll wait, my sentinel daughter, until she sees that I'm going into the house.

Barbara, her husband Dick, and their two children had been

contemplating a move when I went into the hospital three years ago. It was decided that it would work out well for everyone if she and her family moved into my house when I came home from the hospital. Shaky and acutely mindful of the emptiness of the big house, I had not resisted, had indeed been grateful for the arrangement.

I approach the porch. Barbara says, "It's getting dark. I was afraid you might get chilled."

"Yes," I agree, "I think I will get a sweater."

An anxious flash across her eyes. "You're going to come back from your room, aren't you, Dad?" she asks. "There's a very good play on television tonight. I thought we could all watch it."

Dr. Hooper, the psychiatrist, has told her that I'm not to spend too much time alone.

"That sounds great," I say. "I'll just get the sweater and be back out."

Barbara retreats to the living room. I enter my bedroom, sighing in resignation because I'll have to postpone looking through the new seed catalogue that came in the mail today until everyone is in bed. Although Dr. Hooper has released me from his care, he and his advice hang about the house like iron-willed specters.

The children are both out for the evening. Dick, Barbara, and I settle into our tacitly appointed places before the television. The play proves to be avant-garde, hard to follow. My mind wanders. I think about the cabbage again. Just the under-leaves seem a bit ragged. I remind myself to question Mr. Miggs about a possible culprit. Not cabbage worms, I know, because those are easy to see. Maybe —

"Dad, did you notice the way these sets have been designed for the scene changes? Isn't that clever?"

I start. No need to panic. Calm, cool. Maybe just a nod will do. I nod. She buys it. I try again to concentrate on the show. Lucky Dick has fallen asleep, unnoticed. God, I'm weary of Barbara's concern.

She's tired tonight. Dark smudges have appeared under her eyes. She's relaxed and forgets to hold her chin up. The telltale sag in her jawline touches me.

She was more frightened than my other two children, I think, when I went to the hospital. She's more frightened still by the changes in the man who came home from the hospital.

I've overheard her on the phone, explaining to her friends, explaining to herself what happened. "It was Mother's death. It simply undid him. You know how devoted they were."

It's true what she says. Peg's death had much to do with it, but not in any way she might imagine. It wasn't as if we were young. Peg was sixty-three and I was sixty-five. That was four years ago last winter.

The devotion? Well, I'll concede a mutual respect. If there was devotion, it was the formal and dutiful devotion of habit — until the end, that is.

Peg died of a peculiar slow-growing form of cancer. We knew she had it for five years. She bore it with the serenity of people who have been forced to acknowledge their own deaths. I bore it barely believing in its existence.

Almost precisely a year before she died, Peg told me one evening, in nothing more than a conversational tone, "Walter, there's something that's bothered me for more than thirty years. I think I'd feel better if you knew."

"What is it?"

"I had an affair when we were living in Shreveport." Then she laughed very girlishly and shrugged.

"With whom?" I asked.

"You didn't know him."

"For how long?"

"Two years."

I said, "Peg, I can't believe this. Then you were in love with him."

"I thought I was at the time," she said. Then she reached out and touched my arm. "Walter, I've never had any regrets about being married to you. Can you understand that?"

I jumped up and strode about the room, slamming the fist of one hand into the palm of the other. I wonder if I harbored some notion of beating up my wife's lover. I don't remember. All I remember is the gesture. I said, "I'll have to think about this."

For several days, I sorted through the feeling her confession had raised in me. There was an odd quality to my sense of betrayal in that it seemed to have so little to do with the other man. He seemed only a part, but certainly not the cause, of my agitation.

No, the element in it that ached with the persistence of a stubborn thorn was that I would have been absolutely certain that Peg was incapable of having the affair in the first place. It was a breach of trust, to be sure, but that seemed too small to describe the abyss that opened between us.

In those days after her confession, I had no reason to doubt her ability to have carried the secret for thirty years without my slightest suspicion. If I had been the sort of man then who doubted his own perceptions, I might have thought she had never told me, so unchanged was her customary equanimity. Freshly wounded, I saw her calm dignity as an added treachery.

The incident might have slipped silently below the surface of our lives, like so many things in the past, had I not pinpointed the source of my pain.

We were sitting at a late supper one night. Peg said, "Do you think Charlotte would like to come away with us this summer?"

I glanced up from my plate. Her face, lit by the one lamp in the room, was suddenly vivid, like a blurry photo coming into sharp focus. With a stupefying panic I realized that I didn't know this woman who had borne my three children, who had slept beside me for most of my life, who had been the one constancy in my life. And now she was dying.

I blurted, "I've had a couple of affairs myself." That lay flatly over us for a moment. What a foolish thing to say. I tried again.

"What I mean is, it doesn't matter — your affair. I want — I want —"

"You want what, Walter?"

I couldn't put my mouth around the enormity of what I wanted. "I want to talk" was the best I could do.

We lay awake most of the night, uncertain where to begin: haphazardly evoking memories, questioning each other. Toward morning, I held her, already so thin from the voraciousness of her illness. Her fragility was terrifying in its awful mortality. Peg. Peg. Peg o' my heart, did I sing to you as a young man?

Each time together then brought surprises: the joy of discovering each other without the expectancy of first love, deepened by the chill breath of Peg's measured time.

I loved her for the first time, was bound to her in parts of myself I had never known. Later, when she lay in the hospital, her skin tugged firmly, quite youthfully over her face by the rapacious disease, when tears were no longer strange to me, I cried, "Peg, all the years we wasted together. That loss is unbearable to me."

She said, "We couldn't have done this at any other time. We were far too much the sort of people that we were."

She offered it as comfort, I know, but it resounded down the empty well of my soul and continued to echo long after she died.

So Barbara was right in thinking that her mother's death had caused the eventual darkness that descended over my life. With Peg gone, I became the only one who heard those echoes.

The show ends. Barbara stirs in her chair, nudges Dick awake. I'm free to go now. We've all done our duty.

She rises. I sit quietly, not to appear too eager. "Well, Dad, I'll see you in the morning. Are you going to watch more television?"

"No, I don't think so," I say with a well-placed yawn. "I'm going to go to bed."

Good night. Good night.

In my room, I quickly search out the new seed catalogue and position the lamp for the best light.

Fruit trees, shrubs. I'm idly flipping the pages. Flowers require slightly more attention. Maybe next year I'll try some flowers.

I linger for a moment over the red grapes. I've considered an arbor — not so much from any particular fondness for grapes but because of memories of sitting in the opulent shade of my grandmother's arbor as a boy. Yes, grapes might be interesting.

The vegetable section begins. I glance at the clock and listen for sounds in the house. The children when they come home will see my light, but fortunately they are teenagers — an age when whatever I do holds so little interest as to be invisible.

I pore over each picture, read the printed section underneath. I'm convinced that the people who compose the written information are rabid gardeners, too. Who but a gardener could describe rhubarb in such terms as "blushing red, clear through to the heart," "full shapely leaves"?

I'm captured by the catalogue, entranced by the possibilities presented in the glossy pictures of potatoes, corn, and . . .

The doorknob has turned so softly that I don't know Barbara is there until she speaks. "Dad, it's three o'clock."

I shove the catalogue guiltily into a shelf in the night table. Easy, easy. "I'm just going to bed, Barbara," I say. "You could have knocked." That, as Dr. Hooper would say, is a reasonable demand.

"I'm sorry," she says. "I thought you had fallen asleep with your light on."

She remains in the doorway in uncomfortable silence. Then

says, "I don't like to check up on you." She's pleading because she really doesn't like it. "But you know Dr. Hooper spoke to us very specifically about your getting enough rest."

"I'm old enough to decide when to go to bed."

"Dad," she says, "I know I annoy you, but I don't know what else to do to get you to take care of yourself."

I wonder if she means she annoys me in general. During the bleak time right before I went to the hospital, Barbara confronted me tearfully, "You have always loved Charlotte better than me," and I — too raw, too naked in my desire to lie to her — said nothing. She remembers, I know.

"I'm fine," I say.

She hesitates, then says in a rush, "The garden scares me. It reminds me of the CB."

"It wasn't a CB," I say and turn from her.

"Okay, Dad, okay. Will you just promise you'll go to bed?"

"Yes," I say, and climb obediently into bed after she leaves.

The earth smell blowing through the window makes me anxious to be in the garden in the morning. I'm only slightly sleepy. Old men don't need much sleep.

I think of the radio. It wasn't a CB. It was a ham outfit. I built it myself from a kit. At first my son, John, and Barbara had been quite happy about my interest. Good therapy, Dr. Hooper had pronounced.

Barbara, uneasy as my keeper, was grateful for the time I spent with the radio, I suppose.

It was a wonderful radio. I could send signals nearly anywhere in the world, and because night is the best time for reception and transmission, I was many times bent over my set, headphones over my ears, when the sun came up. I slept most of the day, saw Dr. Hooper once a week, and operated my radio at night.

I should have seen it coming — the end of my radio. Dr. Hooper was very insistent that I talk about something besides the radio when I saw him. That made the sessions all the more arduous, as I thought of little else.

Especially after Cecelia. I contacted her in the Philippines. The signal was amazingly clear. Her voice held all the lush mystery of her home. Its cadence described a tropical fragrance around my room. Her English was quite good, and I began to call her every night.

She was twenty, a student of philosophy at the University of

Manila. For her I played the experienced older man, seasoned and unsurprised by life. "How wise you are, Walter," she said many times, and I would chuckle comfortably. The distance between us secured the fraud.

Because she loved Aristotle particularly, I studied him, searching for ideas to intrigue her. I must have done well enough, because she spent a great deal of time with me nearly every night.

The evenings with the family seemed interminable. I paced. I checked my watch, sat restlessly watching television — waiting for the time to pass.

There were times when it was difficult to reach her, but with the patience of love I turned the dials for as long as it took, straining to hear her voice, however faint.

I don't know what happened. She was young, after all. Perhaps she simply lost interest. Perhaps her radio had been damaged in some way, but weeks went by and I couldn't reach her. I did everything I knew to do. I checked with the shop where I had bought the kit, but nothing helped.

My agitation became apparent. I was aware of low-voiced telephone conversations. Barbara was alerting the rest of the family. Even sensing their growing concern, I couldn't control the panic of my loss.

Early one morning, after a night of frantic searching for Cecelia, I rose to the window and began to shout in desperation, "Cecelia, Cecelia. Oh please, Cecelia."

Barbara and Dick crashed into the room — Barbara shaking visibly at the sight of my tear-stained face, Dick circling me warily.

Dr. Hooper was called, medication secured. I began to see him three times a week.

I disliked going to see Dr. Hooper. In fact, I probably dislike Dr. Hooper. He has a sharp nose that points downward, seeming always to be calling attention to his shoes. He is a hard-faced man who makes much of small things. As though seeing him three times a week weren't punishment enough for alarming my family, he neatly disposed of my radio as well.

"Walter, you must see what this radio has meant to you," he said. "Your need for communication was served without your having to risk any real intimacy. This is why it became such an obsession. Because you need the communication.

"I think, and I have told your family the same thing, that it's fine for you to enjoy the radio, but you must put it into balance with the rest of your life."

But I didn't enjoy the radio any more. I had seen the radio as a great benevolent spider spinning a shining web over the world at the touch of my fingers. After Dr. Hooper, it became only a perverse instrument of a crazy old man. It gathered dust in my room until my grandson dismantled it for parts.

At last, I'm sleepy. Ah, Cecelia, why did you leave me?

•

Barbara and Dick are off to work, the children still sleeping. In the garden the lettuce holds the dew in its fluted depths. Last year tiny black insects riddled the leaves with holes. Mr. Miggs suggested planting radishes in their rows, "to draw them devils off the lettuce." This year the leaves are unblemished and the little bugs reside, apparently oblivious to the lettuce, on the tough, useless radish leaves.

I kneel, carefully sliding my fingers along the stem of a weed that has grown hidden within the lettuce leaves, then shoved its imprudent head above them. It crows there among the cultivated plants. I place my fingers as close to the ground as possible. Otherwise the stem will break off from the root and the weed will put out another shoot within days. Broken off at the ground, weeds enlarge in the root to return tougher than ever. I must pull up the entire root.

I give a light tug. It remains fixed. I exert more pressure. The root begins to give. Rolling my wrist, I give it a final yank. Too hard. It comes out, the stem broken. You son of a bitch, I'll get you. I thrust my hand into the lettuce, gently pushing the leaves aside, and see the end of the weed. It has broken right at the ground. I dig with my fingers around the shaft, losing a lettuce leaf in the process. All right, now I'm angry. I'm going to get you if I have to stay out here all day. With only my fingertips, I get a sturdy hold and pull. Hah! There you are. That's the end of you.

Inspection, inspection everybody. Corn, you have a goal — knee-high by the Fourth of July. Kale, recovering nicely from an insect attack. And my beauties, the tomatoes, are in flower, yellow blossoms dotting the dark green vines. I have such plans for you at the fair this year.

"Dad?"

I turn. My younger daughter, Charlotte, stands at the edge of the garden. She is the baby and the rebel of the family. I smile in welcome.

"You look so peaceful out here," she says.

Her remark makes me love her very much.

"Hello, dear." I embrace her.

She has been dieting again. Her face is gaunt beneath a deep tan.

"Come on," I say, "I'll get you a cup of coffee."

"No, no, you go on with what you've been doing."

She teases me — the only one of the three who dares to do that. "So what are you doing today, Farmer Brinkman?"

"I'm pea picking. I'm going to freeze them."

She seldom visits when Barbara is here. Their views of the world have been irreconcilable since childhood.

She sees where I'm going to work and sits down at the end of the row. Because the sun has risen in the sky, I roll my shirtsleeves up. The harsh sunlight shines on my arms; the scars on the inside of my wrists are as bright as lightning. Charlotte sees. She winces with an almost imperceptible shudder.

I'm told that Charlotte was the one who found me lying on the blood-soaked bed. So much blood, they all agreed, and yet I didn't die.

I wanted to die. There was no fear when I slid the razor painlessly across my wrists — just a relief as though it made no difference whether that red flow emptied onto the crisp white sheets or remained encased in my veins.

I pull my gloves from my pocket, slip them on, adjust them over my wrists. Charlotte and I are relieved.

She talks of a recent trip to Bermuda she has made. I haven't been there in a long time and don't care to go. The pea pods strike the pail with hollow thuds.

Later, in the kitchen, the blancher sends up great clouds of steam, I'm proud to have my daughter know that I'm efficient about the business of preserving food.

Charlotte shells peas, admires their sweet odor, and we make each other laugh. It's a wonderful day.

The grandchildren, Carrie and Mike, straggle sleepily into the kitchen and stay. They too love Charlotte. She makes us all laugh with a story of a drunken man on a plane trying to pick her up.

She uses words that make me flinch, and that makes me laugh all the more.

Carrying several plastic bags for her freezer, Charlotte kisses us all and leaves.'

At dinner that evening my son, John, drops by. I know Barbara has told him she is worried about me. She and her family are silent as John and I talk.

"So, how're you doing, Dad?" he asks.

"Fine, John. How are you?"

"Oh, I'm fine," he says, with an "of course" just barely unspoken.

"Barbara tells me you're getting pretty hung up on this garden of yours."

"I enjoy it. I wouldn't say I was hung up on it," I answer evenly.

"Hey, you know what I think?" he says as though the idea has just occurred to him. "It would be good for you to get back to work. That's what you need. Will you consider it?" John and I have had this conversation many times.

"No, I will not."

"For God's sake, why not? You're wasting away with nothing to do."

Mike, still warmed, I suppose, by the camaraderie of the morning in the kitchen, says, "Maybe he's tired of being a corporate robber."

"Michael," Dick and Barbara admonish in unison. Mike looks to me for affirmation. I can't meet his eye, nor can I claim his romantic motive. I can't explain to John why I won't return to work — John who loves the family business with all the devotion I imbued in him, loves it just as I did, building from the sturdy foundation my father had laid.

I have no words to tell him how that which had been central to my life has moved so irretrievably to the periphery, how the finely honed heavy-machinery parts manufactured there no longer seem to have much to do with me.

John runs the business with a competence I don't question, and I am satisfied.

No, John, no. He leaves defeated by an old man's stubbornness.

Barbara and I are alone at the table. She regards me sharply. "Dad, will you at least think about what John said?"

"I have thought about it. A lot. I'm not going back to work."

"Why not?" Her voice rises.

"Because I don't want to."

"Dad —"

"I don't want to discuss it." I rise from the table and pick up a light jacket.

"I'm going out now," I say, walking toward the door.

"Where?" she demands.

"To visit a friend," I reply shortly, slamming the door behind me.

I walk down the long driveway and turn left toward the shopping center.

If I hurry, I can catch the nine-thirty bus. Mr. Miggs will be riding home from work now. I quicken my pace and am soon at the shopping center. I can see a bus in the distance. It pulls to the curb and picks up the large crowd of people there. My bus comes into view several minutes later. I reach the corner as it stops, step aboard, and drop my money into the coin box as the doors close behind me with a pneumatic sigh.

I look expectantly toward the back of the bus. Mr. Miggs is there. He doesn't sit in the back because he is black, he has assured me, but because that's the best vantage point for watching the other passengers. "You can see everybody without turning your head," he explains. "People don't like it if they think you're watching them."

Mr. Miggs waves and smiles. He is tall and reedlike. He is missing half his upper teeth. The remaining teeth are strong and large. The even division of the missing and existing teeth gives his dignified face a comic aspect. Despite his children's embarrassment he refuses to wear the dentures they have bought for him.

I place my hand on the back of each seat to keep my balance. I sit down next to Mr. Miggs, who welcomes me as always: "Good evening, Mr. Brinkman. How are you tonight?"

Our friendship is contained within the bus. He rides the bus home from work each evening and I catch it at nine-thirty at my stop, riding to the end of the line in the city, where he gets off. Then the bus turns around, and I ride home alone. I don't know where Mr. Miggs lives.

Tonight, as we ride through the night into the city, we talk of our dead wives. When I leave the bus, I'm pleasantly lost in memories of my college days and meeting Peg.

I met Mr. Miggs two years ago, shortly after the demise of my radio. I was buoyed in my loss by the drug Dr. Hooper prescribed for me. It was a comfortless tranquillity. The mild summer evenings hung heavily without the radio, and I began to take long walks.

I discovered the new shopping center to be a place of constant activity. I enjoyed strolling there or sitting on a bench watching the crowds.

One night, feeling particularly aimless, I was attracted by the self-contained mobility of the passing buses. I boarded a bus to the city on impulse.

Almost immediately I regretted it. As I stepped aboard, I was hit by a wave of heavy, still, hot air. The driver intoned in a weary voice, "Air conditioning's broke. Got fans but no cooling."

Unable to think of a graceful retreat, I paid and sat down. There were few people on the bus. Two young boys jostled each other and made faces out the windows. A young woman cradled a small child, tired and irritable in the heat. I was touched by her patience as he squirmed and whined, smudging the window with his restless hands. In the rear seat, an elderly black man sat nearly immobile, his eyelids lowered. I might have thought he was dozing off except that the eyes visible below the lids were as alert and sagacious as the hawks' that occasionally perch atop our fence. He divided his attention among the passengers with a judicious liveliness.

I was not, however, too interested in my fellow passengers, because the bouncing of the bus and the closeness of the air seemed to collect inside my head. We passed several empty stops. I felt dizzy and nauseous. I leaned forward, resting my head on the back of the next seat. A fuzzy panic grew as I felt more and more faint.

Disoriented and weak, I was only vaguely aware of a hand on my shoulder. "You all right?" The black man's face was blurry as he leaned over me. The nausea had reached my throat. Afraid to speak, I shook my head.

"Driver, driver, open a window. You got a sick man back here," the black man called with authority.

The bus lurched and the driver called irritably, "Windows don't open no more. Goddamned bus is supposed to be air conditioned."

"Well, it ain't. So stop the bus."

The bus came to a halt and the doors swung open. With the first rush of air into the bus, I began to feel better.

"Can you walk?" he asked.

"I think so."

He supported my elbows. I was conscious of the tautness of the muscles in his thin arms.

"We get you out in the air, you perk right up," he said, guiding me toward the door.

The driver shouted, "I can't wait for you. You hear me, you two?"

"Don't worry about us," my new friend called.

"Please," I said, much revived, "I don't want you to miss your bus."

"That's all right. I catch another one. Us old mens has got to stick together."

We found a bench at the nearest bus stop and sat down. We were in a rundown black neighborhood at the very outskirts of the city.

"I'm very grateful to you," I said, "but I'm fine now. Please take the next bus."

He studied my face with the same keenness I had noticed on the bus. "You better let me call your family come and get you. You awful pale. I don't know if you be all right." We both glanced around the shabby neighborhood surrounding us, and began to laugh.

"You awful pale. You awful pale. Oh my," he chortled.

Serious again, he repeated, "You let me call your family. I wait 'til they come."

The thought of Barbara swooping down in all her frantic concern was chilling.

"Oh no, I can't do that. I can't call my children. They don't even know where I am tonight. They'll just —" I stopped, hearing how foolishly fearful of my children I must sound.

"Yes, children," he said, "can sure be vexatious when you get old. I think they don't ever forget all them times you made them mad when they was little ones. They just been waiting for us to get old and weak. Then they got the upper hand. It funny how it go like that."

"It is funny, isn't it?" I said, delighted by his understanding. "My name is Walter Brinkman," I said, extending my hand.

"Good evening, Mr. Brinkman. I'm Mason Miggs."

And for all of our friendship we have retained this formality. We decided that I should take a cab. With an air of abashment, Mr. Miggs went to a phone booth to call the son with whom he lived, to explain his lateness. "They worry, you know," he said, shrugging. "Then they make a racket." I knew he would lie about his lateness to his son, just as I would lie to Barbara.

As Mr. Miggs and I waited, he mentioned that he rode the same bus every evening. The next night, wishing only to thank him again, I boarded the nine-thirty bus. It surprised me to find that Mr. Miggs and I seemed to have so many things to talk about. His wry humor and enthusiasm were compelling. After that first evening, I have found myself more and more often riding the bus simply to visit with Mr. Miggs. He seems unconcerned that I ride the bus with no particular destination.

Now, two years later, my family still knows nothing of Mr. Miggs. I tell them I visit Stan Garrity, an old friend whose face I barely remember.

•

Good, the cabbage is heading. The middle leaves turn inward and press against each other to form the concise heads. How do you know to perform this way? Why not turn outward to create leafy bunches like the kale?

I'm going to learn to make sauerkraut this year. There's always more cabbage than we can possibly eat fresh.

The tomatoes cling to the vines like small green fists. The fruit is well formed, the skin smooth. They are Chesapeake variety, well suited to this soil. It seems as though one plant is producing particularly well. I reach down into the wire hoops that support them to trim the yellow leaves.

It's time for a pep talk, tomatoes. You will represent all of us assembled here at the county fair! You will compete for ribbons. I fully expect to see a blue ribbon laid across the best of you. It's something you should be striving for, going to the fair. Enough said. I have confidence in you.

Last year at the fair, laid on the long tables in the produce exhibits, were squash, green beans heaped on white paper plates, fiery red peppers and waxy green ones, potatoes, pumpkins, pungent onions, precisely rowed ears of corn, fat red tomatoes, and so many more. Some could only boast of size, ostentatious and grotesque. Oh, but the serious competitors — perfection of their kind. This year mine will be there, too.

Yes, I'll start with one entry, but in a prestige event: tomatoes, the crown of any garden.

I pace the garden, smiling, snapping my fingers in anticipation.

"Dad?" Barbara so soon? I check my watch. It's early. Puzzled, I go into the house.

"Hi, you're home early," I say.

Barbara purses her lips in exasperation. "Oh Dad, did you forget? The party is tonight."

Uh-oh. A weak chuckle. "I'm sorry. It did slip my mind."

"Did you at least check the liquor when it came, as I asked you?"

"Yes, yes, I did do that. All accounted for." I resist an urge to salute. Barbara wouldn't laugh.

"Thanks," she says, kissing me on the cheek. "I'm sorry I barked at you. I feel a little overwhelmed right now."

"Sure. Well, look, let me help."

"Would you? I could really use it."

Barbara organizes well. We work together smoothly with little conversation.

I'm glad to help her, comfortable in her company until she begins to tidy the living room.

She takes a copy of a news magazine and lays it atop a carefully arranged stack of magazines on the coffee table. The magazine is six years old. Inside, there is an article on my business with a picture of me interposed in the column.

I reread it not long ago. It describes me as "dynamic, inexhaustible." It goes on to say that "at sixty-three, there is no sign of the energetic Walter Brinkman releasing the reins of absolute power he holds at Brinkman International."

Barbara has several copies of these magazines. She continues to display them for reasons I refuse to dwell upon.

She often tells Dick when she thinks I don't hear her, "He's just lost his confidence, that's all. In no time at all he'll be wise, wonderful Dad again." She tells him as though Dick needed the reassurance.

Every time she says it, I want to shout at her, just as I want to shout at her now: "That man is dead. What's more, I don't mourn him. He crept out in the blood that stained the bed. There was so little of him left by then. Indeed, he had unraveled to a sad, gray tatter, that man, and left me behind to pay his debts."

But I'm not brave enough to tell my children this late in their lives that I was wrong about so many things; that, as sincere as my certainty was, it served me so poorly when I needed it.

I had wanted to protect them, to arm them, as any parent

does. As Peg observed, I was too much the sort of person that I was to have done any differently. Nevertheless, I'm frightened for their vulnerability, frightened that they have shaped their lives around the wisdom of a man who thought the only vanity he need be forgiven was his pleasure in looking well in a dinner jacket.

Barbara starts out of the room, saying over her shoulder, "I invited the Garveys. I thought you'd enjoy seeing them." I wouldn't, but say nothing.

When she is gone, I take the magazine and slip it out of sight.

Later at the party, the magazine has reappeared on the table. I sit, with a smile I'm hoping is friendly and relaxed. My dinner jacket, it seems to me, drapes unevenly across my chest.

Frank Garvey is pushing a conversation along with the rugged determination of loyalty to an old friendship.

"So, when are you going back to work?" he asks.

"I'm not going back."

"Ho well, you've got something going. I know you, Walter. You're the man who said he'd never retire." He is jovial and pokes me in the chest.

Without a trace of compassion, I say, "You're right. No retirement for me, Frank. I've taken up gardening, in fact."

He recovers quickly. "No kidding? You'll be interested in this, then. We're having our place landscaped."

Then he pins me to the chair with a lengthy story of the laying of the piping to a new fountain he and his wife have had sent from Italy.

Despite his best efforts, long silences fall. Finally, I allow my chin to drop gradually onto my chest; a reasonable picture of a man caught in a doze. I peer through slitted lids as Frank's back recedes. He's not less relieved than I, I'm sure, to be done with the conversation.

"Dad." Barbara touches my shoulder.

"Oh, I'm sorry." I shake my head. "I must have dropped off."

"Are you tired?"

"Yes. If you don't mind, Barbara, I'll go to bed now. The party can probably get along without me. Everyone seems to be having a good time."

Barbara isn't pleased. "Well, if you feel you simply can't stay awake, go ahead."

I pretend I don't hear the pique in her voice. "Thanks, dear. I'll see you in the morning."

I walk straight through the house and out of the back door.

The air is pleasant. I walk toward the closing shopping center. I look at my watch — nine-twenty. I can catch the bus.

The bus and I arrive at the corner at the same moment. I board and approach Mr. Miggs at the back of the bus. He gestures toward my dinner jacket. "You going to a dance?"

I laugh, unembarrassed. I know Mr. Miggs will relish my escape from the party as much as I do.

"My daughter was giving a party. She insisted I put in an appearance. There didn't seem to be much to say to anyone."

Mr. Miggs nods, smiling. "Yes, yes," he says, "they put you out for looks, just like the cookies.

"Before I had my heart attack, they'd let me drink at their parties. When I used to get to dancing, they all stand around and say, 'Ain't that something, that old man do them funny dances?' but back of that, they saying, 'That old man a fool. He too old for all of that.'

"Then if you don't get up and dance, they say, 'Ain't that sad, and he used to be so lively.' " We laugh.

"They don't want you to be old, they just want you to act old," he says, "or leastways how they see old before they get there. That's because they don't know about being old."

"No, they don't."

"But that's all right," he says slyly, "because they don't know the bad of it but they don't know the good of it either. Like how you get to loving little things you wouldn't have thought much about when you was a young man."

"Little things like my garden," I add.

"And like my job," he says. "Anyway, getting old going to take them by surprise just like it did you and me."

Mr. Miggs works, although his children don't want him to. They don't like his working because of his heart condition, but they more especially don't like his job. Yet every weekday afternoon he rides out of the city into the suburbs to a house where he was a gardener until the heart attack made him unable to handle the heavy work. Mr. Miggs often speaks of his illness. I never speak of mine.

On his job now, he stays in the kitchen, drinking coffee and reading the paper, until nine, when the man who has hired him comes home from work. The man's wife is afraid to be alone in the house, and she can't find a maid who will stay past five. Mr. Miggs says she will call through the kitchen door, "Mason, Mason, what is that noise?" He has only to call back, "That's the dog" or "Only the wind," and she is comforted.

His children, all professionals whom he worked to educate, are ashamed of his job.

It's the having somewhere to go every day that's important enough for him to resist all his children's threats and cajolery. He explains, "The days, they don't just run together, all the same, no more. You know how they can do.

"And as for the children, I give in a lot of times because I'm plain too tired to fight. But everybody know when enough is enough. Then you can't give no ground."

Because the bus is more crowded than usual tonight, Mr. Miggs and I must share the rear seat with three teen-aged girls who comb their hair and giggle. We lower our voices. He asks after the garden as one might inquire after relatives.

Everything is doing well, I tell him, but I'm worried about late blight in the tomatoes. I hate to think of the disfigurement the disease could cause so close to the fair.

He consoles me, "You don't get that unless you got a real wet summer. We ain't had that. They be fine. You listen to me because I know."

He shakes a long finger at me. "You got a good garden. All them things you bring me taste just fine. I don't get no flavor from the things in the grocery stores. Back home when I was a child, my mama always had a garden. When she'd start canning and line all them jars up in the cupboard, why, we thought we was rich." His eyes have a faraway look. "Yes, I always did love a garden and yours is a fine one, I can tell."

"It is, Mr. Miggs," I say. "I wish you could see it. Perhaps you could . . ."

I stop. Buoyed by his compliments, I have nearly invited Mr. Miggs to my house. I shudder, picturing Barbara at the sight of him. He would hear as well as I the warning bells behind her politely impassive face.

I feel a sharp twist of anguish at having hurt my friend. But he says without rancor, "Mr. Brinkman, it might surprise you, but it wouldn't be easy for me to take you home either. You see, they'd all start, 'What that white man want with you?' because they'd never think you and me could be friends. And when you look at it, it is peculiar. So it's all right because I know how it is."

A heaviness settles in me that lingers after we say good-bye. Mr. Miggs forgives what I cannot.

•

The fair is two weeks away. The garden pulses with a common breath in its full-blown extravagance. The plants enfold the night-time dampness in their dense depths, releasing it in steady clouds when the morning sun lies in shadowless lengths along the rows. The cabbage heads are tight-skinned and shiny, like bald men. The stems of the string beans stagger beneath the weight of the pods. The cucumber vines greedily creep over every available inch of soil. The cornstalks tower above the rest of the garden, shaking their long, thin leaves like nervous fingers.

I've decided to have a greenhouse built this fall. The winter won't press so heavily this year.

A greenhouse! I have plans that I've copied from a library book: glass for the life-giving sunlight, water, and heat. With cold frames outside, I can plant well into December.

In the fall, I'll have a greenhouse. After the fair, when I'm not so busy, I'll call a builder.

The tomatoes are tinged a faint red. They're round, their pulp pressing evenly against the skin. They're prize tomatoes, for certain. Their pungent odor rises in the heat. In untangling several vines, my hand is yellow to the wrist from the fine powder under the leaves. Prize tomatoes, going to the fair.

I make excuses to go out in the evenings. Barbara is anxious. I tell her I visit Stan Garrity. Instead, Mr. Miggs and I ride the bus — he with a protective arm encircling a large bag of canned vegetables I have brought for him, and I exuberant and talkative about the fair.

Barbara is attentive to me. I see the mental pacing she does when she regards me. "Out again tonight, Dad?" she asks, her eyes fixed to draw an answer larger than her casual question demands.

I'm careless, too excited by the fair to conceal it. I hear my laugh — a loud, sharp bark that makes her jump. I walk to my garden, rubbing my hands, thinking of the fair. I leave the house without explanation to meet Mr. Miggs, sometimes in defiance, sometimes only because I've forgotten the danger in alarming Barbara.

•

The sun slants low in the sky. Tomorrow is the fair, and this evening I select the tomatoes I will take.

I stoop in the garden, poking a sure hand through the wide wire hoops around the tomato plants. I carefully pull six from the vine. I chose these six, weeks ago, while they were still green. None is a disappointment. My eye was that sure! How beautiful you are, your symmetry, your uniform color. Six glossy red globes, the pick of the vines. The jewels of my garden.

I lay them in a small basket beside me, delicately and gently, so as not to bruise them. They're perfect. They're . . .

"Dad." Barbara stands by the garden, her arms folded ominously.

"I ran into Stan Garrity in the supermarket today," she says. "He said he hasn't seen you in years."

"Oh, really? It doesn't seem that long. Old age showing up, I guess."

"Where are you going in the evenings?" she demands.

I stand, staked by the resolution of her stare. "I don't think that at my age I should have to account for my whereabouts," I say in a voice braver than I feel.

"I would agree with you, except for the — the — the trouble you've had. I'm responsible for you, and I think you owe me this much just to put my mind at ease."

"Good God, Barbara, I'm not running a diamond-smuggling operation or patronizing the local ladies of the evening."

"You're not going to tell me, are you?" she says, and the idea that she expects that I will not tell her crystallizes a decision I hadn't made.

"No."

"I'm sorry to hear that," she says, starting for the house. I feel a pang of fear at the genuine regret in her voice.

That fear pricks at me as I lift the basket. I worry that leaving tonight will antagonize her further, but Mr. Miggs must see the tomatoes that will go to the fair. Cradling the basket tenderly under one arm, I walk toward the shopping center to meet the bus.

On the bus, Mr. Miggs examines each tomato with meticulous

scrutiny. He pronounces them all as fine as any he's seen. I'm ready for the fair.

●

I'm awake before first light this morning. I don't rise until I hear the rest of the family. Sleeplessness is a bad sign, Dr. Hooper has told us all.

In the clarity of the early morning, I see the threat of Barbara's anxiety. With the fair nearly here, I'm afraid I've waited too long to mollify her. I lay my plans. The tomatoes wait atop my dresser.

"What are you going to do today?" Barbara asks at breakfast.

"I'd planned to go out for a while. Might play a little golf. I'm rather tired of the garden just now."

Bingo! Right on target. Barbara leans over to kiss me. "Oh, that sounds wonderful. Have a good time."

"I will," I say, chiding myself for considering Barbara so formidable.

Later, I walk the rows of the garden, touching a leaf here and there and thinking of the fair. I took the tomatoes there this morning to enter them into exhibit for tonight's judging. I placed them in a basket and covered them with a small towel. I've seen people carrying their pets in just such a way. Traveling in the direction opposite that I take with Mr. Miggs, I took a bus ride to the fairgrounds in the next town.

What a place, the fair! So early in the morning, and already a large cow was being coaxed and pushed into a stall by two children who barely rose above her flank. A nanny goat bleated in an alarming human wail when her kid was taken from the truck before her. Pigs grunted as they slammed their ponderous bodies against the slats of their pens. Roosters crowed, people shouted, the horses in the vans moved restlessly in the excitement. The rides on the midway sat hunched and silent, great metallic beasts. A wondrous place, the fair.

Although I stayed as long as I dared, I couldn't wait long enough to see the tomatoes put into exhibit. It would be late in the day, I was told, and I've promised myself that Barbara shall have nothing to fault in my behavior. Just as I have my plan, so I know does she — to be sprung into action at the first sign of what she deems craziness.

When she comes home from work, she will find me in the house, reddened from the sun and speaking of a pleasant golf game.

I stay home in the evening and play canasta with Dick and Barbara. She says several times, "Isn't this nice, Dad? Isn't this fun?" I heartily agree each time.

I'm badly beaten in the game because although I didn't see the tomatoes put into exhibit, I know how they must look. The exhibits are all displayed on the starkness of white paper plates. Perhaps the tomatoes reflect a pinkness on the plate from the lights overhead. People walk by the tables, and how the tomatoes must shine. Of the ones I saw brought in, surely none were better than mine.

I don't dwell on the image as I can't appear distracted to Barbara. I'm very tired when I go to bed.

The next day I run some errands for the family. This takes longer than I expect. There is not time to go to the fair without risking being late for dinner. Even with so much to do, time passes with the perversity I remember from waiting for Christmas as a child. By dinnertime, the anticipation has compressed into a solid warmth in my chest.

The judging begins at six-thirty. If I leave right after dinner, I'll arrive just in time. The children aren't home for dinner. An extra burden of conversation falls on me. I'm holding my own and Barbara seems relaxed.

Slowly, deliberately, fork to mouth and back to plate; again fork to mouth and back to plate until the plate is empty. I thank Barbara for the meal, then say offhandedly, "I think I'll take a little walk." It's a quarter to six.

Barbara's head snaps up. "Where are you going?" There's a hard edge to her voice that warns me to be very cautious. Dick looks away. This is it.

"I'm going to the shopping center," I say, starting for the door. "I have a few things I want to pick up."

"I'll drive you up."

"I'd rather walk, Barbara."

"No." Her eyes never leave my face.

The bubble of excitement explodes into anger. "You can't keep me here," I shout.

Dick rises and comes toward me. "Now, take it easy, Walter. We think it's best if you stay around the house for awhile, until you get yourself calmed down."

"I was perfectly calm until my daughter began treating me like a ten-year-old."

I take a step toward the door. Dick catches my arm firmly. "Come on, Walter." He is pleading.

"Dad," Barbara says, "you haven't fooled me for one minute in the last few days. This garden has been exactly like the CB."

"It wasn't a CB, goddamnit!" I shout.

"Whatever. I want you to see Dr. Hooper again. In the meantime, I want you to stay home where the people who love you can protect you."

"Protect me from what?" Dick still grips my arms.

"From yourself, for right now. I'm not going to stand by and allow you to slide into — into what we had before."

"This isn't the same thing, I swear to you." I'm seized by desperation at the implacability of her expression.

"Dad, people who have your — problem often don't recognize it themselves."

"I simply won't stand for this," I say. "I'm leaving." The pressure of Dick's hand on my arm increases. He guides me to a chair and presses my shoulder until I sit down.

"Who are you, Dick, Barbara's goon?" My cheeks are hot with humiliation. Dick is embarrassed. "I'm sorry, Walter. I wish it were different."

"Dad, listen please." Barbara sits opposite me at the table. "I'm going to stay home from work tomorrow. Then you and I will go to see Dr. Hooper. He's told me that we could have an appointment at a moment's notice."

I'm defeated, too uncertain that what they say is untrue. "All right." I rise. "I'm going to my room now, if that's permitted these days."

"Of course, Dad. Listen —" I go to my room.

I sit on the edge of my bed, blank, drained, a crazy old man, not to be trusted out alone. My eyes scan the room and come to rest on the basket that carried the tomatoes to the fair.

No, by God, they're not going to do this. Mr. Miggs is right. Everybody knows when enough is enough. I pace around the room, hot with rage. Then I hurriedly pick up the phone and dial. It rings so many times. At last, "Hello?"

"Charlotte, Charlotte," I say, "you must help me."

Charlotte laughs in confusion. "Dad, slow down. What is it?"

"I made plans to go out tonight for something very important, and Barbara has refused to allow me out, if you can imagine anything so absurd. She even has Dick acting like some sort of hench-man. He was actually muscling me around."

Charlotte is wary. "I can hardly believe that. Why?"

"You know how Barbara is. Because I haven't been to the coun-try club and don't socialize with people she considers acceptable, she thinks I'm off the track again. Once her mind's set, well, you know how she is." I feel only a faint pang of shame for exploiting my daughters' rivalry.

"What do you want me to do?" she asks.

"Come plead my case for me."

"Be right there." She hangs up.

I stand by the window, watching the road in front of the house. Car after car goes by. Charlotte doesn't live far away, but it's a long time until she pulls into the driveway. It's seven-thirty.

I leave my room and let her in the back door. "Thanks for coming, honey," I say. Barbara enters the room behind me.

Charlotte is brisk. "What's going on here, Barbara? Dad says you've refused to let him go out. Who in the hell gave you that right?"

Barbara's face reddens. "How dare you come marching in here, telling me what to do about Dad? You see him only when it suits you. You've refused to even listen to anything I've tried to tell you about him. You know nothing about what's been going on around here. If you were here, you'd know he's — he's having trouble again."

"And you're a psychiatrist, I suppose," Charlotte says. "What wild, strange things is he doing?"

Dick appears behind Barbara as she says, "He's obsessed with that garden, Charlotte. He disappears at night until all hours, and won't tell me where he's going."

"I'm home by eleven every night," I say quietly.

Charlotte laughs. "He gardens and he stays out until eleven. Yes, indeed, Barbara, that's certainly bizarre behavior. I think you're the one that's crazy."

Barbara's voice chokes with rage. "I don't expect you to under-stand. You weren't even in the country when we had the CB inci-dent a couple of years ago."

"It wasn't a CB," I say, almost to myself.

Charlotte clicks her tongue in disgust, and turns to me. "Come on, Dad, I'll take you where you want to go."

"Oh no you don't," Barbara screams. "Dick."

"Just let them go," Dick says. "This is ridiculous."

Barbara wheels on him. She is utterly betrayed. "Dick, do something. Call the police."

Dick starts toward us, reluctantly. "Charlotte, come on, now. Leave Dad here with us. We'll take care of him."

Charlotte's feet are planted in a combative stance. Her eyes gleam with the joy of the contest. "Stop right there, fucker," she says.

Dick stops as though she has pointed a gun at him. He sputters, "There's no need for that sort of language."

"Oh," shrieks Barbara.

Charlotte turns again to me. "Where do you want to go, Dad?"

"To the fair. To the fair, James," I crow.

She takes my hand and we hurry out to her car. It's a small sports car. The top is down. As we speed up the road, the wind catches our hair and waves it like banners around our heads. I laugh in great hiccups of exhilaration. Charlotte is perhaps now a little doubtful, but she drives me to the fairgrounds. She stops at the gate, saying, "I can't stay. Can you get home?" I assure her I can.

"Okay," she says. "Take care of yourself, will you, or Barbara will have my head on a platter."

"I'm fine, honey."

I walk through the fairgrounds. The sun is setting. Throngs of people walk between the buildings housing the livestock. The animals are quiet here at the end of the day. They have given over the activity to the people. The aroma around the pens, however, attests to their presence.

The rides on the midway scream and thunder, streaking into the darkening sky in garish bolts, then plummeting again toward the ground.

I push through the crowds toward the produce display building. I'm caught again in the celebration of the fair. I think the excitement I feel is a premonition that I won't miss the tomato judging.

Closer, closer. I can see the wide doors propped open and a flow of people issuing through them. It's not over. It can't be. I glance again at my watch. It's 8:35.

I hurry toward the door. I question a man I've seen descend the ramp of the building. "Is the produce judging over?"

"Yes," he says, "they just finished."

Feeling hot tears pressing my eyelids, I retreat into the shadow of the building. These tears are ludicrous, of course. Here I am hiding in the shadows from a crowd of strangers, and weeping. Over what? Six tomatoes!

The tomatoes. The way they looked lying in the basket in the garden; round and perfect. Yes, perfect. I wasn't there for the judging, but then I didn't need to be. The judges saw the tomatoes, turned them over, looked with knowing eyes.

I walk slowly toward the door. I'm afraid now to know, afraid of being wrong in my judgment of the tomatoes. I reach the door and, squaring my shoulders, walk into the vast, harshly lit room. The tomato exhibits are set on a central table. I can see them from the door. There are ribbons laid across some of them. Some are blue ribbons. One in each class of tomato.

When I reach the table, I walk alongside as I imagine a disinterested observer might. I turn over several ribbons in other classes, read the names of the exhibitors: "Tomato-Rutgers — Henry Ames." Henry has taken a second place. "Tomato-Hybrid Red — Lucille Banks." Lucille has taken a blue ribbon.

The Chesapeakes — my class — are set near the end of the table. I hestiate, then turn over the white ribbon, third place. My name isn't there. I turn over the red ribbon, second place, thinking, "Second would be nothing to be ashamed of." My name isn't there.

I inspect the losers. Some I know aren't mine. Their flaws are too obvious. My hand trembles as I reach for the blue ribbon. I turn it over and read, "Tomato-Chesapeake — Walter Brinkman."

Prize tomatoes! My tomatoes! Blue-ribbon tomatoes!

I lay the ribbon down on the plate and touch the tomatoes gently. I feel light, as though my body were no more than air. I smile. I want to laugh out loud, to clap my hands, point out the tomatoes to whoever passes by. Mr. Miggs, I wish that you were here.

Mr. Miggs. I check my watch. I'm only a stop or two above his stop. There's plenty of time to catch his bus. I take a last look at the tomatoes, the ribbon. Tomorrow I'll come with a camera. Good-bye, my beauties.

I walk slowly. I consider going home, but Barbara's enraged face is far too vivid. I stop, stand gazing into the trees at the edge of the fairgrounds. The sun has sunk below the horizon. The sky behind the trees, still softly lit in gold, casts a long shadow behind me.

A strange peace settles over me as the sky fades into gray. I feel whole again, for the first time since Peg's death — not the same, to be sure, but no less than I was before. A man who has raised prize tomatoes must know something, something of great value perhaps. Surely I have something yet to teach my children. I, still with much to learn from the pain that disassembled and rearranged me, am different but not lost.

Oddly, Barbara's anger has lost its threat. The worst she can do is to send me back to Dr. Hooper, and he, after all, doesn't know everything. He wouldn't know a prize tomato if he saw one.

I begin to walk toward the gate. Ah, Barbara, I do love you. With effort we could be friends, you and I. I believe I have the courage now to try to explain to you some of what has happened to me. I was quite a persuasive man at one time; perhaps I still am. Who knows? You may find you can love me just as well now as before. Ours are primal ties that go far beyond appearances. We'll test those ties, Barbara, I promise.

Yes, I'll ride the bus home, talk to Barbara tonight. But first I have one more thing to do.

My strides feel long and strong. The bus stop is an easy distance away. The bus pulls up just as I reach the curb. I climb aboard and take the seat at the back.

Mr. Miggs will be surprised to see me already on the bus. So much has happened and we have so little time to talk.

The familiar jostling of the bus seems to heighten my exhilaration. I watch the lights glide over the windows as we near Mr. Miggs's stop.

Through the window I see him rise from the bench, his back erect. Boarding the bus, he blinks in the glare. As he turns toward the back, he spots me. His half-and-half grin splits his face.

Unable to wait until he sits down, I say as he approaches, "Mr. Miggs, next Saturday you must come to see my garden and stay to dinner afterward. I won't take 'no' for an answer."

He halts, his hand clutching the back of a seat in the rocking aisle of the bus. "Well, I'll be," he says, "then I guess you better call me Mason."

IAN MacMILLAN

Proud Monster — Sketches

(FROM THE CAROLINA QUARTERLY)

Treblinka, Eastern Poland: Summer, 1943 — Horror Stories

JAN KRATKO AND Anton Zydovska have worked this detail for two days, and are finally over the shock of discovering that this remote section of the camp is laid out in large burial pits in the yellow, sandy earth. They speak in low tones whenever the German guard walks away, upwind of the tangy smell of death. The nude bodies arrive in a metal dump cart on narrow-gauge rails, some old and emaciated, some young and healthy, and they must drag them into the pit and arrange them in rows, six tiers deep. They rest before the cart arrives again, standing at the edge of the pit and getting their breath from the heavy work, grimacing from the painful, acidic vacuum of hunger.

"Chelmno," Zydovska says. "There an officer used to hang men close to the ground and force them to look into his eyes — then he would laugh very loud like a madman."

"Yes, these little jokes," Kratko says. "I have heard of this. At Maidaneck they would lecture to us, always about what low beasts in human form we were, about how all this is nature's way," and he sweeps his hand out over the pit. "Then they'd take a man and boil his hand in a pot until his skin slid off like a glove."

The cart arrives, pushed by two sullen Kapos who tip it up so that the bodies flop out in a limp and angular little avalanche. Then they turn and push the cart back toward the large brick building where the people are killed. On top of the pile of bodies is a young girl different from the others, who are old and thin and dark-haired. Although her hair has been cut short, they can see it is the color of wheat, and she is plump and buxom and has a chubby, angelic face. Mildly stunned, Kratko looks away from her face, bothered by the eyes, one of which is open wide, with a pale blue iris, while the other is half shut. On the other side of the pit the German guard smokes and looks away toward the distant pines. Kratko becomes locked in a weary and catatonic sadness, a hollow swoon of memory. Such beauty, he thinks. He reaches out and places his hand on the girl's full breast, and the pressure of the hand makes a soft hiss of air escape from her mouth. "It is a shame," he says.

"Don't do that!" Zydovska whispers harshly.

"It is a shame."

"Don't. Don't!"

Soon she is made anonymous in the sea of flesh. Across the pit smoke curls away from the guard's head. Struggling for balance on the flesh, Kratko and Zydovska carry the last body, an old woman with a wart on her cheek, and set her out in her final resting place. Returning to the edge of the pit, staggering with exhaustion and aching with hunger, Kratko barely notices that they walk on the girl's back.

Resting, they wait for the cart. "Here," Zydovska says, "there is supposed to be an officer who shoots children for fun. From his porch. A guard throws the child in the air and — " Kratko nods, understanding. "He has a little daughter who watches, too," Zydovska says. "It is said that she enjoys it very much."

Seeing the dump cart approaching, feet and heads rocking at the rim, Kratko grimaces at the thought. "It is not a thing to let children see," he says.

Auschwitz, Poland: Fall, 1944 — Children of Wing 22

The children do not know what book it is that Andreas Larkos reads. He is close to no one because he does not speak their language, and because one side of his face is marked by a large blotch the color of wine. In their segregated groups of ten or twelve, each tied to the other by common language or dialect, they speculate that the book, either found in the stone quarry or smuggled into the camp, is on some religious subject. There is no time to ask him about it, using either sign language or the halting German a few of them know from school. In the early morning, when dusty shafts of light come through the little windows and travel up the tiers of dirty bunks, he sits tipping it into the sun, whispering to himself. When the block manageress comes in and whacks her truncheon on the wall, he quickly puts the book out of sight and unconsciously covers the blemish with his hand. The manageress herds the children without food or water out to the quarry to gather small stones all day, each of them moaning with hunger and thirst. The weaker ones, swollen in the legs and sleepy, wilt over the stones and cannot get up. They are carted away, a few each afternoon.

Deep in the night they are marched back to Wing 22 and fed a watery soup made with sawdust and potato peelings. Then they immediately crawl into their bunks. Sleep comes quickly.

No one is awakened by the moans or the crying of tomorrow's dead.

Andreas Larkos wakes up. When he sits up on the edge of his bunk, an acid stab of hunger thrusts upward into his chest. He rubs the sleep from his eyes and looks around, then reaches under his mattress for the book, feeling among pebbles, snips of paper. It is about science, the universe, the history of beings on earth. Today, on page 37, he reads about the linear magnitude of time, that the earth is billions of years old and that it takes a thousand times a thousand to make a million and another thousand times that to gauge half the life of the planet. In his half sleep he labors over the comparison: *I am nine, man is a thousand times a hundred, a speck in a billion — Father was four times my nine when . . .* And he sees him again, how strange the way the wind ruffled his black hair, which usually bore the impression made by his tight hat. And his cheeks so strangely puffed, and the rope gone in the flesh under his jaw.

In the quarry a boy ahead of him drops on the stones and seems to study the ground close to him with patient, glassy eyes. Then a string of brown bile comes from the corner of his mouth. Andreas puts his hand on the blemish and turns from him to his own shadow . . . *made by the sun, and there are stars a million times bigger, we see only as tiny points of light in the night sky, a million times the size of the sun.*

When he stands on his shadow at midday and fatigue threatens to overcome him, he finds a flat, gray pebble with the imprint of a fossil shell in it, delicate rills fanning outward from the squared base. His heart thumps with excitement at this discovery. It is one of the best he has seen. He has no pockets, so he places the stone in his mouth for safekeeping, to add to the little collection he keeps next to the book under his mattress.

Berlin: Summer, 1945 — Night Visit

Aichele sits in the dim candlelight, looking for the line from Rilke. He hears them coming, shouting Frau, Frau! They will be in his house shortly. Still he looks for the line, his throat thickening with the familiar despair that is now tinged with a sense of mounting absurdity. Today he saw the Russians herding the new prisoners toward the camps. They were frightened, dirty boys, some pimply, all the same age as the ones he once shooed away from his plum trees. The Führer is dead. Next door, Grubner's daughter, only fourteen, cowers in the useless bathroom waiting for the Russians to pass. Aichele can see from his bedroom window upstairs that she hides there. He fears for her.

It was something like "Ich habe mein Glück und ich habe mein Weh und ich habe jedes allein." He tires, flipping the pages. His luck and his grief. All alone. Upstairs his wife and daughter lie under a quilt on the floor, their fronts untouched as if they sleep, and their backs blasted, punctured with thick splinters of wood from the force of the shattering wall they sat trembling against during the bombing two days ago. He has requested help to remove them and is indignant at the absence of propriety concerning burial.

Now on the porch, Frau, Frau! He rises, thinking Only a short time ago, on the Potsdamerplatz, there were English poets, German intellectuals, women . . . He opens the door. They smile without malice. What victor needs to display it? One has malevolent Kirghiz eyes, not unlike Elizabeth's. Aichele backs away and permits them to enter. They look around. He smells liquor on their breath. Aichele points to the stairs, and they stamp up, disregarding the ancient rug that is threadbare in the middle from a million former steps. Aichele winces.

He follows, holding the candle high and placing his feet on the thicker edges of the carpet as he has done for many years. The two soldiers see the covered forms in the candlelight that casts moving shadows on the wall from Aichele's unsteady hand. The air is touched with the odor of their decomposition, which is just beginning. One soldier falls to his knees and uncovers them. He crosses himself, rises. The soldiers cross themselves again and utter brief prayers. The one with the Kirghiz eyes pats Aichele on the shoulder and looks gravely at his face. They depart, leaving him staring down at the still forms of his wife and daughter.

The Russians continue down the street, saying Frau, Frau! They find the Grubner girl. It is as if they had known always that she would be there. *How horrible!* he thinks. They do not bother to blow out their candle. She only cries, does not fight. Aichele steps to the window, now that they have found her. His candle dulls his vision, so he blows it out and looks down into the little soft orange rectangle of window at the hunched forms of the soldiers.

Lvov, Poland: Fall, 1941 — Street Cleaning

Obersturmführer Fischer sits at the table at the edge of the square, looking into the pale amber wine. At his side his aide Heppler laughs as he watches the proceedings, Fischer's idea, which Heppler had called "first prize for inventiveness." The tablecloth balloons in the breeze, and Fischer notes that the heat of summer has finally passed, which should make his job of eliminating the city's ubiquitous vermin nearly tolerable. Across the table, out in the square, his men peer down the muzzles of their rifles at the hunched backs of perhaps a hundred Jews. Before being relocated at the Janowska Camp, they are cleaning the stones of the square with their tongues. The only resistance was taken care of an hour before, when a young man refused Fischer's jovial order and got his head cracked by the handsome young soldier who now struts around the perimeter of the cleaning crew, lightly slapping his truncheon against his thigh, saying, "Good! Excellent! You! You missed a spot, you idiot! You'll be punished for such sloppiness!"

Heppler laughs again. "Our friend struts like a rooster, no?"

"He has a weakness for these women," Fischer says. "His only fault. Where is this wine from?"

"Oberwesel."

At the near edge of the group Fischer sees a boy who, unlike the others, seems to have become fascinated with his work. He pauses, looking at the flat stone, spits, then continues licking. Heppler sees him too, and squints. Curious about the boy's lack of inclination toward the backward glance or moan of protest, they lean forward to observe him more closely. "A dolt?" Heppler asks.

"It is likely. They are all dolts of one degree or another."

Born deaf, the boy has experienced all with a clarity of vision exaggerated by silence. Assuming that they were involved in some enforced but necessary rite, that the men of the black uniforms were perhaps priests imposing their harsh penance on them, he obeyed the frightened language of his father's face, and began to lick the cool stone. Gradually he wore the surface of dirt away, and there emerged before his eyes a jagged vein of white embedded in the gray. Deep in the white there was a finely fractured translucence that riveted his attention: It was warm ice, the winter season suspended in stone, and it struck him as he revealed it all to himself — a diagonal line dividing like the branch of a tree — that he would never forget the smooth, pale transparency that disappeared down into itself, or the fine, glistening cracks, or the sheets of particolored brilliance with the points of blue and green light.

"I've had enough," Fischer says, sighing. "Order them to the camp."

Spitting and wiping their mouths, the Jews line up for the short march to their new and last home. Fischer sees the boy looking back toward the square with a dumbstruck expression, as if none of all this could penetrate his slavish attention to the stone he had licked.

As they are marched off, Fischer crosses the square, feeling strange at the thought of walking where the Jews had licked the stones, as if the ground under him might drop out at any moment. He is suddenly uneasy, and he no longer enjoys his jest. He stops at the boy's stone, leans over, and studies the vein of quartz. After a few seconds of looking into it, his mind becomes suspended in a ticklish half memory, as if his brain were clumsily laboring at recalling something important, like a familiar but forgotten name. Then he thinks, I must go home soon. This infernal business. I must go home.

"Are you ill?" Heppler asks from behind him.

Fischer stands, and is dizzy, so that spots of light sweep across his vison. "No," he says. "No, it must be the wine. It makes me homesick. It is very good, no?"

Near Essen: Spring, 1945 — Bad Dreams

Gretchen Beck has walked half the afternoon, carrying the small bag of belongings in one hand and holding her daugher's hand in the other. The child, walking two steps to her mother's one, clutches her doll and views the devastated villages with bright curiosity, while her mother averts her eyes from blackened buildings and overturned trucks and occasional neat rows of prone bodies.

Each kilometer or so they encounter more unshaven Americans, who search their belongings and wave them on, pointing in the direction of the village where a camp has been set up for refugees like herself. "Mama!" She turns. The child laughs, holds the doll to her chest. Hanging by the neck from the splintered branch of a dead tree is another doll like her own, pink and smiling, but nude and without arms. It swings in the breeze, the black holes in its shoulders turning across their vision each time the head reaches its button- nosed profile. The child stares at it, the smile slowly passing from her face. Her mother shudders and pulls her along, feeling hunger twist in her stomach. She wonders how the girl can stand it.

The camp is a low metal-roofed building surrounded by fence and tents. Inside, tired soldiers organize the aged and the women and children in lines before steaming pots of soup and mounds of hard bread. She cannot separate the child from the doll while they eat, and reasons that if it makes her secure, then it is all right. Watching the child, she thinks again of the loss of her husband and brother.

Past twilight, they are given a single battered cot to sleep on. She is still hungry, but the child is at least exhausted enough to sleep. They lie nestled like spoons, the mother, child, and doll.

She orders dinner at a country Gasthaus. The proprietor, a fat Bavarian, shakes his head at her order for a simple meal and suggests the specialty of the evening with a cryptic, inarticulate speech. Even though it costs more, she nods, laughing. The meat is pale, swimming in a translucent butter sauce. He stands across the room nodding and gesturing, patting his stomach. Good, no? Yes, excellent! But the meat is too tender, too pale. When she cuts it the flaccid, pale skin slides away and folds heavily into the sauce.

Stunned, she realizes that it is the upper arm of a child. She drops her fork . . .

Sweat trickles across her face. She rises to her elbows breathing quickly. Across the building somewhere, an old man yells in his sleep. Her heart thumps and she trembles, trying to calm herself. Just as she lies down again, the child screams out, clutching at the blanket, at the air, then at the doll. She feels it, babbling shrill and urgent gibberish. "What?" her mothers says. "What is it? What's the matter?" She holds the child's hands, then remembers. "Here," she says. "Here, see? See? She has arms. Oh yes! See the arms? Right here — see them? Oh yes, she has arms.

Near Lublin, Poland: June, 1941 — The Collector

I had known Pervant in Kassel before the war, and that day, as the battalion entered the village, Pervant's place of exile since 1939, I sensed a nearly perfect completion of a process, thinking, as I looked out over the green plains, It will be in some safe place, perhaps a dresser, those same albums. I pictured Pervant years ago, holding the magnifying glass up and smiling with pride and a certain baiting smugness that angered me. Pervant was to be hanged summarily, a confirmed enemy of the Reich. This was the business of the younger SS, robust and boisterous, who arrived in trucks, while I arrived in a limousine, my function administrative.

My heart rose in my chest when I saw him — yes, the records were correct. He was drawn from one of the larger houses by the soldiers, while his wife trailed behind, pleading in German. The difficult preparations for this day were the result of careful calculation: I had to convince the regional administrators that Pervant was dangerous, a partisan involved in sabotage, along with other members of the village. I walked the perimeter of the square as the portable scaffolds were erected, and an officer read a speech to the populace, the preface to the execution selections.

I entered Pervant's house. Yes, there was the old Victorian chair he had in Kassel. The case, too, in which he displayed his collection of glassware — Murano, Meissen figurines, bright but worthless trash. Below the shelves were two drawers. I opened one and the musty smell of old leather wafted up. It was at the beginning of a section reserved for the British Colonies under British Guiana —

my hands trembled as I flipped the pages, and there it was, the four-cent blue, 1856, *Damus Petimus — Que Vicissim*, a ship on a square of blue paper. Such fine, clear type, a nearly perfect specimen. I tore the page out of the album and folded it carefully around the stamp — the others in Pervant's collection were useless to me. I was then suddenly anxious for a leave from this dirty business, and my heart raced in my chest. I now had to protect the stamp until I could arrange a leave. It could not be stained, nubbed, lost.

Outside, the executions were in progress. Men and women swung under the single bar of the scaffold. Holding my hand over my pocket, I passed them on my way to my business. I would distribute leaflets detailing the new laws of the district until my fingers became dark with ink stains. I saw Pervant then, swinging from the middle of the scaffold, his mouth distended as if stuffed with food. Next to him hung a pregnant woman. One officer took snapshots of another, who leaned against the scaffold advising him about focus and depth of field without moving his mouth. I felt that everything was too confused, too chaotic, that the stamp would somehow disappear.

There was a movement at the scaffold — the woman next to Pervant, her midsection. Across the fabric of her dress slid a soft lump that changed the shape of her pregnancy with a slow undulation. I pressed my pocket, afraid of the possibility of some accident, panic, gunfire. Feeling giddy and secretive, I returned to the car to open the page and study the minute printing of the ship, perfect lines under the dim, hundred-year-old pen cancellation. My fears of losing the stamp were groundless. Inside of a month I had it mounted in my collection, safe in the strongbox at home. But experience teaches us that nothing is complete. To my deep sadness I discovered in consultation with an expert that the stamp is a forgery. The horror of it all is that I never will know if Pervant himself was duped, or has done so to me.

Inside Western Russia: Winter, 1943 — Lebensraum

Haas, our officer, believed that we were near the border of Poland, and with renewed hope the three of us trudged on, so that little explosions of snow came off our knees. The brightness drove our eyes nearly shut, so that we saw the endless flat expanse of western Russia only through blazing slits of vision. We had marched for two days and had seen little, until we approached a rise speckled with the black forms of tree stumps. Five kilometers ahead, across snow lifted by the wind like steam off the glittering surface, there was a low peak from which we would see if we would survive or not. We were numb with exhaustion and only half conscious. The bright snow seemed to penetrate and burn out our reason, attention, hope. Our unit lay frozen two days behind us, lined up in the yard of a burned-out church, their greatcoats over them. We walked strung out, Haas far ahead, myself in the middle; and Grebauer, who had joined us from another lost unit the day before, struggled far behind me. Haas was suspicious of him because he told us that he saw SS soldiers killing women and children in Siedlice. "These are lies, Bolshevik deceptions," Haas said. Grebauer laughed, and continued from time to time to tell these stories, always as if to test the limits of Haas's disbelief. Later Haas whispered to me, "A deserter, I think."

Walking toward the peak, I saw the horizon divide so that there was a blue, boiling space in the center, through which torrents of water rushed. At a point where the water would achieve visual particularity, the strange mass became a multitude of pale horses, their snouts, breath vapor, manes all distinct in the middle distance. Cavalry perhaps. I was about to warn Haas about them when I realized that it was a mirage.

Grebauer marched out of the trench Haas and I made in the snow, and came to rest, looking off toward a shattered tree stump on our left. Then he saw down. "I will rest here, until someone comes," he called to me. Then he laughed. *"Lebensraum,"* he said, "we have more than we can use, I think."

"No one will come," I said. "You'll die." He looked small and dirty, sitting there in the snow.

"I will rest here."

Haas came back to us. "Grebauer, get up." The man laughed, leaning back. "I order you to get up." Grebauer gazed at him as if not comprehending the order.

"Come," I said, "we'll get to the top of the hill, then rest."

"One man put a baby's foot on the ground and stepped on it, then pulled it up by the other leg and killed it."

"Get up," Haas said.

"The mother watched. She looked strange, as if she were trying to remember something. A name, perhaps." Haas looked at Grebauer, his face fixed in a mask of thoughtful speculation, as if he were trying to visualize Grebauer's story.

We got him up and continued to climb in the snow, trudging through the vapor of our breath. Haas was first to break to the top. Then I joined him there. Ahead there was a stunning perfection of snow, an infinity of blinding, bluish white under the sky, as if we had emerged on the hilltop to face the vast expanse we had just crossed. Only our trail proved our direction. In the far distance the horizon was speckled with shimmering lakes, and beyond, strange forms, cities of ice, the suggestion of bright onion domes.

Haas reached inside his coat and I heard a ripping sound. Then he held his insignia in his hand, absurdly dense in color. He blinked at them, his eyes flooding, and dropped them into the snow. Some farmer, I imagined, would find them in the spring down among the soft shoots of wheat.

Grebauer was lying behind us. Haas trudged back to him and leaned down. "Come, Grebauer," he said. He lifted the dazed little man and wrapped one arm over his shoulder. "Come, we might be in Poland already. Perhaps only a short distance."

"Here, let me help," I said, taking Grebauer's free arm.

"I feel warm," Grebauer said. "I'm not even cold any more. The earth underneath is warm to the touch, did you notice?"

"Tell me, my friend," Haas said, plowing into the glittering plain before us, "what else did you see in Siedlice?"

"One would think that the snow would melt, with the earth so warm," Grebauer said.

Near Lodz, Poland: Spring, 1945 — Sniper's War

Today there are sounds of jubilation in the distance. A welcoming group of partisans emerges from the village and moves in my direction. Behind them, villagers cheer the advancing Russians as they had thought it best to cheer the Germans, years ago, and the partisan groups who moved by night at those times when they raided the town in search of supplies and comfort. I have waited on the perimeter of this village three days, and my partisan contact, an emaciated man with thick glasses and hands so arthritic that they look like crushed spiders, has come once, with food and warning: We shall start normal life once more, and the communists are our saviors.

Since the first lightning blow of the Germans I have lived a life of movement and solitude. One forced into these circumstances develops isolated forms of genius. In my case, it is the full understanding of the properties of my Mauser, and the perfection of my craft, including my discovery of the mysterious tricks of camouflage — in a plain as flat and vast as my country's there is no place to hide, so that, according to the principle of inversion, no one can find me. My life is a movement across a shimmering plain in search of targets: the black-uniformed SS, the mustard-colored soldiers. I float my target in the circle of liquid light crossed by the hairs, and watch him drop on the boiling horizon. The report fills the sky with divine applause, a hollow chorus of angels' voices. Satisfied, I retreat into the distance, avoiding sparse woodland and stream beds where I will be looked for. I clean and oil the Mauser and inspect it closely for evidence of wear or rust, knowing that the reprisal for one target's death is dozens of villagers hanged, turning in the breeze.

Only rarely have I been forced to approach my targets, when they fought death, clawing at the wound made by an imperfect shot. When they looked up at me, with that instinctively lucid perception bred by pain, I would realize the full genius of the mechanism — to throw metal at such speed!

I study the approaching villagers through the scope, while in the foreground of the liquid circle, hay stubble shimmers in the sun. I sweep the circle over thatch houses, seeking appropriate targets: a dog, a child, a military vehicle. Behind the village, clouds of dust mark the advance of the Russians. Now the contingent of villagers fills the circle. They are led by the arthritic partisan. I slide back, dragging my pack on the ground. Then I sit and wait for the imperfections of muscular control to fade, and for the eye to become one with the magical device that swallows distance up. The largest man drops on the horizon in a dreamlike limpness, while the rest scatter in surprise. The sky fills with divine applause.

ROSANNE COGGESHALL

Lamb Says

(FROM THE SOUTH CAROLINA REVIEW)

HE WAS FOUR YEARS OLD, not much taller than a cypress knee, and his corn-colored hair closed in around his face like ivy around a window. His round eyes fixed your eyes as if he were a hypnotist, their relentless gaze charged by irises the blue of cobalt. His parents called him Lamb, though his real name was Lambert Charles Harroday IV and he thought of himself secretly as Bert. His parents, Althea Bledsoe and Lambert Charles Harroday III, treated him consistently with warmth and tact, and he thought them nearly perfect. Still, he had not yet felt like speaking to them. Lamb's four-year silence had begun long ago to alarm Althea Harroday, and, since his second birthday, she had daily suggested, less and less gently, to Charles that they take him to Atlanta, to a famous clinic there for children with speech disabilities. But Charles was firm. There was nothing the matter with Lamb, he repeated, the boy was just taking his time. After all, the first words of a famous man are the stock of history, and his son was simply making damn sure his would be profound, because the Harrodays knew, knew for a fact, that Lamb would be a famous man — probably not president, he would be too short — but possibly an Einstein or a Mark Twain or, at least, a Harroday Wills. (Harroday Wills was Charles's distant cousin who had moved to Michigan and become a popular author of mystery novels. His pen name, T. Z. Lilly, was a household word in Indian Grove, the small Georgia town where the Harrodays lived.)

The reason that Lamb's parents were so certain of their son's grown-up success was because they had been able to tell, ever since the child began to walk, that he was a genius. At twenty-two months, he expressed interest (by pointing and reaching) in the *Encyclopaedia Britannica,* and it was not long after he had been allowed to hold a volume that Althea discovered him propped up in an armchair, concentrating deeply on the page before him. By the time he was three he had been through (read, his parents insisted) every volume and had begun to spend his time with literature. He "finished" the *Complete Works of Robert Louis Stevenson* in a matter of days; Sir Walter Scott detained him somewhat longer, Thackeray longer still. Then he tackled, one by one, Dickens's novels. These occupied him for quite some time and during that time he showed every indication, his parents thought, of being on the verge of speech. He would push himself out of the heavy armchair and walk into the kitchen where they were usually sitting and purse his lips and lift his hands in a precipitate gesture and they would stiffen in anticipation, but, it never failed, he would not follow through. Instead, he would close his eyes, drop his hands, unscrew his mouth and yawn widely, his tongue as pink as the Harroday Empress, the rose his mother had developed two summers before. He would then turn around, and with a little shuffle that resembled a bird scratching for worms (his mother called it his "dance"), he would return to the library and climb into the chair where his book waited.

During his Dickens days, Lamb began to demonstrate other new and curious tendencies: He started looping his mother's cast-off dress sashes around his throat and knotting them in front as if they were ties; he found Aunt Valentine's forgotten parasol and somehow ripped the fabric and spines away so that he made himself a spindly cane that he carried with him everywhere; and every morning he appeared in his Sunday clothes, the long white trousers and navy-blue brass-buttoned jacket that had come in the mail from Atlanta. Even when the trousers were more gray than white from his escapades in the back yard and nearby woods he persisted in wearing them, so that Althea, in a characteristically accommodating gesture, bought two new pair of white linen trousers for him in the Young Men's Store in town. Not only did his dress take on a certain rakishness, but Lamb's whole manner of deportment also changed. His "dance" became an integral part of his every movement; he shuffled wherever he went. He held his narrow shoulders very straight and kept his arms close to his body. The elder Harrodays were amused and observed to each other in private that their son was surely imitating a Dickens character; they bemoaned their ragged memories and sometimes stole into the library after Lamb was in bed and leafed through the volume he was presently engaged in to find clues as to which hero he emulated, but to no avail. So they simply bided their time, each anticipating the day Lamb moved on to another author and, perhaps, changed his image again.

"Do put those Chesnutt books high up on the shelf, Charles," Althea said one night that spring. "We don't want Lamb coming in with soot all over his face and arms and in rags. Valentine and the girls talk bad enough as it is."

So the Chesnutt books were moved, as were the Steinbeck books and the Caldwell books and the set of Joel Chandler Harris. Althea had a horror of her sister Valentine's tongue, a tongue that had had much exercise since Lamb had begun to grow up so silently. It was that summer, the summer that Lamb was four and had just begun his second trip through the works of Charles Dickens, that Althea was reminded by her sister that it was the Harrodays' turn to host the Fourth of July picnic. Even though these celebrations had become far less elaborate since Wilkins and Mendal (Althea's brothers) had moved out of state with their families, Althea still dreaded them because they meant that not only Valentine and Rudy, her husband, but all six of their girls would be on hand for what seemed to her to be days; actually the picnic was usually only a four- or five-hour affair, but during those hours, Althea knew, the Lucases would have more than enough time to observe Lamb and both his new and his old peculiarities to their hearts' content, which meant until she herself was close to, if not in, tears. So when Val called and offered to have the picnic at her house, because the neighbors would be away and had volunteered the use of their pool, Althea was both grateful and relieved; she knew that she and Charles and Lamb could leave early, curtailing any conversation that became too tortuous. In a fit of appreciation she told Val that she would fry all of the chicken.

The night of the third, with the sound of frying chicken in the kitchen below him like a downpour of rain, Lamb sat in the bottom half of his trundle bed, thinking excitedly. He was looking forward to the picnic. Aunt Valentine made him want to close his eyes and disappear, but he liked the girls, all of them, from Tine to Puff, the baby. He knew that they were outrageous, silly, and mindless, but he found himself carried away by their stories and serpentine arguments, their boasts and complaints. He especially liked Caroline, who was seven and, he thought, very dignified, even wise. She told him about the tulip poplar, how it grew straight up, defying gravity, not like other trees; and she had shown him where the pea hen had hidden her eggs. Lamb liked the way she looked, too. She looked different from the others. Her hair was about the length of his, just covering her ears, and it was light brown, streaked by the sun with blond; her eyes were large and black, her nose small and straight. She was snaggletoothed, but, generally, nobody noticed, because she seldom spoke and when she laughed she gave way to such a frenzy of motion, running in circles or somersaulting, that there was no opportunity to observe her mouth. These transports of amusement were rare, but when they occurred there was a good reason for them, and Lamb knew to look out and to listen. Caroline could make him laugh like no one else could. So Lamb sat in bed and considered what he would say to Caroline if he were to decide to talk. He supposed he would begin with the story of Oliver Twist. He thought she would like that. Or perhaps he would tell her about the fauna in New Zealand or the Lincoln-Douglas debates. There were so many things he had learned about, and they were all jammed up in his head like pickles in a jar. And never once had he spoken of them aloud. He had worried for some time that his head was growing larger as he packed the information in and that soon he would look like poor Bidley Hanes, whose head was like a pumpkin on a hat rack, but he had spent considerable time reading the *Britannica* entry on the brain and he had been relieved to find that his greatest danger was having a brain more creased and wrinkled than a prune. But this would be inside, where no one could see. This comforted him, and as he debated with himself which fascinating facts he would lay before his cousin, if he were to want to speak to her at all, he pictured the creases in his brain and what each crease signified.

The rain sound in the kitchen had stopped.

"Lamb, honey, bedtime!" Althea called.

He climbed out of bed and slipped off his clothes, put on his nightshirt, and went down the stairs for his juice. As his mother arranged some freshly baked brownies on a plate for him, she talked steadily: "And if Aunt Valentine begins to fiddle with your clothes, you just push her hands away — politely, I mean. Just move away, there's no earthly reason why you should stand there and let her rearrange you. And, mind, whatever she or Uncle Rudy says, don't you let it trouble you. They are wonderful people and I love them, but they do not know anything whatsoever about you and your ways. They don't understand. Just ignore them. Politely. And if those girls tease you, why you just smile and walk off somewhere; or you can jump in the pool and swim for a little bit. Under water. Now just don't you worry about it. We won't be there long, just a few hours, and then soon it will be all over and you and I and Daddy can come back here and read or listen to Mantovani or play Crazy Eights or something. Fun. We'll do something fun."

Lamb nodded solemnly but he reflected to himself that the real fun would be when he was there at the picnic, off listening to his cousins or with Caroline alone. He dreamed that night that he and Caroline were sitting on a fat limb in a live oak tree and that he sang a song for her. The song was one he had sung in his head over and over for nearly a year now: "Hearts Are Spades." He had heard it one day when he was visiting Danny next door; Danny's cook sang it for them while she pounded dough to make bread.

When Lamb woke up, it was to sound of thunder, and he looked out of his window into a heavily clouded sky. The gray clouds looked like huge furry animals running into each other and chasing around above the trees. He sat for a while looking out and, as he watched, big raindrops pelted the screen, leaving shiny streaks. He began to review in his mind the processes of precipitation, then went on to run through the annual averages of rainfall in each of the United States. He was on North Dakota when he heard his mother in the hall already in mid-paragraph. ". . . Why come, anyway, I said to her, it will be bedlam in that house with all of us cooped up, you know, they don't use the living room and there is so much furniture in that den; can you imagine, the eight of them and us three, and the Pritchards and old Wilhelmena Pine. Eighteen. And the children won't be able to go out. And that dog of theirs, not to mention the rabbit. But she says to come on, that it might let up, and that anyway she's made a barrel of potato salad and sliced up a peck of peaches, but I know it's not going to let up, just look at that sky."

Althea paused for breath, then continued, now standing in Lamb's doorway, "Rain, honey, but Aunt Valentine says for us to come on. Now you get dressed, quick like a rabbit, and come down for some breakfast and then you can help me pack up the chicken. We'll have to leave by three to get there in time, and I want everything all ready before lunch so I can take a little nap before we go."

Lamb packed his fourth of the basket of chicken expertly; he was, his mother told anyone who would listen, a marvel in the kitchen. He began when he was just three by surprising the Harrodays one afternoon with a pot of tea and scrupulously made cinnamon toast that he arranged on the best silver tray; he had not been able to lift the tray but when he beckoned his parents to follow him into the kitchen they found the food arranged neatly, complete with china cups and saucers and fresh linen napkins.

From that day on, he was constantly amazing them with demonstrations of culinary prowess: He often created elaborate omelettes for breakfast or supper, standing on a small stool next to the kitchen counter, and once, for his father's birthday, he had produced a perfect charlotte russe. It took the puzzled Harrodays some time to make a connection between their son's new preoccupation and the Julia Child cookbook that lay within his reach on a shelf in the kitchen.

After he had helped his mother, Lamb took the book he was rereading (*Great Expectations*) up to his room and sat in bed and read. From time to time he would pause and look out at the rain, which fell harder and harder and made him think of hurricanes and tornadoes. He debated with himself the possibility of seeing Caroline alone and perhaps talking to her; it was not, he knew, a question of ability, for he could talk — he talked, in fact, inside of his head almost as much as his mother talked aloud. No, it was not a question of his being afraid to speak because of failure; it was a question of desire. So far in his four years Lamb had simply found no occasion that inspired in him the want to speak. Every time he had been urged by his family or his friends to participate in a conversation or just to answer a question, he had been struck by an absence of necessity, an utter lack of true purpose.

He always replied in his head and sometimes at great length, but he had early discovered the essential preciousness of language and had determined never to exploit or waste it.

Consequently, he had never heard his own voice. Never once had he practiced or experimented; he just took it for granted that when the time came, he would be ready, fluent, exact, and even eloquent. But that time had not yet come, and, often now, Lamb wondered if it would ever come.

In the car on the way over to Twin Hills where the Lucases lived, Mr. and Mrs. Harroday went through their annual Fourth of July litany of names, ages, and present concerns of all of the cousins and friends who would be on hand.

". . . and Charles, please, do try to remember that the baby, the youngest girl, she's a year now, is called Puff, not Poof. Last Christmas you spent the entire evening addressing her as 'Poof,' and I thought Valentine was going to explode. And it's Mary Dell, not Hattie, who keeps winning the spelling prizes. Mary Dell's eight, no nine, she's the tall, gangly one with bug eyes, hums a lot, you know. And do try to refrain from talking to Rudy about fishing. Ever since he took that trip to the coast and came back two days late, Valentine just goes wild at the very mention; she thinks he met someone, a woman, you know, or something, and the slightest hint can set her off."

"Might be the only fireworks we see today," Mr. Harroday interjected, then, finding an unexpected pause in the conversation, went on to ask: "And the odd one, the small one with the pretty eyes who's so quiet, she's?"

"Caroline." Mrs. Harroday was quick. "Yes. Caroline. There have been some problems with Caroline lately." She made a meditative sound like the buzz of a dozen bees, while Lamb sat up straight and waited. His father also waited, and, when Mrs. Harroday did not continue, prompted her: "Yes? Trouble?"

"Well," Mrs. Harroday glanced toward the back seat where Lamb sat tensed and expectant. She hesitated a moment, as if weighing consequences, and then she plunged, reassuring herself no doubt that her son would repeat nothing he heard. "Well, Caroline's a quiet child, as you said, and she's always been a little peculiar. Kept to herself, that kind of thing. No real rapport with her sisters. A loner, you know. Well, it seems she's always had this imaginary friend, Chrystal she calls her, who goes with her everywhere, even to school. At first, Valentine and Rudy thought it was cute and they asked about Chrystal and even allowed Caroline to have extra cookies and things so that her friend could share. They assumed she'd outgrow it. But she hasn't, and several times last spring during school Caroline caused quite a stir by leaving the playground and walking home because, she would tell them later, Chrystal had a call to make. They punished her of course and began to try to reason with her, but it did no good. And the real trouble began when they found that these calls Chrystal was making were to her brothers and sisters in London — she's an orphan, but she has several, I don't know how many, siblings. The calls were about the others coming over to live with her and Caroline."

Mr. Harroday laughed loudly.

"Well, you can laugh, but I don't think it's particularly funny. Now, Valentine says, there are three of them, Chrystal and Riley and Asberry, and Caroline spends all of her time with them. She never plays with the other children. Valentine says she has to watch her very closely all of the time because she keeps taking food for them — from her own plate, I mean, wrapping it in her napkin, then, well, I don't know, she must eat it herself. Valentine says she never finds traces later."

Mr. Harroday was obviously enjoying his wife's story tremendously; he kept shaking his head and laughing softly to himself. When he asked if Riley and Asberry were boys, brothers, Mrs. Harroday said, "Well, Riley is a girl; Asberry is a boy. They are all seven, Caroline's age. Valentine says they must be nice children, Caroline does not get into any mischief now that school's out, but she doesn't know what they are going to do when school begins, because it seems that Caroline always insisted that Chrystal have a desk and the teacher, a wispy little young thing, just out of school herself, let her have an extra desk. But if she demands *three* chairs . . . well, that's just a part of it, what worries Valentine most is that Caroline is always alone and that when she talks to them at all, it's about Chrystal or Riley or Asberry. Val is afraid Chrystal's going to send for the others . . . why there might be a dozen of them, for all we know."

Lamb was leaning forward, biting his lower lip. He had listened attentively to everything his mother said. He had known about Chrystal last year because Caroline had left him after they had been playing, saying that she and Chrystal had plans to make. He had wanted to go with her but assumed she didn't want more company. Now there were three, and one was a boy. He wondered if his cousin might let him play with them today. He knew about imaginary friends; he had read an article in *Psychology* not long ago with them. He didn't think that having imaginary friends could be bad for Caroline; it was just like the game he played when he pretended one of the characters in a book was his friend. Surely Caroline knew that Chyrstal and her brother and sister were not real; she probably liked them so much because they could be any way she wanted them to be. She could decide what they played, what they talked about, and how they behaved. Lamb thought it was possible that imaginary friends were the best kind of friends to have.

When the Harrodays reached the Lucases' house, which Mr. Harroday referred to privately as "the motel" because, he said, it was so long and so tacky, the rain still fell in huge wind-slanted waves, and they found all of the family and guests inside. All, that is, but Caroline. Lamb missed Caroline the moment he entered, but apparently no one else was concerned because no one mentioned her, not even his parents. Valentine and Rudy and their friends, Weezer and Cal Pritchard, were sitting around the kitchen table drinking mint juleps. Miss Wilhelmena Pine, who was 82 and looked 102 and who wore make-up as if it were somehow a shield against some dread infestation of insects and the more she wore the more she was protected, had perched herself on a backless barstool and balanced precariously there, weaving almost imperceptibly back and forth. Four of the Lucas girls and the Pritchard children were draped over the furniture in the den watching Spiderman and crushing potato chips into each other's mouths. Puff sat in the middle of the kitchen floor calmly playing with a bottle of ketchup, while Frances, the collie, pressed her body close against the refrigerator door and yawned. The crowd's greeting was subdued, as was the Harrodays'; even Althea and Valentine, who had not seen each other in six weeks, refrained from their usual enthusiasm.

After his parents had settled at the table with drinks and he had been urged to join the TV watchers in the den, Lamb began his search for Caroline. He passed through the darkened den without being noticed, and proceeded down the long hall slowly, listening as he walked for Caroline's voice. When he reached the end of the hall and turned around, he began to wonder if Caroline was in the house at all; he had heard nothing, not even when he listened at her door, and her family seemed to take her absence for granted. Pausing again before Caroline's door, he decided to be bold; he knocked, softly, three times. Inside he heard a muffled rustling, then nothing. He stuffed his hands into his trousers pockets and lowered his head. Then Caroline opened the door. She was wear-

ing an Indian suit and her face had been painted all over with
horizontal and vertical stripes of red and brown. Her headdress
was magnificent; it looked to Lamb as if she had a turkey perched
on her head.

"Hey, Lamb," Caroline said.

He couldn't tell whether she was glad to see him or not. He
smiled at her and gave a little wave. She looked at him carefully,
as if she were judging him in a contest, but Lamb didn't mind. He
wore a real tie this afternoon, one his mother had given him, and
his shirt and white trousers had been recently laundered. He stood
quite still beneath Caroline's wandering gaze and finally she
stepped back, opening the door for him to follow her into the
room. In the room, which Caroline shared with Puff, was an iron
double bed painted gold, a battered crib, a tall white chest of
drawers, and a child's bureau covered with open jars of finger
paint. Under it all stretched a heavy dark green rug with men's
faces printed onto it, presidents' faces. In the far corner of the
room there were some pillows, arranged in a rough circle, and
Caroline headed there and sat down. Uncertain of what she meant
for him to do, Lamb followed and stood beside one of the pillows,
his eyes on his cousin.

"We all were just having our tea," she told him; then, cordially,
"why don't you sit over here by Asberry and have a cup and a
bun."

Lamb sat down carefully on the rug in the place she had indicated.

"Asberry was just telling us about the time in London the boar
got loose in the picture show. He said it ran up and down the aisles
oinking and nobody could catch it and it kept grabbing away everybody's popcorn and just snuffing it up until he trapped it himself."

Lamb raised his pale eyebrows to show that he was impressed.

Caroline continued: "You see he had this whip he used to carry,
for rats and stuff; there are lots of rats and stuff in London; so he
took this whip and formed it into a lasso and then he stood up in
his seat and when the wild boar ran by he threw the lasso and got
him. Then he dragged it outside and found a bobby — that's a
London policeman, Lamb — he found one and gave it to him. He
said the bobby handcuffed the boar with some special handcuffs
he had and hooked him to his horse. And he gave Asberry a badge.
See? Isn't it splendid?"

Lamb looked at Asberry's imaginary badge and nodded vigor-
ously his agreement. Caroline offered him more tea and another
bun, both of which, to his disappointment, were imaginary too, but
he accepted them, although he did not taste them. He hoped he
would not offend Caroline but he could not make himself pretend
certain things in front of other people. Even though Caroline herself seemed to be enjoying her repast immensely, Lamb just sat
there with the invisible cup and plate balanced on his spotless
knees.

"Riley, now, Riley just got a letter from the queen," Caroline
informed him. She then produced the letter, which was as invisible
as the tea, and handed it to him. Lamb took it, screwed up his eyes
and tried to appear as if he were reading, but his cousin somewhat
rudely snatched it back.

"Here, I'll help you," she offered. "Riley's bashful, ain't you? She
would rather that I read it. It says, 'Dear Riley Rose' (Rose is her
middle name), 'It was splendid of you to go on the ship to America
to live with your sister and her friend Caroline. They sound so
charming: I miss you. And when you come back you can come
have cake again and ride the horse and play in the royal den. Also,
you can visit the princess and teach her the new games you learn.
Tell Chrystal and Asberry and Caroline *cheerio* and please write
me a letter soon. Lots of love, Your Highness, the Queen.' See,
Lamb, what a nice letter?"

Lamb nodded, but he was beginning to feel uncomfortable. He
felt like Caroline was very far away and he wanted her to come
back and talk to him about things and people he could see and
hear. He was not so sure as he had been that imaginary friends
were such good friends to have.

When Caroline next began to address Chrystal, Riley, and Asberry, Lamb could hardly believe his ears: "Y'all," she said. "Lamb
says that his new tie came from Jimmy Carter. He told me that the
president came to his house for supper last Monday night and
brought him this present and some money. Real new fresh-made
quarters and fifty-cent pieces and two whole real silver dollars.
And the president played Frisbee with him and then they watched
the NBC news. Just think."

Lamb's mouth opened and stayed open. *He* had said? Was Caroline turning him into an imaginary friend too? He saw that she
was looking at him somewhat slyly when she continued her one-

sided conversation with the other three: "Well, it's true, too, and Lamb says that next week he is going on a camping trip, all by himself, in Stevens Woods, where snakes and wild boars and wild-cats live, and he has a real tent with a door and a window in it and he's going to set it up out by a creek and stay a whole week out there by himself. And Lamb says . . ."

"No," Lamb said. His voice was low but firm. Caroline stopped and stared at him, her dark eyes serious and challenging. The silence that rushed into the room after his "no" thrilled Lamb, it was wonderful, it made him want to cry out or to sing. He relaxed in the quiet, still acutely conscious of Caroline's gaze. They sat there on the floor for a long while, neither of them speaking, each with his eyes on the other's. The rain outside had suddenly become loud and the splattering rhythm became to Lamb as comforting as the silence had been. He began to smile at Caroline, just slightly at first and then his face brightened into the best smile he had to give. She remained solemn only until she had made certain there was no irony in his look, and then Caroline too smiled tremendously.

JOYCE CAROL OATES

Theft

(FROM THE NORTHWEST REVIEW)

THE SEMESTER MARYA became acquainted with Imogene Skillman, a thief appeared out of nowhere in Maynard House, where Marya roomed after her freshman year at the University: striking at odd, daring hours, sometimes in the early morning when a girl was out of her room and showering in the bathroom down the corridor, sometimes late at night when some of the girls sat about in the kitchen, drinking coffee or hot chocolate, their voices kept low so that the resident adviser would not hear. Seven dollars was taken from a room on the first floor, at the busiest time of day, just before dinner; twenty-five from another room, down the hall from Marya's on the third floor; a secondhand but still costly edition of Shakespeare's plays was taken from the telephone desk in the front hall. The thief was obviously one of the residents — one of the twenty-six girls — but no one could discover who it was. There were wild rumors, cruel rumors. Marya once heard the tail end of a conversation in which her own name was mentioned. She had brushed by, her expression stonily neutral.

One Saturday morning in November, in her sophomore year, Marya returned to her room after having been gone only five minutes — she had run downstairs to check the mail, though she rarely received letters — to see, with a sickening pang, that the door was ajar. Oh God, Marya thought. Please *no*.

She ran to her purse, which lay where she'd left it on the bed; and, lifting it, she knew it was too light: the wallet was gone.

Her heart was beating desperately. She began to feel faint. The afternoon before, she had cashed her check, thirty-two dollars from the University library where she worked, and she'd had time

to spend only a few dollars of it . . . She pawed wildly through the
purse, but of course the wallet was gone. God, Marya thought. *Shit.*
She stood without moving for several seconds, holding the purse,
before it slipped from her fingers. The sensation of faintness in-
creased; her vision dimmed around the edges; the inside of her
mouth had gone numb.

Someone stood in the doorway behind her saying Marya? It was
Phyllis whose room was across the hall, but Marya did not hear;
she ran to her bureau and pulled open the drawers one by one
and saw, with a sensation of disgust that went through her like a
hot blade, that the thief had been here too — rooting around in
Marya's woolen socks and sweaters and frayed underwear. And
the fountain pen was gone. Of course. She rarely used it, it was
too much trouble, so she kept it in the top drawer with a few pieces
of inexpensive jewelry (which the thief had *not* bothered with): and
it was gone. A handsome black Parker pen with a thick, sporty
nub.

With a scream Marya yanked the drawer all the way out, and it
fell to the floor, making a terrific noise, and the idiot behind her
was crying Marya, what's wrong? — Marya! — as she tore blindly
at the bedspread, at a pile of books and papers on her desk, even
at the cheerful Chagall print — of a gouache called simply *Vase of
Flowers* — she had framed and hung on her rather unattractive
wall only a week or two ago. She swore in a thick, choked, guttural
voice. Every word that flew into her head, every profane phrase,
every obscenity!

She was too angry even to cry. It was so unfair, she needed that
money, she needed every penny, she'd worked in the library until
she staggered with exhaustion, and even then she had begged her
supervisor to allow her a few more hours . . . Her scholarship was
only for tuition: she needed that money. And the pen, she could
never replace the pen. She shouted and kicked at the things on
the floor as if she wanted to destroy them.

Finally she did burst into tears, and Phyllis — timid, frightened
Phyllis, who had probably never seen anyone in such a rage — was
actually holding her in her arms and trying to comfort her. By
now a half-dozen girls had gathered just outside the door. Was it
the thief? Was something stolen? Marya's voice was hoarse and
cracked. What am I going to do, she wept helplessly, what the hell
am I going to *do* . . .

For a long time afterward Marya hated her room. She dreaded climbing the narrow stairs to the third floor, opening the door and stepping inside, though of course she always locked the door now. (Sometimes she was halfway up the long cruel hill to Stafford Hall when she turned impulsively and ran back to her dormitory — seven blocks back, through the wind and frequent pelting rain — to see if she'd remembered to lock the door. And of course she always had. But she couldn't trust herself.)

In the early decades of the century Maynard House must have been impressive: it was a small Victorian mansion, with high, handsome windows, a wide verandah rimmed with elaborate fretwork, a cupola, a half-dozen fireplaces, walnut paneling in several of the downstairs rooms. But now it was dim and shabby. The outside needed painting, and the wallpaper in most of the rooms was discolored. For many years a rooming house, renting to University people, recently it had been taken over by the University housing bureau, and converted into a dormitory of sorts for undergraduate girls. Because it was so far from the main campus, and because its rooms were so cramped (Marya could stand at her full height on only one side of her room: the ceiling on the other slanted sharply down), it was one of the lowest-priced residences, and the girls who lived there were all scholarship students from what might be called, Marya thought wryly, using her newly acquired intellectual jargon, the upper lower class. They worked hard, they stayed up late studying, and a few of them, like Marya, even had part-time jobs; they were not so humorless and unattractive as Maynard House's reputation would have it, but they did share a superficial family resemblance — they might have been cousins, grimly energetic, a little vain (for they *were* scholarship students, after all, and competition for these scholarships was intense throughout the state), badly frightened at the prospect of failure. For then of course they would return home, and their anxious labors at Port Oriskany would have come to nothing, and their lives would never be different from their parents'.

Before the thief entered her room Marya had been absurdly fond of it. Even the standard university furniture did not displease her — the same minimal bed, desk, chair, bureau, bedside table, lamp in every room — and the sloped ceiling gave the room a cavelike, warmly intimate air, especially at night when only her desk lamp was burning. Though she could not really afford it Marya had gone downtown on the bus to buy a woven rug at Grant's, and a new lampshade edged with a festive orange braid; she had bought the Chagall print (for sale at the University bookstore, ninety-eight cents because it was somewhat soiled); she had even decorated the room with rough unframed charcoal drawings she had done herself, mainly self-portraits, when, her first year at the University, she'd been too tense to sleep after hours of writing papers or studying for exams. From the room's four walls smudged and shadowy variants of her own sober face contemplated her. Knowing herself ugly she had made the portraits uglier still. But they pleased her, secretly — the hard prim set of the lips, the strong cheekbones, the dark eyes and thick dark brows. Who is *that,* girls asked, not knowing exactly whether the face was meant to be Marya's or whether it belonged to someone else, perhaps even a man.

Room 35 of Maynard House: the privacy, the isolation, the monastic calm: she gloated over that room, and, sitting in a crowded lecture hall, feeling despair at the numbers of her fellow classmates — the sheer numbers — wouldn't they resemble ants, seen from a distance? — seen even from the professor's podium? — she thought of the room, *her* room, to which she would soon return. All her life, before coming to Port Oriskany, Marya had shared a room with someone else; for years she had shared a bed with her younger sister Alice. Her stepmother Wilma was a gregarious woman, always ready to open her house to relatives, willing to take in strays — just as she had taken in Marya and her two brothers, in fact — and though the Knauers couldn't afford it, they were always crowded at the kitchen table; someone was always "staying for a few days"; a woman might appear out of nowhere, sallow-faced, obviously pregnant, and turn out to be a cousin of Wilma's, or a cousin, even, of Marya's (for everyone was related to everyone else in Invemere), and of course she was welcome to stay as long as she liked, using an extra cot in the girls' room. Wilma is the most generous person I know, someone once said to Marya, probably the mother of a friend, or a salesperson in one of the downtown stores, and Marya had said rudely: That's because she's so stupid, everyone takes advantage of her, then they call her *generous.*

But at Port Oriskany she lived alone. No one stumbled about the

room while she slept, no one poked and pried, or rattled the doorknob. If she wanted to skip breakfast — and she frequently did —
no one scolded her; if she wanted to stay up until four or five in
the morning, reading for pleasure once her assignments were out
of the way, no one protested. (The reading she did late at night
acquired, for some reason, an aura, a value, that did not usually
belong to daylight. It seemed to her at such times that she was
capable of — indeed, could not resist — slipping out of her own
consciousness and into that of the writer's. Bodiless, weightless,
she traversed the landscape of another's mind. It was a secret
process, an almost erotic pleasure, yet it was not at all forbidden
— she made her way with the elated stealth of the thief, through
another's imagination, and risked no harm, no punishment. The
later the hour and the more exhausted she was, the greater her
powers of concentration; nothing in her resisted, nothing stood
aside to doubt or ridicule; and the books she read seemed to take
life, through no exertion of her own. The journals of Wallace
Stevens, the letters of Emily Dickinson, *Ulysses*, *The Magic Mountain*, Nietzsche's *Genealogy of Morals*, the short stories of Chekhov,
Melville's *Pierre* and *The Confidence-Man:* They leapt into an almost
frightening life, their language dazzlingly compelling, their au-
thors' souls [for Marya could be sentimental, in her innermost
heart] laid open to her. So long as she was reverent, and cautious,
so long as she allowed the voice of the work to course unimpeded
through her mind, and to silence her own habitual voice that so
frequently dismayed her . . . She was mesmerized, nothing of
Marya Knauer remained to distract her. The author's real personality, she believed, lay in his writing, and not in his life; it was the
landscape of his imagination that mattered, and not simply because it had outlived him. "Mere" life was the husk, the actor's
performance, books were the reality. She could not have explained
her curious dogmatic certainty but she knew that it was so. When,
her freshman year, she discovered Kafka, and Kafka's famous
remark, *Books are an ax for the frozen sea within*, she saw with excitement how closely it resembled her own belief — and yet it wasn't
her own, for she couldn't believe that the imagination was ever
really frozen. It was kept discreetly hidden, that was all.)
  Sometimes, after reading late, she couldn't sleep despite her
fatigue, her brain so dinned with another's voice. She got out of
bed in the dark and opened her window as far as it would go —

which wasn't very far, the frame was warped — and leaned out, letting her hair blow in the wind. For long vacant moments she stared at the sky, her eyes filling with tears. Her vision absorbed, without recording, the illuminated water tower two miles north of the campus, the flickering red lights of a radio station, the passage of clouds blown livid across the moon. She was desperately lonely. And worried about the future. Yet at the same time she was happy: that was her peculiar secret; she was really quite happy. Her loneliness somehow pleased her. (She hadn't any friends at Port Oriskany, and she had broken off with her three or four friends from high school.) Her isolation, her sense of having pushed herself to the limit, and a little beyond. She even liked those sleep-dazed mornings when she woke before seven, and trudged over to the dining hall three blocks away (for Maynard House hadn't, of course, its own dining hall — the girls had to eat at one of the larger dormitories, where both boys and girls roomed), no matter that it was freezing cold and the sidewalks hadn't been shoveled and the sun wouldn't rise for another hour or more, and there would be, in the cafeteria, only a few subdued individuals, lonely and sleep-groggy as herself. The experience was perhaps an unpleasant one but it was uniquely her own. No one back in Invemere could appropriate it, or mock it, or question her about it, and the chattery high spirits of the other girls at Maynard House, with whom she sometimes ate her meals, could not dispel it. Even her frequent nightmares, which threw her up out of sleep with the dry brownish taste of panic in her mouth, and her heart racing on the very edge of tachycardia, were curiously precious because they were hers. Such dreams were a secret language of her own like the language of the books she read throughout the night. Though she had not the knowledge to decode them she recognized how fiercely and how incontestably they belonged to *her*.

The privacy and sanctity of dreams, Marya noted: but how to decode them . . .

The first time Imogene Skillman climbed, uninvited, to Marya's room at the top of the old house, she stood in the doorway and exclaimed in her low throaty amused voice, What a depressing little room, Marya! So *this* is where you hide out . . .

She stood with her hands on her hips, her cheeks flushed, her eyes moving restlessly about. Why, this is just an attic room, isn't it, she said shrewdly, you can see how they partitioned the attic and made this into a room — but it's far too small — I hope you don't pay much, Marya? — and that tiny window, no wonder it's stifling in here! — and that Chagall print, Marya, you must know that everyone ,has one, everyone on campus, and it's an extremely poor reproduction at that. The wallpaper is filthy, and that bedspread looks as if it's been here for twenty years — or is it your own? — it *is?* — from home? Well. But the drawings are all right, Imogene said, coming closer to investigate. The drawings are very interesting, I wouldn't mind being surrounded by *them.*

Marya was astonished by the girl's outburst, and could only stammer in reply; but Imogene paid no attention. She was staring at the charcoal drawings. She even touched one with her forefinger, smudging it — since the drawing hadn't been sprayed.

So this is where Marya Knauer lives, Imogene said, her eyes darting quickly about. They were a pellucid blue, blank as china. And you're by yourself, of course? — you haven't a roommate?

•

The loss of the fountain pen and the wallet was so upsetting to Marya, and so bitterly ironic, partly because Marya herself was a thief.

(The wallet, of course, was returned. Later that day. It had been found in a trash barrel on campus, with Marya's identification cards in it. Naturally all the money — change as well as bills — was gone.)

Marya thought, I deserve this.

She thought, I will never steal anything again.

A package of chewing gum from Rexall's . . . a pink plastic comb from Woolworth's . . . sunglasses with bright orange frames and very dark lenses from Grant's . . . A tube of scarlet lipstick from out of the drawer, the middle drawer, of her second-grade teacher's desk . . . Stray items, each unimaginably exhilarating: a large brass button out of a classmate's sewing box in seventh grade (the sewing boxes, neatly covered with fabrics of various colors and textures, were for the girls' home economics class); nickels, dimes, fifty-cent pieces from out of change purses, drawers, the pockets of clothing hanging in closets, or picked up jubilantly from the sidewalk; here and there a dollar bill; a small address book of Mr. Schwilke's, her ninth-grade English teacher; a ring with a fake ruby stone, found beneath the folded clothing of a girl Marya had always admired, someone's older sister, in the women's bathhouse at Wolf's Head Lake; a package of cigarettes — Camel's — taken from the front seat of a parked car just last year; and of course the fountain pen. The thefts were always impulsive. Marya saw her hand dart out, sometimes to open a drawer; sometimes simply to snatch an item up. You held it in your hand and if it was small enough you simply closed your hand over it — and it was yours.

That moment when something passed over from belonging to another person to belonging to Marya: that moment interested her greatly.

And of course the excitement — the near-panic — the elation.

But at the moment, at the very moment of theft, she came close to feeling nothing at all. The heart-hammering excitement came afterward. For hours, for days afterward, it would return, lessening each time, until finally it disappeared except as a memory. Whether she felt panic or intense elation, whether she was terrified of being caught or euphoric because she knew she would never be caught, Marya could not say.

She thought from time to time, in disgust, It's a child's habit. It must have something to do with being bad. Wanting to be bad — deliberately bad — wanting to be punished.

How odd, Marya thought, that I've never been caught. When I haven't tried not to be caught — when I haven't *cared*.

It was odd too that the thefts she hadn't committed, the thefts she had refused to commit, should remain so vivid in her memory . . . A key chain that had slipped out of someone's pocket; a small change purse belonging to an older girl at the high school, whose prettiness she envied; miscellaneous pencils, pens, erasers, combs that were hers for the taking; the wristwatch on the bedside table of a priest whom she had visited in the hospital, as he died, by degrees, of cancer. At times her fingers tingled, her heartbeat accelerated, she thought helplessly, Something is going to happen! — and though her instinct was to steal, she managed to overcome it; she simply did nothing at all. A few thefts her freshman year . . . or perhaps they weren't thefts, precisely: she found things in the library, in a classroom, on the stairs of the rooming house in which she'd lived, and appropriated them for herself. When she found money (and this was, unfortunately, rare) she thought, But I need this! I need this. If she came across a library book, checked out of the library but lost, she always returned it: there was her feeling about books, but also a feeling that a library book was impersonal, it belonged to no one, it could not interest her as an object of theft.

In her classes she found herself staring at certain people, at certain of their belongings. Her imagination settled upon certain individuals whom she saw, usually three times a week, week after week, in the same desks and in the same spatial relationship to herself, throughout a semester. What began as simple curiosity shaded into an intense interest. And then she found herself staring covertly at a boy's scribbled-over notebook, for instance, in her American history lecture. (She would have liked to steal the notebook and read it. Read through it, in a safe place. Simply to see what he'd written. Simply to contemplate the elaborate ingenious fretwork of his doodlings.) There was an antique opal ring worn on the smallest finger of a girl who sat just to the left of Marya in her English literature class: the girl had waist-long black hair, straight and coarse, and Marya could not determine whether she was exceptionally attractive or really quite ugly. Many of the students at Port Oriskany were from well-to-do families (so Marya called them, as neutrally as possible, for *well-to-do* didn't sound as crassly naive or as envious as *rich*) and so there were many items of clothing, many hand-tooled leather bags, and boots, and wristwatches, and earrings, upon which her eye might drift with interest. That she could not possibly steal any of these things did not discourage her; if anything, her curiosity was all the more provoked. At times she caught herself gazing at an especially arresting profile, or a head of curly flame-orange hair, or a long slender delicate hand . . .

Beautiful knee-high leather boots. Expensive. Blatantly expensive. Kid gloves, a handsome camel's-hair coat, a blue cashmere muffler. That enormous purse with all the zippers, into which the horsy blonde girl stuffed everything — the girl who turned out to be Imogene Skillman. (And afterward Marya could not comprehend how she'd thought Imogene horsy, or even what she meant by that word. Everyone else considered Imogene beautiful. Though they might dislike her intensely, and dislike even her style — exaggerated, dramatic, intrusive — of beauty.) The girl who sat a few seats from Marya in political science class, with her camel's hair coat rumpled beneath her, her long blonde hair falling in a braid over one shoulder, her nervous china-blue mocking eyes jumping about the class. She rarely took notes. And when she did spend a period writing frantically, Marya observed that she tore the pages out of her notebook and stuffed them into the oversized purse; so perhaps she was writing letters; or oddly hectic notes to herself. She wore an engagement ring with a large square-cut diamond. Very nice, Marya thought spitefully. Very impressive. But it wasn't the engagement ring that interested her — it seemed so undistinguished, so impersonal — it was the girl's other pieces of jewelry. From time to time she wore a big silver ring with a turquoise stone, on her right hand; and a long sporty necklace that seemed to be fashioned out of copper coins; and a succession of earrings in her pierced ears — gold loops that swung and caught the light, tiny black stones, ceramic disks in which gold-burnished reds and blues flashed beautifully. Marya stared and stared, her heart quickening with envy.

Imogene Skillman was a theatre arts major; she belonged to one of the sororities on Masefield Avenue; Marya even knew (how, she couldn't have said) that Imogene was from Laurel Park, Long Island, and that her fiancé was "older" — which meant in his late twenties. After she became acquainted with Imogene it would have deeply humiliated her to inform Imogene that she knew so much about her. Not only her background, and her interest in acting, but that purse, those boots, the silver ring, the ceramic earrings . . .

It might have been Imogene's presence in class that inspired Marya to answer certain of the professor's questions, and to answer them in such detail, in such self-consciously structured sentences. (For though Marya was shy in most of her classes, as she was shy generally, she could quite suddenly become both articulate and emphatic; the tenor of her firm, confident voice caused people to turn around in their seats, and greatly interested, when it did not alarm, her professors.) These little speeches, averaging perhaps one a week, were preceded by the most extraordinary bouts of nervousness, which only faded when Marya actually began to talk. She planned what she would say, her mind jumped wildly about, her hand wavered into the air, and was sometimes withdrawn; and then raised again; and when the professor finally saw her, and called upon her, she felt as if she were running blindly forward to dive off a diving board . . . But still she forced herself to speak slowly and clearly and forcefully, showing none of the panic she felt. It was not simply that most of her professors *seemed* to want intelligent discussions — *seemed, in fact, to depend* upon them — or even that her grade might depend in part upon her classroom performance: she became caught up, sometimes quite passionately, in the subjects themselves. And apart from her genuine interest in such matters was the fact that when she spoke, Imogene Skillman turned about in her desk, almost rudely, to stare at her.

Once, Imogene left behind an angora glove. It was badly worn, and rather soiled. Marya stopped to snatch it up and, without thinking, ran after the girl — who was already out of the room, striding along, laughing, in a high-spirited conversation with two boys — and handed it to her, saying only, You dropped this, and not even waiting for Imogene's surprised thanks.

Afterward Marya felt unaccountably fatigued, as if she had experienced some powerful drain on her energy. She did not know: Had she come close to stealing the glove, or did she feel upset simply because she had made herself known, however fleetingly, to Imogene Skillman . . .

                    •

Marya's friendship with Imogene began, as it was to end, with a disconcerting abruptness.

One morning Imogene simply caught up with Marya, saying, Are you walking this way? — and fell in step with her. It was done as easily and as effortlessly as if they were old friends; as if Imogene had been reading Marya's thoughts. (She stammered and blushed, answering Imogene's candid questions about the course they were both taking, and the general caliber of the University itself, which Marya had never thought to criticize. She felt, during the first several minutes of their conversation, a peculiar sense of guilt, and even shame; for perhaps she had drawn Imogene Skillman to her by the very intensity of her interest, and Imogene was too charitable, too unsuspicious, to hold back.) You say interesting things in class, Imogene said airily, or at least some of my friends think so. I wouldn't know, I have to confess that it's your voice that intrigues me, what if she was playing (so I ask myself, I'm always trying on things for other people) Hedda Gabler with that voice, and there's something about your chin, too, the way you hold it, it looks as if you're gritting your teeth but you *are* making yourself perfectly audible, don't be offended! — the thing is, I'm doing Hedda myself, I can't help but be jealous of how you might do her though it's all in *my* imagination of course. Are you free for lunch? Yes? We'll have to hurry, though, I have a class at one.

It gave Marya a feeling of distinct uneasiness, afterward, that Imogene had pursued *her*. Or, rather, that Imogene imagined herself the pursuer, and kept up, for weeks, the more active, the more charitably outgoing and inquisitive, of their two roles.

For if Imogene reached out, Marya naturally drew back. She shared her family's peasant shrewdness — what does this person want with me, what is lacking in her that she would pursue *me* — and though it gratified her that Imogene Skillman should profess any interest in her at all, it also puzzled her. And there was the problem of Imogene's flippancy, which certain of her friends adored, or anyway encouraged: Marya was not accustomed to such adroit reversals, friendly sunny warmth switched suddenly to mockery, a low-throated serious conversation about religion (Imogene was an atheist who feared, she said, lapsing into Anglicanism — it ran in her family) raised suddenly to a good-natured bawdy exchange of insults simply because one of Imogene's theatre friends appeared. While Marya was too reserved to ask Imogene much about herself, despite her great curiosity, Imogene was pitiless in her interrogation of Marya, and seemed at times, quite artlessly, quite innocently, to be poking about in Marya's chest, her china-blue eyes wide as a child's. Has your family always lived in that part of the state, do you like the mountains, how long ago did your father die, how did he die, are you close to your stepmother, do you remember much about your mother, are you close to your brothers, are you close to your stepsister, do you keep in touch with your high school friends, are you happy here, are you lonely, do you go out very often, are you in love, have you ever been in love, are you a virgin, do you have any plans for this summer, what will you do after graduation? — for the rest of your life? Instinctively Marya distorted the truth, while not exactly lying; she feared that her brash brazen golden-haired friend would recognize a lie immediately, and be offended or amused, as she frequently was when Marya answered in vague evasive words. But half-truths went down very well. Half-truths, Marya often thought, were so much more reasonable than whole truths. For surely Imogene would not care to know the truth about Marya's father's death — it was far more agreeable, as well as plausible, for her to be told that he'd suffered a "fatal" heart attack at the age of thirty-six. And that her mother had moved away from the family, and eventually married another man, and disappeared into another part of the country, probably the mid-South — didn't that sound, Marya thought wryly, far more plausible than the truth, which was that the woman had simply — quite simply, one weekend — disappeared? She sensed that Imogene's keen interest in her might falter if she encountered, in Marya, the sad bitter self-bemused truth that was Marya's innermost core.

Years ago Marya had had an English teacher, a frazzled good-natured doomed young man, who claimed, perhaps for the fun of it, that he could read his students' minds. It turned out that he couldn't read their minds; he wasn't, at least, able to influence their minds. Marya had known he was joking and yet she had sometimes thought . . . she had sometimes thought, watching the man's gaze drift about the class, fixing upon one face after another, that there might be something to it. So she stiffened when he looked at her. Though he was usually smiling, though he sometimes winked at her, because he liked her and imagined her an ally. She could not stop all sorts of crude, ugly, obscene things from flying into her mind at such moments, simply because there was the terrible danger that Mr. Schwilk could read her mind . . . And so it was with Imogene, when Marya endured the girl's long intense immensely flattering interrogations. She was exhausted by the experience, but also pleased; she resented Imogene's frankness, her assumption of an easygoing intimacy that was all one-sided, but at the same time she quickened and brightened in Imogene's presence, and noted that others — in the coffee shop, in the restaurants on Fairfield Street, in the pub, anywhere where Imogene Skillman was known — watched them with curiosity, and must have wondered who Imogene's new friend was.

They would have quarreled almost at once if Marya had not drawn back, with a nervous smile, choosing to admire rather than to be annoyed by Imogene's impetuousness. (*Are you happy, are you lonely, have you ever been in love, are you a virgin?* — no one had ever dared ask Marya such questions.) Imogene was as tall as Marya, and her gold-gleaming hair and ebullient manner made her seem taller still. Set beside her, Marya knew herself shabby and unattractive; it was not *her* prerogative to take offense. And despite Imogene's high spirits there was usually something harried about her. She hadn't studied for an exam, the play rehearsals were going badly and she might have to withdraw from the cast, she'd had a very upsetting telephone call from home the night before

. . . In her imagination Marya saw Imogene's wide white-toothed smile marred by small tics of vexation. Imogene turned the diamond ring round and round her long finger, with a brutal unconsciousness; on cold windy mornings she ran panting up Stafford Hill as the bell sounded, her five-foot-long red muffler wound carelessly about her neck, her coat unbuttoned and flapping about her as if she hadn't had time to dress. But even her distress was enviable. There are certain modes of unhappiness, Marya observed, one would prefer to happiness.

Imogene insisted that Marya accompany her to a coffee shop on Fairfield where all her friends — all her nonsorority and nonfraternity friends — gathered. Marya shrank from their critical eyes; she suspected that she might be one of their subjects for imitation and mockery, once she was out of earshot. (They did devastating imitations of their professors, and even of one another. Marya had to admit, laughing, that they were really quite good.) She knew, in their presence, that if she offered any opinions at all she should be emphatic, even dogmatic, for they would not respect her otherwise, and would probably interrupt her. They were always interrupting one another — they even interrupted Imogene. With her excellent memory Marya could quote passages from the most difficult texts by heart. Her vocabulary, which seemed to atrophy when she was by herself and brooding over her private thoughts, blossomed wonderfully in the presence of a slightly hostile audience she knew she *must* impress. (For didn't Imogene expect her to be articulate, wasn't Imogene always laughing and jabbing her, crying, Yes, that's right, go on, you're absolutely right, Marya, you've got him now!) In the midst of the most spirited discussions about Strindberg, or Whitman, or Yeats, or the surrealists, or Henry James, or Dostoyevsky, or campus politics, or whether Imogene should quit the play, or whether everyone should or should not boycott classes to protest the administration's stupidity, Marya, who began by degrees to thoroughly enjoy herself, could not help but think that she must get out of here, she must leave immediately: wasn't she wasting time, and wasn't time the element that would carry her along to her salvation? Yet she could argue about the Platonic forms (which she thought ridiculous — for where *were* they?), and she could disagree even with Imogene about Hedda Gabler's "secret" compulsion, her voice raised, her manner as confident and strident as the others', though she was already late for work at the library, and had a dismaying amount of reading to do that night.

The coffee shop was several blocks from the University's main gates, a narrow, tunnel-like place devoid of charm, where tables were crowded together and framed photographs of old, vanished athletes lined the walls. The food was mediocre, the coffee far too strong, but everyone — "everyone," that is, in Imogene's vocabulary — went there, simply to get away from their living residences, and to sit for hours, talking loudly and importantly, smoking cigarettes, littering the floor with butts and napkins, trapped by inertia. (They were quick to inform one another that they were missing classes — they couldn't be bothered to get up, and face the cold, and trudge up the hill to sit through a boring lecture.) Marya saw that several of the boys were in love with Imogene. There was Scott, and Andy; there was Matthew, who had taken a sort of provocative dislike to Marya; there was a small dark ferret-faced pre-med student whom Imogene had known in high school, named Trevor. But of course Imogene was engaged: her fiancé's name was Richard, he would not allow himself to be called Dick, though Imogene had the privilege of calling him Dickie. The other girls in the group — Brenda, Jane, Max, occasionally Florence — were attractive enough, and certainly outspoken; but they were no match for Imogene.

One wintry afternoon when Imogene and the others were discussing, in vehement detail, the many failings of the drama school, Marya found herself examining one of the photographs on the wall beside her. It was sepia-tinted, and very old: the 1899 University rowing team. Beside it was a photograph of the 1902 football team. How young they must have felt, as the century turned, Marya thought. It must have seemed to them *theirs*.

Another rowing team. A basketball team. A fencing team. Sad hopeful faces, peculiar clothes, an air of doom.

She felt suddenly that she must run out of here — run back to her room — in order to be alone with her thoughts. But Imogene poked her, and said, Marya? What's wrong? Do you disapprove of Max's theory?

Marya shook her head, embarrassed.

But *you* don't have any opinion?

No, I don't have any opinion.

Imogene said, with a petulant little smile, Well, I was just won-

dering. You looked so abstract. You looked so censorious, as if you were passing judgment on us all.
Marya began to protest, but went unaccountably silent. She smiled at them with Imogene's wide impenetrable grin.

Later that night Imogene came to Maynard House, for the first time, and took Marya by surprise. Her rudeness about the room passed almost unremarked; she chattered brightly, and seemed in an especially amiable mood; and she'd brought Marya an enormous apple, a Golden Delicious, which she tossed into Marya's lap. (The father of one of Imogene's sorority sisters had shipped several baskets of fruit up for them: the girls all helped themselves.) Tell me about those drawings, Imogene said, peering at them. But Marya said, There's nothing to tell. You never said you were an artist, Imogene said, half-scolding. I'm not an artist, Marya said, those are just doodlings. If I get nervous . . . Yes, you're an artist, Imogene said, and d'you know how I can tell? Because these things are so rough, they aren't pretty at all, you haven't bothered to finish them, and yet they catch the eye: there's something unnerving about them. But you don't see yourself like that, do you? Like *that?*

Marya said nothing. Her friend's presence in the small room dazzled and discomfited her. She was waiting for Imogene to leave, though she smiled at her with a queer perplexed smile.

So this is where you live, Imogene said slowly. Her eyes darted quickly about: they were merciless, they would miss nothing. And you're by yourself, you haven't a roommate — you have a whole other life, don't you, she said, inexplicably, with a queer pouting downward turn of her lips.

Friendship, thought Marya uneasily, is a puzzle.

She knew that one had to work at it, had to cultivate it; yet nothing seemed worthwhile except her studies and her grades, and of course her reading. She really had no time for anything else. Now and then a boy from one of her classes or the dining hall approached her, but she drew away brusquely, with so little charm that he never approached her again. In her larger classes she might find herself contemplating a young man, studying his profile, his features, wondering idly who he was, what he might be like as a lover; but then she didn't want a lover; she had no time for *that*. Marya had gradually acquired a reputation for being brilliant — the word was not hers, but Imogene's: Don't you know everyone thinks you're brilliant, everyone is afraid of you? — and it struck her as helpful, for perhaps, like a glass barrier, her reputation would protect her; it would allow her privacy.

And then again she sometimes looked up from her reading, and saw that hours had passed. Had someone called her? It was often very late at such times; her vision was somewhat blurred; she felt light-headed. Had someone called her name . . . ? She rose from her desk, frightened, thinking that great handfuls of her life were being stolen from her and she would never retrieve them.

She had, however, become friendly with a number of girls in Maynard House; more or less friendly. She frequently ate meals with them, though she was inclined — though knowing it was bad manners — to bring along a book. Do you mind, she would ask Phyllis or Catherine or Sally, apologetically, I have so much reading to do . . .

Of course they didn't mind. They too were scholarship students, they understood.

(Though behind her back Marya knew they talked about her. They were envious of her grades . . . they feared her sarcasm . . . they could not comprehend how Imogene Skillman had befriended her . . . they suspected that she was the thief. For the thief still walked off with things, sporadically. The thief whose pronoun was, curiously, "he," though certainly everyone knew it was one of the girls; it was a "she"; whose most recent theft was simply mean-spirited — a letter had been stolen out of the residence adviser's mailbox, a letter from the poor woman's parents containing snapshots of her sister's new baby, and it was found, a few days later, partly shredded, in a gutter not far from Maynard House.)

When Marya told Imogene about the thief Imogene said, People take things all the time, there are thefts everywhere on campus, and worse things too, but nobody wants to talk about it, the newspaper isn't allowed to print certain stories. *I've* never stolen anything in my life, she said slowly, because why would I want anything that somebody else has already had?

Your friend Imogene, people began to say to her. Imogene this, Imogene that. *Your friend Imogene* . . . Marya was flattered but doubtful, for perhaps they weren't really friends. In a sense she liked one or two of the girls in Maynard House better than she liked Imogene — Phyllis, for example, who was a mathematics major, and said to be extremely bright; and a chunky farm girl named Dolores, from a tiny settlement near Marya's home town, who was unfailingly good-natured though the residence buzzed with rumors that she was doing badly in several of her courses. She "liked" them in the sense that she recognized them as superior individuals, really much nicer, much kinder than Imogene. Yet it would not have deeply troubled her if she never saw them again . . . And the loss of Imogene would have been a blow.

She went twice to see *Hedda Gabler,* alone both times. Imogene was very good, in her opinion: hard, bright, sardonic, quick, and languid by turns; and very beautiful. Her golden hair had been expertly fashioned into a heavy Victorian twist, her broad cheeks had been rouged discreetly, her eyes so skillfully made up, and so naturally distinctive, that they were capable of conveying subtleties of emotion throughout the theatre. Or so Marya imagined. Perhaps at times Imogene's voice was too strident, especially when she was sparring with Judge Brack, and there was something wooden, even mechanical, about her stage movements; but after all, Marya thought admiringly, this is an amateur production, Imogene is only twenty years old, she's obviously very gifted . . .

Backstage, however, Marya had not wanted to push through the crowd that surrounded Imogene, she had not cared to compete with the others' praise, nor did she want to kiss and hug Imogene. So much emotion, such a display! It was rather repulsive, exaggerated like the actors' make-up, their rouged cheeks and heavily lipsticked mouths; and Imogene had embarrassed Marya by saying loudly, Marya will tell the truth, here she is, *was* I any good, Marya? — was I really Hedda? She pushed past her admiring friends to seize Marya's reluctant hands and grip them hard, staring at Marya with great shining painted eyes. An odor was released of grease paint and perspiration; it seemed to Marya that Imogene towered over her.

Marya made a joke of it, stammering, But *you* don't need *me* to assess you!

What are you saying, Imogene cried in a hoarse stage voice, are you saying I failed? — I failed?

Of course you didn't fail, Marya said, blushing, you must know you were excellent —

Excellent! — But that doesn't sound like one of your words, Marya, Imogene said.

She was still gripping Marya's hands. Marya had to draw away, her face burning.

Afterward she decided that the scene had been nothing more than an overwrought extension of Imogene's play-acting. It must be difficult, she supposed, for an actor to step out of his role — not the role so much, not the specific play, as the intoxicating activity itself.

Friendship, Marya wrote in her journal, is possibly nothing more than play-acting.

Friendship, she wrote, with hard angry motion of her pen, is a puzzle that exacts too much from the imagination.

So she withdrew from Imogene, and threw herself into her work with more passion than before. Mid-term exams were upon her, papers were due: she recognized the formalities as academic and parochial; yet they were great dark weedy mucky ditches that had to be jumped and *would* be jumped, even if they cost her her eyesight and her health.

She worked, she worked. Hour upon hour. Reading in her room, in bed, taking notes throughout the night. Reading in one of her secret places — on the fifth floor of the library, in the stacks, near a shuddering ventilator; in a corner of the law college library, where one might turn a high-backed leather chair to face a corner; in an alcove in the dreary deserted geology library; a quarter-mile away in the old brick mansion that had been converted into the music school, where she might read and scribble notes and day-dream, the pleasant regularity of her heartbeat underscored by the muffled sounds of pianos, horns, violins, cellos, flutes, coming from the rows of practice rooms. A curious harmony there, if one did not try to hear it. If one did not try to theorize upon it.

She worked in the library, sometimes for as long as five hours at a stretch, and the fact that the University paid her very little — after taxes, her salary was very little indeed: she had almost burst into tears when she received her first check — seemed to arouse in her a frantic need to work even more, to clock more hours each week. Over the weeks she had made up for the loss she had suf-fered (though of course the fountain pen would not be replaced) by disciplining herself severely, and by being as grubby as she dared (she washed her hair now once a week, though it should have been washed much more frequently, and she did not really need toothpaste, why did one *need* toothpaste? — she was sparing with her deodorant, or stealthily used one belonging to another girl that had been left behind in the bathroom; in fact, almost without thinking she used other girls' things if they were left behind — shampoo, soap, mouthwash). Unlike most of the other girls she did not wander down to Fairfield Street for coffee and doughnuts, she never bought cigarettes, when she did her laundry every twelve days or so she prowled about the laundromat looking for leftover boxes of soap so that she needn't waste money; she could appropriate cheap mimeograph paper from a supply room in the library basement; she never had to buy ballpoint pens since they were always lying about, in the library or in classrooms or in the parlor of Maynard House, hers for the taking.

She worked in the library, coming home as late as eleven-fifteen, quite exhausted, yet exhilarated, eager to get to her room for a night of study. Once she nearly fainted on the second-floor landing, and one of the girls said, Marya, maybe you should come in my room, maybe you should lie down, you look terrible, and she had wanted to call the residence adviser, but Marya had brushed her aside, annoyed at the fuss. It's just the stairs, she said, I'm really all right now.

(Imogene telephoned, just before the switchboard closed for the night. Where was she, why did she hurry out of class every day before Imogene could talk to her, was she going out with someone, was she working longer hours at the library, would she like to come to dinner sometime this week, at the sorority? — next week, then? Or in December, before Christmas break?)

Schopenhauer, Dickens, Marx, Euripides. Oscar Wilde. Henry Adams. Sir Thomas More. Thomas Hobbes. Bertolt Brecht. She read, and took notes, and daydreamed, and it sometimes disturbed her that nothing of what she read had been written by women: but then she told herself, with touching arrogance, that *she* would change all that.

Sometimes she trembled with an inexplicable ravenous need: she wanted to snatch up everything in sight, she wanted to run out into the street, she wanted to laugh wildly. Her long periods of concentration began to be punctuated by bouts of sheer directionless emotion. The girls in Maynard House — dutiful-subdued-grateful-scholarship-students — were known for their industry and sobriety, but within the house no one was considered more industrious and sober, more relentless, than Marya Knauer. It was said of her that she was, in fact, a genius: she had an exceptionally high IQ and a near-photographic memory: so her grade-point average *wasn't* so remarkable. (Marya's average was perfect — she had never received any grade lower than A — but the achievement had not been an effortless one.) Then again it was said of her, snidely, by girls in Maynard House who were not doing well, that she managed by studying and studying and studying, and reading every book on reserve for every course, and ingratiating herself with her professors, to get high grades though she didn't really deserve them. She had plotted out her college years, she had plotted out her life, there was nothing to be envied about her, *nothing.* (Two years later Marya was to be told, by a friend who had known one of the girls in Maynard House, that there had even been a rumor she'd been involved with one of her professors — simply to get a high grade in his course.)

Sometimes she walked along Masefield Avenue, past the enormous sorority and fraternity houses. There was Imogene's, with the absurdly pretentious white columns. Four white columns. Southern Colonial. Immense . . . In the winter twilight, in the cold, the houses appeared especially warm, and secretive: every window of their several floors blazed. Marya thought, Why don't I feel anything, can't I feel even envy . . . ? It would have been normal, she supposed, to feel envy; even jealousy and spite; most of the other girls of her acquaintance, who were not in sororities, who were doomed to University housing, were openly bitter about sorority girls and their "privileges" (though what these privileges were Marya could not guess, the sororities were grotesquely expensive, their activities were centered almost exclusively on the fraternities, on "men" — that is, boys — and Imogene complained constantly of the silly little rituals, the handshake, the secret password, the ludicrous reverential tones with which one was obliged to address alums). It would have been normal, however, Marya supposed, to wish to acquire these privileges simply for the sake of being able to jeer at them. They are such assholes, Imogene said airily of her sorority sisters, such *frantic* assholes, and it was part of Imogene's style, part of her great charm, that she could be both contemptuous of aristocratic pretensions and aristocratic — in her disdain, in her beauty — herself.

But nothing really matters, Marya noted in her journal, underscoring the words with slow hard sad strokes of her pen, except individual success.

By which she meant success in the University — success on record — success that might be measured in simple, grave numerical terms. (For it was all very well for idealistic people to prattle about a love of knowledge for its own sake. *Love* and *knowledge:* Marya did know how they were related, as well as anyone. But people were always preaching idealism as a way of boasting of their own privilege, like Imogene saying smugly that *she* had never stolen a thing in her life — for who possessed anything worth stealing? "Knowledge for its own sake" was an attractive fiction.)

Sometimes Marya thought, alarmed, that everything — every moment of her life — that was not calculated to advance her career was a mistake.

Lying in bed after she had awakened, those drowsy luxurious five or ten minutes. Conversations with most people. Conversations with *all* people. Showering, cleaning her room, staring out the window, eating three meals a day (unless of course she brought a book along — which she usually did though she knew the other girls had begun to mock her). All thoughts about home. All brooding over the past. All activities that would not be measured and graded and recorded on her transcript. (In high school Marya had been quite an athlete. She had been captain of the girls' field hockey team, and the basketball team; she had been so skillful at volleyball that it was decided she should play only about half the games, since the other girls were intimidated by her. With her long slender legs, tight with muscle, and her strong shoulders, and quickness, and a certain high-spirited competitive zest that did not come naturally to the others, Marya acquired the reputation — which only amused her, she did not mind at all — of being unscrupulous. She was shrewd, she was cunning, she always took advantage of another player's ineptitude, which seemed to her only reasonable — for wasn't the idea of the game to win, after all? — the boys, when they played their noisy games, were certainly not sentimental about one another. But the other girls resented her, the girls who were her friends, whom she genuinely liked, were baffled by her indifference to them as individuals, on the hockey field or the basketball court, and after one astonishing incident [she had snatched a basketball out of the air, and turned gracefully and leapt and made a basket, her fourteenth or fifteenth in that

single gym class, and the girl who was guarding her, a girl from
the country like herself, somewhat out of place in Invemere, like
herself, grabbed her by the shoulders and spat directly in her face]
she had thought, suddenly, Why do I bother, why do I give a
damn, isn't it just a waste of time? At Port Oriskany she performed
in her two obligatory gym courses just well enough to be assured
of A's, and that was it.)

It was not true, as the other girls whispered, that Marya Knauer
plotted out everything she did beforehand; that she had a plan for
her four years as an undergraduate; that she cared only for her
grade-point average. But it was true that she puzzled over her
grades, she daydreamed, she speculated, she deliberately sum-
moned up, in herself, interludes of anxiety that she theorized
might be necessary for a good performance. Simply because she
was intelligent — and she had always known she was intelligent —
she did not dare allow herself to become complacent. If she failed
there were too many people who would gloat. And what was failure, after all, but a single misstep, a hair's-breadth from perfection . . . ?

She had been at the top of her high school class, and she intended to be at the top of her college class. She would be inducted
into Phi Beta Kappa her junior year. She would win prizes, she
would win scholarships to graduate school; she would not return
home to Invemere, as young people occasionally did, humbled and
grateful for its insularity. (So many families in the area were now
on welfare, since the mines were closing, that there was, along with
the apathy and drunkenness and lazy despair, a queer sort of bliss:
for it was very like being a child again, a child perpetually, with no
need even to contemplate leaving home.)

You're going to have a breakdown, Imogene had said, catching
Marya on the run, vexed that Marya didn't have time to go down
to Fairfield Street with her. You drive yourself and drive yourself,
and what's the point? — I mean, if you ruin your health.

Marya laughed, it struck her as so incongruous, Imogene Skillman's concern for *her* health. (For Imogene had the reputation of
staying up all night too. And she had a reputation along Masefield
Avenue for doing a great deal of drinking at fraternity parties.)

Marya said, My health isn't of any use to me, if I don't get
anything accomplished.

When she was exhausted and depressed she raised her spirits by a deliberate act of will, by contemplating how well she had done so far. It was a superb record, wasn't it; it was enviable. Before arriving at Pork Oriskany she had imagined her classmates would be superior to her, and that she would have to work desperately to keep up with them; within a few weeks of her freshman year, however, she had discovered, to her astonishment and amusement, that a good number of her college classmates were no more intelligent than the boys and girls she had known in high school. (Those idiots, Marya had often thought. Those contemptible *idiots* — for of course they had not always been fond of her.) During freshman orientation week they were herded from place to place, to listen to talks that alternated between piety and what was meant to be humor, and Marya had noted how often it was said — how uncannily often — that one's university career was much more than a matter of grades. The entire person, the *entire person*, was to be educated. It was a time of fertility, and promise, a time for exploring numerous pathways, a time for making lifetime friends. Ah yes, thought Marya, who felt no pity for the half-dozen scholarship students of her acquaintance who went on probation their first semester, and flunked out (for flunking, for them, was simply the failure to maintain a B average) in the spring. The University preached one ethic but acted upon another, and since the ethic acted upon made a good deal of sense to pragmatic Marya, she saw no reasons for objecting. (She did feel pity, though, for students who appeared to be working hard, yet received poor grades anyway. In Maynard House this term three girls were evidently in academic trouble, among them Marya's friend Phyllis. She was failing an advanced calculus class, someone told Marya.) The second semester of her freshman year, Marya had come close to losing her perfect grade-point average. She had unwisely signed up for a course in religion, having been attracted by the books to be taught, and the supplementary reading list (the *Upanishads; Bhagavad-Gītā; Holy Bible;* the *Koran; Hymns of the Rigveda;* books on Gnosticism, and Taoism, and medieval Christianity, and the Christian heresies, and animism, magic, witchcraft, Babylonia, Alexander the Great, Renaissance ideas of Platonic love). All very promising, very exciting, but the professor turned out to be a cheerful popinjay who lectured from old notes, giving out ideas obviously thrown together from others' books and articles. He appeared to want nothing more than these ideas given back to him, and he did not particularly encourage questions from the class. Marya might have done well — she transcribed notes faultlessly, even when she was contemptuous of their content — but she could not resist sitting stonily silent, refusing to laugh, when the professor embarked upon certain good-natured jocular anecdotes. (It was one of his classroom mannerisms, almost a sort of tic, that each time he alluded to something female he lowered his voice and added a wry observation, meant not so much to be insulting as affectionately teasing. He was a popular lecturer, everyone liked him, or liked him well enough; most of Marya's classmates did not mind the banality of the man's observations, and were childishly grateful that he joked often enough to keep them awake.) So it came about that though Marya received high grades throughout the course, and an A on her final paper, the grade posted for her final examination was C; and the final grade for the course was B +.

Now what could be more petty, Marya reasoned, trying to keep calm, the professor for what he had done (for she never doubted that she had written an excellent exam), or Marya herself for her consternation . . . ? She knew, she knew very well, it was absurd to feel so thunderstruck and so helpless, so sick with rage, she would probably remember this for the rest of her life: the humiliating *pettiness* of the transaction. But though she knew she had suffered no disaster, she felt, in fact, as if she had discovered a hard little tumor in her breast; possibly she felt even worse; for the tumor would be out of her control, and the grade of B + really was not. She had the option of protesting. Perhaps he wanted her to protest, perhaps he was expecting her; he certainly knew who Marya Knauer was, sitting there in the third row, frowning at him, judging him with her dark pitiless gaze all semester. Now I have a choice, Marya thought, I can forget this insult and forget him, or I can humble myself and go to him, and try to get the grade raised.

She stayed away a day, and during that time she was too agitated to eat.

Of course she went to him, and of course, after a few minutes' clucking and fretting (he pretended she hadn't answered one of the questions, that she had not handed in both examination booklets, but there the second one was, at the bottom of a heap of bluebooks — what a surprise, wasn't it!), he changed her grade to A. And smiled roguishly at her, as if she had been caught out in mischief, or some sort of deception, for which he was forgiving her. You seem like a grim young woman, he said, you never smile, do you? — or maybe you are simply thinking your own thoughts during class, maybe you believe you know everything I have to say beforehand? Is that it? Marya stared at his sandaled foot. He was a satyrish middle-aged man, with red-brown tufts of hair in his ears, and a strangely vulnerable smile; she could quite see why everyone liked him, and why they signed up for his course; he was probably quite a decent person, altogether. But she hated him, she wished him dead. She would not have wanted to kill him herself — for one thing, the act would then be embedded in her memory — but she would have gazed with indifference upon his death agonies; or so she imagined. He said again, teasing, You *do* seem like a fairly grim young woman, Miss Knauer, did you know that? — and Marya quite calmly resisted the impulse to say something sarcastic, or vulgar. For she had, after all, triumphed. She had humbled herself, she had amused and disgusted herself, she *would* remember this forever, as a craven act not very different from giving herself up sexually to the man; yet it was a triumph; her record was still perfect; he had not wounded her. She waited, and said with careful timing, My mother is dying of cancer, I know I shouldn't act depressed and make other people unhappy but sometimes I can't help it, she isn't expected to live much longer, I'm sorry if I have offended you . . .

He stammered his apologies, actually rising from his desk, putting a hand out to her. Suddenly he was deeply moved, suddenly everything had changed between them. Miss Knauer, I didn't know . . . I'm so very sorry . . . I hadn't any idea . . .

A minute later Marya was striding down the corridor, trying to keep from laughing. In her hard right fist was the fountain pen she had lifted from his cluttered desk.

It turned out to be an expensive pen, a Parker pen. With a handsome squarish blunt nub, and the man's engraved initials.

How marvelous, how perfect! — how beautifully it had gone! The shame of having humbled herself had been erased by the shame — or what would have been the shame — of theft.

She used the pen occasionally, until it ran out of ink. Sometimes she wrote in her journal with it. Or in the margins of her notes. Marya, she wrote languidly, in the attractive hand she used when not hurried, Marya Knauer, admiring the appearance of the words, Marya Marya Marya Marya Knauer, which really looked as if they had been written by someone else.

Phyllis, they began to say, was very unhappy. She was going out nearly every night. With different boys. Out as far as the Rosewood (a popular tavern, to which Marya had never gone), out along the lake, to the water-tower hill, even to some of the fraternity houses. One night she came in staggering drunk, and was violently sick to her stomach on the stairs.

Phyllis, they whispered, was failing two courses. And now she couldn't study at all.

One night she did not return by the time Maynard House was closed for the night. So Marya forged her signature downstairs. (For which she might have been expelled — though who, she reasoned nervously, could identify the forgery as *hers?*) Evidently Phyllis came back sometime in the morning when the rest of the girls were in class, in so disheveled and agitated a condition that she had to be taken to the infirmary, and from there to the city hospital; and in a day or two her family came to take her back home; and no one saw her again.

How quickly it can happen, Marya thought, dazed. How quickly . . . And then the waters close over your head.

(For though everyone in Maynard House talked about Phyllis for days, and certainly pitied her, her absence was hardly a palpable thing. There were papers to write, exams to study for . . . Poor Phyllis, they said. Poor Phyllis. She had gotten in over her head in certain courses, she just wasn't bright enough, you would think she might have known better than to take such difficult subjects . . . In the end her breakdown had something to do with imprudence, possibly even impracticality.)

One Saturday Phyllis's mother and older sister arrived to clean out her room. How is she, everyone asked, and Mrs. Myer said brightly that she was fine, really fine, resting and eating right again, almost completely recovered. Marya asked whether she would be returning second semester. No, not that soon, Mrs. Myer said. She and the older sister were emptying drawers, packing suitcases briskly. Marya helped with Phyllis's books and papers, which lay in an untidy heap on her desk and on the floor beneath the desk. There were dust balls everywhere. Stiffened crumpled Kleenex, and tiny balls of Kleenex, like pellets, underfoot. Loose hairs. An odor of grime and despair. Marya held her breath, hoping she wouldn't faint. Phyllis was more real to her now than she had been in the past, even when she had comforted Marya, taking her in her arms. But it was disappointing: when Marya introduced herself to Phyllis's mother and sister they had been friendly enough, but clearly not interested; Phyllis had never mentioned Marya to them, evidently; and of course there was no special message for her . . . I might have been her closest friend at Port Oriskany, Marya thought. The idea was sobering.

Then something occurred that Marya was to marvel at for months afterward, and to attempt to recount for Imogene, who couldn't of course have been expected to fully understand — she was straightening, a pile of books in her arms, her hair in her face, when she happened to see, simply happened to see, Mrs. Myer dumping loose items out of a drawer into a suitcase, and one of the items was — she saw it clearly, and had to fight the impulse to exclaim — her black fountain pen.

My God, Marya said aloud.

Mrs. Myer turned to her, smiling faintly. Yes? Did you say something? she asked.

Marya stared and could not speak for a moment. She tottered, the stack of books in her arms. She *was* light-headed. Then she said, politely, sadly, Oh — nothing. Nothing at all.

Weeks afterward, months afterward, someone was to exclaim suddenly, There aren't any more thefts! — since Phyllis moved out. And the rest of them took it up, amazed, reluctant, wondering. Do you think —? Do you really think —? Phyllis?

I wouldn't say such things, Marya said roughly. It isn't anything you can prove. It could be slander.

Wednesday dinner, a formal dinner, in the Chi Omega house, Marya seated beside Imogene, sullen and self-conscious, eating her food without tasting it. She *can* appreciate the thick slabs of roast beef, the handsome china, the white tablecloth and linen napkins, the crystal water goblets, the candles, the silver-green wallpaper, the housemother's elegant social chatter at the head table, the girls' animation, their stylized beauty. Imogene, in this context, is much more obviously a sorority girl; she is even wearing her pin with its tiny diamonds and rubies, just above her left breast. Her laughter echoes that of the other girls', the way she leans forward, slightly hunching her shoulders as she laughs, as if thrilled, slightly shocked, the way she allows her heavy hair to swing from side to side, brushing most becomingly against her chin; the way she uses her knife and fork, and passes dishes about, or calls for one of the uniformed houseboys with a perfunctory confidence. (Marya is embarrassed: one of the white-uniformed houseboys is a boy who sits beside her in English: it is extremely difficult for her to see him in this new context, which she naively interprets as being somewhat shameful.)

A mistake, Marya thinks, drinking from her water goblet and noting with dismay the greasy marks from her lips. Should she wipe them away —? Or try not to notice —?

A mistake, she thinks, making little effort to take part in the table's silly conversation — where are you going, where is your family going, over the holidays, Miami Beach Sarasota Bermuda the Barbados Trinidad. From time to time she smiles unconvincingly, a small pinched smile that seems almost calculated to annoy (so Imogene might interpret it, Imogene who knows Marya's sly selfishness well), and fixes her dark gloomy shadow-ringed eyes upon whoever happens to be speaking.

Beforehand, all that day, Marya anticipated the dinner and the evening with excited apprehension, though she had accepted Imogene's invitation reluctantly. (But we're allowed to invite guests every few weeks, Imogene complained, and it's my turn, and I want *you* — and some of my friends want to meet you — is that so strange?) She had been excited, and hopeful, and nervous, wondering if perhaps she should eat something beforehand so that she wouldn't stuff herself out of anxiety at the table — but now that she is actually seated at the table, now that she sees what Imogene's life is here, she isn't hungry at all, and has to force herself to eat, to be polite . . . The presence of the houseboys is also distracting. That they are undergraduates at the University, the same age as the girls they are waiting upon, strikes her as unfair — unjust. She is *certain* they must be uncomfortable, though their expressions are as neutrally composed as her own.

In her quick light entertaining voice Imogene is talking about someone whose name means nothing to Marya. Imogene isn't the most beautiful girl in the sorority — there are lovely, *lovely* girls here — but she is by far the most articulate, the most amusing.

Now she lowers her voice, does a comic imitation, the other girls are loudly amused, the housemother at the head table glances over, frowning, even one of the houseboys grins. Hilarious Imogene Skillman! Cruel Imogene! (Marya knows that Imogene has mimicked *her.* Exactly how maliciously she wasn't told: she had parodied Marya's recitation of the concluding stanza of Stevens's "Sunday Morning," performed spontaneously and passionately one day at the coffee shop months ago. At the time Imogene had appeared to be moved by Marya's ecstatic recitation, so Marya supposed, afterward, knowing Imogene, she would feel she *must* mock it.) But the girls are supposed to behave in a ladylike fashion, especially on Wednesday evenings, when the dinner hour is moved back to 7:30 and they are required to wear stockings and high heels and attractive dresses; so the laughter is quickly muffled.

Now the subject shifts to a party several girls are attending this weekend, at another university; now it shifts to clothing; now to an angry editorial in the student newspaper; now to politicking — "politicking," that word, is used — in the sorority, over some issue Marya knows nothing about and has no interest in. She is thinking about friendship. She is thinking about Phyllis, and Imogene, and herself; and there is no connection between them. Phyllis whom she had not actually *seen* . . . had not looked at . . . A thin girl, with very short blonde hair, a perpetually worried expression, tortoiseshell glasses. She had had the look and the manner of a much younger girl. Always shyly smiling on the stairs, at the mailboxes, in the dining hall. (More than once, in the dining hall, Marya had pretended not to see her sitting alone and looking her way expectantly; she had hurried with her cafeteria tray to another table because she wanted to read or be alone with her thoughts.) Now that she was gone, now that she had vanished — and she had completely vanished, for no one ever spoke of her — she had acquired in Marya's imagination an ethereal doomed quality. Phyllis might have been her friend, she might have been Phyllis's friend, hadn't Phyllis been sympathetic with her that Saturday . . . It seemed not to matter very much that Phyllis had stolen from her. Thinking of Phyllis, brooding about Phyllis, Marya rarely remembered that she had stolen so many things, so much money (they estimated it to be more than $220, and this from girls who really hadn't much money at all), and that she had specifically stolen from *her.* They might have been friends if Marya had been more attentive. If there had been more time . . .

But it is a fiction, Marya supposes. A fictitious imagining of the past.

Imogene and a dark-haired beauty named Maddy are discussing recent courses. Or are they merely discussing their grades. Marya pretends to listen, thinking that this too is a fiction: her very presence in the Chi Omega dining room, the effort she took to subdue her hair, to wrap it about in a twist in imitation of one of Imogene's styles, the labor — performed with ironic grimaces, and a great deal of irritation — to make herself up with liquid flesh-toned makeup, and dark red lipstick, and even eyebrow pencil. You look halfway civilized, Imogene said, squeezing her arm in delight, though perhaps she was disappointed because she went on to say: But they're expecting some sort of barbarian princess —!

The past is a fiction because it is reinvented, and always distorted. The process might be interpreted as tragic but Marya suspects it is merely comic. Somewhere in the past "reality" lies, broken and jumbled, and, in the present, fictitious replicas of that reality dominate — but of course it isn't "reality" any longer since it does not exist. Lies replace truth, good-natured and well-intentioned lies as well as malicious ones, and the process is irreversible, it is the very process of life itself, and Marya cannot fairly condemn it. What *is* fiction, and what is "real" . . . ? Imogene, for instance, had been genuinely moved by Marya's recitation of the Stevens poem, as she had been, from time to time, oddly moved and excited by other flashes of Marya's passion, or wit, or audacity: it had been quite clear at the time that Imogene *had* admired her. That much was true. At the same time Imogene had certainly mocked her, at a later date, as she mocked everyone, eventually, whether she "liked" them or not. And that too was real. Her mockery, her cruelty, her dazzling malice — her energy for demolishing others, and for demolishing her own sentimental states of mind. Marya had been angrily hurt when told of the incident, and she'd said something wittily cruel about Imogene in return, hoping it would be repeated to her; but a few days later, encountering Imogene in the bookstore, she had been delighted to see her, and the two had talked as warmly and as animatedly as if they'd been close friends for years. The present swallows up the past, and not only eradicates it — which wouldn't be too terrible, perhaps — but offers a fictitious past in its place . . . So Marya, drawing her thumbnail hard against the tablecloth, making secret indentations in it, thinks ahead to a time when she will have erased Imogene Skillman from her memory, and supplanted her with an "Imogene Skillman" both flattened and enhanced in order to embody the dominating idea she might represent in Marya's life. How could it be otherwise! She knows she cannot keep Imogene — that much is clear — for Imogene has a reputation for being gaily and recklessly improvident with her girl friends as well as with her boy friends (and she continues to go out regularly, despite the fact that she is engaged) — so why make the effort?

Imogene once said, The measure of a person's love for you is his hurt at your betrayal — that's how you can tell your value, or how little you mean. Her face had fairly glowed in triumph: she *knew*.

Marya studies Imogene covertly. She doesn't know, cannot decide, whether she likes this beautiful strident young woman very much, whether she halfway loves her, or whether she detests her . . . Imogene glances at her, smiling roguishly. Oh Marya won't approve of this! she laughs, nudging her. Marya is such a puritan, she's a throwback to an earlier simpler duller era.

Yes, says Marya, what —?

That paper on Wordsworth we had to do, you know I got an A on it? — last week? Well, she says, lowering her voice, well, I didn't have time to write it, actually type it up, so I gave Andy a few pages of notes — I could hardly read them myself, they were so messy — and asked him if he would please compose something around them — you know how well he writes, and he seems to like the Romantics! — and he'd done a fifty-page paper on Romantic theory last year so of course he didn't mind, he was very sweet, he gave me back twenty-five pages and what I read of them were brilliant — and so — well — I *did* get an A, which gives me a chance for a B in the course — but you can imagine how worried I was, what if I was called in and interrogated on the paper and didn't even know what it *said* —?

Everyone laughs, for Imogene is so sheepish, so childlike, and at the same time so sinful.

Even Marya laughs, though her laughter is startled.

Then suddenly she is no longer laughing. She says, That was a dishonest thing to do — I don't like that at all.

Imogene chooses not to hear the tone of Marya's remark. She says gaily: Oh you mean leading poor Andy on? Making him think —? But otherwise he wouldn't have written so *well*.

Marya says softly, Yes. That too.

Imogene says, Well — puritans are puritans. I wouldn't ask *you* to give me the slightest shred of help.

(Though in fact she has, occasionally. And Marya has been happy enough to oblige.)

Marya does not reply. The subject shifts again, the girls take up the conversation with relief, saving Imogene from a display of bad temper rather than embarrassment; and in a few minutes the lengthy dinner is over.

Come upstairs for a while, Imogene says. She is smiling insincerely, there are strain lines around her mouth.

Thank you, Marya says, but I have to leave.

You *are* angry —?

Marya shrugs her shoulders.

Well — are *you* so honest? Imogene cries.

Marya turns to walk away, pushes through the little crowd of girls in the foyer of the sorority house, her face burning. Are *you* so honest! *You!* She thinks calmly that she will never see Imogene Skillman again.

There's no reason why you shouldn't take this coat, it's a perfectly good coat but I don't want it any longer, Imogene said, in her "frank" voice. You've complained all winter that you hate your own coat and yes I *know* you didn't mean you wanted mine — for Christ's sake, Marya, of course I know that — but anyway here it is: and I think it would look wonderful on you.

Marya stared at the coat. Camel's hair, pleasantly scratchy beneath her fingers, with a belt in back, priced at — how much? — $200, $250 in the downtown Port Oriskany stores. Marya's own coat must have cost about $45; she had bought it at a spring sale in Grant's, back in Invemere, several years before.

If you're thinking that people will know it's my coat — it was my coat — don't worry: camel's-hair coats all look alike. Except they don't look like wool imitations, Imogene said.

But won't your mother, won't your parents . . .

What? I can't hear you, you're mumbling again.

Won't your parents wonder what happened to it?

Imogene fixed Marya with a quizzical look. But why ever should they? — it's *my* coat.

But I can't just take it, Marya said.

Why not?

Because —

I have a new coat, in fact I have three or four coats right here at college with me, you've seen the cashmere with the fox collar? — and I have that parka — and of course the rabbit fur — it's absurd for me to hold onto this. I like it well enough, it's very warm, it *is* attractive, but I think it would look better on you than it does on me . . . on account of your dark hair . . .

But I can't, Marya said.

She was thinking, I am ten years old. I am eight years old, I might as well be standing with my forefinger stuck in my mouth, big-eyed and stricken. I can't refuse and I can't accept and I can't imagine a way out of this conversation . . .

Imogene, however, imagined a way out. She said, Don't be offensive, Knauer, you know I can't stand it! — and left the coat on Marya's bed and ran down the two flights of stairs, so heavily Marya could feel the affrighted old house shudder.

So you are Marya, Mrs. Skillman said warmly, in the drab front room of Maynard House. She and Mr. Skillman and Imogene had arrived to take Marya out to dinner, downtown at the Statler Chop House. We've heard so much about you from Imogene, I think we expected someone more . . .

Now Mother, what on earth —! Imogene laughed sharply.

. . . I was only going to say *taller,* and perhaps *older,* Mrs. Skillman said, offended.

Marya, blushing, shook hands with both the Skillmans. She saw that they were quite ordinary decent well-intentioned people, nothing like their daughter. Mrs. Skillman wore a mid-calf dark fur coat Marya supposed must be mink. Mr. Skillman wore a hat, and showed his gums when he smiled.

In their presence Imogene was a subtly different Imogene. She wore the beautiful rabbit coat, and the boots, and the ceramic earrings that shone in the January sunshine, and she looked pretty rather than striking; and Marya noted that her laughter was delicate and girlish, never coarse, as it was so frequently. Sweet little Imogene, Marya thought, eleven years old.

In the hotel lobby Marya observed the other guests with interest. Like Mr. and Mrs. Skillman they were expensively dressed, and wore their clothes without self-consciousness. It is possible, Marya thought wryly, that the body is conscious of expensive clothing — it moves differently, it gives some thought to its impulses.

Graceful clothes, graceful motions. Masking, Marya wondered, what sort of souls . . . ?

It's a sophisticated form of theft, Imogene giggled.

Marya smiled blankly, looking from one Skillman to the other to the other.

The waiter was pouring more wine into Marya's glass. It was white wine, unpleasantly sweet, but Mr. Skillman had said it would go perfectly with her trout. Imogene too had had white wine — several quick glasses.

You aren't funny, Mrs. Skillman said.

She's just teasing, Mr. Skillman said. She likes to tease.

Imogene giggled, nudging Marya who continued to look blank and uncomprehending. (Conversation had lighted upon Mr. Skillman's business — he owned a savings and loan company in Jamaica, Long Island — and many of his clients were, evidently, according to Imogene, impoverished blacks who bought expensive cars.)

I do like to tease, don't I, Marya, Imogene said, nudging her again.

Later, Mrs. Skillman was saying to Imogene, You don't answer questions, dear. Your letters are just dashed off. If only you would *call*. If we try to call you the line is busy for hours, and if we get through you aren't in, and you never return our calls . . .

My sorority sisters are very negligent at taking messages, Imogene said. They find it difficult — holding a pencil, writing down words. They're functionally literate — they must be, or they wouldn't be in college — but that doesn't include *writing*. That only means reading.

We asked you about Richard, and you never replied . . .

Dickie's hurt, he's keeping his distance, Imogene said. He's pretending to be angry.

Pretending to be angry . . . ? Mrs. Skillman said.

He's in Costa Rica with the embassy, you said, Mr. Skillman murmured. That was in November.

I don't care to discuss my private matters in a restaurant, Imogene said haughtily. Anyway — Marya hears enough about Dickie. She *really* isn't interested. Can't we talk about lofty intellectual matters?

You and Richard haven't quarreled, have you? Mrs. Skillman asked.

Notice, Imogene whispered loudly in Marya's ear, how Mother checks my hand . . . ? She'd be mortified if I lost my engagement ring. If Dickie demanded it back.

Imogene, Mrs. Skillman said, smiling weakly, you really shouldn't tease so much, didn't one of your high school teachers say, do you remember, such teasing is a form of aggression . . . ?

Not that I'd give it back if he *did* demand it, Imogene laughed. It's mine to keep.

But have you and Richard quarreled? Is something wrong? Mr. Skillman asked.

Waiter, more wine, Imogene said in a pre-emptory voice.

But then, on the way back to the campus, she became the Skillmans' daughter again — sweet and girlish and suddenly quite sentimental. I'm so happy you could all meet, she said, I only wish Marya would come home with me sometime, you'd like each other *very* much, if only you could all relax. But Marya works so hard . . . I can barely tear her away from her books . . . D'you know, Mother, Marya is ruining her eyes?

Mrs. Skillman smiled uncertainly, staring not at Marya but at Imogene, from the front seat of Mr. Skillman's enormous Lincoln. Is that so, dear, she murmured, that's very . . . that's very unfortunate.

"Dickie."

Am I jealous of "Dickie," Marya wondered. She lay sprawled on her bed, listless, too tired to write in her journal. There were now more than fifty pages, each line of each page crowded with words in Marya's small tight meticulous secretive hand. A stingy hand, most likely. But then she was poor — she was from Invemere, not Laurel Park, Long Island — she couldn't afford new notebooks very often and she didn't want to experience the temptation to steal.

In Imogene's cluttered room on the second floor of the baronial Chi Omega house Marya came across, jeering, copies of *Bride* magazine. She leafed through them while Imogene protested, laughing, hiding her face. Wedding gowns! Satin and pearls! Orange blossoms! Veils! Lace! Bridesmaids' dresses! And look here, Marya crowed, flapping the pages in Imogene's face, a wedding-cake bridegroom to go with all this shit — though he *is* out of focus in the photograph.

Ah but you'll have to be a bridesmaid, Imogene laughed. Or maid of honor. Or whatever the hell the terminology is.

They studied snapshots of Richard, flicking them at one another like playing cards. Would you like, you know . . . Sometime . . . Imogene said softly.

Marya did not understand, and did not speak.

Imogene lay on her back, across the bed, and let her long hair dangle to the floor. Her belly was very flat; her pelvic bones protruded. She smoothed her shirt across her abdomen with long nervous fingers.

The first time I came with him, she said hesitantly, but with a little giggle, it wasn't — you know — it wasn't with him inside me, the way you're supposed to — that way left me dry, and sore. He was too big, I thought, they're *very* big compared to us, but in another way he wasn't big enough. The first time it worked for me, he was, well, you know, kissing me there, he'd gotten all crazy and wild and I couldn't stop him, and I never thought I would let anyone do that — go down on me — because — am I embarrassing you? — because afterward, she said, laughing, they want to kiss you: and it's disgusting.

She rolled over, away from Marya, and hid her face.

After a long while she said, her breath labored: Am I embarrassing you?

Marya's throat and chest were so constricted, she couldn't reply.

•

A Marya Knauer anecdote, told by Imogene with peals of ribald laughter:

Imogene finally talked Marya into coming along with her on a date. (It was commonly thought that Marya was afraid of men — or did she merely hate them? Stony-faced impassive Marya, with her formidable brain.)

Marya's date was Andy Fein, a senior majoring in advertising and business administration, of whom Imogene was fond. (He was a very handsome boy of twenty-one, and though Marya saw at once that he disliked her she supposed he was attractive enough. For whatever that was worth.)

They went to a movie at a suburban mall, and then to a local pizza restaurant, and then to the water-tower hill, where numerous other cars were parked. Marya stiffened. Andy had not yet touched her, but she knew he would be kissing her in a minute, and she couldn't think how to get out of the situation gracefully.

. . . few minutes? Imogene murmured from the front seat.

By the time Marya and Andy got out of the car, to stroll along a darkened path, Imogene and her date were locked in a ravenous embrace. Marya's heart was beating frantically. She felt that she might suffocate — she couldn't seem to catch her breath.

Andy took her hand. Then slipped his arm around her shoulders.

They walked together awkwardly. He was saying something — making a joke about something — alluding to the movie they had just seen? — or to Imogene's flamboyant behavior? Isn't she supposed to be engaged, Marya said. Sure, said Andy, but she does this all the time. She does this all the *time*, Marya said, but why —? Andy laughed uncomfortably. He was not quite Marya's height, and his dark eyes shied away from hers. I don't know, he said. Why shouldn't she? You know how Imogene is — she does things.

She's an idiot, Marya said roughly.

Please don't be angry at *me*, Andy said, laughing. He was nervous, yet keenly excited; Marya sensed his sexual agitation . . . Behind them, parked along the drive, were lovers' cars, their headlights extinguished. From this distance the car in which Imogene and her "date" were pawing at each other was undistinguishable from the others.

You don't approve? Andy said. But, well, Imogene's like that. I've been out with her before — I mean, on double dates — she does what she likes — I don't think she lies to her fiancé. He'd have to allow her her freedom, you know, or she'd break off the engagement.

You know a lot about her, Marya said.

I don't *know*, I'm only speculating.

It's all so . . . it's all so trivial, Marya said flatly.

What do you mean? said Andy.

Oh — this.

This —?

Marya made a brusque gesture toward the cars parked behind them on the drive.

You take an awfully superior attitude, Andy said.

Marya said nothing. He tightened his arm around her shoulders.

Is this idiot really going to kiss me, Marya wondered. Her heart was still beating heavily; she kept seeing Imogene's profile, the cameo-clear outline of her face, illuminated for a moment as the headlights were extinguished. Then she moved into the boy's embrace, she kissed him, and half-turned sleepily to Marya and Andy in the back seat, and asked if they would like to go for a walk for a few minutes . . .

Does she make love with them? Marya asked.

Them?

Different boys. Men. One week after another.

I don't know, Andy said resentfully. I suppose so.

I thought *you* were in love with her, Marya said in a mocking voice.

Andy said, offended, We're just friends. We're very good friends.

Oh no, said Marya, I thought you were in *love* with her.

Andy withdrew his arm from her shoulders and walked beside her without speaking. There was nothing for them to do; it was still March, and quite cold; their footsteps sounded dully on the crusted snow.

At the top of the hill Marya squinted, trying to bring the city's lights in focus. A sad thing, her eyes had weakened; she would probably have to get glasses soon. But she put off the task. She couldn't afford an eye doctor, and glasses, and it would take up too much of her time . . . Andy was saying something about the dark, the night, the stars, the city lights, something about infinity, and Pascal, and Marya supposed it was meant to be conciliatory — it was meant to be, certainly, "intellectual" — but she could not concentrate on his words. She kept seeing Imogene, Imogene kissing that near-stranger, Imogene locking her arms about his neck. She kept hearing that lazy low voice.

Suddenly Andy took hold of her shoulders and did try to kiss her. It was a brave gesture, it must have required some calculating, but it failed utterly — Marya simply stepped back, astonished.

What the hell are you *doing*, Marya said.

Marya for Christ's sake —

But this is a charade! — it's ridiculous! Marya said. You don't like me, we haven't anything to say to each other, we've been made

fools of, the entire situation is absurd! And now you want to kiss
me, she said, jeering. Simply for something to do.

Marya, you don't understand —

Go away, go on back there and peep in the window, Marya said,
turning aside in disgust. I'm walking home.

Andy shouted after her: You're crazy, Marya! It must be two
miles back —

But she walked down anyway, alone, past the slow stream of cars
ascending the hill, her hands in the pockets of the camel's-hair
coat. At first she was angry — her head rang with accusations —
but the cold still night air invigorated her, and by the time she
thumped up the steps of Maynard House, past midnight, she felt
quite good. She felt *very* good.

Next day, Sunday, Imogene stood at the downstairs desk ringing
Marya's buzzer repeatedly, one two three four, one two three four,
and then one long rude ring, until Marya appeared at the top of
the stairs, her hair in a towel, crying, Who the hell is it —! She and
Imogene stared at each other. Then Imogene said, Here's your
purse, you walked away and left your purse in the back seat, do
you know you're getting eccentric, your behavior is getting piti-
able, what if someone had picked you up last night, don't you think
Lyle and Andy and I would have been responsible? But *you* — you
haven't the first sense of — of — of responsibility to other people,
or —

Just leave the purse, Marya said, leaning over the banister. Leave
it on the desk and get out. And don't talk to *me* about responsibility, after screwing what's-his-name —

Go screw yourself! Imogene shouted. Go fuck yourself!

Go fuck *yourself!* Marya shouted.

Ironically, the anecdote shifted its contours and took on, after a
brief while, an even more comic aura: for hadn't Marya Knauer
been more or less raped, hadn't she fought off her assailant and
run panting and sobbing all the way back to campus, in the cold,
and in the snow, to pound on the door of Maynard House . . . ?
She hadn't her key, the poor luckless girl had even left her purse
behind.

The stories varied. Sometimes Marya hadn't been raped, exactly
— not *exactly*. She had escaped in time, or her would-be lover had
given up in time. (But why would anyone want to rape her, the
boys joked. How would you even go about it?)

Uglier still was the rumor that Marya had been embarrassingly aggressive with Imogene's fiancé Richard, who had flown up to visit. They had all gone out together, Marya had had too much to drink, Richard offered to drive her back to her residence, she threw herself on him in the car and had to be pushed away . . .

Marya was astounded. A preposterous story, an obviously fabricated story . . . Surely no one would believe it . . .

I've never even met Richard, Marya said faintly. Imogene has never introduced us. Why the hell is she *saying* such things . . . !

There were hints, too, that Marya had borrowed money from Imogene. And items of clothing as well — the camel's-hair coat, for example. She can keep it, Imogene was reported to have said, I really don't want it back, I was never very fond of it.

Marya telephoned Imogene and began shouting at her: Why are you saying these things, are you crazy! — do you think I don't know *you* are making up these lies — But Imogene hung up; Imogene wouldn't let her speak.

Marya saw how everyone watched her, smiling covertly as she passed. Marya Knauer who had made a fool of herself with another girl's fiancé, Marya Knauer who was supposed to be so intelligent, with so high an opinion of herself . . .

In the dining hall she sat alone. Turning the pages of a book with trembling fingers. Two boys passed behind her, carrying their trays . . . *That* the one? one whispered. They laughed softly and sat at the end of the table to watch her.

I won't be driven out of here, Marya thought, forcing herself to finish the tepid food on her plate. (Many years later she will remember the food distinctly, as she will remember the sad mild resigned feeling of nausea it evoked: heated-up macaroni-cheese-and-hamburger with some sort of gluey tomato base.)

She was late for philosophy class. The bell in Stafford Hall had just stopped tolling. She ran, she ran, whimpering, for an examination was scheduled for that morning, and she couldn't be late . . . but she was late . . . somehow it happened that she was nearly five minutes late . . . Just outside the door she paused, trying to catch her breath. She would open it, and hurry to her seat, and begin to write. Five minutes would not make any difference. She could explain to the professor, who in any case liked her, she could say anything that flew into her head, he would be sympathetic, of course he wouldn't penalize her; this wasn't high school. But the thought of opening the door and stepping into the room paralyzed

her. Everyone would glance up: everyone would stare. Marya
Knauer, that's Marya Knauer, that's the one who . . . isn't that the
one who . . . ? Here and there and there, throughout the lecture
hall, small flicking smiles would appear. Isn't that the one Imogene
was telling us about . . . ? Such an ugly horse of a girl!

At a distance she saw Imogene, days later. Imogene in the company of several boys. They were laughing, they were very much
together, no doubt they were intimate friends . . . Imogene wearing sunglasses, her hair partly hidden behind a black silk scarf;
Imogene in blue jeans and a bulky-knit gray sweater. Marya
shrank back. She stared, but with her head slightly averted. A
comic figure. Of course Imogene saw her — who could fail to see
her — of course Imogene said something to the boys, who glanced
her way, grinning — but Marya did not dare to call to her. Afterward she discovered that she was trembling.

Why did you lie about me? Why did you betray me?

Imogene —

She sent Imogene a note, the first week of April. *Things aren't
going well for me, I missed a philosophy exam, I'm behind in all my courses,
I don't know if I am unhappy or coming down with some sort of exotic
illness, why don't you drop by and see me sometime . . . or could I come over
to the Chi O house and see you . . .*

She had written Imogene innumerable notes. And lengthy letters. Some of them were incoherent, some were carefully composed on the typewriter, a few were obscene. As she wrote them
she saw again and again her friend's languorous movements, the
way her arms slipped about that stranger's neck, cozily companion-
able, lazy, the way they kissed open-mouthed, before Imogene
half-turned to her. Would you like to let us alone for a few minutes. Would you like to go for a walk, for a few minutes.

I'll come over there one night, Marya wrote feverishly, *and strangle
you with that pretentious braid of yours . . .*

She wrote many messages, but sent only the briefest one, asking
if she might come over to visit. But Imogene failed to answer.

Oddly, when she happened to see Imogene on campus (she had
given up going to her English class — she couldn't bear the risk of
seeing Imogene up close) she usually turned sharply away. Even if
Imogene had sighted her she turned away, pretending not to have
seen *her*. Once Imogene half-raised a hand in greeting but Marya
pretended not to notice.

What is fiction, and what is real, Marya wondered, writing in her journal. She could easily imagine herself killing Imogene; or at least standing by indifferently as Imogene died. She wouldn't lift a hand to prevent that death, she knew. At the same time she quizzed herself about how to respond, should Imogene ask her to be a bridesmaid. For the dresses, the shoes, the shoes alone, would be staggeringly expensive . . .

•

One rainy April afternoon Marya went quite boldly to the Chi Omega house, and up to Imogene's room on the second floor. The door to the room was closed: she rapped hard on it, and opened it before Imogene could call out, Who is it . . . ?

The shades were drawn. Imogene lay half-undressed across the bed, with the spread pulled over her. The room smelled of something acrid and medicinal.

Oh Marya, Imogene said guiltily.

Are you sick? Marya said at once.

They had both spoken at the same time.

. . . a headache, a bad cold, nothing worth mentioning, Imogene said hoarsely. But my throat is sore.

Marya stood with her hands on her hips in the center of the room, staring.

Well, she said. Do you need a doctor, you think . . . ? Or . . . ?

I'm all right, Imogene said. I'm resting.

Marya glanced about the room nervously. Clothes lay everywhere — thrown across chairs, even across Imogene's desk. A half-pleasant odor of cough medicine, spilled perfume, unwashed clothes. Marya could see that Imogene's hair lay in spent greasy tangles on the bed, and spilled off the edge of the bed in a lazily becoming way.

You told so many lies about me, Marya said.

Yes, well . . . Well, said Imogene, coughing, they weren't exactly lies.

I wanted to strangle you.

They weren't exactly *lies*. There's an essence . . .

I'm all right now, Marya said, pacing about, the balls of her feet springy, the tendons of her calves strained, I've gotten over the worst of it, I don't intend to fail my courses.

I might have exaggerated but the essence is true, Imogene said, groping for the pillow behind her. She managed to sit up. She brushed her hair out of her face with an impatient gesture . . . There's a poetic truth, a hidden truth, she said.

I don't intend even to do poorly in my courses, Marya said. Her voice was fairly even. She worried that it might swerve out of control; but the pacing-about helped. You can't make me lose my perfect record.

Can't I, said Imogene.

Why did you lie about Richard? You know I've never met Richard, Marya said. I never *wanted* to meet Richard.

Because you're jealous of him. Of him and me.

Yes. All right. I was. I was jealous, Marya said, laughing. But why did you lie about it? I wouldn't have wanted to sleep with *your* precious lover.

You think so highly of yourself, don't you, Imogene said. She reached for a box of Kleenex; Marya approached her, and with a slow, diffident, formal gesture pushed the box within Imogene's reach . . . You can't be cracked, can you, you're a nut that can't be cracked, Imogene laughed. A tight little virgin. And very proud of yourself.

I won't stay, Marya said shakily. You must want to sleep.

I do want to sleep, Imogene said.

Why didn't you talk to me on the phone, why didn't you answer my note? Marya whispered.

Why did you look the other way all the time? Imogene said.

When —?

All the time.

You were laughing at me, Marya said. You were spreading lies about me. I don't understand why.

I'm transferring out of here, next semester, Imogene said. The drama school is hopeless; I can't stand the staff, and I can't stand the other students. As for my sorority sisters . . .

I don't understand *why*, Marya said miserably.

Oh for Christ's sake what are you talking about! Imogene cried. I don't feel well, you barge in here, you can see I want to sleep, I haven't gotten to a single class in two weeks and I don't give a damn but I refuse to give *you* the satisfaction . . . What are you but a hillbilly character, a hillbilly intellectual, putting on airs.

You *gave* me that coat.

Your jealousy, your morbid possessiveness . . .

I never met your fiancé. I never even asked you much about

him, and when I did, Marya said, her voice trembling, it was only to be polite . . . only because I thought you wanted me to. I wasn't jealous, I don't even know what you're talking about . . .

My parents didn't care for you either, Imogene said, blowing her nose into the tissue. My mother said —

It was only one of the things we talked about, your precious Richard, Marya said wildly, we talked about hundreds of things, it doesn't make sense for you to accuse me of wanting to sleep with him: I don't want to sleep with any of them!

D'you know what my mother said, Marya? Imogene said lazily. She said — Oh Marya could be charming if she tried, if she didn't have that horse face and didn't exaggerate it with that hair hanging down and that long mournful self-pitying look of hers — she *could* be charming but she probably won't be, she's too selfish. No one will ever marry her. You could help her, Imogene, but I wouldn't advise it — your strays and misfits have a way of backfiring on you — they're *never* grateful —

You gave me that fucking coat, Marya said helplessly, striking her hands together. And then afterward — afterward —

Oh let me alone! Imogene said. Her voice was hoarse, her exclamation sounded like a half-sob. I could get you thrown out of here for trespassing — you don't *belong* here — you deliberately made a fool of me, downstairs at dinner that time, afterward my sorority sisters said, Well *she* isn't anything so hot, what's special about her! — I couldn't possibly defend you when you sat there tongue-tied for an hour, then babbled something asinine on your way out — just precisely the sort of thing you always do! Will you close the door on your way out, please? I've taken a half-dozen aspirin and I want to sleep.

She drew the spread roughly over her long restless body and let her head fall back against the flattened pillow . . . Good-bye, Marya! she whispered.

On the stairs, on the sidewalk outside the sorority house, Marya examined the earrings. The Aztec ones, the barbarian ones, bronze and red and blue, burnished, gleaming . . . She had dreamt, evidently, that her hand reached out to take the earrings, for she remembered the dream quite clearly, but she did not remember *taking* the earrings up in the room. Imogene had turned over impatiently on the rumpled bed, had drawn the spread across her legs, and Marya had watched, from a distance, her hand leap calmly out.

No one, Marya thought in triumph, can keep me from my perfect record.

She then did a very strange thing: she went immediately to an earring shop on Fairfield Street, at the very foot of the hill, and despite her aversion for the proprietor — a soft-eyed, soft-bearded, "sensitive" young man in his late twenties — she asked to have her ears pierced at once, and Imogene's earrings inserted.

The young man said, But that isn't how we do it. First we put in gold studs, then a few weeks later when the wound is healed . . .

No, said Marya, put in these earrings, and hurry up.

But we put in studs first, everything has to be antiseptic so you won't become infected . . .

I don't give a damn about that, Marya said fiercely. These earrings *are* gold. Put antiseptic on *them* . . . Are you going to pierce my ears or not? Or do I have to go somewhere else?

Do you have five dollars? the young man asked sullenly.

Crossing the quadrangle between Stafford Hall and Roebaum Memorial Chapel at 9:45 one chilly May morning, Marya caught sight of Imogene slowly approaching her. It had been more than two weeks since the theft of the earrings — two weeks, during which she had worn the earrings everywhere, for everyone to see, quite brazenly. She and Imogene had frequently seen each other, usually at a distance, though once in rather close quarters on a crowded stairway, and Marya had been amused at Imogene's pale stricken look: and the way she turned aside, pretending she hadn't seen Marya.

How unconvincing an actress you are, Marya gloated.

But now Imogene approached her directly, though her movements were rather wooden. Marya did not slacken her pace: she was headed for the library: she wore jeans that fitted her snugly, and a handsome inexpensive cotton shirt, open at the neck, and a lightweight plastic raincoat, and of course the beautiful earrings, which swung heavily as she walked, and tugged at her earlobes. (The earlobes *were* sore. Probably infected, Marya thought indifferently, waking in the night to small stabs of pain.)

Imogene's face was dead white, and distorted. A horsy face after all, Marya thought. There were strain lines around her mouth and on her forehead, she looked much older than twenty, and the tendons in her neck were clearly visible as she ran the remaining five or six yards to Marya. You — you hillbilly bitch! Thief! Imogene screamed. She snatched at Marya's left ear, she would have seized the earring and ripped it out of Marya's flesh, but Marya was too quick for her — she must have known instinctively what Imogene would try to do.

She struck Imogene's hand away, and gave her a violent shove backward. But Imogene recovered at once and slapped Marya — slapped her hard across the face. You bitch! she screamed. You won't get away with this!

Marya's books and purse had fallen to the sidewalk. Passers-by stopped to stare. What a sight, two tall, slender, attractive girls fighting, in front of the chapel — both in blue jeans, their long hair wild, their faces angrily contorted. Marya was shouting, Don't you touch me! What do you mean, touching *me*! She crouched, her knees bent, and, like a man, like a trained fighter, swung upon Imogene, and struck her on the side of her face. It wasn't a slap but a punch: Marya's hand was closed into a hard angry fist.

The blow must have been a powerful one, for Marya struck from the shoulder, and Imogene's head snapped back, and almost immediately blood appeared on her mouth. She staggered backward and swayed but did not fall. Oh Marya — she said.

But Marya was walking away, her books and purse gathered up in her arms. Her long fast stride and the set of her shoulders, the set of her head, must have given onlookers the impression of confidence, but in fact she was badly shaken, and it was some time before she could catch her breath . . . She turned to look back, and saw Imogene sitting on the ground, and a small crowd gathered around her. Two or three persons were squatting before her. You'll be all right, Marya thought sullenly, someone will always take care of *you*.

•

And then nothing further happened.

Marya kept the earrings, and Imogene never again confronted her; nor did anyone dare bring the subject up to either of the girls. Marya was correct in declaring that her perfect record would not be marred — it remained perfect — but Imogene did poorly at the end of the year, failing two subjects, and in place of transferring to another university she quit college altogether.

In the fall Marya heard that Imogene was living in New York

City. She had broken off her engagement over the summer; she had joined a troupe of amateur actors, and lived in a two-room apartment off St. Mark's Square. It was said that she had a part in an off-Broadway play, to open in October, but Marya was never able to learn the title of the play, or when, precisely, it opened, or how successful it was.

Biographical Notes
Other Distinguished Short Stories
of 1981
Editorial Addresses

Biographical Notes

NICHOLSON BAKER was born in 1957 and grew up in Rochester, New York. Before graduating from Haverford College, he played bassoon for a short while with the Rochester Philharmonic Orchestra. Other stories of his have appeared in *The Atlantic, The New Yorker,* and *StoryQuarterly.*

CHARLES BAXTER was born in Minneaplis and now teaches at Wayne State University in Detroit. He has published two books of poetry, *Chameleon* and *The South Dakota Guidebook.* His essays, fiction, and poetry have appeared in many periodicals, and his fiction has been included in the *Pushcart Prize* volume of 1982.

RAYMOND CARVER has published three collections of short stories — *Will You Please Be Quiet, Please?, Furious Seasons,* and, most recently, *What We Talk About When We Talk About Love* — and three collections of poetry — *Winter Insomnia, At Night the Salmon Move,* and *Near Klamath.* Capra Press will publish a collection of his stories, poems, and essays in the spring of 1983, and Knopf will bring out a fourth book of his stories in the fall of 1983. Mr. Carver teaches in the Creative Writing Program at Syracuse University.

ROSANNE COGGESHALL was born in Hartsville, South Carolina. Her stories have appeared in *Southern Review, Epoch, South Carolina Review, Artemis,* and *The New Virginia Review.* Her long poem, *Hymn for Drum,* was published in 1978 by the Louisiana State University Press.

JAMES FERRY was born in Chicago. He graduated from the University of Michigan, where he received an Avery Hopwood Prize for Fiction. He is currently living in Syracuse, New York, having done graduate work at Syracuse University. "Dancing Ducks and Talking Anus" is his first published short story.

ANNE HOBSON FREEMAN was born in Richmond, Virginia, and now lives there again, after being raised and educated in New York, Philadelphia, and London. Her stories have been published in *Mademoiselle, Cosmopolitan, McCall's, The Virginia Quarterly Review, The New Virginia Review,* and *The Richmond Quarterly.* Also a widely published writer of essays and articles, Mrs. Freeman teaches prose writing at the University of Virginia.

ALVIN GREENBERG was born in 1932 in Cincinnati, Ohio, and grew up there. He attended Brown University, the University of Cincinnati, and the University of Washington, and since 1965 has lived in St. Paul, Minnesota, and taught at Macalester College. He has published two novels and — most recently — a collection of short stories entitled *The Discovery of America* (Louisiana State University Press), as well as several volumes of poetry.

ROBERTA GUPTA was born in Wales, and grew up there. She has lived near Washington, D.C., for the past twelve years and has two sons. Her stories have appeared in *The Georgia Review, MSS,* and other literary magazines.

WILLIAM HAUPTMAN was born in Texas and is a graduate of the Yale School of Drama. His plays *Heat* and *Domino Courts,* have been produced at numerous theaters in the United States, Canada, England, and France. He received a *Village Voice* Obie Award for Distinguished Playwrighting, and has held a Guggenheim Fellowship. He has also written scripts for public television and the studios. "Good Rockin' Tonight" is his first published fiction.

JOANNA HIGGINS lives in Little Meadows, Pennsylvania, and is finishing a first novel, *Marie Stelmak.* Her fiction has appeared in *MSS* and *Passages North.* "The Courtship of Widow Sobcek" is her first published story.

CHARLES JOHNSON is the author of two novels, *Faith and the Good Thing* and *Oxherding Tale,* two collections of drawings, *Black*

Humor and *Half-Past Nation-Time,* and the PBS Vision's drama "Charlie Smith and the Fritter Tree." He is an Associate Professor of English at the University of Washington, fiction editor of *The Seattle Review,* a producer-writer for the PBS series *Up and Coming,* creator and host of the PBS series *Charlie's Pad,* and was formerly director of the AWP Award Series in Short Fiction, and Northwest director of the Fiction Collective. He has published over 1000 drawings, as a cartoonist, and numerous short stories.

FRED LICHT teaches art history at Boston University, specializing in European and American sculpture. His short stories have appeared in various American periodicals over the past twenty years. His best-known art book is *Goya: The Origins of the Modern Temper in Art.* Recently he finished a monograph on Antonio Ganova that will appear in 1983 in English and German editions.

IAN MACMILLAN has published fiction in *Yankee, TriQuarterly, Western Humanities Review, Carolina Quarterly,* and elsewhere. *Light and Power,* a collection of stories, won the 1979 Associated Writing Programs Award for Short Fiction and was published in 1980 by the University of Missouri Press. *Blakely's Ark,* a novel, was published by Berkley/Putnam in 1981. Mr. MacMillan teaches at the University of Hawaii.

LISSA MCLAUGHLIN was born in Olean, New York, and educated at Oberlin College and Brown University. She now lives in Providence, Rhode Island, where she alternately teaches English to college students and creative writing to grade-school students. She has published two collections of prose poems, *Approached by Fur* and *Seeing the Multitudes Delayed.* Her stories have appeared in *The Massachusetts Review* and *The North American Review.* Ms. McLaughlin is also a childrens'-book illustrator and is currently working on her first picture book for Lothrap, Lee and Shepard.

EDITH MILTON was born in Germany, grew up in England during the Second World War, and came to the United States in 1946. In addition to her short stories, she has written a novel, *Corridors,* and is working on another novel. She and her husband, an artist, live in New Hampshire with their two college-age children.

JOYCE CAROL OATES, who lives and works in Princeton, New Jersey, is the author of a number of short-story collections and novels, including, most recently, *A Bloodsmoor Romance* (Dutton). Her stories have appeared in *The Best American Short Stories* and the *O. Henry Awards,* and she is currently at work on a new collection.

JOYCE RENWICK studied nursing at the University of Pennsylvania, writing at the University of Virginia, and English literature at the Bread Loaf School of English and at Lincoln College, Oxford. Her short stories and interviews of writers have appeared in *Horizon, The New England Review, Choice,* and *Newsday,* and have been aired on National Public Radio, Pacifica, and the Voice of America.

MARY ROBISON teaches at Harvard. Her books are *Days,* a collection, and *Oh!,* a novel, both published by Knopf. Her short stories appear regularly in *The New Yorker,* and *Esquire* has printed her nonfiction. A Guggenheim Fellow for 1980/81, she has a master's degree in writing from Johns Hopkins. Ms. Robison lives south of Boston, in Hull.

ANNE F. ROSNER has published short stories in *The Yale Review, Antioch Review,* and *TriQuarterly.* Several of her poems have appeared in various other "small" magazines, and she is, at present, at work on a novel.

R. E. SMITH lives in West Lafayette, Indiana, though he frequently returns to Texas for prolonged visits. His stories have appeared variously in such literary magazines as *Descant, Cimarron Review,* and *The Texas Review.* He teaches in the Department of Communication, Purdue University, where his special interest is oral interpretation, the oral communication of literature.

100 Other Distinguished
Short Stories of the Year 1981

Selected by Shannon Ravenel

LLOYD, LINDA
Poor Boy. The Antioch Review, Summer.

LOWRY, BEVERLY
If You're Not Going to Stay Then Please Don't Bother to Come. Mississippi Review, Spring/Summer.

MASON, BOBBIE ANN
Old Things. The North American Review, September.
Recreation. Bloodroot, Winter.

MERWIN, W. S.
A House Abroad. The New Yorker, March 23.

METCALF, JOHN
The Eastmill Reception Centre. The Fiddlehead, Winter.

MILLMAN, LAWRENCE
Annie Bardwell Gets Back Her Cutlery. TriQuarterly, No. 51.

MUNRO, ALICE
Labor Day Dinner. The New Yorker, September 28.

NUDELMAN, JANE
Taste of Apples. New England Review, Winter.

OATES, JOYCE CAROL
The Lovers. Canto, Vol. 3, No. 4.
Minor Characters. The Massachusetts Review, Summer.

PANCAKE, B. D'J.
The Honored Dead. The Atlantic Monthly, January.

PENNER, JONATHAN
Amarillo. TriQuarterly, No. 50.

PETERSON, LEVI S.
Trinity. Ascent, Vol. 7, No. 1.

POPE, ROBERT
The Dispossessed Children. The Antioch Review, Winter.
The Man at the Window. Adena, Spring.

ROBISON, MARY
Happy Boy, Allen. Mississippi Review, Winter.

SCHMIDT, STEPHEN
The End of the Week. The Kenyon Review, Winter.

SHELNUTT, EVE
The Pilot-Messenger. Ploughshares, Vol. 6, No. 4.

SHEPARD, JIM
Runway. Harper's, April.

SINGER, ISAAC BASHEVIS
Advice. The New Yorker, December 28.

SMILEY, JANE
The Pleasure of Her Company. Mademoiselle, March.

SMITH, LEE
Oral History. Carolina Quarterly, Winter.

SOUTHERN, TERRY
Heavy Put-Away *or* A Hustle Not Wholly Devoid of a Certain Grossness, Granted. The Paris Review, No. 79.

STARK, SHARON SHEENE
Janka-Doodle. Cimarron Review, October.

STUBBLEFIELD, CHARLES
Folklorist. Denver Quarterly, Summer.

SZELL, TIMEA K.
The Roadside Cross. Quarterly West, Spring/Summer.

TAYLOR, PETER
The Gift of the Prodigal. The New Yorker, June 1.

TAYLOR, ROBERT, JR.
The History of Frank James. Cimarron Review, January.
Mourning. The Ontario Review, Spring/Summer.
Passing Away. The Agni Review, No. 14.

TELEKY, RICHARD
Notes on Parking. The Tamarack Review, Winter.

THOMPSON, ROBERT
Under the Swaying Curtain. The Missouri Review, Fall.

UPDIKE, JOHN
The City. The New Yorker, November 16.
The Lovely Troubled Daughters of Our Old Crowd. The New Yorker, April 6.
URDANG, CONSTANCE
A Leg. Ascent, Vol. 6, No. 2.

VAUGHN, STEPHANIE
Other Women. Antaeus, 40/41, Fall/Winter.

WEAVER, GORDON
Fearing What Dreams? New England Review, Spring.
Parker *Lacrimans.* The Georgia Review, Summer.

WEISBROD, R. R.
The Accompanist. The Sewanee Review, Summer.
WETHERELL, W. D.
If a Woodchuck Could Chuck Wood. The Virginia Quarterly Review, Autumn.
WIEBE, DALLAS
Omega I. The Paris Review, No. 81.
WILLIAMS, DONALD
Period of Grace. Southwest Review, Summer.
WILLIAMS, JOY
Breakfast. Esquire, August.
Summer. The New Yorker, May 25.
WILSON, MILES
Figuring the Quiet. The Texas Review, Fall.
WOLFF, TOBIAS
Next Door. Antaeus, 40/41, Fall/Winter.
Passengers. TriQuarterly, No. 51.

ZELVER, PATRICIA
Unglued. The Ohio Review. No. 26.

Editorial Addresses of American and Canadian Magazines Publishing Short Stories

Adena, Kentuckiana Metroversity, Garden Court, Alta Vista Road, Louisville, Kentucky 40205

Agni Review, P.O. Box 349, Cambridge, Massachusetts 02138

Akros Review, University of Akron, Akron, Ohio 44325

Analog, 380 Lexington Avenue, New York, New York 10017

Antaeus, 1 West 30th Street, New York, New York 10001

Antioch Review, P. O. Box 148, Yellow Springs, Ohio 45387

Apalachee Quarterly, P.O. Box 20106, Tallahassee, Florida 32304

Aphra, RFD, Box 355, Springtown, Pennsylvania 18081

Ararat, 628 Second Avenue, New York, New York 10016

Arizona Quarterly, University of Arizona, Tucson, Arizona 85721

Ascent, English Department, University of Illinois, Urbana, Illinois 61801

Aspen Anthology, The Aspen Leaves Literary Foundation, Box 3185, Aspen, Colorado 81611

Atlantic Monthly, 8 Arlington Street, Boston, Massachusetts 02116

Aura Literary/Arts Review, 117 Campbell Hall, University Station, Birmingham, Alabama 35294

Ball State Forum, Ball State University, Muncie, Indiana 47306

Bennington Review, Bennington College, Bennington, Vermont 05201

Black Messiah, Vagabond Press, 1610 North Water Street, Ellensburg, Washington 98926

Bloodroot, P.O. Box 891, Grand Forks, North Dakota 58201

California Quarterly, 100 Sproul Hall, University of California, Davis, California, 95616

Canadian Fiction, Box 46422, Station G, Vancouver, British Columbia V6R 4G7, Canada

Canto, Canto, Inc., 9 Bartlet Street, Andover, Massachusetts 01810

Capilano Review, Capilano College, 2055 Purcell Way, North Vancouver, British Columbia, Canada

Carolina Quarterly, Greenlaw Hall 066A, University of North Carolina, Chapel Hill, North Carolina 27514

Chariton Review, Division of Language & Literature, Northeast Missouri State University, Kirksville, Missouri 63501

Chicago, 500 North Michigan Avenue, Chicago, Illinois 60611

Chicago Review, 5700 South Ingleside, Box C, University of Chicago, Chicago, Illinois 60637

Choice, Box Z, State University of New York, Binghamton, New York 13907

Cimarron Review, 208 Life Sciences East, Oklahoma State University, Stillwater, Oklahoma 74074

Colorado Quarterly, Hellems 134, University of Colorado, Boulder, Colorado 80309

Commentary, 165 East 56th Street, New York, New York 10022

Confrontation, English Department, Brooklyn Center for Long Island University, Brooklyn, New York 11201

Cosmopolitan, 224 West 57th Street, New York, New York 10019

Creative Pittsburgh, P.O. Box 7346, Pittsburgh, Pennsylvania 15213

Cumberlands (formerly Twigs), Pikeville College Press, Pikeville College, Pikeville, New York 41501

CutBank, Department of English, University of Montana, Bainville, Montana 59812

December, December Press, 6232 N. Hoyne, Chicago, Illinois 60659

Denver Quarterly, University of Denver, Denver, Colorado 80210

Descant, P.O. Box 314, Station P, Toronto, Ontario M5S 2S5, Canada

descant, Department of English, Texas Christian University Station, Fort Worth, Texas 76129

Ellery Queen's Mystery Magazine, 380 Lexington Avenue, New York, New York 10017

Esquire, 2 Park Avenue, New York, New York 10016

Event, Douglas College, P.O. Box 2503, New Westminster, British Columbia V3L 5B2, Canada

Fantasy & Science Fiction, Box 56, Cornwall, Connecticut 06753

Fiction, c/o Department of English, City College of New York, New York, New York 10031

Fiction International, Department of English, Saint Lawrence University, Canton, New York 13617

Fiction-Texas, College of the Mainland, Texas City, Texas 77590

Fiddlehead, The Observatory, University of New Brunswick, Fredericton, New Brunswick E3B 5A3, Canada

Four Quarters, La Salle College, 20th and Olney Avenues, Philadelphia, Pennsylvania 19141

Gargoyle, P.O. Box 57206, Washington, D.C. 20037

Georgia Review, University of Georgia, Athens, Georgia 30602

Good Housekeeping, 959 Eighth Avenue, New York, New York 10019

Grain, Box 1885, Saskatoon, Saskatchewan S7K 3S2, Canada

Great River Review, 59 Seymour Avenue, S.E., Minneapolis, Minnesota 55987

Greensboro Review, Department of English, University of North Carolina at Greensboro, Greensboro, North Carolina 27412

Harper's Magazine, 2 Park Avenue, New York, New York 10016

Harpoon, P.O. Box 2581, Anchorage, Alaska 99510

Helicon Nine, 6 Petticoat Lane, Kansas City, Missouri 64106

Hudson Review, 65 East 55th Street, New York, New York 10022

Indiana Writes, 110 Morgan Hall, Indiana University, Bloomington, Indiana 47401

Iowa Review, EPB 321, University of Iowa, Iowa City, Iowa 52242

Jewish Dialog, JD Publishing Company, 1498 Yonge Street, Suite 7, Toronto, Ontario M4T 1Z6, Canada

Kansas Quarterly, Department of English, Denison Hall, Kansas State University, Manhattan, Kansas 66506

Kenyon Review, Kenyon College, Gambier, Ohio 43022

Ladies' Home Journal, 641 Lexington Avenue, New York, New York 10022

Lilith, The Jewish Women's Magazine, 250 West 57th Street, New York, New York 10019

Literary Review, Fairleigh Dickinson University, Madison, New Jersey 07940

Little Magazine, Box 207, Cathedral Station, New York, New York 10025

Mademoiselle, 350 Madison Avenue, New York, New York 10017

Malahat Review, University of Victoria, Box 1700, Victoria, British Columbia, Canada

Massachusetts Review, Memorial Hall, University of Massachusetts, Amherst, Massachusetts 01002

McCall's, 230 Park Avenue, New York, New York 10017

Michigan Quarterly Review, 3032 Rackham Building, University of Michigan, Ann Arbor, Michigan 48109

Mid-American Review, 106 Hanna Hall, Department of English, Bowling Green State University, Bowling Green, Ohio 43403

Midstream, 515 Park Avenue, New York, New York 10022

Mississippi Review, Department of English, Box 37, Southern Station, University of Southern Mississippi, Hattiesburg, Mississippi 39401

Missouri Review, Department of English 231 A & S, University of Missouri, Columbia, Missouri 65211

Mother Jones, 607 Market Street, San Francisco, California 94105

Ms., 370 Lexington Avenue, New York, New York 10017

MSS, Department of English, State University of New York, Binghamton, New York 13901

Nantucket Review, P.O. Box 1234, Nantucket, Massachusetts 02554

National Jewish Monthly, 1640 Rhode Island Avenue, N.W., Washington, D.C. 20036

New England Review, Box 170, Hanover, New Hampshire 03755

New Letters, University of Missouri at Kansas City, 5346 Charlotte, Kansas City, Missouri 64110

New Mexico Humanities Review, Box A, New Mexico Tech, Socorro, New Mexico 87801

New Orleans Review, Loyola University, New Orleans, Louisiana 70118

New Renaissance, 9 Heath Road, Arlington, Massachusetts 02174

New Yorker, 25 West 43rd Street, New York, New York 10036

North American Review, University of Northern Iowa, Cedar Falls, Iowa 50613

Northwest Review, University of Oregon, Eugene, Oregon 97403

Ohio Journal, Department of English, Ohio State University, 164 West 17th Avenue, Columbus, Ohio 43210

Ohio Review, Ellis Hall, Ohio University, Athens, Ohio 45701

Old Hickory Review, P.O. Box 1178, Jackson, Tennessee 38301

Omni, 909 Third Avenue, New York, New York 10022

Only Prose, 54 East 7th Street, New York, New York 10003

Ontario Review, 9 Honey Brook, Princeton, New Jersey 08540

Paris Review, 45-39 171 Place, Flushing, New York 11358

Partisan Review, 128 Bay State Road, Boston, Massachusetts 02215

Passages North, William Bonifas Fine Arts Center, 7th Street & First Avenue South, Escanaba, Michigan 49829

Pequod, P.O. Box 491, Forest Knolls, California 94933

phoebe, George Mason University, 400 University Drive, Fairfax, Virginia 22030

Playboy, 919 North Michigan Avenue, Chicago, Illinois 60611

Ploughshares, P.O. Box 529, Cambridge, Massachusetts 02139

Plum, 1121 First Avenue, #4, Salt Lake City, Utah 84103

Prairie Schooner, 201 Andrews Hall, University of Nebraska, Lincoln, Nebraska 68588

Present Tense, 165 East 56th Street, New York, New York 10022

Primavera, Ida Noyes Hall, University of Chicago, 1212 East 59th Street, Chicago, Illinois 60637

Prism International, University of British Columbia, Vancouver, British Columbia, Canada

Quarry West, College V, University of California, Santa Cruz, California 95060

Quarterly West, 312 Olpin Union, University of Utah, Salt Lake City, Utah 84112

RE:AL, Stephen F. Austin State University, Nacogdoches, Texas 75962
Redbook, 230 Park Avenue, New York, New York 10017
Richmond Quarterly, P.O. Box 12263, Richmond, Virginia 23241
Salmagundi Magazine, Skidmore College, Saratoga Springs, New York 12866
San Jose Studies, San Jose State University, San Jose, California 95192
Sands, 7170 Briar Cove, Dallas, Texas 75240
Saturday Night, 69 Front Street East, Toronto, Ontario M5E 1R3, Canada
Seattle Review, Padelford Hall GN-30, University of Washington, Seattle, Washington 98195
Seventeen, 850 Third Avenue, New York, New York 10022
Sewanee Review, University of the South, Sewanee, Tennessee 37375
Shenandoah, Box 722, Lexington, Virginia 24450
Shout in the Street, Queen's College of the City University of New York, 63-30 Kissena Boulevard, Flushing, New York 11367
South Carolina Review, Department of English, Clemson University, Clemson, South Carolina 29631
South Dakota Review, University of South Dakota, Vermillion, South Dakota 57069
Southern Review, Drawer D, University Station, Baton Rouge, Louisiana 70893
Southwest Review, Southern Methodist University, Dallas, Texas 75275
Sou'wester, Department of English, Southern Illinois University, Edwardsville, Illinois 62026
StoryQuarterly, P.O. Box 1416, Northbrook, Illinois 60062
St. Andrews Review, St. Andrews Presbyterian College, Laurinburg, North Carolina 28352
Sun and Moon, 433 Hartwick Road, College Park, Maryland 20740
Swift River, Box 264, Leverett, Massachusetts 01054
Texas Review, English Department, Sam Houston State University, Huntsville, Texas 77341
Three Penny Review, P.O. Box 335, Berkeley, California 94701
TriQuarterly, Northwestern University, 1735 Benson Avenue, Evanston, Illinois 60201
Twilight Zone Magazine, 800 Second Avenue, New York, New York 10017
U.S. Catholic, 221 West Madison Street, Chicago, Illinois 60606
University of Windsor Review, Department of English, University of Windsor, Windsor, Ontario N9B 3P4, Canada
Vanderbilt Review, 911 West Vanderbilt Street, Stephenville, Texas 76401
Virginia Quarterly Review, 1 West Range, Charlottesville, Virginia 22903
Vision, 3000 Harry Hines Boulevard, Dallas, Texas 75201
Wascana Review, Wascana Parkway, Regina, Saskatchewan, Canada

Waves, 79 Denham Drive, Thornhill, Ontario L4J 1P2, Canada

Webster Review, Webster College, Webster Groves, Missouri 63119

West Branch, Department of English, Bucknell University, Lewisburg, Pennsylvania 17837

Western Humanities Review, University of Utah, Salt Lake City, Utah 84112

William and Mary Review, College of William and Mary, Williamsburg, Virginia 23185

Wind/Literary Review, RFD Route #1, Box 809K, Pikeville, Kentucky 41501

Wittenberg Review, Box 1, Recitation Hall, Wittenberg University, Springfield, Ohio 45501

Writers Forum, University of Colorado, Colorado Springs, Colorado 80907

Yale Review, 250 Church Street, 1902A Yale Station, New Haven, Connecticut 06520

Yankee, Yankee, Inc., Dublin, New Hampshire 03444